As his mother began to wash the white man's head and face, the boy turned away.

She used a strip of dirty, stiffened white cloth—one of the dead soldier's stockings. If only these white men wore moccasins instead of the clumsy black boots that made their feet hot and sticky. With moccasins the white men would not need to wear these silly stockings. He smiled and began to feel better for it.

This was his seventh summer. He was too old to act like a child, the boy decided.

Finally he turned back to watch his mother scrub the last of the black grainy smudges from the edges of the bullet hole in the soldier's left temple. Little blood had oozed from the wound.

Perhaps this pale man had already been dying from that messy bullet wound in his side. The boy had seen enough deer and elk, antelope and buffalo, brought down with bullets. And he knew no man could live long after suffering a wound in the chest as terrible as this. This soldier had been dying, and he was shot in the head to assure his death.

Someone had wanted to make certain that this soldier was not taken alive. Someone had saved this pale-skinned soldier from the possibility of torture by sending a bullet through his brain.

*George Armstrong Custer, in one of the
last portraits made of him in April, 1876.
(courtesy of Custer Battlefield National Monument)*

SON OF THE PLAINS—VOLUME 2

SEIZE THE SKY

TERRY C. JOHNSTON

BANTAM BOOKS

NEW YORK · TORONTO · LONDON · SYDNEY · AUCKLAND

SEIZE THE SKY

A Bantam Book / April 1991

Quote from Cavalier in Buckskin: George Armstrong Custer
and the Western Military Frontier, *by Robert M. Utley.*
Copyright © 1988 by the University of Oklahoma Press.

Quote from New Sources of Indian History *by Stanley*
Vestal, courtesy of Dorothy Callaway and Malory C.
Ausland.

Map design by GDS/Jeffrey L. Ward

ISBN 0-553-28910-1

Published simultaneously in the United States and Canada

Bantam Books are published by Bantam Books, a division of Bantam
Doubleday Dell Publishing Group, Inc. Its trademark, consisting of the
words "Bantam Books" and the portrayal of a rooster, is Registered in U.S.
Patent and Trademark Office and in other countries. Marca Registrada.
Bantam Books, 1540 Broadway, New York, New York 10036.

PRINTED IN THE UNITED STATES OF AMERICA

OPM   14 13 12 11 10

I dedicate this book to
Richard Wheeler
the gentle poet and philosopher
of the high plains of Montana

On Custer Hill the knot of fallen men graphically portrayed the drama of the last stand. Although Cooke and Tom Custer had been badly butchered, most in this group escaped severe mutilation. "The bodies were as recognizable as if they were in life," Benteen wrote to his wife a few days later.

Although naked, "The General was not mutilated at all," Lt. Godfrey later wrote. "He laid on his back, his upper arms on the ground, the hands folded or so placed as to cross the body above the stomach: his position was natural and one that we had seen hundreds of times while taking cat naps during halts on the march."

ROBERT M. UTLEY,
Cavalier in Buckskin

I believe anyone familiar with old-time Indians will prefer their version of a fight to that of other eye-witnesses. The Indian was by nature and training a very close observer, objective and unimaginative as few white men can be. Moreover, the Indian was a veteran who went on the warpath several times each year from early adolescence until he became too old to fight. . . . He was therefore cooler and more experienced, as a rule, than his white opponents. . . . War was his absorbing sport. His rating in the tribe depended upon his proven exploits in battle and he took good care to claim all honors to which he was entitled, and to demolish any false claims advanced by his comrades. Therefore in any kind of a fracas he had all the keen, clear-eyed alertness of a professional sportsman. And as long as he lived, whenever he had an opportunity, he recounted his exploits in battle publicly and in the presence of his rivals.

—STANLEY VESTAL
New Sources of Indian History

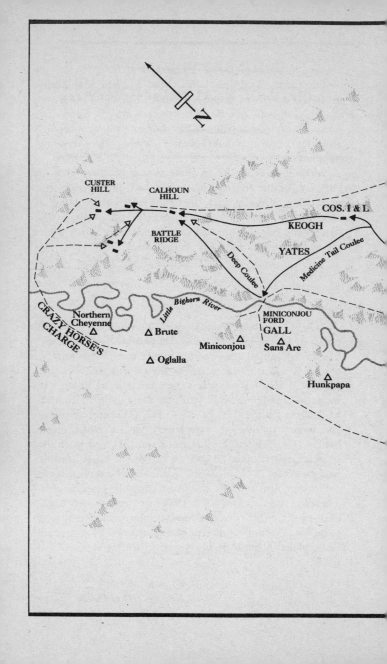

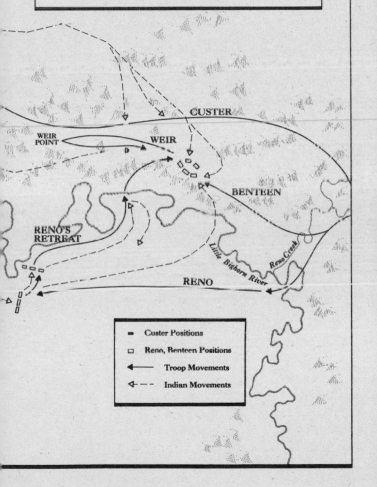

THE BATTLE OF
THE LITTLE BIGHORN

0   1

Miles

CUSTER

WEIR POINT   WEIR

BENTEEN

RENO'S RETREAT

Little Bighorn River

Reno Creek

RENO

▬	Custer Positions
▢	Reno, Benteen Positions
◄━━	Troop Movements
◄- - -	Indian Movements

SEIZE THE SKY

THE HILLSIDE

CLOUDS of black powder smudged the late-afternoon ridges like yesterday's coal-oil smoke. Yellow dust floated into the broiling air beneath the countless unshod pony hooves and moccasined feet scurrying through the gray sage and stunted grasses beneath a relentless summer sun. There weren't many of the big, weary, iron-shod army horses left on the hillside now. A few carcasses lay stiffening, bloated, their legs rigid. But most of the big iron-shod horses had clattered down to water.

He cried out. Not wanting to go up that hill. Terrified of what he saw. More terrified of what he heard.

Wailing, screeching, and hideous cries assaulted the ears. So many keened in mourning. Still others cried out their songs of victory. Many more lips screeched bowel-puckering shouts of vengeance as they attended their deadly labors of conquest. The side of the hill ran dark with blood.

He dared not look, covered his eyes. But just as quickly

his mother jerked his hand away from his dirty face. She wanted him to see, to remember.

The parched, sandy slope was littered with the stinking refuse of battle: bodies pale and lifeless, scattered across the dusty sage and brown grasses. Their dark blood soaked into the eager, thirsty soil that stretched all the way up to those mule-spine ridges far to the east where the sun, now into its western quadrant, glared down like a cruel, unblinking eye.

He tripped, stumbling to his knees. He cried out as he was dragged to his feet again, as his spindly copper-skinned legs bled. Quickly he cut off his own yelp. Long ago he had been taught that a boy of the People does not cry out in pain.

There were several women and men clustered around each of the pale bodies on this knoll. Mostly it was the women, hunched over their crude handiwork. These bodies were as white as fish bellies—except for bloodied, leathery faces, necks, and hands.

What hairy creatures these fish-bellied men are.

Some of these browned-hide faces were almost copper enough to belong to the People. Had it not been for all the hair on their faces that made him shudder with the sharp memory of childhood nightmares, he would not have believed these bodies were what the neighbor tribes called the dreaded *wasichus*.

His mother halted near the crest of the hill. There she knelt and enclosed him within her arms. At first her teary eyes moved about before gazing at last into her son's face. She instructed him to stay by her side. Fearfully his own dark-cherry eyes darted about the hillside, and he understood why she admonished him not to wander. Here in this place existed a mad fury he had never seen in his few summers of life.

Women, children, old men—running about carrying knives and axes, stone mallets and tomahawks, lances and bows, pistol butts and rifle barrels . . . cutting, slashing, clubbing, tearing, and gouging.

The little boy huddled against his mother. Fear formed a hard, hot knot in his belly.

She bent, putting her face right next to his so she would not have to speak so loudly. Instead, she began to sob again before any words could come out.

Another woman of their tribe came up beside the mother and son, kneeling in the blood-soaked soil. Bighead Woman was a good friend of his mother. He called her *aunt* because he had no real blood relatives among the People. The woman smiled down at him, brushing the tears from one of his dirty cheeks. When she looked into his wide, frightened, small-animal eyes, he saw in hers a sorrow he had never before seen on her face.

"Monaseetah," the older woman whispered hoarsely, like a trickle of water running over a drought-parched creek bed, "you must be quick about this now. I wish to leave and go with the others across the hills. To touch these pale men who came with such foolish hearts to strike our camps of women and children again. Always they come to strike the women and children first—"

Her words snapped off in midsentence like dry kindling as the boy's mother lifted her face, a mask of utter sadness and despair. Bighead Woman understood that despair and hopelessness immediately.

"This I did for you, Monaseetah." Her gnarled, scarred hand pointed down at the three bodies crumpled on the ground nearby. "I watched so that none would touch his body. Many came here to mutilate him . . . as they do now with the others who rode against us when the sun rode high in the sky. But I told them your story. Most left without a word to find other bodies they could revenge themselves upon. Some said a small prayer for you before they turned to go. My heart shares how you must feel. Long ago I lost a man in battle—in a time of cold when the Winter Man's breath blew white out of the northlands. My man was killed in a battle just like this with the pony soldiers. It was the time you lost your father. You will remember . . . must remember—that time those cowardly white warriors of winter followed their chief . . . this one!"

Bighead Woman gestured violently toward the naked corpse beside them in the dust. She waited for Monaseetah to speak.

"I thank you for your care this day, sister. I will stay here now. My son and I will stay to watch over the body until dark fills the sky. We will see that no harm comes to this man. You need wait no longer. Leave us now."

The older woman reached into a small quilled pouch hung at her belt and removed a bone awl, its point hardened in fire and sharpened for punching holes in the thickest of bull hides. With that awl clasped in one hand, Bighead Woman twisted the white soldier's head to the side. Monaseetah grabbed the woman's hand to still it.

For a long moment they stared at one another, the older woman able to read what lay within the liquid depths of the young mother's eyes.

"What I do now is not for you, my young friend," Bighead Woman explained softly. "This I do for him. *Hiestzi* did not heed the words told him long ago during his days in those lands to the south. Eight winters it has been now since the elders of our tribe warned him not to attack the women and children and villages of the People. Yet Yellow Hair did not hear our clear, strong words. This I do for him. So that Yellow Hair may hear better in the life to come—I wish to open his ears up to the songs he should have heard long ago."

Eventually Monaseetah's fingers loosened their frantic grip on the older woman's brown wrist. "It is understood," she replied as she pulled her hand away in resignation.

Cautiously Bighead Woman inserted the point of the bone awl into the left ear canal, then suddenly rammed it all the harder when she encountered resistance. She brought the bone spindle out accompanied with a slight trickle of blood. When she had twisted the man's head to the left, she punctured the right ear as well. Finally she wiped the bone awl on her dusty buckskin dress and dropped it back into her pouch.

"It is right, this that you do," Monaseetah sighed. Her voice was like a dry wind that scoured the distant prairie home of her Southern Cheyenne people.

"Yes, it is right, little sister." The older woman shakily rose to her feet. "Perhaps you will be granted another time together with *Hiestzi*. In another place, in some dream yet to come."

"Perhaps." Monaseetah did not look up to see her friend hurry away to join the others scurrying like maddened red ants across the yellow hillsides, where the heat rose in shimmering waves to the bone white sky.

Frightened still, her son looked down the slope. Here and there warriors had turned the fish-belly bodies of their white victims facedown after mutilation and desecration. He remembered the Cheyenne belief taught him by the old ones: It was bad luck to leave an enemy facing the sky, because his soul could more easily escape the earthly plane.

Many of the hairy tanned heads had been smashed to jelly. The congealing ooze was already attracting both crawling and flying insects. Some heads had been severed from the bodies. Among the sage and yellow dust lay other body parts: hands, feet, penises, legs, and arms. Practically every man's torso bristled like a porcupine with a score or more arrows, most fired into the dead bodies by eager young boys or infuriated, wrinkled old men who could not remember ever celebrating such a resounding victory. Truly, this was a day for joy and singing the old songs.

Farther down the slope two older youths played a game of shinny-ball with a soldier's head, batting the bloody trophy back and forth with discarded rifles that could be found beside every dead soldier. The bearded head rolled into the sticky entrails that had tumbled from another soldier's belly wound. Suddenly the two youths had a new game to play. They yanked and pulled, tore and ripped the warm, snakelike intestines from the man's belly.

The little boy turned away, his mind already numb to the shrieking crimson spectacle all round him. Even here at his feet he could not escape the gore. Here lay three of the white-bellies, looking like helpless fish flopped on the creek bank. All three had been stripped by the women. Yet while two had been desecrated and horribly mutilated, their genitals hacked off and tossed aside, their thighs gashed, a hand gone or foot cleaved away, heads scalped and pummeled to a sticky jelly—the hairy-face in the middle remained untouched.

Why had his aunt protected this one from desecration? Why had she stood guard while his mother hauled him up the hillside to view this body? Why would they want this one, solitary soldier out of all the others to hear better in Seyan—his people's Life After Crossing Over?

This soldier's face bore a look of peace.

The boy felt something very different boiling inside his own belly. In summer all he ever wore was the little breechclout and his buffalo-hide moccasins. The sun's scorching fingers raked his naked back. Trickles of sweat coursed down his heaving chest. It seemed the sun's rays grew hotter, the stench more suffocating. He imagined the white-belly corpses inching in on him here where he sat near the crest of the hill.

"Aiyeeee!"

He jerked up, his nose inches from the frightening glare of an ancient, shriveled woman. The skin on her face sagged, as did the wrinkled pair of old dugs he saw as he peered down the loose neckline of her ill-fitting skin dress. The boy swallowed sickly.

Her wild eyes darted like accusing black marbles from him, to the white soldier, to Monaseetah, and back to the soldier's body again.

"You have not touched this one yet!" Her teeth showed black gaps from which burst a hideous odor.

"No." Monaseetah placed a hand on the dead soldier's chest, over his heart just above the bloody wound. "He is a . . . my relative."

"Aieee!" Her head fell back as she cackled, and the boy feared it would fall off the old harpy's shoulders. "A *relative*, sister?"

"You are Sioux—yes?" Monaseetah did not remove her hand from the soldier's heart.

"Miniconjou."

"I am Tsistsistas. I know this soldier from long ago. Several winters now. In my land to the south. This one, he was foolish to come north. But, he is my relative."

Slowly the old one bent forward, studying the young mother's face with a rheumy eye. "You see to him, Cheyenne sister." The old hag peered at him closely a long moment before he pulled away, hiding behind his mother. "I want his boots, Tsistsistas. Only his boots!"

She cackled once more as Monaseetah scooped up the knee-high dusty black boots she had set aside for herself. The scuffed cavalry boots belonging to two other soldiers were nowhere near as tall as these. Running her hands over the soft, pliant black leather, the wrinkled one smiled now that the precious treasure belonged to her.

"These, little sister, will make fine bullet pouches . . . perhaps a quiver for some man's arrows. Maybe a hiding place for a man's love charms or war medicine. So very soft."

"Take them and go, old one!" Monaseetah snapped. "Just go!"

Her fiery words caught the boy by surprise. He rarely heard his mother bark at others. She almost never shouted at him or his older brother—only when they had really deserved it.

"He is your relative, you say?" She squinted the cloudy eye again, stooping close to the young Cheyenne mother, glaring with suspicion and disbelief at Monaseetah.

"He is."

With a bony finger the old one brushed a lock of the boy's light hair out of his eye before she took that same finger and dipped some of the drying blood from the massive oozing wound at the soldier's left side. With that blood she smeared something on the man's left cheek. Again she dipped and painted, dipped and painted, until she had enough of a symbol brushed dark against the sun-burnished skin and reddish blond whisker stubble.

"I put this here to tell all Sioux they must leave this body alone." The old woman's face softened. Perhaps she remembered years without number gone by, remembered little ones at her breasts, remembered a man she had loved long before there were too many years to count any longer. "My people will not bother him, seeing this sign on his body, little sister. Do not worry your heart."

Monaseetah sat stunned, not at all sure what she should say. "Thank you . . . for your great kindness." She dropped her gaze, ashamed of her tears.

"Little niece, it is always better to grieve. Later you can heal from that mourning for those who have gone before us to the Other Side. It is always better to forget after some time has passed . . . and you go on into the days granted you by the Father of us all."

"But I do not want to forget. I will never forget."

Monaseetah's words turned the old woman around after a few hobbling steps. She looked at the tall, dusty cavalry boots clutched securely beneath her withered arms like a rare treasure.

"I will always remember this day, little one. Remember for all the time that is left me. I too can never forget. Sometimes it might be better to carry the hurt inside . . . and remember what happened here beneath this sun."

The wrinkled one turned away and was gone.

More frightened now, the boy clung to the back of his mother's buckskin dress. Monaseetah pulled free a butcher knife and set to work with its sharp blade.

He could not see what she was cutting until he stepped around her shoulder. His wide, wondering eyes watched as she finished hacking off one of the pale man's fingertips. Monaseetah let the soldier's right hand fall before she dropped the fingertip into a small pouch hung round her neck.

Why would she take part of this soldier's body to keep when everywhere else on the hillside all the others hacked at the white bodies with pure, unfettered blood-lust?

He studied the soldier's head and saw that it would truly make for a very poor scalp. The short reddish blond bristles were thinning, the hairline receding. No wonder no one had torn this skimpy head of hair from the white man's skull.

"Here, my son." Monaseetah gave him an elk-horn ladle she had pulled from her wide belt. "Bring me water from the river. Take it. Go now."

She nudged him down the hill toward the river that lay

like a silver ribbon beneath the wide white sky. At least it would be cool beside the water, he thought.

Dodging the huge bloating horses and gleaming soldier corpses, he went to the river and scooped water into the ladle. Mounted warriors screeched past him as they rode to the south. Shaking, the boy spilled half of the cool water on his lonely, frightening climb back up the long hillside. He slid to a halt beside his mother and choked back the sudden foul taste of bile washing his throat.

It surprised him. For the first time this afternoon he wanted to vomit. He gulped and swallowed, fighting down the urge to rid himself of that breakfast eaten so long ago.

As his mother began to wash the white man's head and face, the boy turned away.

She used a strip of dirty, stiffened white cloth—one of the dead soldier's stockings. If only these white men wore moccasins instead of the clumsy black boots that made their feet hot and sticky. With moccasins the white men would not need to wear these silly stockings. He smiled and began to feel better for it.

This was his seventh summer. He was too old to act like a child, the boy decided.

Finally he turned back to watch his mother scrub the last of the black grainy smudges from the edges of the bullet hole in the soldier's left temple. Little blood had oozed from the wound.

Perhaps this pale man had already been dying from that messy bullet wound in his side. The boy had seen enough deer and elk, antelope and buffalo, brought down with bullets. And he knew no man could live long after suffering a wound in the chest as terrible as this. This soldier had been dying, and he was shot in the head to assure his death. Someone had wanted to make certain that this soldier was not taken alive. Someone had saved this pale-skinned soldier from the possibility of torture by sending a bullet through his brain.

Strange. As the boy looked about the hillside, he could see that the warriors had taken no prisoners. As far as his young eyes could see along the ridges of shimmering heat and yellow dust and black smoke and red death—none of these pony soldiers had lived for longer than it took the sun to move from one lodgepole to the next.

The boy sat quietly and watched his mother at work. With care she washed the white man's entire face, scrubbing the dirty sock dipped in river water over the bristling stubble of red gold sprouting on the burnished cheeks and strong chin. The lips were cracked, peeling and bloody from days in the sun and from drinking alkali water.

The boy's eyes wandered down the pony soldier's frame until they froze on the wound in the man's left side, just the length of two of his little hands below the white man's heart. An ugly, gaping hole; he imagined the exit wound had to be even bigger. Surely the warrior who had shot this pony soldier had been no more than one arrow flight away when he fired his gun—no more than fifteen of his own short little-boy strides. A shot fired far enough away not to bring instant death—but close enough to insure that death would be soon in coming.

He wondered: In his last moments had this soldier gazed down this slope, seeing all the lodges and wickiups where slept the young unmarried warriors along the bank? Hadn't the soldier seen the great village stretched for miles along the Greasy Grass? Or had he seen and refused to believe his own pale blue eyes now staring in death at the summer sky of the same robin's-egg hue? Had he plunged on down toward the villages and his own death?

How could his mother treat this soldier as she would a member of her family? They had no relatives. Monaseetah and her two sons were alone in this world. It had been twelve winters since Monaseetah's mother was killed by pony soldiers far to the south along the Little Dried River. Eight winters now since Monaseetah's father had suffered the same fate at the hand of other soldiers in another dawn attack. His thoughts and fears tumbled: Why had his mother told the old Miniconjou woman this white-bellied soldier was a relative?

The stench of dried blood and putrefying gore clung strong on the breeze. He rubbed his nose and fidgeted, wanting to be gone. His mother's hand quieted his nervousness.

"I am finished at last, my son." She pulled him round to her gently. "I want you to listen to my words with all your heart. Listen to me with your soul, son of my body."

The boy nodded, wanting only to be gone from this terrible hillside.

Monaseetah tossed aside the dirty stocking she had used to bathe the dead soldier. When he studied her eyes for some answer to his confusion, the boy discovered tears glistening in her dark eyes, streaming down her coppery cheeks. He thought, *She is the prettiest woman I have ever seen.*

With a tiny dirty finger he touched her cheek, wiping away a single tear. Without a word Monaseetah took his tiny hand, directing him to touch the white soldier's hair.

"The red gold of a winter's sunrise," his mother whispered as she touched the soldier's hair.

Monaseetah guided his hand to stroke her own dark, silky hair falling unfettered in the hot breezes across her quaking shoulders.

"Black, my son. Sleek as the raven's shiny wing when it snags the sun's rays in high flight."

She took the boy's hand and brought it up to touch his own head. She held some of his own long hair before his eyes.

"Your hair is not like your mother's."

"I do not understand," he said, quivering.

Again Monaseetah took his hand to touch first the soldier's thinning, close-cropped hair. Then her own long, loose hair. Finally his own. Looking at it perhaps for the first time in his young life, the boy found himself growing scared, with a cold creeping right down to his toes.

"You were named Yellow Bird because of the color of your hair, my son."

He watched her choke back a sob that made his mother shudder. She swiped at her wet cheeks before he worked up courage to ask.

"You are my mother, aren't you?"

"Yes." She smiled through the haze. "I am your mother."

Anxiously Yellow Bird wrung his hands through his hair, not understanding, afraid to accept what his mother had told him. He did not like the feeling at all. He had been scared before, he remembered. Like last summer when his pony had been spooked by a rattler, bolting into the hills as he clung to its mane in desperation. Yet right now he was more frightened than he had ever been.

Yellow Bird bolted to his feet. As quickly his mother snagged his wrist and yanked him down beside her. He fell to his knees, sprawling over the naked pony soldier.

He cried out as his face brushed the pony soldier's cold, bristling cheek.

Fiercely he clamped his eyes to shut off the flow of hot tears. In a flood he figured out what she wanted him to tell her. But Yellow Bird knew his mother wanted him to say the words himself.

Desperately he hungered for escape. The hillside filled his nostrils with the stench of blood and bowels released in death, gore scattered across the gray-backed sage and yellow dirt and dry red-brown grasses in savage, sudden, welcome death. At once Yellow Bird could not breathe.

"No!" he shouted. It scared him to hear the unbridled fear in his own voice.

"Yes," his mother cooed. She cradled his little hands within hers, holding him in this place of terror.

"No-o-o!" Yellow Bird whimpered like a wounded animal caught in a snare.

Again and again he whipped his head from side to side, whimpering his word of denial.

"It is so, my son."

Suddenly he let his tense, cold muscles go. Yellow Bird stopped fighting his mother. Instead he collapsed against her, sobbing as he stared down at the soldier. Once again he took up some long strands of his own loose, unbraided hair, lifting it into the bright, truthful sunlight. There before his eyes it shimmered, each strand much lighter than the dark, coarse hair of any other Cheyenne he had ever known in his few summers of life.

After what seemed like another lifetime, Yellow Bird brought his face away from his mother's soft breast where his tears had soaked through her soft buckskin dress. Already the sun had begun to cast long shadows in its relentless march to the west.

"Yes, Yellow Bird," Monaseetah said quietly. "This is your father."

BOOK I

THE MARCH

CHAPTER 1

THE dawn air was filled with that heady, earthy fragrance of fresh dung dropped by a few of the hundreds upon hundreds of mules and horses crowding the parade ground.

Springtime brought with it at least one blessing to this land of tractless, far-reaching prairie: enough rain to hold down the thick yellow dust. But rain also brought mud and great, swampy puddles that collected across the swales and at the foot of every hillock. Those puddles in turn bred mosquitoes, winged tormentors soon to rise over this northland as they had for his last three springs here on the Missouri. Huge creatures swarming above these great grasslands in a dark cloak like the horde of locusts swarming above the Egypt of ancient pharoahs.

Still, it would take something far hardier than a plague of mosquitoes to drive him from this western frontier. Perhaps only a call to Washington City itself.

"Mr. Burkman." He turned to his personal aide. "I see you scribbling in your little book again."

The short, dark orderly looked at that tall soldier beside him with something akin to worship. "Yes, General."

"So tell me what you've written about this momentous morning so far . . . a morning of which grand destinies are made, Mr. Burkman."

The young private cleared his throat and glanced up at his benefactor nervously. "Uhhh, all I've written so far is *Wednesday, seventeen May, 1876*, sir."

"Nothing else?" His azure blue eyes scanned the activity on the parade ground. "All this time here on the porch this morning, and all you've been inspired to write is the date?"

"There's more, sir—but I'm a little at the loss for words, General. I've never been on a campaign before . . . it's all a bit overwhelming to me right now."

"I quite understand, Private," the officer replied with that famous, peg-toothed smile of his, slapping his orderly on the back. "Tell me, then, have you scribbled anything else of note?"

"Only . . . *Fort Abraham Lincoln, Dakota Territory*," John Burkman said. Then he uttered the rest more softly. "We prepare to embark on a mission of national importance, one that will spell the final subjugation of these plains for the settlement of white civilization, or the continuation of the Indian Wars, which have so long plagued this great land."

The officer smiled beneath the bushy mustache that hung like corn straw over his mouth. "Very good, John. I like it. But—you ought to scratch the last part of that. We're going to put an end to the Indian Wars once and for all."

The young private licked nervously at the dulled point of his pencil, then set it to work, scratching across the sheet of his ledger, attempting to capture more of his commander's words for history. "Yes, sir," he replied absently as his hand flew across the page.

"Keep at it, Striker!" He patted the young man's shoulder again. "You'll have much to tell your grandchildren about this campaign. There won't be a man, woman, or child across this great republic of ours who won't know about the glory-bidden U.S. Seventh Cavalry."

He stepped toward the edge of the porch, eyes raking

the parade ground approvingly. Finally he stuffed his pale fingers into the skintight yellow doeskin gloves and tugged at the tall fringed gauntlets as he plodded down two steps and stopped, breathing deeply of the air of anticipation that hung thick over the parade.

"John, there won't be a soul from Washington City to St. Louis who fails to know about George Armstrong Custer when the dust settles and my personal standard flies over the battlefield."

"Yes, General!" Burkman hopped down the steps of the Custer home constructed just west of the massive parade ground so he would stand beside the taller man. He truly idolized the dashing "Boy General," hero of the Union Army of the Potomac during the Civil War.

He turned to Burkman and again smiled engagingly beneath the bristly mustache. "St. Louis is the site of the Democratic convention next month."

Burkman was purely muddled now. "I thought you hated politics and politicians both, sir. Why, after what President Grant and the Congressional Committee did to you—"

"Power brokers, Mr. Burkman." Some of that bright smile had drained from a face beginning to show the signs of age and the toll exacted by years lived at the mercy of wind and rain, sun and cold. The march of time was marked like a war map on that face. "Power to accomplish much of what needs to be done rests in the hands of a few power brokers . . . and they can select men who will grab the reins of our nation and lead it into our second century."

"Yes! Our centennial, sir. What an opportunity—"

"Let us take that opportunity in hand—a destiny thrust on few men, Mr. Burkman, a destiny most men would shrink from. Stay at my side, young man, and I'll take you into this great republic's second century."

"I'd be privileged to stand beside you under any circumstances, sir."

"For the time being, Private Burkman, what say we just head for the Yellowstone?" Custer tugged the cream-colored, wide-brimmed slouch hat over the short, uncharacteristic stubble that covered his head. He worried the new hat's sweatband into place. "It'll take some time getting used to this damned haircut Libbie gave me yesterday."

"Why so short, sir?"

"I wasn't the only one. Lieutenant Varnum, who heads up our detail of scouts talked me into it, really. Seemed like a good idea at the time. Easier to care for and a hell of a lot cooler. So I got a pair of horse clippers from the livery sergeant and set Libbie to work in the parlor." He yanked the hat off again and ran a callused, freckled hand over the reddish, thinning stubble. "Not a bad job of it either."

Custer quickly added, "Not a bad job for a green recruit going west on his first campaign to fight hostiles along the Yellowstone! A dad-blamed shavetail! That's just the way I feel with this jack-gagger haircut."

He skipped on down the rest of the wide steps that spilled onto the parade ground from the front veranda of the second home he had built for Libbie at this northern post. Standing across the river from the frontier town of Bismarck, Dakota Territory, the first army outpost built nearby in 1872 had been christened Fort McKeen, home then for the Sixth U.S. Infantry. Not far from it the new buildings of Fort Abraham Lincoln had sprung up on the northern prairie to house some nine companies so that when Custer's regiment arrived late in the summer of 1873 after a futile pursuit of the Sioux along the Yellowstone, this new home of the Seventh Cavalry sat ready in its fresh coat of paint. Army gray, a color known only for its distinction of losing itself against the prairie background. For some time, quarters were cramped, as the post had room enough for only half the regiment.

Winters could be murderous, with subzero temperatures for weeks at a time, brutal temperatures requiring one soldier's full-time efforts to keep the numerous fireplaces stoked in the Custer household: six fireplaces on the ground floor and four on the second story. It had been one of those second-floor fireplaces that caused the house to burn to its foundation in the frigid month of February 1874. Just about everything the Custers owned had been destroyed in that disaster, but Libbie mourned most the loss

of but one cherished item: a wig she had woven from
trimmings of her beloved husband Autie's long, curly, red
blond hair.

As soon as the ground thawed that spring, a second
luxurious home had risen on the same foundation. The
pride not only of the Custers, but of the entire Seventh as
well, it boasted a thirty-two-foot living room with a wide
bay window, and a billiard room on the second floor.

No home with so much style would be complete without
a library adorned with Custer's favorite classics, along with
biographies of famous generals, history texts, and a smat-
tering of fiction. In addition, there were several rooms
where he exhibited his collection of guns, Indian artifacts,
and stuffed animal trophies collected over his years in the
west. In that decade Custer had harvested quite a collection
of trophies, each taken with a nonregulation sporting
weapon. His reputation with a rifle had spread far and wide.
Even Richard A. Roberts, civilian secretary assigned to
General Alfred H. Terry for this summer's Sioux campaign,
had written, "Custer is the best shot with a Creedmore
rifle."

Over the door to Custer's study, where many of his most
prized mementos were displayed, hung a hand-lettered
sign reading:

MY ROOM
Lasiate Ogni Speranza, Voi Ch'entrate
(All hope abandon, ye who enter here)
CAVE CANUM
(Beware the Dog)

In that study Custer had spent many hours toiling over
his memoirs the last couple of years, insisting that Libbie
be in the room with him while he wrote "Battling with the
Sioux on the Yellowstone" and began his "War Memoirs"
for *Galaxy* magazine readers back east. It seemed everyone
on the other side of the Missouri River thirsted for his vivid
tales of action and adventure, danger and bloodshed along
the western frontier. So important was reading and writing
to his own life, Custer even enjoyed teaching others to

read. Many were the hours he would spend on idle winter afternoons with servants' and enlisted men's children gathered round his knee, a reader in one hand, a speller in the other. These scenes were a delight for Elizabeth Custer to watch, for Libbie and her darling Autie had long ago given up the hope of ever having children of their own.

Custer ordered a huge garden planted behind his house, enclosed by a tall, stout fence to keep his numerous hunting dogs and staghounds out. The general preferred a lot of fresh vegetables to the usual army rations. Family cook Mary saw to it that the general and his lady were fed appetizing meals envied all along Officers' Row.

In the spring of 1875 a ballroom had been added to the house so that Custer and his lady Elizabeth could entertain in a much grander style. Libbie was fond of inviting young ladies from their hometown of Monroe, Michigan, or even new acquaintances from their visits to New York City, all to come spend their summers at the fort as guests of the regimental commander. That warm, exhilarating laughter of young women went a long way toward brightening the dull prairie duty of many a young officer himself far from home. Elizabeth had seen to it that a special chandelier was purchased and hung in the ballroom, along with a harp and a grand piano she had rented in St. Paul, Minnesota, and freighted all the way back to Fort Lincoln in an army wagon.

Music and plays contributed to a livelier atmosphere than existed at most frontier posts of the time. The minuets, waltzes, and Virginia reels played in the Custer's grand ballroom provided some diversion for an otherwise drab existence. One might hear some soldier plucking out tunes such as "La Paloma," "Susan James," or "Little Annie Roonie" on a banjo or guitar, or scratched on a fiddle. Whenever Libbie found any trooper to have even the slightest talent at anything musical, that ability was exploited for everyone's amusement and entertainment.

Even a Swiss cavalryman recently immigrated from his mountain homeland became a regular visitor to the Custer home. While the general lounged on a bearskin rug in his parlor, the Swiss musician performed Tyrolean melodies on his zither. So fond of music itself and a bird's cheerful songs, Custer had even brought a pet mockingbird all the way from Kentucky when his Seventh Cavalry had been transferred back to frontier duty.

Still Custer had grown restless after a short time in Dakota. Even during the busy social season at Fort Abraham Lincoln, with the fames and the charades and those vignettes played before backdrops of painted canvas, Custer grew restive and bored. Those costume balls and plays were not enough to satisfy this commander of an isolated fortress on the far western edge of an immense frontier. There was something unnamed lacking in his life, and for so long now he had dared not admit it to himself.

Each fall Libbie would join him on a trip back east, perhaps going on to Chicago or New York for some of the bright lights and bustling activity of those teeming cities. Yet the sophisticated veneer wore thin all too quickly, and he found himself suffering that gnawing emptiness once more . . . needing to replenish the well of his own soul with those desolate prairies and high plains of the far west. Only there on the wild land did he feel himself near whole again—as near to being whole as he had been for the seven years since that long winter gone.

Only then did Custer feel somewhat closer to the Cheyenne woman's wildness once more.

"Your mount is ready, Mr. Burkman?"

"It is, General." The private shoved the stub of the pencil back in his pocket and stuffed his notebook in his blue tunic. "I saddled Vic for you, sir. And the troop farrier has Dandy ready for Mrs. Custer—just as you requested, sir."

"Splendid! I want both those fine animals to get their fill of clean prairie air on this campaign."

Burkman watched the general remove his hat and swipe his forearm across his brow. In the short time he had known Custer, the young private had watched the general's hairline recede at a steady pace. Burkman declared cheerily, "Gonna be a hot one for sure today, General."

He winked at his orderly. "Not even summer yet, John. I'll just bet you can't wait."

Custer stood in Dakota Territory after all, where every scorching summer the land lay blistered like steamy rawhide beneath a merciless one-eyed sun. Winters were just as deadly if not even more brutal, with nothing to slow the arctic wind but the grasslands of Canada.

Still, winter or summer, one of the biggest problems remained that the fort had no well, not even a cistern. Every day water wagons made that bumpy ride down to the river to draw the day's rations. By late December or early January, those on the water detail would have to chop through as much as five feet of ice before they could haul water up from the Missouri.

If it wasn't the snow swirling like white buckshot in an eye-stinging winter blizzard, then the soldiers of the Seventh found the summer sky turned black with grasshoppers. If the grasshoppers clinging to everything and everybody wasn't enough, all a man had to do was wait until the cool of the evening for relief from the excruciating temperatures, when the hordes of mosquitoes would rise up above the Big Muddy like a biting, bloody curse suffered upon the land. Some of the soldiers who had to be outdoors at that time of day had even taken to wearing a balloonlike helmet made with wire and draped with a special netting for protection from the bloodsucking monsters.

After a while a lot of those old-timers with the Seventh Cavalry cursed their lot, wondering what they had done to deserve their imprisonment in this hellhole on the Upper Missouri. Many of them joked that Satan's roaring fires of sulfur and brimstone could be no worse than late summer at Fort Abraham Lincoln when the thermometer still hovered at better than ninety degrees come sunset and the clock chiming off nine bells.

"Thank you, Mr. Burkman." Custer admired his stocking-footed, blaze-faced sorrel. "Vic looks ready as ever, doesn't she?"

Handing the general his reins, John said, "She does that, sir. Even more splendid when you're in the saddle."

"If I didn't know better, I'd say my orderly was bucking for a promotion!"

Custer laughed easily as he tightened Vic's reins to turn his mare toward the massive parade where the troops gathered for review. Most of the men had spent the last few nights in tents off a distance from the post on a shakedown to ready them for what lay ahead on their march across the western prairie.

"Be sure to fetch Dandy for Mrs. Custer and have him saddled promptly, John," Custer reminded as he pranced away, waving his big cream-colored hat in the humid dawn air. "Her luggage is down in the foyer, just inside the front door. Have it thrown in my wagon, will you?"

Burkman nodded. He watched the general bring the hat down to strike Vic on her right flank, spurring the mare into that bustle of activity that was the Seventh U.S. Cavalry marching to war.

CHAPTER 2

THE sun hung a hand high above the horizon when the last wagon was hitched and all troopers stood in formation for parade review through the fort. Libbie, and Custer's own sister Margaret, who had married handsome, solemn James Calhoun of L Company, both sat sidesaddle, anxious and waiting to get under way. Earlier that spring Custer had applied for, and won, a transfer of Calhoun's younger brother, Fred, from General Terry's infantry to his own regiment of cavalry. Fred Calhoun, everyone knew, had married Custer's young niece, Emma Reed. Custer wanted his family gathered round him with the coming campaign and his approaching hour of glory.

"Is all in readiness, Custer?"

General Alfred H. Terry, commander of the Department of Dakota, sat ramrod straight atop his gray charger.

"We're ready, sir!" Custer exclaimed exuberantly. "Shall we press on?"

"By all means, Custer. Let's march."

He shouted to his bugler, Henry Voss. "'Boots and Saddles,' Sergeant!"

With the brassy explosion of those first few notes from Voss's bugle, there arose over the baked-mud parade a chorus of cheers and huzzahs. The army would be hard-pressed to find a single one of these men clambering aboard their mounts who didn't consider a march across the prairie highly preferable to a summer spent lollygagging around Fort Lincoln. Each and every one of these men in blue cheered and slapped themselves onto saddle leather, happy as only a horse soldier could be. Each knew he had a grand opportunity to whip some Sioux and come riding back home with a victory beneath his army belt. Word from the scouts themselves was that they'd have an easy time of it—what with joining up with Colonel John Gibbon riding out of the west leading his cavalry and infantry both, and General George Crook marching up from the south with thirteen hundred more.

A few of the old files had been grumbling over the last few days despite the promising odds, asking themselves why they had to go along anyway. With that many soldiers and those few redskins . . . why, there damn sure wouldn't be enough warriors to go around to make this trip worth a teetotaler's spit. Hardly enough Sioux bucks to make the fight worth the trouble of loading a carbine or working up a sweat arguing with a pack mule.

"Boston! Autie! You ride back with Tom. Hear, now?" ordered Custer.

The two young men pulled their horses out, whipping them back to Captain Tom Custer's C Company. Brother Boston, youngest of the Custer boys, all of twenty-five and a civilian forager on the army payroll for seventy-five dollars per month for these past five years, had taken a leave of absence since the third of March to accompany his two older brothers on this Sioux campaign. And young Autie—Harry Armstrong Reed—named after his famous uncle, an adventuresome, fresh-faced farm boy of eighteen years, loped after his Uncle Boston back to join Uncle Tom's troops.

"Bugler!" Custer roared at Voss. "Sound the advance! Center guide, forward, *ho!*"

Custer nodded to General Terry before he spurred off to fetch Libbie. Sister Margaret would await the passing of husband James Calhoun's L Company.

Behind General Terry arose that familiar creak of slat bed, freight-wagon wood, tire iron, and harness leather, the slaps and curses of wagon master and teamsters as they set the regiments in motion. Custer's cavalry and Terry's infantry, hooves and boots and wheels all cutting and chopping at the rain-soaked, sun-hardened dreariness of the parade. Having spent the last two days and nights on Cannon Ball Creek some three miles below the fort in preparation for this campaign, the men were itching to head west at last.

Out from the fringes of Officers' Row stepped the genteel wives, each waving a handkerchief in farewell and dabbing at her eyes with that most private, painful sorrow of parting. Many more women and children surged out from along Soapsuds Row, where the wives of enlisted men and noncommissioned officers, some mopping at their own red eyes with apron corners, gathered to see their men off. Some of the children marched and skipped beside the procession itself, singing along with the troopers as it seemed the entire fort bellowed out that stirring theme for the gallant Seventh Cavalry. Some of the young boys even waved scraps of cloth tied to the ends of sticks held high overhead, while toddlers furiously beat on old tin pans like drums.

Everyone at Fort Abraham Lincoln knew the words to "GarryOwen," a sprightly Irish drinking song adopted by Custer upon the formation of the Seventh Cavalry after the end of the Civil War:

> We'll break windows, break the doors,
> The watch knock down by threes and fours;
> Then let the doctors work their cures,
> And tinker up our bruises.

As Custer and Libbie passed by the Indian camp just west of the fort, Lieutenant Charles Varnum signaled his thirty Arikara scouts to fall into formation. Weeping squaws and wailing copper-skinned children trotted along the column, grasping for one last touch of a loved one riding off to fight ancient tribal enemies—the feared Lakota Sioux.

Warriors all, these Ree scouts wore their finest feathers and smeared themselves with paint for this grandest of marches, every man among them singing his personal chant of war medicine more loudly than the man beside him. The air filled with a high-pitched screeching, wailing din that for a moment threatened to drown out the lusty bass voices of the troopers belting out their favorite song. Yet as blood stopping as was that scene played out beside the Indian lodges, no clamor could overshadow the bright, courageous verses of the Seventh's fighting song.

> We'll beat the bailiffs, out of fun,
> We'll make the mayor and sheriffs run;
> We are the boys no man dares dun,
> If he regards his whole skin!

That pounding of Arikara drums along with the singsong wail of Indian scouts was almost too much for Libbie. Somewhere deep inside she sensed this campaign was not to be the easy, surgical strike into the Indian heartland everyone claimed it would be. Something told her all too many of these men who trotted behind her husband this bright May morning would not be coming back.

"By all the saints!" Custer exclaimed, suddenly rescuing Elizabeth from her melancholy reverie. "Take a look behind you, Libbie. Now, isn't that as grand a sight as you'd ever hope to see?"

She turned for a moment to watch the long, snaking bullwhip procession in column-of-twos winding its way out of that cluster of gray buildings, leaving the squalid prairie post far behind.

"Yes, Autie!" she agreed, calling him by that nickname used only by family. "I couldn't imagine being anywhere else but by your side."

He peered into those dark, calf brown eyes framed by

that shimmering chestnut hair tied up around her face, every strand neatly stuffed beneath a riding bonnet and veil. "You are a spoiled little girl, Elizabeth Bacon Custer."

"Just what makes you call me spoiled, General Custer?"

"First, there was your father, the esteemed Judge Daniel Stanton Bacon of Monroe, Michigan—God rest his soul—to give you everything your heart desired. And now you have me to do the very same thing for you."

"My darling, darling Bo," she said, pouting her full, lightly rouged lips. "Daddy gave me but one thing I ever truly wanted."

"And . . . what was that, Rosebud?"

"Why, George Armstrong Custer," she slapped a glove at his buckskinned forearm. "The one and only thing I ever truly wanted I had to get myself! And that was *you!*"

To her surprise Custer tore up the bottom of her veil and pressed his lips to hers—surprised, for she had never allowed him any more than a sterile peck on the cheek when in public. As he drew away, Custer found her eyes had grown as big as china saucers: full of wonder, a coy haughtiness, but not without a hint of genuine pleasure.

"I'll miss you, Libbie . . . truly I will," he whispered above the noisy clamor.

She turned away before her tears began to flow. "We have such a splendid life together, you and I, don't we? I shall miss you while you're away. These are always the darkest hours . . . your leaving."

Suddenly she swirled back to look at him with a start, compelled by something to do so. The sun hung directly behind his head in its rising, its light refracting a reddish gold off the bristles of his hogged haircut. In that instant it appeared Custer had cloaked about him a strange light, an aura of some otherworldliness, not unlike the halos that encircled the heads of saints in those Bible storybooks back in Monroe, where she had attended seminary.

"My dear, dear Bo—I will miss you so very . . . very much."

> Instead of Spa we'll drink brown ale,
> And pay the reckoning on the nail,

No man for debt shall go to jail
From GarryOwen in glory!

More than a half mile in advance of the columns now, Custer reined up atop a hill and turned to watch the advance.

Like some old wooden bucket spilled on the dry, thirsty ground and pouring forth its contents, Fort Abraham Lincoln sat forlorn and abandoned, emptied of men and life and purpose. All three two-storied barracks and those six detached officers' quarters. The granary, administrative offices, a dispensary for the regimental surgeons . . . the guardhouse, ordnance depot, and powder magazine along with the commissary and quartermaster storehouses. Soap-suds Row, where the laundresses plied their varied trades, in addition to the quartermaster stables. Six cavalry stables capable of holding more than six hundred mounts, and the sutler's store with a small, squat barbershop hunkered right against it. Not that far away sat a cabin of peeled cotton-wood logs, crudely roofed with oiled canvas that served as a photographer's cabin, where for the nominal price of a dollar, any soldier could send a tintype home to family and loved ones.

In the early morning's cool breezes, the stars-and-stripes swallowtail guidons snapped feverishly, popping alongside the blue regimental flag bearing the proud eagle of the Seventh. Forward of them all sailed Custer's own personal standard—a deep blue-and-scarlet silk of his own design, crossed silver sabers nearly covering the entire field.

Two full miles of army wound its way up the hills from Fort Abraham Lincoln, twelve hundred men: Terry's single company of Sixth Infantry, two companies of the Seventeenth Infantry, Custer's Seventh, plus one hundred seventy-six civilians—the entire procession mounted on or pulled by some seventeen hundred animals parading out of the badlands of the Missouri River. The spectacle included one hundred fourteen six-mule-team wagons, along with the thirty-seven two-horse teams and some seventy other vehicles.

At about two o'clock Custer chose a pleasant campsite

appropriate for the entire command and the grazing of so many animals on the banks of the Little Heart River thirteen miles out from the fort. With Libbie beside him he rode to a gentle swell of land to watch the columns approach, his own heart pounding with martial pride at the sight spread before him across the gold and brown and green of prairie, the great land sprinkled with a bright carpet of its spring flowers.

"They're your soldiers, Autie. No mistake of that," she sighed as he slid the hat from his head and rubbed at the bristles of thinning hair. "You must care for each and every one of them as your own children."

Custer looked at her strangely for a moment. "I always put the welfare of my men first, Libbie. What a strange thing for you to tell me."

She shook her head, not at all knowing now why she herself had said it. "Look, Bo!" Libbie pointed down at the approaching columns. "You can see dear Tom down there!"

"Sure enough!" He laughed as they both waved to that tiny figure in creamy buckskins and a white slouch hat perched astride his dun mare.

"How much he dresses like you, Autie. That man fairly worships you, like young Boston, even little nephew Harry. Big brother, brave uncle—you are every bit of that and more to the whole family now. What would any of them do without you?"

Custer stared absently at Tom, still such a tiny, almost indistinct figure among that sea of blue tunics. "After this campaign, he'll be his own man, Libbie. No longer any need of him following on my coattails. I'll see to it. Tom is destined to ascend the upper rungs of the army ladder. And I—I'd like to take you on to Washington, my dear."

"Washington?" She placed a delicate hand against her breast in surprise.

"No . . . you might fool others, Libbie," he chided, "but you can't convince me you haven't thought of it many times."

"Why, the last time we were there together was during the war. Our abbreviated honeymoon, as I recall."

"Just start getting used to the idea!"

He swept her chin into his cupped palm, planting a kiss on her parted lips. Custer held his mouth to hers for a long time, until he finally opened his eyes to find her staring mule-eyed at him.

"At least you didn't pull away this time," he said, licking his lips, tasting the tantalizing flavor of her lip rouge. "Perhaps you enjoyed my touch."

"Y-yes," she finally stammered. "I have . . . have always enjoyed your touch—oh, how I will miss you, Autie!"

Libbie raised her ivory chin and closed her eyes for him this time. Her lips parted slightly, inviting.

Custer had never refused her.

CHAPTER 3

Just before dawn on the eighteenth, a summer squall rumbled over the valley of the Little Heart River, soaking everything that hadn't been covered with gum ponchos or rubber sheets, leaving cargo, wagons, and tents steaming beneath the new sun.

At eight A.M. the air still hung heavy as the regimental paymaster completed his issuance to the men of the Seventh Cavalry. Custer had purposely ordered him to accompany his troops west on the first day's march so that no soldier could be tempted to spend his meager pay with the post sutler, or with those painted prostitutes at Sadie's Shady Bower or Clementine's Retreat, Bismarck's infamous fleshpots.

In addition, the general gave his troops a few minutes to write a letter home, as Custer knew many would be sending money back to family in the States.

"Mr. Cooke! Have trumpeter Voss sound 'The General,'" Custer ordered his adjutant, Lieutenant W. W. Cooke. "Let's be pulling for the Powder River!"

"Aye, General!" Cooke snapped his heels together, giving a smart salute.

Custer said to Libbie: "Every time I think about it, I'm glad I made Cooke adjutant before we moved the regiment to Kentucky to control those infernal sheet-draped night riders. He's been a blessing ever since. Not that Moylan wasn't competent. Just that, well—Mr. Cooke adds a dash of something to our corps."

"Because he's a Canadian?" she asked, hinting at a grin.

He shook his head. "I'm not quite sure just what it is, really. He has a way with the ladies, as does brother Tom. Why, I'd dare venture to say those two dandies have seen more—well, let's just say those two make a rounding pair, they do. Dashing, gallant gentlemen. Exactly what I want folks to think of the Seventh when they lay eyes on officers like Cookey or Tom."

"You've surrounded yourself with the very best, dear," she reminded him, handing her empty coffee tin to Custer.

"More, Mrs. Custer?" he asked.

"No." She rose, combing her hands down that long buckskin riding habit her husband had ordered tailored in St. Paul especially for her. "The darkest of hours is upon me, dear, sweet man. I must tear myself from you and let you go off to your other mistress now."

Custer twitched at her sudden declaration. "Whatever can you mean by that?"

After all these years and all these miles, he brooded, *how did she . . . what can she be thinking of . . . who would have told—*

"That beautiful, dark-eyed, seductive young mistress who keeps calling you away from my arms with her siren song, Autie." Libbie turned west, gazing down that gentle slope where the bustle of twelve hundred men and many more animals raised a deafening clamor.

As that noise rumbled up the hillside toward their informal officers' row, she continued. "I've known about her for a long . . . long time, Bo. But, kept it to myself, not wishing to clutter up our lives with decisions . . . having to choose. Let's face it—I knew I would lose if it ever came down to it. So why force you to choose between me and her?"

He had struggled to keep the young dark-eyed one out of his mind—out of his mind completely but for those long, soul-chilling winter nights when he found himself recalling a long winter gone. . . . Only when he was lacking what Libbie had for too long neglected to give him of herself . . . only when he could no longer force down that memory of the dark-skinned one he had kept hidden away inside him for these seven long years . . . only then did Custer admit to himself that he had always wanted to go back . . . back in time and—

How had Libbie found out about Monaseetah? Was it Benteen?

Libbie was in his arms suddenly, spilling the remaining coffee in his cup all over a boot and a forearm. He was even more surprised by her impulsive embrace.

"You silly," she murmured into the linsey-woolsey shirt she had personally sewn for him. "You can be so thick-headed at times."

"Thick-headed?"

"Your mistress." She stepped back, cocked her head at him with a stern gleam of reproachment in her calf-brown eyes and balled both hands atop the hips of her buckskin riding skirt.

"My . . . my mistress?" he squeaked.

"If you had to choose," she wagged a parental finger at him disapprovingly, "Elizabeth Bacon Custer would be the one to loose, wouldn't she?"

He swallowed hard, not believing it had come to this.

"Your love affair with the army, Bo!" She giggled, rallying a brave smile she let rain over him as she took a step closer, gazing up into his sapphire eyes.

He stared down at her in disbelief, the sting of some tears already smarting his eyes, totally dumbstruck in the wonder of this woman he had known for all these years and perhaps never really known at all.

"That's what I'm jealous of—the truth be known," she went on. "Your love affair with the wildness and freedom of it. And I'm bitter toward the army because they allow you to run away from me out there and play at being a soldier—just like a schoolboy."

Custer swept her into his arms and held her close.

"I've always known, Autie," she admitted quietly. "Known that if you had to choose, I would rate second best . . . only what you came home to when you couldn't be anywhere else. But I've taken what I could of you, when I could . . . and I've lived a very full life."

"But, it isn't over—"

"I'll always be there when you decide to come riding back home to me, my darling Bo." She flashed him a valiant smile even though her watering eyes told him something far darker.

Elizabeth turned away, smoothing her palms across the buckskin skirt, then fussed with those mother-of-pearl buttons on the front of her jacket. Looking down the slope, she noticed Custer's sister Margaret striding uphill, arm in arm with husband James Calhoun.

She turned back to Custer suddenly, desperately. "It is come. The hour I dread the most, dear heart. Come . . . kiss me. And with those lips tell me you have inside some very private and special place reserved just for me still. Kiss me."

He swept her up and held her fiercely, pressing his lips against her with a consuming passion that surprised him. He too realized the time had come to part—her blackest hour.

Calhoun and Maggie stood some ten feet away, appearing as nonchalant as possible without interrupting the embrace. James stared at the trees, the ground, his fingers—anything. Margaret, on the other hand, grinned impishly at the couple, as if she had just been let in on the biggest secret ever.

"Maggie!" Custer exploded when he noticed her out of the corner of his eye. "How long've you been standing there?"

"Long enough!" Libbie answered with a grin, winking at Margaret. "Plain to tell by the smile on your sister's face!"

"Sure enough." Margaret winked back with her own Custer blue eyes. "This isn't a pleasant time for any of us . . . but it needs something special in the doing. Might as well do it as well as you two in your private parting . . . if there's a parting to take place. Right, Jimbo?"

The tall, strapping lieutenant blushed.

She nudged him with her elbow. "Am I ready to bid you farewell, my love?"

Custer had always liked that about his freckle-faced younger sister—her straightforwardness that cut straight to the core or the quick, depending which side you found yourself on. He had always supposed that trait came from growing up the only girl in a family of prank-pulling, mercilessly teasing boys.

Calhoun said, "The corporal with your horse should be—"

"Here," she answered, turning to watch the young soldier bringing an animal up the slope, followed closely by Tom Custer, who waved his wide-brimmed hat.

"What the devil are you doing here?" Custer asked of his brother.

"Say—that's a fine ticket you've just handed me!" Tom answered as he halted, handing the reins of the saddled mare over to Libbie. "Here I have a sister of blood and a sister of marriage bidding us a sad farewell, and you actually think I'm going to book out on it?"

"Tom is a dashing, gallant young cavalry captain," Libbie said approvingly. "And you must keep in mind, Autie—he is *very* available."

Tom rushed at Libbie, sweeping her off her feet and swinging her round and round several times to the accompaniment of cascading giggles. Finally he dropped Libbie to the ground and kissed her warmly, ending his embrace with a stout hug.

"Libbie . . . Libbie . . . Libbie, you dear old lady," he said, staring down at her brown liquid eyes. "You will get me married off yet, won't you?"

"I promise, Tom." And she laid a lovely white hand over her heart in oath. "You're next. Then Boston and nephew Harry. I keep trying—"

"Oh, you must keep trying," he begged, smiling larger than life as he gazed into her teary eyes. "Later this summer, after we return from whipping these damned Indians—excuse my swearing, sisters—but you must have some of your lady friends come back out west and join us for vacation. Perhaps Emma Wadsworth or Agnes Bates. I'll have to get truly serious about this marrying matter this summer, old lady. Will you still help me, sister? Promise?"

She gazed into her brother-in-law's eyes, that scarlet spot on his cheek from the bullet wound at Saylor's Creek still very much a rosy birthmark. "You silly man. You're everything your older brother is not. Of course, I'll help see you married off to a fine young maiden from Monroe."

Tom stepped back, sighed, and swept her hand up for a chivalrous kiss. "Thank you, lady fair. If you find for me but half the lady my big brother married, I shall reside in heavenly bliss for the rest of my days on this mortal plane."

"You're an errant knight, Thomas Ward Custer."

"Farewell, m'lady." And he swept his hat across the ground in a grand bow, then plopped it back atop his head. "I must be off to the Indian wars. Be-damned—appears my company leaves without me!"

Tom scrambled off downhill, turning once as he dashed through the scrubby brush to wave a farewell to his sister and sister-in-law. "I'll take proper care of James for you, Maggie!" he hollered back to the little group atop the sun-drenched slope.

"I have no fear you will, you naughty boy!" Margaret teased at her brother.

At that very moment the regimental band struck up the plaintive chords of "The Girl I Left Behind Me."

> The hour was sad I left the maid,
> A ling'ring farewell taking;
> Her sighs and tears my steps delay'd—
> I thought her heart was breaking.
>
> In hurried words her name I bless'd,
> I breathed the vows that bind me,
> And to my heart in anguish press'd
> The girl I left behind me.

Maggie went to Custer. Placing her hands alongside his ruddy cheeks, she boosted herself up on her toes, planting an uncharacteristic kiss on his lips.

"Until I see all those lovely freckles again, brother dear." Her hands slipped away, swiping at the tears caught in the corners of her eyes.

"Freckles again?"

"You can't help the sun, Autie," Libbie remonstrated as she slipped an arm in his.

"I suppose I can't. A man whose life is outdoors, and me cursed with this fair skin."

"Just make certain it's a thick skin, dear," she reminded, leading him over to her horse. "Able to turn any warrior's arrow, do you hear?"

He stopped her, turning her round to face him. "The problem I'll face is not arrows, Rosebud. My main concern is to keep the Indians from running on me. My only fear is that they won't stand and fight. I don't want to be left holding onto an empty village again . . . a hollow victory. If only they'll stand and fight."

"Well," she cleared her throat, thick with sadness, "I myself can't stand here any longer, dear." She pressed against him with a fierce, clinging embrace, the way ivy clings to the oak.

Custer himself stood like a plank of rough-hewn timber, arms nailed at his sides, while she hugged him. It was so uncharacteristic of her. In fact, this whole morning had been unlike Libbie. Last night, while she drifted off to sleep with her fragrant chestnut hair spread across his bare chest, he loved sensing her bare breasts rise and fall against his own cool flesh. The closeness of her naked, heated skin . . . and not being able to have her. All these years—she denied them both their intimacy because it was too painful a reminder. Unable to conceive children, she saw no sense in any intimacy between them at all.

But last night. After all those years. . . .

Libbie pulled away, running the back of her hand under her nose, and yanked on that scarlet hunting cap he liked her to wear. When she had a bow in the ribbon beneath her chin, right near the ever-present cameo brooch, Elizabeth finally turned to her horse, allowing John Burkman to cup his hands and boost her to the saddle.

For a long, pensive moment, she peered down at the young striker, looking all the shorter against the massive backdrop of tall George Armstrong Custer and the mountainous James Calhoun.

"Good-bye, John." She finally scratched the words out of her dry throat, wearing a sad smile. "You'll look after the general for me, won't you?"

"Why, yes ma'am. I surely will. . . ." He wrinkled his brow at her woeful expression and was fixing to ask her why she thought her husband needed someone to look after him, but Libbie suddenly whirled away, tapping her high-buttoned boots against the army mount to speed away. She was leaving Dandy behind with her husband. He would take both Vic and Dandy to the Yellowstone.

Margaret galloped off right behind Elizabeth with a wave and a final kiss blown to Calhoun. She trotted up beside Elizabeth before reining back, both women heading east up the bank of the Little Heart River, letting their horses lope frisky and playful in the cool morning air still heavy with the remnants of last night's thunderstorm.

Libbie couldn't look back.

She dared not.

Custer stood with his arms hanging useless at his sides, watching her go. Wondering what to do with his big hands, he finally stuffed them into his pockets, feeling like a schoolboy detained after everyone else had headed out to the schoolyard, caught someplace he shouldn't be. For the first time in their lives together—he sensed something different between them, something sour tasting at the back of his throat.

John Burkman watched Custer staring after Libbie, remembering that sad, somber smile Mrs. Custer had on her lovely china-doll face. For as little a time as Private Burkman had known the general, he had come to love him. And Burkman's heart more so than his head had sworn a fierce allegiance to George Armstrong Custer. He didn't mind all those other soldiers jealous of his cushy assignment. They called him dog-robber, the common, derisive term applied to orderlies who cared for their superior's personal needs. Such abuse was a small price to pay to be allowed closeness to this great and noble being.

Custer turned to Burkman, hearing the young soldier step up behind him. Calhoun drew close on Custer's left, all three intently watching the two women ride the breast of the flowing land beneath a climbing sun.

"You know, gentlemen"—Custer boyishly stuffed his hands deeper into his leather pants pockets and hunched his shoulders up—"a good soldier really has two mistresses. Exactly as Libbie told me."

He stared at the ground, scuffing a boot-toe into the sodden grass and kicking up some wet soil. "While he's loyal to one mistress, the other must suffer." Of a sudden he looked up and said, "Gentlemen! It's nearly eight-thirty. Let's ride for the Yellowstone!"

Turning, Libbie gazed back at the two-mile-long columns winding their way up from the valley of the Little Heart in the cool, morning breezes that would have tugged at the women's dresses had it not been for the buckshot sewn in the hems.

As their horses blew, only then did the faint, faraway strains of "GarryOwen" reach her ears. Off to the Yellowstone and the land of the mighty Sioux. Off to whip Sitting Bull and Crazy Horse.

> Our hearts, so stout, have got us fame,
> For soon 'tis known from whence we came;
> Where'ere we go they dread the name
> Of GarryOwen in glory!

In the next heartbeat a solitary figure raced out of the long, dark columns and stopped, wheeling round on his stockinged sorrel mare to peer back at that distant knoll to the east. He pulled away from the lines of blue-clad troopers a few yards, rising to stand like a ramrod in his stirrups, gazing back at the women on top of their rise, silhouetted against the morning sky. He was waving his hat at the end of his long arm, back and forth in long sweeps before he slapped his big charger on the rump with that cream-colored hat and raced pell-mell for the head of the march like the Devil himself was larruping at Vic's tail.

Almost like a prayer, Libbie whispered a few lines of poetry she once memorized while a school-girl in Monroe, waiting like school-girls always had for their one true beau to gallop into their life.

> He who leaves is happier still,
> Than she who's left behind.

As the last words fell from her trembling lips, the first rays of sunlight broke through that muslin-thin overcast, making for a strange light as fractured sunbeams spread over the long columns winding west.

With tiny, dewy particles of moisture drenching the morning air, a sudden and eerie mirage spun itself before her eyes as Libbie watched that long, blue snake poke its way toward the yawning land like a hungry abyss that opened itself to greet the Seventh. Reflected in those particles of moisture like a huge mirror stretched across the blue-gray canopy was the image of the U.S. Seventh Cavalry . . . marching . . . marching equidistant between earth and sky.

A stifled gasp caught in her throat. She put a trembling hand to her lips.

Oh, if she had only realized it before . . . all those years gone, years bitterly wasted. Years she had no idea would end so soon.

"What is it, Libbie?" Maggie whispered.

"Nothing," she declared bravely, swiping at her eyes. Swallowing against the knot in her chest, Libbie watched the mirage riding half-way between earth and sky, and knew as certainly as she knew she loved Autie that it was a premonition of some great catastrophe to befall those gallant men.

> Our hearts so stout, have got us fame,
> For soon 'tis known from whence we came;
> Where'ere we go they dread the name
> Of GarryOwen in glory!

CHAPTER 4

Bʏ the time the Seventh had rendezvoused on the Yellowstone with Colonel John Gibbon's forces drawn from both Fort Ellis and Fort Shaw in Montana Territory, Custer's troops felt as if they had marched through hell itself to arrive at the mouth of Rosebud Creek.

Besides the surprising snowstorm that kept them sitting for two days back in May, the men had also suffered through drenching spring rains and stinging hail, and more recently had blistered beneath a relentless sun interrupted each afternoon by a brief interlude of thunderstorms before sunset. It could be that way this time of year on the northern plains. Good reason for a man to keep his "rubber blanket" handy—what others called their "gum blanket"—a rubber poncho to turn the rain. Slipped over the head and measuring some four feet by six feet, it had already proved itself on this campaign.

Certain fragments of the regiment had marched off on one or the other of two long, tough scouts that convinced the expedition commanders they were narrowing the noose around the hostiles. Now that General Alfred H. Terry's Dakota column had joined up with Gibbon's Montana column, everyone figured the Sioux were gathering to the south of them.

At three P.M. on 21 June, General Terry brought to order a conference of the high-echelon officers of his combined regiments aboard the *Far West*, the stern-wheeled river steamer anchored against the north bank of the Yellowstone River. Its pilothouse lined with thick iron boiler plate, the steamboat was fortified against a probable attack by hostiles along these western rivers. The boiler plate had been curved slightly to deflect enemy bullets, in addition to having a head-high opening in front so the wheelman would have a full view of the river ahead. The lower deck was protected by sacks of grain along with four-foot cordwood stacked on end all round the gunwales.

What had so far been a hot and sultry Wednesday appeared to offer some relief on the far horizon. Gray and purple thunderheads were building with a fury on the distant rim of the prairie as the officers crammed themselves into Captain Grant Marsh's dining room for their war conference. Custer himself preferred standing by the door as many of Gibbon's officers and most of Terry's infantry commanders set fire to their cheroots, cigars, and pipes. Breathing deep of that freshening breeze slipping along the river, Terry himself eagerly awaited the afternoon's cooling storm.

"The Commissioner of Indian Affairs claims we might see only some five hundred to eight hundred warriors, counting all of fighting age." Terry plunged ahead with his introductory remarks as most every man settled back with a glass of trader Coleman's whiskey.

"He's wrong," declared a new voice.

The room fell silent as the attention shifted toward Custer at the doorway.

"Care to tell us just how the commissioner's figures could be so wrong, sir?"

Custer turned toward the speaker, Colonel John Gibbon. Above his bulbous nose the colonel's dark eyes peered cold like chips of iron. Gibbon had been Custer's artillery instructor during his studies at West Point.

"Those agents, sir, with all due respect," Custer began, pushing himself back into the close, smoky room from the narrow doorway, "either don't know how to count, or they're nothing more than liars."

He waited for the murmurs to quiet themselves before continuing. "I prefer to think they are simply lying through their teeth to their superiors."

"Can you substantiate that, General?" Another officer rose to confront Custer. "And why in blazes would they lie to the army about those goddamned figures?" Major James S. Brisbin, commander of Gibbon's Second Cavalry out of Fort Ellis, was known among his army friends as Grasshopper Jim because of his oft-quick and erratic marches. He stepped near Custer. "What reason would those agents have to give us bad intelligence?"

Custer measured him a moment. "For exactly the same reason those traders become rich men on their meager salaries—sutlering for the government on hardscrabble reservations."

"Explain yourself, Custer," Terry demanded.

"Of course." He stepped into the room that extended the full width of the steamboat. "If those venal traders inform their bosses in the Indian Department how few Indians they really have left on their reservations, they won't get their normal allotments. And when that happens, the traders won't have all those government goods they can continue to sell privately for exorbitant profits at the expense of the Indians living on those godforsaken refuges some call reservations."

"You're claiming those agents have been lying to us, sir?" Brisbin turned to Gibbon as he asked his question. "For the sake of padding their own pockets?"

"Nothing more complicated than that."

The silence grew as thick as the blue smoke in the room until a slight breeze slipped through the open windows and deck doors to stir Terry's papers on the oak table before him.

Terry rose slowly and ground the chair away from him

across the plank flooring. "Appears Custer has presented us with quite a salient dilemma here, gentlemen. A real doozy, in fact. For the moment let's assume he's correct—that there are more Indians flowing from the reservations than anyone really understands, in addition to those noncompliers who were already off the reservations to begin with when any counts were made."

Stuffing the moist stub of a cigar in his mouth, Terry scooped up a handful of coffee-stained papers from the table before him. "Here is my telegram to Division HQ in Chicago last Christmas.

> The Indians at Standing Rock are selling their hides for ammunition, Indians are closely connected to Sitting Bull's band. I ordered a stop to such sales, and I suggested that the Interior Department be requested to give similar orders to the traders."

"Yet those orders weren't issued until the eighteenth of January," Gibbon noted sourly.

"That's correct, John," Terry replied somberly. "Plenty of time for the hostiles to acquire all the Henry repeaters they've wanted for 'hunting purposes.' But allow me to continue the progression of Custer's point. On sixteen February I again wrote Division HQ with my own intelligence, requesting that the three companies of the Seventh Cavalry serving in the Department of the Gulf rejoin their regiment in this department."

Terry looked up from his sheaf of papers, allowing his eyes to touch most of the officers in the room. "I believe every one among you will realize exactly why I was requesting to have every available man, horse, company, and gun made ready for this campaign. Simply because, gentlemen—we weren't all that damned sure just what we'd be facing."

He let that sink in for a moment before continuing. "For if the Indians who passed the winter in the Yellowstone and Powder rivers country should be found gathered in one camp, or in continuous camps, as they usually are so gathered, they could not be attacked without great risk of defeat."

After the embittered mumbling had passed through the assembled officers, Terry emphasized, "Fellas, I want to repeat. Such a great force of Indians could not be attacked by a flimsy force of troops without great risk."

As the last words fell from the general's lips, Custer noticed his commander's eyes were on him. "The Seventh has never let you or General Sheridan down before, sir," Custer stated. "With our full compliment of troops, we aren't about to fail you now."

"Exactly, Custer," Terry said. The smile within the general's dark beard was not lost on a man in the room.

Terry could be quite charming and amiable among his peers—looking more like a professional scholar than a military strategist. Beneath the kind blue eyes and a gently lined face, bronzed by the outdoor life to a hue of old saddle leather, resided a heart brimming with sentiment.

"I merely want all your fellow officers gathered here to understand just what I had to go through to get the Seventh Cavalry put back together for this fight. On twenty-four March I telegraphed Sheridan, asking for the three troops of the Seventh he had stationed down in Louisiana, simply because the most trustworthy scout I had on the Missouri reported not less than two thousand lodges and that the Indians were loaded down with ammunition."

"Two thousand lodges?" Gibbon bolted upright in his ladder-back chair, ripping the dead cigar from his lips.

"Reported as fact, John. He's regarded as one of our best."

"Why, that would make over three thousand warriors ready to fight," Major Brisbin exclaimed in wonder.

Someone else whistled low and long to fill the silence as thick as the storm clouds gathering outside on the Yellowstone prairie.

"More," Custer said. "If you count every weapon-carrying male between thirteen and sixty, you very well could have twice that number to take the field."

"Gentlemen!" Terry held up his hand to quiet the clamor. "Custer could well be right in fearing what numbers we'll confront. Gentlemen, I want to emphasize what I've said. The Indians are confident and intend on making a stand."

"Are you trying to scare us, General?" Gibbon inquired with a wry smile.

"Not in the least, John." Terry flashed a quick grin. "It's just that—well, let me bring in a civilian scout to add some credence to these reports. George! Come on in now!"

From the far door strolled lanky, leathery George Herendeen. Terry had stationed him on the quarterdeck just outside the dining cabin, awaiting his cue from the general.

"This is George Herendeen, a scout of mine who's worked for the army for many years. Not all that long after we pulled out of Lincoln, I called George into consultation regarding the Sioux we'd be meeting and just how many he expected we'd run up against. Would you tell them what you said to me on that occasion, George?"

"Sure, General," the tall, weathered scout answered. "I told you what I felt was the truth. I said that a good many Indians have skipped the reservations, and that if all these various bands leaving the agencies unite with the hostiles of Sitting Bull, they'd probably have a force of some four thousand warriors."

"Besides those sobering numbers, Mr. Herendeen," Terry prompted, "what appears the disposition of the hostiles at this time?"

"What you have gathering up out there, General, is a convention of the hardest, hell, the very best fighting chiefs known on the plains. They are well armed and well supplied with ammunition and provisions."

"Thank you, George," the general nodded to Herendeen as a cue for him to make his exit.

"Excuse me, General. Mr. Herendeen?" Custer pushed off the wall and took a step forward so he could lean on the long, ornate table bolted to the floor in the center of the room. "You brought this scout all the way from Lincoln only to have him tell us this? What is Herendeen to do now?"

"He'll ride along with Colonel Gibbon and myself as one prong of the attack."

"I see," Custer mused, his eyes darting to those maps laid out on the table before Terry. "Mr. Herendeen—"

"Please, General Custer. Call me George."

"All right," and he flashed that famous peg-toothed grin of his, "suppose you tell me, George—are you acquainted with Tullock's Fork—here?"

"Yes, General, I am."

"Do you know where the head of Tullock's Fork lies?"

Herendeen nodded, beginning to catch Custer's drift. "Yep, I do that."

"What's this all about, Custer?" Terry inquired suspiciously and not a little impatiently.

"Tullock's Fork, sir—right here on the divide between the Rosebud and the Little Horn." Custer stabbed a freckled finger on the map. "It flows north to the Yellowstone where we sit at this moment. If Mr. Herendeen here knows that fork and that divide, he's the man I want along with me."

"Pray . . . what the devil for, Custer?" Terry's interest was rubbed sore by now.

"For a moment let's suppose I'll have some need for a man who knows the lay of the land between the Rosebud and the Little Horn and where the hostiles might best be bottled up so they won't run on us."

Terry didn't reply at first. Instead, his eyes shifted from Custer to Herendeen, then dropped to his maps as he studied Tullock's Fork and the Wolf Mountains. At last he peered back at the tall, graying scout.

"George? How would you feel about riding along with the Seventh?"

Herendeen scratched at his heavy beard flecked with some winter iron, pondering the proposal as if it were something tangible and weighty. "All right. It'll be an honor to ride with you, General."

"I'll have you know, Mr. Herendeen—I'm going to work you for your keep!"

Most of the officers in the room chuckled along with Custer and the tall scout.

"He means that, Herendeen," Major Brisbin added,

"that Ol' Iron Butt Custer can ride the pants off any man in this army!"

"Why all this interest in Tullock's Fork, though?" Gibbon interrupted. "To me it appears these Indians of yours are somewhere up the Rosebud." He pulled the stub of a dead cigar from his clenched teeth. "We've flushed them from the Powder and the Tongue. They've got to be far up the Rosebud now—"

"Or . . ." Custer paused, then said: "on the Little Horn itself."

Major James Brisbin watched General Terry wave his hand, shouting for silence against the hubbub in the *Far West*'s dining room, where their afternoon meeting had reached a critical point.

Terry turned to Custer. "Why all this suspicion of the Little Horn?"

"I believe the scout you ordered Major Reno to take—coupled with my own march west to join up with Colonel Gibbon's forces here at the mouth of the Rosebud—pushed them on over to the Little Horn."

"Why the hell would the Sioux move over there if they're reported to be ready and willing to stand and fight?" Gibbon asked, twisting in his chair to look over his shoulder at Custer.

"Simply because Indians choose where they'll stand and fight, as rare as it is. If the place is not right, if their medicine isn't strong enough, or if the odds don't favor them in the slightest—the warriors will run to fight another day."

"Custer here's the most experienced Indian fighter we have," Terry offered by way of explanation.

Brisbin sensed the others in the room give their begrudging agreement.

"They'll find their place," Custer continued. "They'll make their stand. They'll fight, by God. And gentlemen—I might add it will be a fight worthy of any man's career."

"Not just yours, General Custer?" Brisbin growled.

"No, Major." Custer spat it out like slander. "Any officer with the brains—and the balls—to ride down into them when we find that camp."

"Perhaps—" Brisbin slapped a glove along his leg. "Just perhaps you're suggesting a man who's been brought up on charges twice already for not following the orders of a superior officer—"

"Major!" Custer roared.

The small, tight room grew tighter as every man's eyes were suddenly directed toward Custer. No longer a rosy-cheeked "Boy General," the wrinkles of time and sun and wind cut across his brow, crow-footing his eyes and chiseling his cheeks into the thick mustache. A single muscle twitched along his red-stubbled jaw.

"Not once has either of those actions shown that I lost a man on account of what some would *claim* was my refusal to obey orders."

"Nonetheless, General," Brisbin said as he raised a hand for silence in the murmuring room, "without fail you put your men in jeopardy."

"J-jeopardy?" Custer stammered. "We are soldiers, Major Brisbin!"

"Gentlemen!" Terry stepped between the two as the argument heated far too quickly.

"General?" Custer wheeled on Terry. "It appears the major here suffers from Colonel Gibbon's green flu."

Brisbin was certain of it now. He'd struck a raw nerve with Custer. "Green flu?"

"Explain this flu, Custer," Gibbon himself echoed, glaring at the young cavalry commander.

"Yes, sir. Looks as if Major Brisbin—like you, sir—has grown jealous of General Terry's decision to have the Seventh deliver the death blow to these Sioux."

There followed a long moment of silence in the room before Gibbon spoke. "If you do go, it will be a death blow. But not to the Indians, Custer. You'll be lucky if you get out of there with the shirt on your back and what you have left for a scalp still clinging to your head!"

Custer turned to Terry, winking. As if to say Gibbon was proving his own jealousy.

"You know well enough my plan doesn't allow Custer a solitary hand in this action, John." General Terry laid his papers on the table and gazed steadily at Gibbon. "He'll be moving in concert with us."

Gibbon scoffed. "Hardly, General. This man has never moved in concert with anything but his own ambitions. He may appear ready to work with us in this maneuver . . . but he's most able and indeed ready to seek a way out of the confines of what you've planned for him, sir."

"John"—and this time Terry's voice was quieter than normal—"I don't believe I'm hearing you say this. Could it be true that you do indeed find my plan somewhat distasteful?"

Gibbon glared at Terry a moment as if found out, then his eyes softened as he stared out the window at the water of the Yellowstone whipping past. "Alfred, with all due respect, my four troops of Second Cavalry from Fort Ellis have been in the field since the twenty-second of February. I put my six companies of infantry from Fort Shaw on the trail of these bloody savages back in March. Since that time both my cavalry and foot soldiers haven't returned to their station—"

"What's the point of this, General?" Custer appealed to Terry.

"Point, Custer?" Gibbon snapped. "The point is there isn't a man among those soldiers who hasn't come to regard these Sioux as his very own. Why, we've been waiting some five long months to corral and contain these red buggers! By all that's holy—by all that's just—I again appeal to you, General. Allow my troops the honor of crushing them!"

"John," General Terry whispered, the quiet appeal filling the dining room against the backdrop of rhythmic wavelets lapping along the hull. "I've already decided, and that decision will stand. The strongest unit I can field will make our attack. The unit that is the most ready for battle will spearhead this operation. The Seventh Cavalry."

"We are at full strength, Colonel," Custer jumped quickly to conciliate. "Many of your men and animals are simply worn out. It's been a long spring for them. Surely, sir—we can bury this hatchet and find a way to restore amicable relations between our regiments once more. I want no glory for myself alone. Instead, I seek only to play what role General Terry designs for me in this campaign. Believe me, I don't seek to take anything from you or your men. I want only to perform my duty as a soldier."

"And what duty is that, Custer?" Gibbon inquired.

"To do as ordered, sir."

"Only what General Terry sends you to do?"

"Exactly, yes, sir."

"And if General Terry sends you to scout the location of the hostiles? If he orders you to find them first, then *wait* until you can perform in concert with my forces? What then, Custer?"

He gulped slightly, adjusting his shoulders nervously. "I am a soldier first, sir." Custer's back snapped rigid. "I live as a soldier. I will most certainly die not having forsaken that profession, Colonel."

"I believe, gentlemen," Terry yanked every man's attention back to himself, "that we've answered that question concerning Custer. Suppose we proceed."

"General Terry?" Brisbin bristled, barely containing his disappointment.

Terry looked at the commander of the Second Cavalry under Gibbon. "Yes?"

"Will you take up the matter of Custer's use of Lieutenant Low's Gatling guns now?"

"Yes, we will." Terry nodded, his quick blue eyes a little nervous. "I suppose we should dispense with that consideration as the next order of business."

"Gentlemen," Gibbon interrupted, "I suggested to General Terry that if Custer were indeed going to take the lead in this operation, he should at least take along the Gatlings for the safety of his command."

"I could not agree more, and let the record show my concurrence, sir." Brisbin smiled. "When you consider that they can fire over two hundred fifty rounds per minute at some nine hundred yards—I can't imagine any commander trailing such a massive congregation of hostiles without those guns at his disposal."

"The Gatlings are old," Custer replied firmly. There arose a quiet gasp from those officers sweating in the room. "Since seventy-two the army has preferred the Hotchkiss gun. But whatever the case, as for me—the Gatlings will slow me down. I'm leaving them behind."

"Slow you down?" Gibbon, an old artillery officer and proponent of the Gatlings, could not believe what he heard. "You're on a scout, Custer—intending to find the Indians and prevent them from scattering. That's all, Custer. But for the sake of your men, I implore you to take those guns. For some reason I'm not all that sure you and your Seventh won't stumble into more than you can handle keeping those hostiles contained until my troops can come up. With all those estimates we've heard out of the reports here this afternoon, why—those Gatlings might just save your notable scalp."

"I appreciate the concern for my scalp, Colonel. I consider it a high compliment, to be sure. But with respect, those guns are heavy, and I want to be able to move as fast and as light as I can. Those Gatlings would very likely kill me before they'd ever save a single trooper's neck."

Terry coughed. "You choose to leave the Gatlings behind?"

Custer studied Terry before answering the general's question, as if reconsidering one last time. He had thought it over and knew what unknown factors he was heading into, measuring those odds as best he could. He was, after all, a horse soldier. Pure and simple. Being that and that only had served him well in the Civil War and across the plains, from south to north. Custer was a horse soldier. Cavalry. Nothing more than horses and men . . . and guts.

"Yes, sir. I've chosen to leave the Gatlings behind."

"Very well, gentlemen. This matter of the Gatlings has been decided."

"General Terry?" Gibbon said, his eyes still locked on Custer.

"Yes, John."

"Since Custer refuses to take along the guns for an added measure of safety, has he considered my offer of Brisbin's cavalry to ride along as a means of giving him more strength, yet with that *mobility* of the cavalry he so ardently espouses?"

Terry directed his attention to Custer. "What say you to the offer of Brisbin's Second Cavalry?"

"At my disposal?"

Terry shifted his gaze to Gibbon with that question unspoken between them. In turn Gibbon looked at Brisbin.

Grasshopper Jim found himself nodding reluctantly. "Yes," he sighed. "Major Brisbin and his cavalry completely at your disposal, Colonel Custer."

"I can only thank you for your generous offer, Major. And yours, too, Colonel Gibbon." Custer smiled again. "However, as you say, we are to keep the hostiles from scattering on us once more. Seems that's all they've been doing to Major Brisbin all spring."

Custer let the weight of that affront hang in the air. Brisbin opened his mouth, but Gibbon raised his hand, shutting him up, allowing Custer to continue. Brisbin figured Gibbon wanted Custer to hang himself with his ample tongue.

"No, General Terry," Custer continued. "I don't think we'll run into a thing the Seventh isn't capable of handling all by itself."

Brisbin seethed in silent fury at the breach of military etiquette.

"Shall we take up this matter of the scouts to ride along with Custer on the reconnaissance?"

Gibbon nodded in resignation. It was his only response to Terry's question.

Terry continued, clearing his throat. "Very well. Colonel Gibbon has selected six of his finest Crow scouts to accompany the Seventh. To the Crow the colonel is known as No Hip. His most trusted Crow scouts will be ferried across the Yellowstone this evening and presented to your regiment, Custer. They're to act as a medium of communication between our two commands while in the field. I want to stress this fact—you already have some forty Arikara scouts. Gibbon has but thirty now that these six Crow boys are loaned to you. The Crows are more for our benefit than yours on this exploration of yours up the Rosebud. These six are really for service to Gibbon."

"How can they be of service to Gibbon if they're riding with me?"

"Because you'll use them to communicate with Gibbon's command. When you locate the Indian encampment, find out where the hostiles are going, their strength, then dispatch one or more of the Crows back to Gibbon with word. Only in that way can we execute this pincer movement that will keep the hostiles from escaping our noose. In fact, Gibbon here is even assigning Mitch Bouyer to you. He's got a Crow wife. Been living with the Crow for some time. But he's half Sioux. A good man. Trained under none other than Jim Bridger himself. Gibbon evidently feels you should have the best, Custer."

"I appreciate that," Custer answered.

"Very well," Terry replied with a sigh, staring down at those charts and maps spread across the oak table. "If only we knew what has become of General Crook and his forces." He tapped a finger down the Rosebud. "Somewhere . . . down to the south of us . . . is our third prong. And only God knows where."

As the rest of the officers leaned in round the table, studying the maps, the commander of the Department of Dakota stood tall and cadaverously thin over his papers, deep in thought. "What I propose to do now is to go over this report by Major Reno's scout and look over these charts on the Rosebud and Wolf Mountains. We even have some surveyor's maps given us by the Northern Pacific Railroad."

"Do any of them show us where General Crook is at this moment?"

"No, Custer. We have no idea where Crook is," Terry said. "But more important to this campaign—and to you—is figuring out just where the Indians under Sitting Bull might be gathering."

CHAPTER 5

Nот long after Terry's officers hunkered round the table over those maps and charts, the sky opened up as if someone had slit its underbelly and everything tumbled out.

For the first few minutes it rained, assaulting the *Far West* and all the troops on shore with drops the size of tobacco wads. When the wind suddenly shifted out of the north, the rain just as quickly turned to hail—huge, ugly, sharp-edged weapons from the heavens.

By the time the storm rumbled past and sundown was at hand, the ground lay white and the air chilled John Gibbon to his marrow.

"Isn't that just like the high plains, gentlemen?" Custer asked, as he, Terry, and Gibbon crunched across a thick layer of hail icing the ground as far as a man could see. "One day you broil your brain, . . . and if you're still alive the next, you catch your death of cold."

Both Gibbon and Terry chuckled with the young lieutenant colonel as they drew near Custer's tent at the center of his Officers' Row on the south side on the Yellowstone.

"I wish I had more to offer you in the way of refreshment," Custer apologized. "Just never got a handle on this matter of alcohol."

"No matter." Terry freed some of the top buttons of his tunic. "I think I've had quite enough for the day as it is."

Gibbon glanced at Terry. "We came along for only a moment, Custer. To speak with you in private."

Custer appeared perplexed as he settled on his prairie bed, a tick stuffed with grass. "Why is that?"

"Armstrong," Terry began. He removed his hat and shook the water from the crown. "I need to reemphasize some concerns of mine now that we three are alone. I have only the two of you with me . . . the two who will form the pincers of this campaign."

"Sir?"

"You've made it perfectly clear to everyone that you don't want the Gatlings nor Major Brisbin's cavalry along. I could beg you to reconsider, Armstrong. Hell, I could order you to reconsider . . . if I thought it'd do any good." Terry sounded as morose as his dark beard. "But I'm afraid ordering you to take them wouldn't be an answer either."

"No, sir. It wouldn't in the slightest." His eyes held steadily on Terry's.

"I think I share the general's opinions of your talents here, Custer," Gibbon offered with rare candor. "Even though I don't approve of your methods at times." He slipped his hat from his head, running a hand over his thinning hair. "I haven't spent all these years in this man's army not to recognize a young officer who's going places. But we all want you to understand that you have much more at stake here. Not merely your reputation—"

"A reputation that's been tarnished from time to time," Custer interrupted. "Is that what you mean to say?"

"Only for doing what you felt was right." Terry put a hand up so Gibbon wouldn't reply. "I know. Let's just say you got caught in some political traps through no fault of your own, and we'll leave it at that."

At that moment a black woman appeared at Custer's tent

flaps. Terry's eyes flicked at Gibbon, watching consternation boil across the colonel's face.

"John, this is Maria," Terry introduced Custer's servant. Custer waited for her to curtsy to Gibbon before he explained, "She's been with me since 1873 when my former maid ran off with a teamster after my unit transferred to Fort Rice. Maria's been on both the Yellowstone and Black Hills campaigns with me."

"Ginnel," Mary began, bowing her head politely. "Sorry. I didn't know you had com'ny, sir. I'll come back later on."

"No, that's quite all right, Mary. You go right ahead and work on what you were doing."

"I won't be in the way?"

"Not at all," Custer replied. She slipped past him into the tent. "Maria is quite the cook. Should you both choose to stay the evening, we'll fix up some special dumplings for supper to go along with her sage hens. Including some delicious prairie onions she's dug up hereabouts."

"Thank you—no, Custer," Terry answered for them both. "We'll be heading back to the *Far West*. A lot planned yet for this evening. Still, Mary's sage hen with dumplings does sound inviting. I'll trust you to invite me to dinner when we get back home? Mary?"

She turned, surprised that General Terry had addressed her so directly. "Why, of course, Ginnel. Anytime you say. Anytime you and the Missus wanna have the hens. I'd be much pleased to cook for you."

"Maria here is even taking some live sage hens back to the fort with her when she leaves in the morning."

"Oh?" Terry glanced at the black woman. "You're leaving in the morning?"

"Yessuh."

"I'm sending her east with Chawako and his Rees, who are heading back to your Powder River depot, where she can board a supply steamer, taking our mail and dispatches with her to Lincoln. Since the Seventh pulls out in the morning, there's going to be a lot of mail: letters to family back east . . . sweethearts and wives. I wouldn't doubt but there'll be a lot of greenbacks headed east on that ride too."

"Dollars that sutler Coleman didn't get his hands on yet? Now, that's hard to imagine!" Terry guffawed with Gibbon and Custer. "That trader can smell a man with a coin in his pocket at fifty paces!"

"And pick that man's pocket at ten paces!" Gibbon stated.

"You certainly know the man, don't you?" Terry laughed all the harder. "Mary, I will take you up on that offer. When we return to the fort, Custer—you and Libbie must have us over for dinner."

"Certainly, sir."

"Custer." Terry cleared his throat, then said, "In all confidence—between the three of us—the plan for this campaign awards you and the Seventh the brunt of the action and hence the lion's share of the—"

"Glory, sir?"

"Why, yes. Nothing short of the glory."

"We won't let you down, General." Custer pursed his lips beneath the straw mustache.

"That goes a long way to relieving my anxieties, Custer. In that event I'll issue your written orders in the morning." Terry got to his feet as he slipped his campaign hat over his dark hair. "If you have any further questions at that time, we can go over them before you embark on your scout. For now, however, my mind is quite fogged enough as it is. We were at that meeting from near three o'clock until close to sundown! Life at the War Department in Washington City must be quite a bore compared to field action—eh, gentlemen?

"I plan to rest through the shank of the evening and see you off in the morning. Then I'll get Gibbon's outfit squared away and dispatched down the Bighorn to meet with you."

"An effective plan, General," Custer answered, his azure eyes smiling.

"Custer?" Terry stared at the ground a moment, as if tongue-tied. "One more thing—I'm not all that sure . . . sure just what to say for the last."

That caught Custer completely off-guard. "Say . . . say whatever you want to say, General."

Terry gazed at Gibbon a moment. Gibbon nodded.

The general sighed before he spoke. "Remember this, Custer: use your own judgment and do what you think best if you strike the trail. If you find my concept for this campaign impractical under the circumstances you encounter, you can change it . . . accepting full responsibility for varying from my plan, you understand."

Custer nodded, a hard smile still crow-footing his eyes with tiny wrinkles.

"And, Custer—whatever you do—by God, hold onto your wounded. Just hold onto your wounded."

"Yes, General." Custer squinted quickly, his pale blue eyes gazing past Terry to the deepening indigo of the evening sky outside and the first faint splash of the stars spread across the darkening canopy reaching far across the southern horizon. Up the Rosebud. "The wounded . . . they will be protected. I promise you both that."

Gibbon set his hat over his thinning hair and swiped the back of a hand beneath his huge nose as he turned to step out the tent flaps.

Terry halted at the doorway.

"Custer, I just may be the last to trust in you." The general gripped the young officer's arm paternally. "In fact, this spring it became apparent that not even your old friend Phil Sheridan . . ."

"I understand fully, sir." Custer nodded at Gibbon before looking at Terry. "Thank you, General. The Seventh won't let you down."

"Find the Indians, Custer. We'll help you do the rest."

"I'll do my best, sir." Custer snapped a smart salute.

Terry and Gibbon walked toward the south bank of the Yellowstone, where a rowboat waited to ferry the officers over to the *Far West*.

"Cooke!" Custer called into the twilight.

His adjutant trotted up from a nearby camp fire. "Sir?"

"Have trumpeter Voss sound 'Officers' Call.' I want to speak to the men in an hour."

In fresh paint and their finest outfits, Gibbon's Crow scouts presented themselves to Custer.

To them the soldier-chief would be known as Young

Star, Ihcke Deikdagua. At times they would call Custer the Morning Star. In years to come, none of the Crow would be able to explain to interpreters precisely why he had been given that name.

Young Curley was the first to climb up the bank to Custer's tent, crunching across the frozen hail to present his hand to the famous pony soldier.

"What's this?" Custer asked, peering down at his right palm, where Curley had placed a coin with his vigorous handshake.

"It is good luck that you touch his dollar." Interpreter Mitch Bouyer translated Curley's explanation.

Though only seventeen winters in age, Curley liked what he saw in the cut of the man. This pony soldier stood tall and slim, broad of shoulder as he thought a warrior should be. Most of all, it was those azure eyes that told Curley, *Here is a kind, brave, and thoughtful man*.

He had never before seen any man with such eyes.

Custer said, "Curley, is it? Yes—by jigs, I do believe we'll all be good luck for one another, boys!"

After shaking hands all round with the others, Custer gestured expansively across the entire group. "I have seen most of the other tribes of these mountains and plains except the Crow. And now I see the Crow for the first time. I truly think they are good and brave scouts. I have some scouts here, these Rees. But most of them are worthless to me. I am told the Crows are good scouts, so I sent for you to be part of my command. I myself gave General Terry six hundred dollars for you scouts, and Mitch Bouyer here, to pay for your services."

He motioned the scouts to sit as Burkman and adjutant Cooke came up with stools and a couple of small trunks. After the Crows had settled themselves, Custer spoke through the half-breed Bouyer.

"I want you to understand I have not called you to go with me up the Rosebud to fight. Instead, you need only track the enemy's path and tell me where they are. I do not want, nor do I expect, you to fight these Indians we are trailing. You just find the Indians for me. I will do the fighting."

He turned to his striker. "Burkman, fetch me that pouch I set out on my field desk. The leather one with the fringe down one side."

With pouch in hand, Custer turned again to Curley. "With this money I am giving you," and Custer began to pour some coins out of the pouch into the scout's palm, "I want you to go to the steamboat and buy some paints and new shirts. You must do this now," he directed while he poured more coins into the palms of the rest. "We leave tomorrow as soon as preparations are made. I want you ready to take me to the Indians who took your hunting land and have long been causing your people many problems."

Custer suddenly turned to Cooke, struck with an idea. "Lieutenant! I want you to hurry straightaway to the quartermaster and bring me a wall tent for these boys."

"The Crows, General? A tent?"

"Exactly, Cooke! These boys will stay with me tonight. Eat supper and camp with me . . . won't you boys?"

They nodded their heads after Bouyer interpreted the invitation, smiling for the soldier-chief.

"While supper is being readied for us," Custer motioned for the scouts to stand once more with him, "you go to the steamboat and get your supplies with the money I've given you. By jiggers, I feel all the better already about this scout. With good men like you Crows with me . . . I can't help but find the Sioux quick and finish them off. Now, come back as soon as you've made your purchases, and we'll have something to eat."

Custer escorted the group to the south bank of the Yellowstone, where several boats sat on the sand to ferry soldiers to the far shore or the steamboat itself.

As the Crow were about to board the skiffs that would row them out to the *Far West*, Custer suddenly became drained of his bubbly enthusiasm. The famous smile disappeared from his haggard face.

"I want you scouts to know I understand you don't know a thing about me yet," he explained through Bouyer by the lapping waters of the Yellowstone. "I am known far and wide among the tribes as Charge-the-Camp, because I will not hesitate to wade right into a battle myself. You ask about me. Anyone will tell you how I cleaned up a camp of Cheyenne on the southern plains. That was eight years ago, but I intend to do the very thing to these Sioux. And remember the Crow scouts who ride with me—the scouts who lead me to these Sioux I'm hunting—you will share in the horses captured from the Sioux herds."

Smiles reappeared beneath the greased Crow pompadours as Bouyer translated.

Sioux ponies as an additional reward? What could possibly be better? Curley wondered. *Money from this soldier-chief to buy a new shirt for this journey, and some war paint for our faces when we ride down on the Sioux camps. Aiyeee! Now the promise of Sioux ponies as well! This is a great thing in a young Crow scout' life!*

As Custer turned with a wave to them all, crunching back toward his tents across the icy hail melting in slushy patches up the slope, Curley turned to Half-Yellow-Face and White-Man-Runs-Him.

"This Young Star will be a good soldier to follow. He understands Indians. He will not fall behind. I will like fighting for such a soldier. This one will win. This one will bring us victory over our old enemies. Young Star will not quiver and fall back, afraid of the Lakota."

As the soldier-boatman dipped his oars into the water, dragging the skiff toward the *Far West,* Curley watched the steamboat's lights illuminate the tops of the wind-whipped whitecaps.

"It is decided," Curley said quietly. "I will go with this one wherever he leads me."

A half hour later Custer sent bugler Henry Voss to blow "Officers' Call" through camp.

Tom Custer was the first to appear, as was usually the case. "Something's eating at you, Autie," he remarked as he strode up, watching his older brother slapping the old rawhide quirt against his boot. "Don't often see you this worked up. Reminds me of the time Benteen wrote that letter dragging your name through the mud in papers all over St. Louis, Chicago, and New York."

"Another attack on the Seventh, that's what!"

"What now? Or should I say, who?"

"That infernal Grasshopper Jim!"

"Brisbin?"

"None other!" He glared testily at his brother with those icy marine eyes, flames from the nearby fire dancing off his reddish blond mustache that all but covered his mouth.

"He still pushing to come along?"

"Tried once more to worm his way in on this scout," he flared. "This fight is ours!"

"No man will argue that, Autie!"

"He'll play no part in any of it, not him nor Gibbon! Not even Terry." He slapped the quirt once more for emphasis as others straggled into the ring of firelight.

"I hope you told that bastard what-for!" Tom said

" I did just that!" Custer kneaded the quirt handle into his palm. "I told him the Seventh had no need of his four troops of cavalry."

"Damn, if you can't stir a fighting man's blood, Autie!" Tom slapped his brother on the shoulder. "Why, fellas, we're going to kill us some Sioux just like we done to Johnny Reb down at Saylor's Creek!"

Tom had won his second of two Congressional Medals of Honor during the Civil War at Saylor's Creek, charging a Confederate artillery position and single-handedly bringing back the rebel flag to Union lines. He also brought back a serious wound—a hole in his cheek where a Confederate ball had entered, smashing an exit wound behind the ear. More than eleven years later, Thomas Ward Custer still wore that rosy scar on his cheek. Wore it as proudly as he wore his medals.

"Hear! Hear!" shouted Captain George W. Yates, a hometown Monroe boy like the Custers. "Go, you wolverines!"

"That's the spirit, men!" Tom hollered enthusiastically as he watched friends backslapping.

His was the sort of contagious enthusiasm that his older brother liked to see run through his officer corps. Here on the precipice of their march up the Rosebud, here with the men keyed up tight as a cat-gut fiddle string, brother Tom could work his singular magic on his fellow officers.

Irishman Myles W. Keogh pounded big James Calhoun on the back. Both members of the Custer inner circle cheered lustily with Tom.

"Nothing short of death stands in the way of the Wild I Company!" Captain Keogh growled in his peat-moss brogue.

"Appears nothing will stand in our way now, Myles," Custer said as the huzzahs quieted. "Terry's giving us all the help he can. I believe the old boy knows we'll be the ones to save his hide on this campaign—not Gibbon, not even Crook."

"Custer and the Seventh!" Tom shouted, amid cheers.

"All right!" Custer himself shouted. "Let's get down to business so we can get you back to your units. There's much to do and little time to do it. We are leaving tomorrow."

"Tomorrow?" Captain Frederick W. Benteen croaked.

"Damn! Old Sitting Bull himself better watch out for that mangy scalp of his now!" adjutant Cooke hollered.

"In the morning?"

"Dang-it-all—but I'm itchy for a good scrap a'ready!"

Waving a hand for silence, Custer began, "We'll leave somewhere between late morning to early afternoon."

"How long we expect to be out, General?" Major Marcus Reno shuffled a step forward to inquire. He would be second only to Custer himself on the scout.

"Just as long as it takes, Major. To put it in terms of something you can tell your men, I want to be ready for fifteen days of march."

"Fifteen, sir?" Captain Yates asked.

"That's correct, George. We're being provisioned for fifteen days. For the first few days the marches won't be all that long, but later on I figure the length of each march will be increased as need and circumstance arise."

"Ol' Iron Butt won't go hard to wear us out—eh, Autie?" Tom joked.

"No," he grinned. "It wouldn't do to wear out a single man of you and run you into the ground trying to keep up with me! But on the lighter side, if more of you had done as I have, you would not have to brood on dying and leaving someone behind with nothing but your memory."

"If you're talking about that life-insurance policy you took out in your name for Libbie, I got myself one for Maggie as beneficiary," Lieutenant James Calhoun boasted.

"Metropolitan Life Insurance Company, Jim?"

"That's right, General. Same as you." Calhoun winked to those round him. "While I don't expect to use it—you never know when old Iron Butt here will ride us all to our deaths chasing Sioux up and down some bloody river again!"

As the laughter subsided, Keogh stepped forward, slapping his chest. Many were the times Myles Keogh was not the most-liked man in the regiment. Too often a drunken braggart, strict to a fault with his men and most times prone to violence. There remained an electrifying aura about the man, especially in that effect he had over the fairer sex—and it all carried over to the unquestioned control he held over the men of his "wild" I Company. With Custer's regiment from its inception, brooding Myles Keogh brought the best, and perhaps the worst, out in all his men.

"What's to say 'bout me—eh, mates?" His thick brogue poured over every one.

"Why, who the hell would you name your beneficiary, you lady-humping rounder, you?" Tom Custer swung a fist into Keogh's taut mid-section.

"Why, Tommy, me boy! You know I 'aven't got a dolly to mourn me passing, a'tall . . . a'tall. But, still took me out a policy with the same blooming life insurance drummer. And, should these red buggers be-chance lift my scalp—why, them bankers'll pay me dear ol' mither back in Erin they will!"

Calhoun slapped Keogh on the back, pushing him back into line good-naturedly.

Calhoun and Keogh were quite a pair. Both serving long with Custer and his magical Seventh, both part of the inner clique that drew close around Custer himself, protecting the general. Fiercely loyal to a fault, both Keogh and Calhoun swore that should the day ever come that they could repay Custer's kindnesses to them, neither of them would be found wanting.

"Gentlemen!" Custer held his arm up, and the officers' laughter subsided. "We'll move up the Rosebud tomorrow. There will be no wagons this time. Hence, no tents."

He waited until the good-natured groans and complaints played out. "No wagons means we're taking mules along. A pack train. Twelve mules per company. That forces us to march light, you understand. Fifteen days we'll be out, so fifteen days' rations packed for each man. Hardtack, coffee, and sugar to be carried on each man's mount. Twelve days of bacon only. No more. Don't overburden the mounts, gentlemen. There may well come a time when we can't afford to overtax the animals, and we'll need their energy and strength for a fight of it. Ammunition more than food, fellas. Understood?"

"Yes, sir!" Cooke answered for them all.

Custer peered a moment at the cloudy sky, almost as if hoping for a peek at a star. "Speaking of our mounts, every man will carry twelve pounds of oats and a nose bag for his horse. In case we can't locate good graze, we must be prepared to feed the animals. And every man will keep on him a hundred rounds for his carbine, twenty-four for his revolver. In addition, see that two thousand rounds of carbine ammo are loaded on each company mule. If you feel your assigned mules can take it, I might suggest some extra forage."

"Sounds like you're fixing to have us out even longer than fifteen days, General."

Custer glared at Major Reno's dark face. "We might be. Terry figured five days at the most before the jaws of his trap snap shut. However, I want us ready for fifteen at the least. These Indians won't get away this time. My only fear is that the Sioux are going to run, that I'll have to chase them as they scatter on us. But Sitting Bull won't get away for long if we're prepared to follow."

"Beggin' pardon, General." The big Missourian stepped into the light between lieutenants Edgerly and Smith. "Are you prepared to support any unit that gets itself into trouble this time out?"

Custer tensed, turning slowly toward the strapping Benteen. "Captain, care to tell me just what you mean by your question?"

"Why, I was remembering the Washita and Major Elliott. . . ."

With Benteen's acidic words Tom Custer sensed a stunned silence slash through the assembled officers like a saber.

"Major . . . Major Elliott?" Custer stammered.

"Yes, General. That time on the Washita when you failed to support one of your officers. I want to be assured in front of your officer corps that such an event will not occur again. You will follow and support as you have promised?"

"Promised?" Custer grew bright red. "This is war, Benteen! Not some sterile battle maneuver pitting us against civilized soldiers in the Shenandoah Valley. We're preparing to do battle with hardened warriors. Don't dare speak to me of promised support, for I won't hear of it ever again! We're soldiers, doing our job as best we can. Do you all understand?"

After a moment of reflection, Custer ripped off his hat and ran a hand over his freshly clipped hair. Back to bristles, compliments of barber-trader James Sipes aboard the *Far West*.

"We'll be fighting warriors who have battled us before on the Yellowstone, I'm sure. Led by Gall and American Horse and none other than Crazy Horse himself. So it's reported. I led my cavalry into many battles during the recent rebellion in the south, engaging my horse against the cream of the Confederate horse. But I want each and every one of you to understand that we have never come up against warrior-leaders like this Crazy Horse. He's the kind who likes to hurt you before he kills you, as I understand."

"Let the bastard taste Seventh Cavalry steel!" Tom blurted angrily.

"If anything, he'll have to taste our lead," Custer replied. "The sabers were left behind at Powder River."

"Let it be *my* lead, pray God!" Tom said.

Custer turned back to Benteen. "Captain, I repeat—we

will be fighting warriors." He eyed the rest of his officer corps. "Unlike those you killed at the Washita."

"Seems you have me at a disadvantage now, General," Benteen replied. "I have no idea what you're referring to."

"For those who don't know or may have forgotten about you shooting a young boy during battle—"

"Young boy!" Benteen shrieked.

"A mere youth, Captain!"

"He was over twenty. A full-fledged warrior, by god!"

"Don't lie before these good men. Your fellow officers!"

"By damned, General—with God as my witness . . . that man was a warrior. I daresay a better warrior than many of the soldiers we'll be leading south along the Rosebud in the morning."

"The difference being, Captain—that those young men I'll be leading down the Rosebud will know the difference between warriors and . . . boys."

Benteen shrugged shaking his head as he shuffled back in line, muttering loud enough for most to hear, "A young warrior will kill you just as quick as a gray-headed one . . . any day."

"Any questions?" Custer inquired.

"General?"

"Yes, Myles?" Custer smiled at Captain Myles Moylan. He had always liked the dark Irishman. Moylan was genuine, early on coming to enjoy Custer's respect during his time as adjutant during their Fort Hays duty. Following his years as adjutant, Custer had rewarded Moylan's loyalty with a captaincy at the head of A Company.

"I was wondering, sir, that with two thousand rounds of carbine ammo and extra forage you're suggesting—all that on the backs of just twelve mules—won't that break 'em down before too long?"

Custer studied the flames before he answered. "I trust in each and every one of you men to do what you feel right for your commands. If you think you should carry extra forage, then by all means do so. Carry what you *damn* well please."

With that singular word Tom realized his brother still smoldered with Benteen's insult. Custer rarely if ever swore. And this use of profanity did not go unwasted on these men who knew him best.

"The idea was only a suggestion of mine, Myles. You need not hold to it. But, best that each of you tattoo this on your minds. You'll be held accountable for your companies—both men and animals. Understand once more that we will be following the hostiles' trail . . . no matter how far it takes us. No matter how long it takes us. Understand, gentlemen—we may never see the *Far West* again. We cannot rely on it or its supplies from this point on. If my guess is right, we may not see the other units for some time either. Once we march over those ridges to the south, following the Rosebud in the morning . . . we'll be entirely on our own."

Custer turned toward Calhoun, testy as a sage cock, when he heard his brother-in-law mutter something under his breath to Keogh. "What was that, Jim?"

"I just said it was better that way, General," Calhoun replied self-consciously. "Better that we don't have the rest of those other units bogging us down."

"Bloody right, General!" Keogh growled. "We're a fighting unit. Not like these other shoneens what never seen a fight or scrap before . . . much less a battle with the bloody savages!"

"You can count on Company A, sir!" Moylan joined in.

"In that case," Custer said quietly as he stepped near Moylan, "you all might suggest to your men to bring along a little extra salt."

"Salt, sir?" Lieutenant Edward S. Godfrey asked.

"Yes, Lieutenant. We may have to live on horse meat before this campaign is out. Most certainly mule meat unless some troopers are put afoot . . . or there are some saddles emptied."

"Saddles emptied?" Lieutenant George D. Wallace croaked.

"Casualties."

"Salt certainly makes horse meat taste better to my discriminating palate!" young Tom joked to raise everyone's sudden gloom. "Had it before down to the Indian

Territories chasing old Medicine Arrow himself. Not bad, if the horse isn't a friend . . . and you're hungry enough!"

Custer himself had turned on his heel and taken a couple steps toward his tent when he suddenly turned back again. "I'm sorry, but I forgot to mention something to you men before we break up. General Terry has given his permission to tap the whiskey kegs aboard the steamboat this evening."

He had to wait while wild cheering erupted from the group. "If any of you have the inclination, you might avail yourselves of the army's generosity. I'm aware many of you, like Tom here, make a habit of taking along an extra dram or two in your canteens—just for what Tom calls that 'extra-tired time.'"

"From the sounds of it," Tom stepped beside his brother to face the rest, "looks like my brother here is set on pushing us extra-hard and making us extra-tired!"

The officers laughed along with the younger Custer, wiping the backs of their hands across dry lips or rubbing their bellies to show what they thought of his idea of getting enough whiskey to wet down a month-long thirst. A long, dry trip out from Fort Abraham Lincoln.

"When I have General Terry's written orders in hand come morning, I'll have Cooke come round. Otherwise, have your sergeants pay heed to the bugle calls. We'll strike camp as soon as the regiment is prepared to move out. That'll be all. Good night, gentlemen."

CHAPTER 6

A s Custer slipped back through the open flaps of his Sibley tent where striker John Burkman had three oil lamps glowing, their chimneys lightly smoking, Burkman rose anxiously. The three tufts of oily smudge were carried off on a strong, cool breeze as the general washed in, anxious. John watched the officers move off in pairs and small groups, crunching across what patches remained of the icy hail.

Custer sank on a canvas stool, studying the sounds of the camp whirling about him for the moment. The *heer-haw*s of the mules. The whinnies and snorts of the horses. Among the tents there arose the sudden peal of some man's high laughter followed by the loud blast of another soldier's guttural guffaw. Above it all, here and there, Custer listened to the sweet sound of soft-sung melodies raised from one side of camp, while from the other direction came the faint strains of a banjo or some fiddle, perhaps even a squeezebox keening out a song popular to that particular breed of man who served his nation on the western plains.

"Doesn't much sound like a camp of men marching out on campaign against the Sioux, does it, Mr. Burkman?"

John's eyes darted to Custer, finding the general staring out the tent flaps into the night, apparently hypnotized by those night fires stretching endlessly west across the Yellowstone prairie.

"I wouldn't know, sir."

"Of course," Custer replied softly. He rose, turned to Burkman. "You've never been on campaign before, have you?"

"No, sir. This is my first time against . . . the enemy, sir."

"Enemy," Custer repeated, stepping to the tent flaps, mesmerized still by the twinkling of so many camp fires, together like so many stars dusted across the indigo velvet of the summer prairie. "The enemy, John. Tomorrow we'll tramp down the trail of those Sioux that Reno let slip by."

He turned, a strange and haunting look in those winter-cold eyes of his. Eyes gone tired, like rumpled, worn baggage to Burkman. John glanced down at Custer's hands, held out before him as if clutching something, gripping it for all it was worth. As if he would never let it go. Burkman's eyes crawled back to Custer's face, to those sapphire eyes, which now seemed to peer right through the striker.

"We'll find them, John," he whispered. "Once I find them, I'll have myself a place in history."

Burkman swallowed hard, trembling as he clutched the cream-colored hat he had been brushing clean of dust for Custer's outfit in the morning. "Yes, General. A place in history—"

"Autie!"

With the sound of Tom's voice hailing him from beyond the fire, Custer whirled on his heel. Three forms loomed into the light, all arm in arm, the trio eating ground in huge strides as they marched up to Custer's tent.

"We're headed over to take ol' Terry up on that whiskey!" Tom held up one hand carrying five canteens.

"Those all yours, Tom?"

"Not all," he answered with a snort. "One of 'em belongs to Lieutenant Harrington!"

"Four for you, brother?"

"'At's right, General!" Keogh blared, holding aloft his own four canteens. "Thomas here's a good lad—stout drinking bunkie, if ever there was one. He is, he is. We'd made good bunkies of it, in the old days of the war of rebellion, that is!"

"James," Custer said as he stepped from the tent flaps, looking squarely at Calhoun, "you'll see these two don't get themselves into any serious trouble tonight, will you?"

"Aye, sir!" He saluted. "We don't plan on drinking all that much tonight anyway."

"Glad to hear that, fellas. Save it to drink a little at a time on the march."

"Little at a time?" Tom snorted. "Autie, you've just never learned how to live. You'll be dying a wretched old man—wondering what it was to have lived!"

"I've had my bout with whiskey, Tom—back to Monroe. Sworn off it completely."

"How well we know of that. I'd be the last to blame a man for not holding his liquor!" Tom chuckled along with Keogh and Calhoun. His smile faded as he studied his brother's face. "But you've not truly enjoyed yourself ever since . . . sixty-nine, wasn't it? Sixty-nine when you had to send that Cheyenne gal away. I don't remember her name, Autie."

Keogh found Custer's eyes on him, as if seeking confirmation. "That be the gospel, 'tis, General. You ain't the same man since that Cheyenne girl. Whatever she done to you, it made you a happy soul."

Burkman saw Custer swallow. "Well," he said self-consciously, "you boys take care this evening." He worried a palm over the stubby bristles of his thinning hair a few times, as if he wanted out of a fix but didn't reckon on getting his bearings. "Don't get drunk and scalped while over there round Gibbon's boys. I'll need you three this time out, you know."

"That barber Sipes isn't getting anywhere near us!" Tom roared, slapping Calhoun on the back.

The scene was happy once more. Every bit as happy as it had been somber a brief moment ago. No more talk of the past. Only talk of a future borne up the Rosebud.

"Let's be walking, laddies!" Keogh howled, prodding the other two from Custer's tent. "That bleeming shoneen of a trader's got whiskey . . . and Myles Keogh's got him a thirst to match!"

"See you to the morning, General!" Tom's voice came back from the thickening darkness swallowing the trio.

That stopped Custer dead in his tracks. He turned to stare after the men, certain it was Tom's voice he had heard. Dead certain. But brother Tom had never addressed him by rank before. Tom had never called him *General*. . . .

As he and his friends were rowed over to the *Far West*, moored snugly against the north bank of the Yellowstone, Tom Custer studied the brightly lit steamboat gently rocking atop the river like a glittering tree ornament. From the sounds of the hurrahs and laughter, coupled with the sights of shadowy forms darting across the yellow splash of lights on deck, Tom figured Coleman's whiskey kegs would do a hard business of it tonight.

Not all that unusual, he thought to himself as Keogh laughed with Calhoun.

There had been whiskey sellers dogging the trail of the Dakota Column once it marched away from Fort Abraham Lincoln. Seemed that out in this lonely part of the world, once anyone who had a way to transport cheap whiskey heard of an army unit marching into the field, a whiskey trader of one color or another would be attending each night's stop. Tonight beneath an overcast Yellowstone moon, it appeared the government-licensed trader aboard the *Far West* would make himself a small fortune from army coffers at Terry's behest, as well as taking out of each soldier's pockets whatever the man had left in the way of loose pay after all this time on the trail.

True enough, Tom realized that trader James Coleman had made out quite well along the column's way west.

Coleman and his partner Sipes stayed busy tonight

minding their whiskey kegs. For all but the most hardened of drinkers, the traders' whiskey seemed the best bargain offered beneath that canvas awning. The troopers believed they could get more mileage out of a dollar pint of cheap grain alcohol than they could out of damned near anything else Coleman had for sale. The trader rightfully worried of running out of whiskey this last night at the mouth of the Rosebud, what with so many men from the Seventh filling their canteens with his cheap corn mash.

Growling, Coleman constantly reminded that rowdy, shoving crowd beneath his awning that they had to leave him with something in his whiskey kegs for the party he'd throw after the regiment marched back down the Bighorn— the victorious Seventh Calvary once more.

"The men what bring me Crazy Horse's scalp along with Sitting Bull's . . . I'll let those men finish a keg all on their own!" Coleman promised down at the end of the crude plank bar Tom leaned against.

The tent rang with exuberant voices of hundreds of shoving, sweaty soldiers, each one cursed of an undying thirst yet to be quenched. Coleman's was a promise that made every dry recruit think hard on searching out those two infamous chieftains all on one's own.

"Shit!" a soldier near Tom joked among his friends in a fevered, drunken knot, "how the hell is this trader gonna know if a scalp I raise come from the head of Crazy Horse himself anyway?"

"Hell!" another soldier shouted to the trader pouring his cup full of amber liquid. "Maybe this whiskey of yours'll even stop my damned knees from rattling like nails in a hollow keg!"

Very few Seventh Calvary officers ended up playing poker or monte that night aboard the *Far West*. Most of the gamblers turned out to be members of Gibbon's or Terry's staffs. Custer's officers chose better things to do with their time.

This inky night that had slithered over the mouth of the Rosebud found most of the young men, and old alike penning a last letter home. Their officers had informed them some Rees were heading east in the morning with some of the last mail to be dispatched for a week or more, suggesting the men use the time wisely. Those who couldn't write had those who could pen still more letters. And for a few hours, most minds and hearts were on home. Even those old files who didn't have any other home but the army now still possessed some dim, foggy memory of that warm, secure place where a man's mind will go before he's pushed to think of nothing more basic than staying alive.

Letters to family back in the States. Long, rambling, promising letters to sweethearts . . . pretty faces that stared out at a young, frightened man in blue from a little tintype he guarded in his hand as he scribbled some last words to that special someone back in Ohio or Michigan, New York or South Carolina. A tintype he would eventually slip inside his blouse and wear against his skin over the next few days as they stalked the mighty Lakota bands.

It would never change, no matter what war a man found himself marching off to. There was always someone he could write and tell of the secret fears he didn't dare share with his fellow soldiers. Private words of longing and loneliness scratched across endless pages of foolscap that last night at the Yellowstone beneath a flickering of oil lamps and torches and firelight.

Small clusters of officers huddled in those late hours to pen their wills, then have those solemn testaments witnessed by friends. Grim instructions given, agreed to, and sworn over for the dispersal of personal effects to family members back east should the unthinkable happen in the coming days as they followed Custer up the Rosebud in search of Sioux. What to be done with the few trinkets each man had accumulated during his time in the army— whether he carried his possessions on his back or in his pockets, or they simply lay waiting back at Fort Abraham Lincoln at the bottom of a near-empty trunk.

On the eve of battle every man wanted to know he would have something that could go back to his family to show that he had indeed been of some worth during his short time on this earth . . . each man wanting to pass something on to show for his brief service in the army of the west.

Like some cold fingers slipping around a tin cup at Coleman's tent on that north bank of the Yellowstone, the mood in camp slowly changed as more and more of those men of the Seventh left the whiskey and returned to a somber camp to scratch at their letters, write their wills, swear death pacts with bunkies to see that an old watch made it back to Cape Girardeau, Missouri . . . or a special wedding band made it back to a little cabin near Cold Springs, Arkansas . . . or that neck chain he wore was delivered to a widowed mother somewhere down a holler outside Cross Plains, Tennessee.

As the clock crept into the wee hours, fewer men stood drinking at the trader's kegs. This late only the old, fire-hardened veterans still drank, staring up the Rosebud, wondering what awaited them as they rode in Custer's wake come morning.

Custer scratched a metal nib across sheets of foolscap at his field desk, while striker Burkman polished bridle and crupper, saddle, holsters, and belt, with a nervous energy. With a peculiar flair for understatement, the general was penning his last, long letter to Libbie, though he promised her he would dash off a few lines in the morning before departure.

Terry appears to retain the highest of confidence in me, holding up to others to emulate my zeal, energy, and ability. Yes, Dear Heart Alfred knows all too well he is an administrator and that I am the Indian Fighter. He used his abilities as an administrator to assure that I will do what I do best . . . nay, better than any man in the army.

For the longest time after he had laid his pen aside and stepped to the tent flaps, Custer stared out at the cloudy, starless night, soaking in that somber mood cloaking the camp. It was no stranger to him, this blackness. Veteran of all but one of those battles of the Army of the Potomac.

Veteran of campaigns along the Platte River Road and successful strikes into the heart of Indian Territory itself. Campaigns along the Yellowstone and an exploration of the Black Hills—that most sacred place of the northern plains tribes.

He sighed deeply and turned back to his desk, where he took pen in hand.

> If I were an Indian, he wrote, I often think I would greatly prefer to cast my lot among those of my people adhered to the free, open plains rather than submit to the confined limits of a reservation—there to be the recipient of the blessed benefits of civilization, with its vices thrown in without stint or measure.

"There!" he whispered to himself. He had admitted it to himself and to Libbie at last.

If by a twist of fate he found himself cast as one of the hostile chiefs he would be hunting down come morning, Custer admitted he would have to elect to go on living the free, unfettered nomadic life of old rather than suffer the stifling stagnation of the squalid reservations. To live as wild and free warriors always had, or to die a warrior.

> There were times, Rosebud, when I so desperately hoped to find you aboard one of the steamboats plying the waters of the Yellowstone. To hold not only one of your sweet letters, but to once again hold you close. When the *Josephine* brought us the mail at the Tongue, I prayed you had stolen aboard to surprise me. You might just as well be here as not. . . .
>
> I hope to begin another *Galaxy* article soon, if the spirit moves me. They seem thirsty for my words back east. Perhaps they'd enjoy my speeches? Look on my map and you will find our present location on the Yellowstone, about midway between Tongue River and the Big Horn. . . .
>
> Reno's scouting party has returned. They saw the trail and deserted camps of a village of three hundred and eighty lodges. The trail was about one week old. The scouts

reported that they could have overtaken the village in one day and a half. I am now going to take up the trail where the scouting party turned back. I fear their failure to follow up the Indians has imperiled our plans by giving the village an intimation of our presence. Think of the valuable time lost!

But I feel hopeful of accomplishing great results. I will move directly up the valley of the Rosebud. General Gibbon's command and General Terry, with steamer, will proceed up the Big Horn as far as the boat can go.

I will like campaigning with pack mules much better than with wagons, leaving out the question of luxuries. We take no tents and desire none.

I now have some Crow scouts with me, as they are familiar with the country. They are magnificent-looking men, so much handsomer and more Indian-like than any we have ever seen, and so jolly and sportive; nothing of the gloomy, silent red man about them. They have formally given themselves to me, after the usual talk. In their speech they said they had heard that I never abandoned a trail, that when my food gave out, I ate a mule. That was the kind of man they wanted to fight under; they are willing to eat mule too.

I am sending six Ree scouts to Powder River with the mail; from there it will go with other scouts to Fort Buford.

From here on out the men will sleep in overcoats and saddle blankets. I have arranged for the hounds to be left with the mules when battle is assured. At the very least John can care for them in my absence. Tuck is such a problem tonight. She is in and out, dashing out with a playful yip when a wolf howls, scurrying back in with her tail fast between her legs to cower at my knee. Let us hope the Sioux are as discerning as Tuck . . . to know when to stick their tails between their legs!

I also wanted you to share in the good news—I have seen that Boston and Autie were transferred from Quartermaster Corps for the next fifteen days so they can accompany us on our scout up the Rosebud. Along with Tom, Boston, Autie, James, and Fred Calhoun, I want all the Custer clan in on the fun! We have such a dear, dear family gathered round us, Libbie. We are indeed fortunate in this life to share that family together. . . .

To the end, Custers all!

His pen fell silent above the page as he grew pensive again. Listening to the wolf howl . . . seeing her dark eyes conjured up before him on the tent wall once more. He clenched his eyes, trying to block out the vision. Still they haunted him. Dark black-cherry eyes gleaming out at him from the back of that wagon as it rumbled out of Fort Hays, heading south and out of his life.

Less than fifty yards downstream stood Mark Kellogg's tent where the late-night oil burned just as brightly as Custer's lamps.

Although both Sherman and Sheridan had warned him against taking any reporters along, Custer found it impossible to refuse that fervent request from the former telegraph operator working for the summer in a Bismarck law office and writing an occasional article printed in the Bismarck paper, even the New York *Herald*, under his pen name, Frontier.

After all, Custer had reasoned, the *Herald* was owned by his good and politically powerful friend, James Gordon Bennett, Jr. Without much time given over to wrestling with the problem, Custer had decided to allow Kellogg to accompany the campaign. Besides, why shouldn't Bennett's paper get the scoop on everyone else when he defeated the Sioux and became the darling of the Democractic convention about to meet in St. Louis?

Kellogg was a likable fellow, sharing much in common with Custer anyway. He favored a get-tough policy with the "noncompliers," those Indians refusing to come in to their reservations. Custer was sure Kellogg would write a favorable account of the coming battle, since there had been so much concern after the Washita debacle and how aspects of that winter's campaign had been manhandled in the press. After all, Kellogg had stated publicly, "I say turn the dogs of war loose and drive the savages off the face of the earth, if they do not behave themselves."

A widower with two girls, who smoked Bull Durham, and enjoyed a rare game of chess, the reporter had once preached a temperance lecture at the graveside interment of a drunk who died of consumption. Since he shared Custer's teetotaling habits when it came to whiskey and other spirits, Kellogg was not among those who bolstered trader Coleman's profits that cloudy night of 21 June.

Instead, Mark Kellogg spent the evening rattling off dispatches to be sent back east in the morning in addition to letters to his daughters. The remainder of his time he spent in getting rations and supplies squared away and stuffed securely in his canvas saddlebags, along with an adequate supply of lined paper and pencils he would require up the Rosebud with Custer.

At forty Kellogg was nonetheless youthful in appearance, with but a few small crows'-feet worrying his eyes in addition to the steel-rimmed glasses, and some flecks of gray in his hair that betrayed his age.

Mark brooded needlessly past midnight, concerned that he would have enough bacon and sugar and coffee for the fifteen days, as well as enough paper. More important than food was paper. Kellogg wanted to write the war story to end all war stories. And by riding with an Indian fighter of Custer's caliber and reputation, Kellogg was certain he would see action worth description. Never before had he written anything worthy of much notice, since most of his prose plodded along in a pedestrian manner.

This time, however, Mark Kellogg was certain the drama of the coming chase and the thrill of battle with Custer's cornered quarry would inspire him to lofty prose.

This small, unassuming widower would ride an army mule south along the Rosebud behind Custer, certain this was to be his moment in the spotlight. No longer would he merely report the actions of others. At long last Mark Kellogg, reporter and campaign correspondent for no less than the New York *Herald*, would participate in the *making* of history—a destiny he had waited forty long years to enjoy.

That old mule picketed outside his tent just might carry him farther than the Rosebud and any Sioux camp Custer would assure they would run across.

Well past midnight John Burkman left Custer at his field desk, perched on his cot, finished with his letter to Libbie, and now working on his journal. Always the journal.

The striker headed next door to his small A-tent, with a stop to relieve his bladder swollen from all the coffee he had shared with his commander.

As he watered the ground, Burkman gazed at the lights glittering on board the *Far West* moored against the far shore and remembered that some of the officers from Terry's command had rowed across to join Gibbon's men for a late-night game of monte. For a moment he sensed those soldiers were the lucky ones, not having to suffer this unexplained dread for the coming of day, not having to worry over the noose of despair that his own private premonitions tightened around his heavy heart.

Burkman stuffed himself back in his britches and wiped his hand off on army wool before he nudged the buttons back through their holes. Here in the chill wee hours, all he heard was the sound of Custer's two horses munching dried grass at their picket pins.

That, and the steady beat of the Crow and Ree drums. Burkman was sure it was the distant beat of those drums that helped him fall asleep that last night at the Yellowstone.

The distant beat of Indian drums.

CHAPTER 7

HEADQUARTERS DEPARTMENT OF DAKOTA
(IN THE FIELD)
Camp at Mouth of Rosebud River, Montana,
22 June 1876

Colonel:

The brigadier general commanding directs that as soon as your regiment can be made ready for the march, you proceed up the Rosebud in pursuit of the Indians whose trail was discovered by Major Reno, a few days since. It is, of course, impossible to give you any definite instructions in regard to this movement; and were it not impossible to do so, the department commander places too much confidence in your zeal, energy, and ability to wish to impose upon you precise orders, which might hamper your action when nearly in contact with the enemy. He will, however, indicate to you his own views of what your action should be, and he desires that you should conform to them unless you shall see sufficient reason for departing from them. He thinks that you should proceed up the Rosebud until you ascertain definitely the direction in which the trail above spoken of leads. Should it be found (as it appears to be almost certain that it will be found) to turn toward the Little Horn, he thinks that you should still proceed southward, perhaps as far as the headwaters of the Tongue, and then turn toward the Little Horn, feeling constantly, however, to your left, so as to preclude the possibility of the escape of the Indians to the south or southeast by passing around your left flank.

The column of Colonel Gibbon is now in motion for the mouth of the Big Horn. As soon as it reaches that point, it will cross the Yellowstone and move up at least as far as the forks of the Little and Big Horns. Of course its future movements must be controlled by circumstances as they arise; but it is hoped that the Indians, if upon the Little Horn, may be so nearly enclosed by the two columns that their escape will be impossible. The department commander desires that on your way up the Rosebud, you should thoroughly examine the upper part of Tullock's Creek; and that you should endeavor to send a scout through to Colonel Gibbon's column with information of the result of your examination. The lower part of this creek will be examined by a detachment from Colonel Gibbon's command.

The supply steamer will be pushed up the Big Horn as far as the forks, if the river is found to be navigable for that distance; and the department commander (who will accompany the column of Colonel Gibbon) desires you to report to him there not later than the expiration of the time for which your troops are rationed, unless in the meantime you receive further orders.

Very respectfully, your obedient servant,

Ed. W. Smith, Captain
Eighteenth Infantry, A.A.A.G.

Lieutenant Colonel G. A. Custer, *Seventh Cavalry*

"As soon as my regiment can be made ready to march!" Custer exclaimed, rattling the paper whereon Captain Smith had written General Terry's orders for the Seventh to scout up the Rosebud for the hostile Sioux. "By jove, we'll be ready before Gibbon's swallowed his lunch!"

Burkman was relieved to see Custer so jovial. Several hours ago the striker and the adjutant crept into the regiment commander's tent as those first purple gray streaks of dawn lit up the Yellowstone Valley, hoping to awaken the general, finding Custer sitting upright on his cot, his field desk still perched atop his lap and the pen clutched fiercely in his freckled hand—fast asleep. Burkman had attempted to remove both pen and Custer's letter to Libbie in hopes of nudging the general down on his bed for some decent rest, but Custer awoke instead, greeting them both.

"Balderdash, John!" he roared, standing and stretching. "I feel marvelous, more than rested—I'm invigorated!"

By midmorning adjutant W. W. Cooke had returned, the folded orders in a waving hand, a smile cutting his face wolfishly. Tuck loped through the tent flaps at that moment, tongue lolling, ears flopping, placing her massive head on her master's lap for a morning rub.

"Good day, Cooke!" Custer bellowed as he scratched the hound.

"A great one it is, General!"

"Is that what I think it is?" Custer asked impatiently.

"It is indeed, sir—Terry's orders. We're on our way now!"

Custer tore open the orders, his eyes dancing across the words every bit as fast as they had sailed across General Philip Sheridan's momentous telegram bringing Custer back to duty with the Seventh Cavalry for that winter campaign down in the Indian Territories.

"Cookey, go to Terry's headquarters across the river. Give him my compliments and my sincerest thanks for the issuance of his orders for the march. Tell him I expect to have my regiment ready sometime between late morning and early afternoon. And be certain to inquire if the general would care to review the troops."

Cooke saluted sharply and left.

"Are both horses ready, Mr. Burkman?"

"Yes, General. Just the way you like them, brushed and glossy. Farrier came over at my request and trimmed 'em both this morning for you. Saddle's soaped and polished."

"My standard?"

"That too." Burkman pointed to the bright crimson-and-blue swallowtail guidon in the corner shadows of the tent. "Ready for your bearer."

"Good, Striker." He clapped his hands together characteristically. "I do believe I'll dash off a few more lines to Libbie before I get myself too absorbed in other details and find I can't do what I promised her. See that our mess utensils are stored aboard a mule, in addition to enough paper and pencils for me to use over the next long haul of it."

After Burkman had turned away to busy himself with his chores, Custer plopped on his cot with a sigh and took the pen in hand once again.

> 22 June—11 A.M.
>
> I have but a few minutes to write, as we move at twelve, and I have my hands full of preparations for the scout. Do not be anxious about me. You would be surprised to know how closely I obey your instructions about keeping with the column. I hope to have a good report to send you by the next mail. A success will start us all towards Lincoln.
>
> I send you an extract from General Terry's order, knowing how keenly you appreciate words of commendation and confidence.
>
> Come the historic conclusion of this action against the Sioux, I will have much to tell you, and we will have much to talk about. I want you to think about the whirlwind social life of Washington City, where you will bloom, and all that condition will offer someone of your upbringing and education, Dear Heart.
>
> There is so much on my mind at this point, I will have to wait in sorting it through till next I write. Until then,

know that I have loved you . . . and always will, Libbie.
The door is at last flung open for us both!

Your devoted boy,

Autie

Mark Kellogg could not remember ever feeling quite this
way. The throbbing pulse of excitement that beat through
camp was more than contagious. Finding himself part of
this great procession would be downright humbling if it
weren't so damned exciting. Everywhere he looked, Mark
watched the frantic bustle of men and animals, guns and
guidons—a camp vibrating with an electric energy here on
the plains of the Yellowstone.

With twelve mules assigned for each of the twelve
companies, including some additional animals assigned to
General Custer's headquarters' command and Lieutenant
Varnum's scouts, a pool totaling one hundred sixty mules
had been selected from the wagon-train stock that plodded
this far from Fort Abraham Lincoln.

The ammunition that Custer had specified must be
carried by each company was packed in *aparejos* or leather
packsaddles, not the conventional sawbucks most often
used by mule teams. In addition, the rations for fifteen days
had been assigned each soldier. His daily ration would
consist of eight ounces of hardtack, a hard cracker some four
inches square and dry as these summer plains of Montana
Territory. In addition, there was three-quarters of a pound
in salt pork and a pint of army coffee to wash it all
down—rations that included that extra salt in the event
they had to sacrifice some worn-out mules to the evening
mess fires on a long and costly chase.

Once the rations were drawn and packed, most of the
company captains went back to double-check the ammunition. Only then did the company sergeants inspect each
soldier's saddle gear: nose bag, an extra fore and hind shoe
with nails, and some twelve pounds of oats tied in a grain
bag to each saddle. A haversack was lashed behind each
trooper's McClellan saddle, itself swabbed with a fresh coat
of oil and lampblack to prevent the rawhide from cracking

in the dry, arid air of the northern plains. Beneath the McClellan sat the thick indigo blue wool saddle blanket sporting its gold border. As they had down through the ages, taciturn veterans watched over the great number of raw recruits like anxious mother hens, assuring that the green troopers packed an additional halter, picket rope, and pin in their haversacks.

By this time of the morning most of Custer's soldiers had made their last trip across the Yellowstone to visit trader Coleman's prairie store. With what little money they had kept back for themselves, some of the troopers purchased the large, floppy Hardee hats that would keep the blazing sun off their faces and necks much better than the standard-issue kepi, or forage cap. Many of the old files preferred instead the slouch style they purchased for $2.50, or even the popular manila straw hat they took off the sutler's hands for a mere fifty cents. With the purchase of an additional bandanna or two, which a soldier could use to keep the dust from crusting his nose and mouth, his list of necessities just might be complete.

Now each young trooper would gaze longingly at what he had left in the way of spare change spread across a callused, dirty palm. Most decided to spend the bank on luxuries such as chewing tobacco, cigars, salves for cracked lips or wind-blistered cheeks, raisins, or some hard candy for a sweet tooth. Even a few of the shavetails bought themselves one of the checkered hickory shirts or a pair of lightweight overalls, both immensely more comfortable than standard army issue for a summer march across Montana Territory.

With what Kellogg had learned, it appeared on this trip there would be more than the usual share of shavetails riding up the Rosebud behind Custer, that being the popular army term for a new or green recruit, since the newly purchased army mules had their tails cropped straight away.

As the regiment finished its preparation to march into history, raw youngsters accounted for much of the Seventh's manpower, though most of Custer's officers had gained battlefield experience in the Civil War. While the fact that most of the rank and file had little battle experience was no real cause for concern in this frontier army, the fact that from thirty to sixty percent of some companies were shavetails with less than six months service under their belts could give any veteran fighting man pause when going against battle-hardened Sioux warriors.

Still, most of those raw privates had heard repeatedly of Custer's reputation from the Seventh's lifers. They had heard the ring of confidence in those older voices telling them Custer wasn't a man to let them down in battle. It was as easy for a man like Mark Kellogg as it was for a green recruit to believe that all Custer had to do was flex his military muscle, making a quick charge or two, and any Sioux warriors fighting under the fearsome Crazy Horse would turn tail and scamper off over the sagebrush. Straight back to the reservation.

Confidence ran high in that morning's camp at the mouth of the Rosebud, fueling expectation of a quick and stunning victory to add to the Seventh Cavalry's laurels.

John Burkman laid out Custer's clothing according to the general's request.

Above his buckskin britches and those polished black boots that hugged his knees, Custer donned a gray flannel army blouse over which he pulled his new buckskin jacket. Complete with a large falling collar and sleeves rippling with dancing fringe, the jacket sported two large patch pockets decorated with short fringe and a double row of five brass buttons running down the front.

To top it all he would pull on his cream-colored, wide-brimmed felt hat. He had rolled the brim up slightly on the right side so that he could more easily sight his sporting rifle from horseback. Around his neck he tied that famous oxblood neckerchief. Custer wanted his troops to recognize him in the powder-smoked madness of battle, to know where he was, certain that their leader rode with them into the thick of it. That bright crimson tie, flowing like blood itself from his neck—telling one trooper and all that Custer himself did not cower behind the lines but galloped with them into the fray.

In addition to his field knife stuffed down in a beaded,

fringed scabbard, Custer buckled on a pair of English self-cocking, white-handled Webley pistols, each with a ring in its butt for a lanyard. The general refused the English custom of wearing the lanyard round his neck to prevent
the loss of a pistol during the heat of battle. This belt that carried both scabbard and holsters was a canvas-loop regulation-issue cartridge belt that he preferred to the more cumbersome leather version. Taking his favorite Remington sporting rifle with an octagonal barrel, chambered for .50–70 center-fire cartridges, comfortably slid in a leather scabbard of its own, Custer pulled on his gauntleted gloves, fringe spilling halfway to the elbow.

The final gracing touch came when he buckled on a pair of shiny gold spurs over his gleaming ebony boots. These were spurs originally belonging to General Santa Anna, president of Mexico, then claimed as spoils of war by an American officer at the end of the war with Mexico in 1848. That same American officer made the unfortunate decision of siding with the Confederacy in 1861. G. A. Custer himself claimed those gold spurs as the spoils of war at Appomattox Wood in 1865 as the forces of the Confederacy admitted defeat.

By noon Thursday, 22 June, a harsh northwest wind scoured the prairie at the mouth of the Rosebud, tugging at General Alfred H. Terry's hat. He reined up, bringing his staff to a halt beside Colonel Gibbon's officers.

That same stiff wind tousled the fringe worn by Custer's buckskinned officers in emulation of their beloved commander: Tom and Boston both, in addition to family favorites James Calhoun, Myles Keogh, and Billy Cooke.

The tormented guidons snapped like parching corn in the raw wind as Custer pranced up atop the blaze-faced, white-stockinged sorrel named Vic, shoving his hands into his yellow buckskin gloves. Mark Kellogg rode on his heels.

"Mr. Kellogg!" Colonel John Gibbon hollered in that characteristically gruff bullfrog voice that years ago had struck mortal fear in the heart of plebe G. A. Custer at the United States Military Academy. Gibbon indicated a place at his right hand. "Please do me the honor of standing beside me during the review."

Kellogg glanced at Custer anxiously. With his sapphire eyes twinkling, he nodded with a wide smile that seemed to assure Kellogg that both of Custer's superiors were aware the reporter was destined to ride up the Rosebud with the Seventh. Custer himself came to rest at Terry's left hand, watching with a heart-swelling pride as twelve companies, more than six hundred troopers, rode past—backs ramrod straight, lips clenched in determination, and eyes held dead ahead for the hunt at hand. Following the troopers marched a motley procession of some forty scouts: Arikara and Crow with half-breed Mitch Bouyer included, while the regimental band, which would be staying behind at the Rosebud to await the Seventh's triumphant return, stood on a nearby knoll blowing out the merry strains of "GarryOwen" before they dived into the sentimental favorite of the older veterans, "The Girl I Left Behind Me."

> The to the west we bore away,
> To win a name in story,
> And there where sits the sun of day,
> There dawn'd our sun of glory.
>
> Both blaz'd in noon on Alma's height,
> When in the post assign'd me
> I shared the glory of that fight,
> Sweet girl I left behind me.

"Twelve noon, gentlemen!" Custer roared, and saluted first General Terry then Colonel Gibbon. Unexpectedly he nudged Vic out of formation to stop beside James Brisbin.

"Major." Custer presented his hand to Terry's surprise. "Wish me luck?"

Damn it all, Terry thought to himself watching Custer. *If this doesn't beat all!*

A smile eventually cracked Grasshopper Jim's face. "Good hunting, General! And good luck to all your men!"

"Thank you, Major," Custer replied as he tugged his

glove back on the right hand. "That means a lot to me, it does."

Custer sawed Vic's reins to the left, stopping in front of Terry for a moment, their eyes on the column-of-fours, each troop accompanied by its own twelve pack mules. As they watched, some of the mules began fighting their loads, resisting the cargoes and kicking up heels. The general watched Custer grimace, his cheeks reddening as the men struggled with the mules.

Not quite the grand embarkation Custer was dreaming of, Terry brooded, sympathetic for the Seventh's young commander. *Yet he'll soon be on the trail, where there will be little to dampen his spirits.* He gazed at the shimmering waves of heat rising round that plodding column of blue and gray and yellow heading into the hills bordering the Rosebud.

A bulldog trotted past, loping off behind the departing troopers heading south into history. Major Brisbin whistled, then whistled again, until the bulldog was out of sight.

"That's not one of your hounds is it, General Custer?"

He shook his head. "Not mine, Major. Must belong to one of the men. Tramping all the way from Fort Abraham Lincoln. Appears he's not about to be left behind!"

"A grand sight, Custer!" Terry cheered, something of a chill like January ice water nagging at the base of his spine.

Custer cleared his throat, turned, and lifted his cream-colored hat from the reddish bristles on his head. "Gentlemen! Until I see you next!"

"In a few days, Custer!" Terry reminded, smiling professorially.

"See you then." Custer tapped Vic with those gold spurs, and the big mare spun away.

"Now, Custer!" Gibbon suddenly piped up, standing in his stirrups. "Don't be greedy. Wait for us!"

Custer slapped the big hat back on his head and pranced Vic round in a tight circle before he brought the anxious mare under control.

"I . . . I w-won't, sir!" his stammer floated provocatively on the stiff, chill breeze.

In Terry's next heartbeat Custer jabbed the sorrel with those golden spurs and set off at an astonishing gallop, kicking up moist clods of dirt and grass as Vic sped him along the squeaking, jangling column of cavalry and mules, disappearing into the distance, his back to the superiors he was leaving behind at the Yellowstone.

> The hope of final victory
> Within my bosom burning
> Is mingling with sweet thoughts of thee
> And of my fond returning.
>
> But should I ne'er return again,
> Still worth thy love thou'lt find me;
> Dishonor's breath shall never stain
> The name I'll leave behind me.

BOOK II

THE STALK

CHAPTER 8

For better than a hundred fifty summers, the Sioux had journeyed to Bear Butte with the short-grass time. Bear Butte, close by the east slope of their sacred Paha Sapa.

Every summer the great pilgrimage to the Black Hills had traveled from the four winds, to meet in celebration of their ancient way of life. Summer after summer the mighty Teton bands gathered until their combined herds numbered thirty thousand gnawing at the rich grasses along the forks of Bear Butte Creek.

Here the seven circles of the mighty Lakota nation raised their lodges like bare brown breasts uplifted to the sky in praise, thanksgiving, and celebration of life.

But for the past two summers, the Sioux had been driven from their ancient land where the great Wakan Tanka ministered to His people's needs. Bear Butte lay within shooting distance of the obscene mining camp called Deadwood Gulch, Dakota Territory. Really nothing more than a collection of saloons, sutlers' tents, and prostitutes' cribs.

Yet stain enough still on this holy place, enough to force the Sioux away. No more could the Lakota gather to celebrate with thanksgiving at Bear Butte. Not while the white men tore greedily at the Mother's dark breast, searching voraciously for the yellow rocks that made white men crazy.

So the great council of the Teton Sioux tribes had declared their move to the Rosebud this summer to be good. With the coming of the first snows of last robe season, word had spread from camp to camp, across the agencies and reservations—announcing that the clans would steer far from their Paha Sapa.

This summer, farther west. Not on the Powder. No, not on the Tongue either.

The great summer joy would gather to celebrate under Sitting Bull along the Rosebud.

In the Sore-Eye Moon of last winter, those of Old Bear's band of Northern Cheyenne who had survived Red Beard Crook's attack on their snowy camp huddled in the darkness in the hills above the headwaters of Pumpkin Creek. Below them soldiers set fire to lodges and robes, clothing and dried meat, while some of the brave young warriors slipped in and stole back their fine herd of Cheyenne ponies from Colonel Reynolds's young, foolish soldiers.

"Hush," Monaseetah cooed to her boys, shivering in her one blanket.

"I am hungry," Sees Red snapped. He was seven winters now and had learned that when he wanted something, he had to demand it like a young warrior.

His mother stroked his black hair. "We will eat soon."

"When?" he demanded.

"Soon," she whispered, hunkered down in the scrub oak and cedars with knots of other survivors who had fled from the soldiers. She held her two sons against her body, staring down the long slope at the bright fires. Fires glowing warm and inviting now. Fires that were once their lodges, their lives, in this winter valley.

She was reminded of a camp along the Little Dried River in the southern country when she was but a girl of thirteen summers, a camp where white soldiers butchered and defiled her mother. Then she remembered Black Kettle's village along the Washita in the southern territories as well, when she was seventeen winters. A camp where the soldiers killed her father.

"How long will we stay here?" Sees Red asked.

"You ask too many questions." She pulled him closer. "Why can't you be like Yellow Bird? He is content to sit here with his mother, watching the fires, and wait for the others to begin our long walk."

"Yellow Bird is not like us, Mother," Sees Red said darkly.

She gazed down at the quieter of her two sons, stroking his light-colored hair. Hair not at all like his brother's. "He is your brother."

"Others tell me that we truly are both your sons but with different fathers." Sees Red sniffed, feeling arrogant again. "I am Shahiyena, Mother."

"Yes, you are Cheyenne."

"He is not." Sees Red jabbed a dirty finger at his little brother.

"He is Cheyenne," Monaseetah protested, shivering. "From my body . . . Yellow Bird is Cheyenne."

"No, Mother. He is white, like the soldier-chief who is his father. My father was a Cheyenne warrior."

"Yes, Sees Red. But Yellow Bird's father was also a great warrior."

"No! He was white—an earthman!"

She nodded. "It is true, Yellow Bird's father is white, but he is the greatest of all soldier-chiefs—a powerful warrior among his people."

Sees Red pouted a few moments, glaring flint arrow points at his little brother in his sixth winter now. "He is not like me or my friends. Not like us, Mother."

"Hush," she replied, beginning to rise. "Come, now. The others are going."

"Going where, Mother?" Yellow Bird spoke for the first time since he had been yanked from his warm bed and dragged from the cozy lodge to the safety of this hilltop.

"I do not know, my sons. But," she gazed back over her

shoulder at the blazing twinkle of many fires lighting the snow, reflecting red orange on the low clouds overhead, "we no longer belong here."

She cried silently that Black Night March, tears freezing on her cheeks as she shuddered with more than the cold. Time and again she stopped, rewrapping the one wool blanket around them all, the one blanket she had to share with her two sons. Reminding herself it had been right to leave the Indian Territories of her people, to live with her cousins among the northern bands where she could be free. With the hope still burning in her breast that one day her husband would find her.

Through the deep snow and darkness of that long winter night, Old Bear's Northern Cheyenne struggled on, guided by stars and the wind that hurried them along the ridges of that icy country, carrying only what they had on their backs. They told each other to keep moving. Those who stopped too long would not be with them when the morning sun reached into the sky.

Near daybreak some of the young warriors appeared on the hilltops, signaling with their blankets and robes.

"They ride ponies, Mother!" Yellow Bird cried. "Ponies!"

"Yes . . ." Monaseetah cried too, with silent tears.

Down from the gray slopes, the young men drove their recaptured ponies, leading the mustangs into the scattered remnants of Old Bear's band. First the old ones were lifted out of the snow and set atop the strong young backs of the Cheyenne ponies, clutching manes and thanking the young brave protectors of the helpless ones.

Then the women and children.

"Now! We ride to The Horse's camp," shouted White-Cow-Bull, an unmarried Oglalla warrior from Crazy Horse's village who had been visiting friends among Old Bear's people when Crook and Reynolds attacked.

He directed the rest of his Oglalla brothers and some of the Cheyenne warriors to ride as sentries along the far ridges, searching the land for sign of more soldiers as he led the survivors in the line a bee would take to its hive. Once their noses were pointed north, White-Cow-Bull galloped back along the ragged column of stragglers. He reined up beside the beautiful Cheyenne woman.

"You are warm?" he asked.

"I am." She did not take her eyes off the broken, trampled snow beneath her pony's nose.

"And the boys?"

Monaseetah held them both in front of her on the pony's back. "Warm too." She knew the handsome Oglalla warrior had eyes for her alone.

He waited a long, aggravating moment, as if searching for something more to say to the woman who did not want to talk to him.

"We ride to The Horse's camp now, Monaseetah. You will survive. Your sons will survive as well. We have strong ponies between our legs now, and the Cheyenne have always been a strong people. You will survive—and you will remember the night the soldiers burned your village!"

White-Cow-Bull suddenly yanked his pony away from the slow march, leaving the woman behind. He hammered his heels against the pony's ribs as he galloped toward the front of the column, kicking up a spray of snow into the new red light emerging at the edge of the world.

"Ride, Shahiyena!" the Oglalla shouted down the line. "Follow me to freedom!"

For three days the Cheyenne marched before coming to the camp of Oglalla chief Crazy Horse. There the Sioux took in their friends, giving them clothes to replace the frozen, tattered remnants of what they had carried away on their backs from Old Bear's winter camp.

Empty, gnawing bellies were filled from the store of dried buffalo and antelope put away for this winter season by the Oglalla. Old Bear's people warmed themselves around Sioux fires, talking about the Black Night March they had survived. After three days it was decided that together Crazy Horse would lead them all to join up with Sitting Bull's Hunkpapas.

When at last all three bands would camp together, they could decide how to defend themselves from the soldiers who had come to force them back onto their reservations.

Three more suns rose and fell before they found The

Bull's Hunkpapa village along the Creek of Beavers, nestled for protection against the late-season snows beneath the Blue Mountains.

After many hours of council, it was decided the survivors of Red Beard's attack could travel with the Sioux. The three formed an alliance for the protection of those Northern Cheyenne of Old Bear. After all, the tribes agreed, the soldiers had attacked a Cheyenne village. Not the Sioux. The soldiers had not burned and plundered an Oglalla or Hunkpapa winter camp.

Talk was that the soldiers must be hunting Cheyenne once more, as they did on the Little Dried River in Colorado Territory twelve winters ago. As they stalked down the Cheyenne on the Washita eight winters gone.

This three-way alliance was formed for their mutual safety during the buffalo-hunting season drawing near. And because the Cheyenne themselves were the hunted ones, they would act as the point of the march on these nomadic wanderings come the short-grass time.

Following the march leaders were the Oglallas, while the Hunkpapas of Sitting Bull would act as rear guard. It was The Bull's contention that the best way to avoid trouble was to stay as far from the white man as possible. If they could but avoid the army, he reasoned, there would be no worry of attack.

Slow marches of a few miles each day that winter-into-spring as the three villages moved up the Powder. With the full warming of spring awash over the northern prairies, they marched over to the Tongue.

And slowly, slowly, on to the Rosebud.

Every day The Bull sent out runners to the other bands trapped in bitter despair on the reservations.

"Look what I have!" Bull boasted. "You on the agencies have nothing but what the white man chooses to give you . . . when he chooses to give it. While I and the others have what Wakan Tanka has always given His people. Come, bring your guns! We will hunt in the old way. On our old lands. Where the white man will bother us no longer."

All through the spring and the first reaching of the

short-grass to the sun, many trails from north and south and east slowly began to merge together like strips of sinew wrapped into bowstring. Days of spring sped into summer, and one by one the little tracks of a lodge or two moved off the agencies, eventually joining others, their travois poles scratching the earth like the little streams and creeks feeding the mighty torrent of a river.

The Sioux were now as they had not been for many, many winters. Once again they were gathering with the old spirit, the old courage, the ageless power. There flowed a new life vibrant in every man, woman, and little babe strapped on the travois. They would go where the white man could not reach them.

Sitting Bull would take his people to those ancient hunting grounds, where they would not be bothered by the white man.

Sitting Bull would take them to the Rosebud.

By four o'clock that first afternoon, Custer halted the command on those open, minty bottomlands fragrant along the west bank of the Rosebud. Here the westerly breezes sweeping down from the Wolf Mountains would drive away troublesome mosquitoes come nightfall. The river at this point ran some thirty to forty feet in width, only three to five feet in depth, clear running but slightly alkaline, and with a gravel bottom that caressed the tired feet of many a trooper wishing to cool himself in its pleasant ripples that evening.

At sunset "Officers' Call" was sounded by Custer's chief trumpeter, Henry Voss. Word buzzed through camp that the officers would find Custer's bivouac beneath his headquarters' flag tied to a bullberry bush in the direction of the march.

By the time Fred Benteen, senior captain in the regiment, had squatted in the grass near the general's bedroll, he could see Custer was nowhere near as jovial as he had been that morning nor the previous evening. Benteen unbuttoned his blue blouse and swatted at a troublesome mosquito, sensing a sudden and serious mood seeping along the Rosebud as the last stragglers trotted up.

Fred scratched at the reinforced crotch of his cavalry trousers, then pulled out his ever-present pipe and stoked the bowl to a cheery glow.

"Cooke, how do we stand?" Custer barked with a taste of iron to it.

"All present and accounted for, sir!"

"Very good." Custer paced a moment, gathering his thoughts. "Since we're all here now, let me begin. I'm sure we each have better things to do that spend endless sessions listening to orders of march. Most of you have accompanied me many times before. You'll find little changed on this journey."

Tearing off a small limb from the bullberry bush spread like an awning over his bedroll, Custer continued. "I want to be assured that this scout is successful. And, I believe, success is marked by finding the Sioux. Am I correct, gentlemen?"

"Yes, sir!" Calhoun answered, then nervously glanced around at some of the more silent of his fellow officers.

"To assure our success, I am reminding you all of some of the primary orders of march I must insist upon upholding—the most important of which is that each of you must see that your trumpeters bury their bugles in their saddlebags and don't bring the bloody things out again until I order them brought out. There will be no more trumpet calls except in the gravest of emergencies. Good," he answered himself, slapping the limb across his left palm.

"At five A.M. each day we will begin our march. Five—promptly! That means your troops should be rousted by three for breakfast and to ready their mounts. You company commanders are experienced men and know well enough what to do, plus knowing when to do what's necessary for your men, so there are but two things I feel should be regulated from headquarters: when to move out and when to go into camp at the end of each day's march."

He paced a moment, tapping an index finger against his lips. "All other details, such as reveille, stables, watering, halting, grazing—everything will be left to the judgment and discretion of the troop commanders. I want you all to keep paramount in your minds you must remain in supporting distance of one another and don't dare get ahead of the scouts I will have out at all times in advance of our columns. And please, gentlemen—don't lag behind the main body of the march. I don't want any stragglers butchered. Understood?"

When he heard mumbling agreement from most of the weary men, Custer plunged ahead. "From all the intelligence General Terry has gleaned, in addition to the scout of Major Reno here, who found much evidence of lodge fires on that reconnaissance, we just might meet something in the order a thousand Sioux warriors. Now, fellas—if what the reports say is true about the Indians jumping the reservations like gnats off a hot plate this summer to join up with Sitting Bull and Crazy Horse . . . well, it looks like we might run onto something closer to fifteen hundred warriors."

"Fifteen hundred?" Wallace gulped.

"That's right, Lieutenant." Custer took a couple steps toward Wallace.

"But, sir. There's only some six hundred of us!"

Custer said, "Six hundred of the finest, anvil-hardened troopers who ever sat their asses atop McClellan saddles west of the Missouri—and don't you ever forget that!" He waved the limb over their heads, pointing downstream at the regiment going about its evening mess. "I'll put those six hundred up against twice that fifteen hundred warriors any day, Lieutenant!"

"Hear! Hear!" Tom cried, but quieted when Custer flicked a disapproving glance in his direction.

"But to put your mind at ease—from the reports of Indian agents up to the Commissioner of Indian Affairs, it looks as if we won't find an opposing force of more than fifteen hundred. Now, General Terry offered me Brisbin's cavalry and the Gatlings—"

"General?"

He turned. "Just a moment, Captain Keogh. You must all understand my reasoning. If those fifteen hundred warriors can defeat our Seventh Cavalry, by jiggers, they're gonna defeat a larger force." He looked at Keogh. "Captain, your question?"

"Personally speaking now, General." Keogh pricked all ears with his thick, foggy brogue. "I'm happy you didn't bring them others along. We all know each other here. We're all friends, ain't we now? And we all know just how the next man's going to act in a scrap of it. I say we're far better off not having Grasshopper Jim's Second Cav along to muddle things up for us."

"What Myles says is true, boys. With our regiment acting alone, there won't be a problem with harmony. The addition of Brisbin's unit would've caused jealousy and friction."

"Tell 'em why you turned down the Gatlings, Autie," Tom suggested with a grin as he shoved his hands in his pockets.

"Simply put, I figured the guns are pulled by condemned and inferior animals. Our march will be over terrain difficult enough as it is. The heavy, cumbersome guns and those busted-down animals would hold us back, perhaps at a most critical moment when I must maneuver as cavalry on the field of battle was meant to maneuver—turning in precision at the drop of a hat."

Custer stepped back to the awning. "Now, our marches each day will be from twenty-five to thirty miles each. I remind each of you to husband your troop's rations and be very watchful of the horses' condition. As I said before, we just might be out longer than we've rationed ourselves for. If we strike the hostiles' trail, gentlemen—I intend to follow it . . . right on into Nebraska or back to the Missouri River if need be. We'll find those Sioux and their camp followers. Make no mistake of that. We're not going in to our station until we have those warriors in our death grip!

"Boys," Custer continued, "I'll eat mule jerky and drink bad water if I have to, for as long as I have to. Simply because George Armstrong Custer is going to track those warriors right into hell if he has to!"

Benteen watched Custer bend the bullberry branch in half, finally snapping it with a resounding crack.

"I'll be glad to entertain any suggestions, gentlemen,"

he concluded quietly, "if those suggestions are presented in the proper manner by an officer of this command."

Benteen took notice of some of those faces that had been staring off at the river, gazing up at the clearing sky, or down at their dirty boot-toes, suddenly snap up. Something strange in the commander's comment snagged Benteen's attention like a fishing hook snagging a cutthroat trout.

This just wasn't the Custer he had come to know during their last decade together. Whereas the general was normally snappy and often sarcastic, now Custer's mood appeared contemplative, brooding.

Damned near somber, Benteen mulled.

If you were of the inner circle, then bless you. If you stood on the outside looking in, as did Frederick W. Benteen—then pity you, soldier.

So those who knew Custer best now hung not only on his words at this moment, but his tone and the distant look of those haggard eyes. Tom, Calhoun, Keogh, Cooke, Moylan, and Godfrey. For the general to become something different here on the first day of their march—it was enough to make a sensible man grow edgy, watching over his shoulder for ghosts.

Benteen himself wondered as Custer droned on, thinking Custer must certainly feel trapped within the strictures of Terry's rather general and ambiguous orders. *He grows despondent,* Benteen brooded, *yearning to be free of Terry. Instead, the arrogant, crowing bastard may well hamstring himself on the sharp horns Terry's designed for him.*

Then, while others studied Custer, Benteen's gaze was drawn to brother Tom.

Benteen figured no others would read that hollow despair round his blue eyes. If he knew any man as well as he knew Custer, Fred Benteen thought he understood Tom Custer.

Yet only Tom would truly understand that ever since the Washita, Autie had grown increasingly afraid. Not of death. Never that. No man could ever seriously entertain the idea of George Armstrong Custer wetting his pants over the thought of death.

No, instead it seemed Custer was afraid of risking his last great victory earned along the Washita in Indian Territory eight long winters behind them. Only Tom realized that his brother now stood the chance of winning for himself a seat among Washington's powerful—and this close to the precipice, Custer might also stand to suffer a complete defeat of all his hopes and dreams.

Yes. Benteen understood it now, watching the way Tom gazed at his older brother. *Tom looks at him like Peter himself looked at Christ. The young one knows how crucial it is for big brother to have everything successful and glorious. From here on out there can be no taint of defeat or withdrawal for the Seventh. Custer will be satisfied with nothing short of victory. This close to the edge of greatness, a man often teeters when looking back to see just how far he's come in so short a time.*

"I want it understood," Custer continued, "that I'll allow no grumbling in the slightest and shall demand exact compliance with orders from every officer. Not only my orders, but every officer's as well."

The general wiped his empty palm over his bristling mustache, watching his men with intensity. "It has come to my attention recently that some of my actions have been criticized to Department HQ by a few of you officers."

Here he goes, Benteen thought, fidgeting.

"Criticism going right to Terry's office. Now, I'll always take recommendation from even a junior-grade second lieutenant in my command, but I want that recommendation to come to me in the proper manner."

Bending to rip open the flap of his canvas haversack, Custer yanked forth a smudged, field-weary copy of *Army Regulations* from which he read the pertinent section regarding the offense in criticism of actions of commanding officers.

"I put you each on notice." He ground his words out as he slammed the book shut. "Should there be a repeat of this offense among any one of you in the future, I shall take the necessary steps to punish the guilty party."

To Benteen, Custer's challenge polluted the air like the acrid stench of burnt gunpowder as the general let his words sink all the way to the core of every man. Benteen couldn't let it pass. Although he had never been one to provoke Custer needlessly, neither was he a bootlicker who would let this challenge pass.

"General." Benteen took a step forward. "If I may be so bold. Appears you're lashing the shoulders of *all*—just to get at some. Now, as your entire officer corps is present, wouldn't it do to specify the officers whom you accuse?"

Benteen knew well enough the answer to his own query. He stood toe to toe with Custer, as the same man who years ago mocked the general in his scandalous letter exposing Custer's questionable actions immediately after the Battle of Washita when Major Joel Elliott and his men were abandoned to their fates and the butchery of the Kiowas.

"Captain—" Custer glared at the bulky Missourian with flinty eyes, though the salutation came out barely whispered above the hush. "I want my words to be a steel bit—and that bit shoved in the mouth that should wear it."

Benteen ground a boot-heel into the soft grass. "Then, General, would you be kind enough to tell me—before my fellow officers—if I'm the one who's been grumbling and complaining to HQ about you?"

"Captain, I'll not be catechized by you, or any man on regulations, nor the management of my own command. However, for your information—here before these fine men—I will state that none of my remarks were directed toward you. I know of no grumbling on this or on any other campaign, by you."

A sad smile graced Custer's sunburned face as his sapphire eyes took on a distant glow. "I know I can rely on each and every one of you from here on out. I always have. Whether you knew it or not. I've relied on my officer corps like they were my own family. Sure, there'll be bickering in a family—just like the Custer household back in Monroe. Right, Tom?"

"Sure, Autie." Tom never took his eyes from Benteen.

"We are family, gentlemen. We will support each other in what the future brings. We're horse soldiers, after all."

A man didn't have to be standing right beside Custer to hear sentiment catch in his throat as the general rasped out the name of his beloved regiment: "We're the

Seventh. We'll succeed only by hanging together, above dissension . . . or we'll die alone in miserable solitude because we failed each other."

With those last words Custer flung the limb aside and brought his right hand up, saluting his subordinates in a rare gesture of fellowship. Nervously, as they glanced furtively at one another, one by one the men of this command brought their right arms up to answer the sudden, unexpected salute from their general. It was an odd, uncanny feeling that shot like a thunderbolt through that assembly on the banks of the Rosebud at twilight.

Never before had Custer saluted them first.

He brought his arm down snappily, forcing a grin to crease his sunburned face. "That will be all, gentlemen. We march at five."

CHAPTER 9

THE officers shuffled off downstream, back to their companies and bedrolls.

Uneasy, Lieutenant Edward S. Godfrey wasn't really sure he had caught all of it right, as he was rather deaf in one ear, but he nonetheless sensed an unexplained anxiousness in his pit when he strolled away from Custer's bivouac at that moment. He stopped and turned to glance one last time at the general he had served since the Seventh Cavalry's earliest days at Fort Hays in Kansas Territory.

In Godfrey's way of thinking, Custer had for the first time shown a genuine reliance on his officers. And with this unexplained openness, Godfrey was more than certain there was something inextricably *not* Custer at all. Even something more profound than the mere tone of his voice, which, while normally brusque and somewhat curt, was on this occasion conciliatory and subdued.

Almost like an appeal for help, Godfrey considered. *As close as he can come to making an appeal for help . . . as if something's eating away at him.*

Finding his unshakable commander shaken in this way touched Godfrey clear down to his roots.

Lieutenant George Wallace, the regimental recorder but four years out of West Point himself, strolled along with Godfrey and Lieutenant Donald McIntosh in silence until they reached their bivouac. Lavender light was only then sliding headlong from the western sky. Off in the east a sliver of moon was rising when Wallace tore his eyes from the horizon and studied his two companions.

"Godfrey, McIntosh," he whispered, snagging their attention. "I believe General Custer is going to be killed."

Godfrey's eyes flicked to McIntosh apprehensively, finding him every bit as stunned as he. Then Godfrey found his voice. "Why?"

He was a veteran of the Seventh, after all. He ought to know everything about his commander. He had ridden with Custer at the Washita, down through the Yellowstone campaign and the Black Hills expedition. No, Godfrey himself didn't like the nervous wings rumbling round inside him at this moment.

"What makes you think Custer's going to be killed?"

Wallace waited while a group of soldiers strolled past on their way up from the river.

Already the nighthawks were out, swinging in low overhead, striking a moth or mayfly in the growing darkness. Death leaving no time for a cry for help or a yelp of pain. Swift and efficient. No warning. No sound until too late. Only the swift wings of death asail on the wind above the faint swish of cavalry boots plodding off through the tall grass growing here beside the gurgling Rosebud. Young soldiers returning to bedrolls and their dreams of home.

Finally Wallace answered in a harsh whisper, "Because I've never heard Custer talk that way before."

That was all it took for the hairs to prickle at the back of Godfrey's neck. He was deaf in one ear, but he had caught precisely every single one of Wallace's words. He walked apart from his friends.

As he groped along beneath starry patches among the clouds overhead, Godfrey brooded, as a blind man in need of answers sensing his way upstream, where he hoped he'd find the scouts' camp.

Good God, he told himself. *You've fought Indians with Custer before, Ed. Along the Platte River Road and the Washita and the Yellowstone itself. It's not like you're some ignorant shavetail quaking in your boots before your first fight.*

No, he admitted. *This is something different. Something downright spooky.*

He found a few of the Crow scouts and a dozen or more of the Rees, all gathered round their little fire. They talked quietly through Bouyer and Fred Gerard, the Arikara interpreter, or conversed silently among themselves, their hands gesturing in quick, darting flight like those nighthawks swooping overhead.

Not desiring to interrupt, Godfrey hunkered down on the grass near Mitch Bouyer, behind Bloody Knife, chief of the Ree scouts and a longtime tracker for Custer. He found himself seated beside Half-Yellow-Face, one of the older Crows assigned from Gibbon.

After Godfrey had attentively listened to the various conversations, studying what he could of the facial expressions and the signs used, he was surprised when he saw Half-Yellow-Face nudge the half-breed Sioux interpreter and point out the soldier among them.

Bouyer turned and grunted. Godfrey nodded and rose on his haunches a bit to show his interest in what the scouts were deliberating. Bouyer studied the two shiny bars on Godfrey's collar for the first time, perhaps remembering that the Indian scouts were officially assigned to Godfrey's K Company.

"You, pony soldier," Bouyer began, his voice low, causing Godfrey to lean forward with his one good ear. "You fight Indians before, eh? Ever fight these Sioux?"

Godfrey swallowed at the coarse directness of the question. *Damn*, he thought, *these scouts have a way of cutting right through the underbrush and getting right down to the root of something, don't they?*

"Yes . . ." Ed admitted. "Several times down near Nebraska, but our hottest engagements were along the Yellowstone three summers ago now."

"Hmmm," Bouyer considered as he turned back round to the fire, dallying at the coals with a twig for a few minutes. Only then did he turn back to stare directly at the lieutenant. "Well, then, pony soldier—just how many of them Sioux do you expect to find up there?"

Godfrey watched Bouyer nod upstream and point with his twig toward the hulking Wolf Mountains—the direction Custer was leading them.

"The general briefed us on the reports the army's received."

"How many warriors the army tell you Custer's going to find?"

"They figure we may find between a thousand to fifteen hundred warriors . . . if we find them."

"Oh," Bouyer laughed mirthlessly, "you'll find them all right." His teeth flashed beneath the pale thumbnail moon. "You'll find them if you go riding with Custer."

The half-breed seemed ready to let that settle a moment like a muddy puddle stirred. Then Bouyer continued. "So you tell me your own mind, pony soldier—you think we can whip that many Sioux?"

It was not lost on Godfrey that the half-breed Sioux interpreter had suddenly gone from saying *you* when referring to Custer's command, to now saying *we*.

"Oh, yes," Godfrey said quietly. "I guess so."

At that moment Half-Yellow-Face and White-Man-Runs-Him interrupted, asking Bouyer what had been said between the interpreter and the soldier. Then Bloody Knife sounded his interest, asking Fred Gerard to translate the gist of the conversation for the Rees in the circle. A few minutes passed before the Indians fell silent once more, their somber eyes refusing to talk any longer.

Bouyer tossed the twig into the little fire at his feet, watching it flare, then die out. "Well, pony soldier. I do not know this Custer—but Bloody Knife tells me much of him. I do not know him myself, but it's for sure I know the Sioux. Only thing I can tell you—we are going to have one damned big fight. One—damned—big—fight."

With nothing more than a whisper on the grass, Mitch

Bouyer rose, turned on his heel, and disappeared into the purple twilight.

One damned big fight.

Bouyer's words clung to Godfrey like stale fire smoke, stinging eyes and lungs. Foul on the tongue. Eventually he got to his feet and trudged off, growing nervous and cold and out of place among Gerard and the Indians. An outsider who did not understand their mysticism. An outsider who did not even understand why he shuddered uncontrollably as if he were freezing.

On the way to his bedroll, Godfrey stopped at Lieutenant Winfield Edgerly's D Company bivouac. A few officers had gathered beneath Edgerly's company flag, quietly singing some of their favorites down by the lapping waters of the Rosebud. Not only "Bonny Jean" and "Over the Sea," but also "Mollie Darling" and "Drill, Ye Tarriers" were all raised to the quiet evening stars amid complaints from Benteen of disturbing his sleep.

After "Dinnah's Wedding" and "Grandfather's Clock" were sung, Godfrey himself led them in the "Doxology," or the "Olde Hundredth" as it was popularly known.

> Praise God from whom all blessings flow;
> Praise Him all creatures here below.
> Praise Him above ye heavenly host.
> Praise Father, Son, and Holy Ghost.

With the nervous stammering of *amen*s, most of the men bid good night to their fellow officers and slipped off into the darkness to locate their companies and bedrolls while the chorus of coyotes and wolves took up the nightly serenade where the soldiers left off. Beautiful in its own feral way, though eerie to the uninitiated ear—that blending of high-pitched yips from the younger coyote pups, echoed by the deeper howl of a prairie wolf, was a chorus that thrilled a man accustomed to the high plains.

All round the regiment that summer night sang a lullaby meant only for the innocent.

Past those few lonely sentries on picket duty, a man

here . . . then another there slipped out to find himself some privacy for nature's call. One by one the solitary soldiers crept in among the horses and led an animal over the first hills to the east. Across the Rosebud. Climbed into the saddle—nosing for the Black Hills. Or off to the northwest and the Bozeman Road. Wherever—some men just wanted across those first low hills and away from this place.

It would be easy for their fellow soldiers to accuse them of cowardice. Too damned easy to figure these green recruits and a few fire-hardened old files to boot were all struck with a bad case of the "yellow flu."

Better yet, a clear-thinking man had to figure those soldiers had their eyes trained on the diggings located up in Alder Gulch or meant to head down to Deadwood with gold in mind. Sure enough easy for any man with half his wits who kept his eyes and ears open to understand he was finally within striking distance of the Dakota gold fields or the rich veins near Virginia City, Montana. Easy enough for any man who could keep his mouth shut to get lost among those miners and drummers and traders and gamblers who peopled those places men always went when they wanted to stake it all on one turn of the spade, or a single play of the cards. Such soldiers could always trade in a sturdy army mount branded *US* for a new set of duds, shucking himself of that yellow stripe down the outside of his britches . . . maybe even earn himself a grubstake up in the hills somewhere on some nameless stream.

Damned sure better than dying on some nameless little creek with Custer and his crazy band of zealots, one deserter thought as he slipped off into the noiseless night.

Damned sure better than dying with Custer.

Praise Him above ye heavenly host.
Praise Father, Son, and Holy Ghost.

Just as Custer had ordered, no reveille sounded for the Seventh on the morning of the twenty-third.

Entrusted to awaken the camp, the horse guard checked

their watches beneath the pale, lonesome starlight before groping their way through the sleeping camp, nudging their relief. Each was charged to see that his bunkies were rousted into the predawn darkness to relieve their bladders and start their tiny coffee fires.

By the time the columns moved out as scheduled at five A.M., with the newborn sun peeking red as blood over the eastern rim of the prairie, Lieutenant Charles Varnum and his scouts had been gone the better part of an hour, their own cold breakfast and boiled coffee laying as heavy as wet sand in their bellies.

As the Montana sun streaked like a stalking coyote out of the draws and coulees to the east, Custer leapt aboard Vic, waved farewell to striker Burkman, and set off for the day's scout. Directly behind him rode Sergeant Major William H. Sharrow, charged with carrying the maroon-and-white regimental standard in the company of Sergeant Henry Voss, the regiment's chief trumpeter, who carried the general's crimson-and-blue personal standard, the very same flag Custer had ridden with while commanding his Union cavalry during the Civil War.

The sight of the general heading upriver was the signal for the command to move out.

By the time that sore-eyed red sun climbed a hand high above the horizon, the regiment had crawled better than eight miles. Already the troopers had unbuttoned their shell jackets, leaving them open to catch the breezes from down the valley. Waist length, topped with a short, stiff collar, these shell jackets were the first item of apparel a man shed and tied behind the saddle as the morning warmed.

Custer joined his scouts at the first deserted Indian campsite the trackers ran across.

Tepee rings and fire pits pocked a large area of bottomland along the Rosebud. As the troops rode up, many of the veterans looked over the trampled ground in awe-struck wonder. More Indians had camped here than those hardfiles could ever hope to boast of seeing before in one place. In addition, there was a sobering number of wickiups still present, those willow limbs stuck in the ground, their tips tied together to form a dome over which the warriors had thrown a canvas fly, buffalo robe, or wool blanket for shelter at night.

"I can't believe the Sioux'd treat their dogs this damned good," Lieutenant Varnum chuckled as he trundled along behind Bloody Knife and a handful of Rees who scoured the deserted camp for sign.

Fred Gerard dragged to a halt, turning on Varnum with a death-cold look smeared across his old, weathered face. "Charlie, my boy—the Sioux didn't put these wickiups here for their goddamned dogs," he growled, raking his tongue around a dry mouth as he yanked a tin flask from a back pocket.

Varnum froze under Gerard's glare, growing nervous as some of the Rees studied how their interpreter had confronted the pony soldier. The lieutenant scuffed his jackboots across the ground like an embarrassed schoolboy, kicking up tufts of dry grass with the square toe.

"Not for dogs, Fred? Then what the hell they put in them wickiups?" He tried to chuckle again. No one laughed along with him.

"Charlie, my boy," the prairie-hardened Gerard replied, wagging his head sadly. *A damn shame*, he thought, *this here's the man Custer's put in charge of the regiment's scouts*. "Those wickiups sheltered the older boys and young warriors—the males of the tribes who're too old to live with their families now but too young to marry and have a wife and lodge of their own just yet."

Gerard licked his sore, dry lips, anticipating the taste of the whiskey as he worried the cork from the hip flask. He drank hard at the burning liquid that years ago had ceased to scour his throat with fire. After he raked the back of a hand across his wind-chapped lips, the interpreter went on.

"I'm afraid a lot of them wickiups was used by warriors scampering off the reservations, Charlie. You tell Custer, won't you? Tell him to think hard on all those warriors scampering off the reservations, come to join Sitting Bull."

For a moment Gerard had himself worried, hearing the ring of something foreign in his own voice.

The lieutenant stood gaping as Gerard turned and

walked off, following Bloody Knife, Red Star, and the others.

At one of the wickiups Bull-in-the-Water and Gerard tested the leaves on those limbs that had formed the frame. They were dry. Easy enough to tell that as he rolled those leaves about in his dirty palms. But they weren't crispy dry yet. Just wilted a shade.

"How long?" Mitch Bouyer stepped up beside Gerard with Half-Yellow-Face and Curley.

"Week maybe. From what Red Star figures." Gerard, a former post trader and now the official Ree interpreter at Fort Abraham Lincoln, tore the corner off a tobacco plug with yellowed teeth. Looking over this abandoned campsite, his mouth went dry, and he spit the chaw out.

He and Bouyer watched Custer remount, signaling his soldiers to resume the march. Angrily Custer hollered for Varnum and Bouyer to get their scouts out and moving ahead of his blue columns once more.

"Custer's got his hands plenty full right here, I think," Bouyer whispered gravely from the side of his mouth as he crawled aboard his Crow pony.

Gerard nodded, flushing a yellowed smile. "He's had his hands full ever since he decided to take these Sioux on. It's like he's got a bone stuck down in his throat and can't get shet of it. Shame of it is, I'm afraid the general's gonna choke on that goddamned bone."

Throughout the rest of the morning and into the growing heat of the afternoon, the scouts and a few of the old-timers began to notice a scarcity of game in the area of their march. A rare thing in virgin country such as this. A cavalry column marching across the high plains of Montana Territory would surely kick up some antelope, deer, and elk, or scatter off some of the birds normally roosting in the trees or chattering in complaint from the bushes.

Yes, sir, Gerard thought, shifting himself up on the cantle of his damp saddle. *Downright spooky to follow the Rosebud and not find a mess of wrens or a flock of sparrows swooping overhead out of the summer blue.*

Damned little life we've found dotting the thick marshes among the eddies near shore either.

Gerard knew his scouts and the Crows understood. They and Bouyer alike understood what had driven the game out of the country for miles around. Only an immense village on the march could have scoured the countryside clean of almost every sign of life.

Almost—except the magpies and robber jays that squawked their irritating demands over the abandoned campsites in search of a free morsel here, a bit of fat there. Something left behind by the gathering bands. And always the turkey buzzards overhead, circling, circling Custer's Seventh.

Gerard gazed up into the climbing sun. *It could give a right-thinking man the willies to watch those goddamned buzzards hanging up there over us.* High-flying wing slashes circling lazy on the warm updrafts in that pale, summer-burned sky. *Any right-thinking man damned well knew he ain't dead yet.*

By the time Custer ordered his command into camp near four-thirty P.M., the regiment had put nearly thirty-three miles behind them. At each of the three deserted camping places they had run across through the day, the general had ordered a short halt while the scouts inspected the sites.

Somber and silent, both Crow and Ree had walked the packed lodge circles. Put hands in the ashes of old fires. Broke open bones to inspect both condition and age of the marrow. And they did it all without a single word, shrouded in discomforting silence. Gerard watched them, silent as well, noticing that only Rees' dark eyes talked bravely to one another. Only their eyes talking.

While stable sergeants cussed and fretted over the lack of graze, because every blade of grass for some distance on both sides of the trail and been chewed to the ground, other soldiers speculated on the number of Indians they were following now . . . where the bands were headed . . . and how long ago the hostiles had left the area. In the last camp they had run across, over three hundred fifty lodge rings had been counted.

It didn't take an interpreter like Gerard to compute the simple plainsman arithmetic that added up to better than a thousand men of fighting age right on that one spot.

He could tell from the look on Bouyer's face that the

half-breed understood well enough that the bands were coming together. Gerard himself paid more and more attention to the dark eyes and gloomy faces of his Rees than he did the wild ramblings of loose-lipped army speculators like Varnum.

With a healthy heave Gerard rared back and tossed the empty tin flask toward the west bank of the Rosebud.

"Almost made it!" Lieutenant Varnum cheered his effort. "'Nother few feet . . ."

"Nawww," Gerard shrugged it off. "Not with a empty one, I wouldn't. That's a piece to throw a empty one."

Varnum studied him closely. "You wouldn't have any more of that, would you?"

Varnum's question brought Gerard up short. *The man's army, through and through. It just ain't right for one of Custer's solemn teetotaling churchboys to get his hands on any whiskey.*

He bent over his saddlebags anyway. "What the hell." He pulled out another flask. "Yeah, I got some more. Just want you remember, Varnum—I'm a civilian, and I can carry this along with me if I choose. Just in case you're figuring on showing the general the evidence—"

"I'm not," Varnum interrupted, licking his own dry lips anxiously. "Please. I just want some for myself."

"Yourself, Charlie?" he exclaimed in disbelief. "Why, I'll be damned."

"Just—with all the . . ." Varnum's eyes flicked around nervously. "I was with the Rees, the Crows all day." He wagged his head like someone watching the gallows go up a board and a nail at a time outside his own iron-barred window. "I may be green at this, Gerard. Handling Indians, that is. No old sawbuck like you. But even I could read their eyes. I ain't the smartest man Custer's got working for him—but I can sense we're running right on up the backside of something here that even the general don't know what he's doing."

"Here." Gerard shoved the flask into Varnum's fist. "You pay me when we get back to Lincoln."

The lieutenant clutched it against his chest like an icon, reverently. "Thank you, Fred."

As Varnum wheeled away, Gerard called, "Charlie. Just do me a favor, will you?"

"What's that, Fred?"

"Don't pour all that stuff down at one sitting. Save some for the 'morrow."

Fred watched the chief of scouts lead his weary army mount off through the milling command as the regiment spread out to establish its camp for the night. Gerard dropped beside his horse at his saddlebags to pull out a flask for himself this time. With his mount picketed he settled his shoulders against the saddle and sighed.

Hell, he thought. *You got plenty whiskey to spare.*

Why, between his spacious saddlebags and that generous army haversack, Gerard had brought along enough whiskey to see him through for a good month.

CHAPTER 10

Nearly an hour later the Crow scouts came plodding in, their little ponies nearly bottomed out from what had been required of them. Rule of thumb on the plains stated that a scout traveled twice the distance a cavalry column would march in a day, what with all the back-and-forth and the up-and-down. That meant those little grass-fed cayuses had done something over sixty miles beneath a cruel summer sun.

Yet right now it wasn't only fatigue that Mitch Bouyer could read on his Crows' faces. Something more, in fact altogether primal, that strained and pinched the normally happy faces he knew as well as he knew any friend.

Bouyer understood as few others would, for he had stood at the center of those deserted camps with his scouts. He had walked across the worn earth of the central council lodge, visually ticking off that distance to the farthest of the brush arbors and wickiups used by the youthful warriors. Mitch knew his Crow had read such sign as easily as any white man back east picks up and reads his daily newspaper.

The half-breed knew there wasn't a bit of good news to be found on the front page today.

Custer sought out the Crows while striker Burkman busied himself brushing down both Vic and Dandy with tufts of grass. Bouyer nodded to the general without a word while Custer squatted in his characteristic manner, one knee on the ground as he leaned an elbow on the other.

"This is the main point I want you to tell them, Bouyer," Custer began after Mitch had fed him the intelligence from the scouts' travels. "These Sioux have been killing lots of white people. You explain to your boys here—I've been sent here by the Great Father in Washington City. I'm told either to bring the Sioux back to their reservation or to defeat them in battle. Keep in mind, I'm called Charge-the-Camp. I'm a great war chief, greater than this Sitting Bull or his general, this Crazy Horse they speak of. But—I'll tell you a secret that no soldier who rides with me knows."

Custer slowly eased himself to the ground with Bouyer and his Crows. The significance of that posture wasn't lost on the scouts.

"My friends, I do not know whether I'll get through this summer alive. There'll be nothing more of any good in store for the Sioux from this time on, however. If the Sioux kill me, they will still suffer, for many more soldiers will come in my place and fill my empty boots. Ask your boys if they understand that."

He waited for Bouyer to translate. Some of the Crow nodded in agreement before Custer continued. "And if the Sioux don't kill me, why—I'm going to whip them soundly, right back to their reservations, where they belong. They've disobeyed the orders of the Great Father back east . . . and they will pay. Besides, you'll take home many fine Sioux horses, won't you, boys?"

Custer smiled widely, his sunburned face wrinkling as he waited while Bouyer translated. Young Curley spoke up, and when he was done, Mitch talked in a morose tone.

"These boys don't like you talking this way, not one bit,

Custer," Bouyer whispered with a powder-crack voice. "They figure there's strong medicine on a man who talks about his own death. You've spooked 'em now."

"Now, Mitch. I know some about Indians, mostly Cheyenne. But you tell these Crow not to worry. I'm not going to run, nor will I let my spirit fly away easily in battle."

"This is good," Bouyer answered in English before he translated.

"You tell these boys they're my favorite scouts," Custer continued. "I want them beside me when I go in for the kill. You tell them the strength of my words, Bouyer."

Custer stood and smiled down at the Crow trackers.

"You tell them, Bouyer tell them I'll recommend them to their people, and they will all be leaders among the Crow."

Custer turned on his heel, strode off at a lively pace. Mitch thought the way the general moved wasn't the plodding of a man seriously contemplating his own mortality.

Swinging his cream hat against one powdery leg to knock dust off the brim, Custer waved to some troopers and officers bathing in the cool waters of the Rosebud beneath a purple orange glow of sunset. On the opposite bank upstream a ways, Captain Benteen grumbled sourly under his breath. He had set a seine hoping to snare some trout for supper. But with all the naked swimmers splashing and setting up a playful howl in the rippling waters, the captain's cutthroat had been scared off.

Custer chuckled over Benteen's predicament, at the same time hoping the Sioux would not be scared away from his own trap the way the trout in the Rosebud were fleeing Benteen's seine.

But then, with "Custer's Luck" you always caught the Cheyenne. Old Black Kettle and Medicine Arrow both.

The more Custer thought on it, the more certain he became that his only problem would be one of surprise. The Sioux would run like jackrabbits once they got wind of him on their trail. And that simply wouldn't do.

You need Sitting Bull and the rest to play too important a role

in what you've got planned for the rest of your life, Armstrong.
Whether it's a big village like those we ran across today or nothing
more than five or six lodges. You must have that victory . . .
and you must have it now.

Adjutant W. W. Cooke was already at the Rees' camp
with the headquarter's guidon fluttering in the warm, dry
breath of early evening. Gerard sat to the side, not partak-
ing in the pipe the Arikaras shared in their circle. Custer
went down on one knee as he told Gerard to inform the
scouts of the news just brought in by the Crows.

"They figure there are a great number of lodges," Custer
started. "A great number of Sioux in many camps coming
together. What I want the Rees to tell me: If we catch up
to the Sioux, and I can keep them from running, what will
happen?"

Bloody Knife, veteran of Custer's 1874 expedition into
the Black Hills, nodded, wanting his old friend Stabbed
to reply for them all. Creaking up on his tired knees, then
to his feet, the old medicine man began to hop around and
around, circling, dodging this way, then that. Jumping
here, then there, with a sudden youthful vitality marking a
warrior.

After a moment of pantomime, Custer nudged Gerard.
"What's he trying to say?"

"He's showing you how the Sioux warriors will jump this
way and that, so they don't get hit with any soldier bullets."

Custer chuckled at the old man's primitive charade. "All
right. Now have him tell me what the Rees think will
happen to my soldiers."

Gerard translated, watching the circle of scouts fall
silent. Stabbed stiffened his arms at his sides as if marching
along in formation, then reacted to the impact of a bullet,
falling to the ground. Next he rose to one knee, aiming his
imaginary carbine at a moving object; he was again shot and
rolled to the grass in death throes. Finally he stretched
upon the ground, again shooting his rifle, when struck by a
silent arrow falling from the sky. Trying to pull the shaft
from his back, the old Ree died.

"What's all that?"

Gerard muttered under his whiskey-soaked breath,

"He's telling you the soldiers aren't going to fare all that well when they come up against Crazy Horse's Sioux."

Custer nervously wiped a hand across his straw mustache, irritating his chapped, wind-burned lips. "Don't you think I can see that?"

"General," Gerard whispered hoarsely, glancing around. Seeing some officers and a few young troopers ambling up out of curiosity, Gerard decided he didn't want to cause a scene in front of so many of the general's men.

"It's all right, Fred," Custer sighed. "You tell your boys word for word that I never expected them to fight beside me. Alongside my soldiers. All I want your Rees to do is capture as many of the Sioux ponies as they can run off. Every pony will be theirs. The Sioux won't need all those fine ponies on the reservations, that's for sure."

Gerard finished his translation, which caused the Rees to bob their heads in appreciation.

Growing pensive, Custer sensed a sentimental cord tighten within him. Perhaps the time had arrived for him to let these scouts and others know what the coming fight would mean to him.

"Long have I planned on this campaign to take me far from here—far from Fort Abraham Lincoln. Far from the land of my old friends, the Arikara. With only one small victory over the Sioux, I will become their Great Father in Washington City."

He stopped right there, his words slapping a stunned and dumbstruck Gerard. Behind him Custer overheard the whispered murmurs from his soldiers, as an electric response to his announcement shot through the assembly.

"When I get to Washington City, I won't forget my friends, the Arikara. Believe in that with your hearts. This is my last fight. I must have a victory and I must have it now, even if we defeat only a handful of Sioux warriors and a handful of lodges. With that victory in hand, I must quickly turn around and head back east. The people of my country will want to see me, hear me, take me to Washington City, where I will become your Great Father."

Custer kneeled beside Bloody Knife. "This is my friend. Bloody Knife has ridden down many trails with Custer before. Sad that this is the last war trail we will travel together, old friend."

He slung his buckskinned arm around Bloody Knife's shoulders. "But I tell you all, there will be a big house in Washington City for Bloody Knife to sleep in when he comes to visit me. Then I will send him back home to Dakota and a fine house of his own that I will have built for him. His two arms will be weighed down with the many presents he will bring back for his people to share. As Great Father of the Indians, I will reward those who have helped me win my final, lasting victory against these Sioux."

Custer said to the others in the circle, "The rest of you will have plenty to eat for all time, into the winters of your grandchildren, even unto their grandchildren."

"Hou! Hou!" the Rees answered in a great, spontaneous cheer.

It was not a strange sensation for him, this choking on a hot, sentimental knot in his throat. Nor were these tears hot and stinging new to his eyes.

He often found himself moved to tears when he thought about his men—the gallant Seventh and what they had done to bring him this far down the road to his historic destiny. Here he was, in fact a simple man, who knew to his core that his moment had come. Greatness was at hand.

"To St. Louis, General!"

Mark Kellogg bolted to Custer's side, raising the general's right arm aloft. Soldiers pressed in about them both. Better than a hundred by now, more trotting up, curious at the noisy excitement.

The short bespectacled newsman had wandered through camp, looking for Custer, eventually finding him in council with the Arikara scouts. It took but a few moments for a man like Kellogg to read the portents in Custer's private oaths to his Indian trackers.

Mark felt as swept up in the frenzy as any, leaping to the general's side on heady impulse, one of the few in that camp along the Rosebud this evening who truly understood the importance of Custer's promise. At this moment Kellogg watched that winning smile creep across the freckled face before him, the blue eyes lighting up with a distant glow.

"Y-yes . . . Mr. Kellogg!" Custer shouted over the din of whistling, stomping soldiers.

"You're announcing your candidacy, I take it?" Mark hollered above the bedlam.

"Candidacy? I hadn't . . . no, the Indian Commissioner . . . No—but yes, suppose I could as well as Grant himself, Mark! Suppose I am announcing . . ." He gazed over the swelling, raucous assembly of shouting soldiers and scalp-dancing Rees.

Kellogg allowed Custer's arm to drop, gripping his right hand in both of his, pumping exuberantly. "Congratulations, General—I mean, *Mr. President!* Let me be the first to congratulate you!"

"I haven't had my name placed in nomination, much less been elected—"

"A formality, General! Wait till Bennett himself gets word of you defeating the Sioux! He'll have St. Louis stampeding for you so fast, your head will spin." Kellogg wore a smile that lit up the dark eyes beneath his thick spectacles. "You're a natural for it crowds will love you. I can see it, a grand sweep you'll make across the States. After all, General—this country's always given her highest office to the men who win her wars, don't you know!"

"I suppose she does at that," he stammered.

"Of course, she does," he replied with a genial slap to Custer's shoulder. "First we had Washington, who freed us from that bloody tyrant George the Third! Then Andy Jackson, who shoved the British back into the sea again. And ol' Zach Taylor helped consolidate America's destiny in the southwest, wrenching American soil from the hands of Mexican despots. And finally Ulysses S. Grant himself, the man who saved our great Union for Mr. Lincoln—God rest his soul. With the help of fine officers such as yourself and Phil Sheridan . . . you understand. Those *soldiers* have been rewarded by our grand republic with a term at her helm."

Kellogg suddenly winced as Custer gripped the reporter

on the arm, his powerful hand like an iron vise. Mark watched a strange look cloud Custer's face.

"Mark," he gasped, "I had never before considered the presidency. What had been my dream, my furthest hope—the commissioner of Indian affairs—perhaps secretary of war."

"Dammit, General!" Mark shouted. "Don't you see? You want power? *Power?*" He laughed hysterically. "You have all the damn power any one man could ever want as president!"

A roar followed Kellogg's declaration. Custer slapped Kellogg on the shoulder, then pushed through the crowd to return to headquarters bivouac.

"There's really no better year than this, General!" Kellogg hollered after him, his notepad waved high. "No better time for a political party's nominating convention to be ignited by such raw emotion of the moment—once you defeat this Sitting Bull and his cronies."

"I've never been more ready!" Custer shouted back. "Let's pray Sitting Bull is as well!"

Custer strode off into the deepening twilight.

You have so little time now to find the Sioux, to secure your victory—no matter how small. Then you must get word back to Bennett in St. Louis by telegraph . . . yes! In time to sweep across the floor of the Democratic convention. Who, he thought, would turn down the nomination of a national hero? The youngest general of our recent victory over the rebellious southern states? Why, there's no doubt I could be swept into office following a grand campaign at the nation's centennial celebration in Philadelphia!

But first, he ruminated, he had to get word of his victory to the waiting ears of James Gordon Bennett, Jr., owner of the New York *Herald* and his political adviser and confidante. Surely he could dispatch someone dependable like Charley Reynolds to reach a telegraph key up in Bozeman. The same quiet, dependable scout who had carried news from the Black Hills for Custer back in seventy-four. . . .

But—what if Charley doesn't make it?

It was not a question of defeating the Sioux. No, in Custer's mind it never would be. Instead, it became merely a question of getting word of his victory to the waiting world . . . and on time.

Herendeen and Bouyer! Yes! They could do it. Both take different routes south to the great Platte River Road where they could find telegraph offices . . . anywhere from Fort Laramie to Fort Fetterman. Just pray the wires are up and the operators are at their keys.

Most of all, Custer knew he would assure that his beloved army did not shrivel into a ghost of its former self. With an end of problems in the post-war south along with a temporary calming of the Indian situation out west, there had arisen in Congress a strident hue and cry to cut back the Senatorial appropriations for the nation's army. Many a good man would be thrown out of the only work he had ever known.

If elected, Custer would change that antimilitary mood sweeping Capitol Hill . . . by the force of his personality if nothing else. To assure that his beloved army did not become a eunuch. With what he would do to keep his country's army strong in the future, with all that he had done to lay those victories of the past at his nation's feet . . . he was every bit a natural leader. Certainly after all his successes, this nation could trust the helm to *President* George Armstrong Custer.

And beside him on every train platform, at his arm on every dais and speaker's rostrum of the campaign, would stand Elizabeth Bacon Custer. He had married her, pledging his life to her. Libbie knew he had pledged his life to the army as well.

Pledged your life to Libbie, yes . . . but what of your heart, Armstrong?

Never once had he entertained any thoughts of leaving her.

Once. Once only. But Libbie simply needed him far too much for him to abandon her. It was for that reason that he had never brought himself to tell her the reason they could not have any children rested with her, and her alone.

Custer knew he would never shrink from any charge, any enemy fire—no matter what that enemy threw at him. Yet he could still not bring himself to explain to Libbie that she was the one who could not have children.

He suddenly realized—his boots grinding to a halt.

You're a father already. How long now?

The child would have been born sometime in the fall of sixty-nine. That would make Monaseetah's son some six and a half this summer.

Her son?

As he smiled with the thought of it, Custer was certain for some unexplained reason that he had been blessed with a son.

And just as quickly his paternal joy plummeted from its dizzying heights when he realized odds were he would never see the child . . . his child. Never know this son. It was as if a cold stone had been rolled into his heart.

Dare he think of the boy's mother? Her beauty. Dare he remember the fragrance of her flesh warm and musky as she pressed herself into him, full of fire? *The mother of my child.*

Could Monaseetah find it in her warm, childlike soul to absolve him of his guilt for sending her away . . . more so for abandoning her and the child?

Perhaps this matter of the woman and their child would be something he would have to see to before he took that sacred oath of office.

Yes.

To live up to the oath he had pledged to himself and to her so many summers before this. He had promised . . . no, he had *sworn* he would return for her.

Custer knew now he had to see her again. With every fiber that was at his command. He had to see Monaseetah and the boy.

After all, Yellow Hair had never lied in his life.

CHAPTER 11

I T was nothing more than ignorance really.

These white men—soldiers and scouts alike—they assumed all the deserted camps the regiment ran across during their march of 24 June were merely successive camping sites of the same village on the move.

The Crows and Rees knew better.

Bloody Knife as well as any.

The aging, veteran Arikara tracker understood these converging sites were in fact the continuous camps of several large bands having joined here on the upper Rosebud. What angered him into even stonier silence was that he and the other scouts could not convince the soldiers that they were fools if they refused to see the camps were the same age.

Beginning that long and very hot day, anger became a bitter potion the Indian scouts would be drunk on before another sun had risen.

At each of the abandoned campsites, the convergence of a growing number of lodge rings and fire pits joined the abandoned wickiups along the river's bank. And on the outskirts of every abandoned camp, the grass was found close cropped for miles around, the herd-trampled meadows generously speckled with droppings already dry and crumbly beneath a relentless Montana sun.

Site after site passed, each the same as the last, except that most of the soldiers found they had to agree it appeared the camps were growing larger, until it appeared as if the circles no longer had any room for the normal camp horn but needed instead to raise more and more lodges back in every bend and twist of the riverbank.

At the upper end of each abandoned campsite, the scouts drew up their horses and read each other's expressions on their stony copper faces. No need of saying anything more. For here, on the southern edge of every camp, the many trails converged into one broad road, plowed and furrowed by Indian ponies, the thousands upon thousands pulling travois.

Half Sioux himself, Bloody Knife realized by now that the hostiles were heading over the spine of the Wolf Mountains. And his medicine helper told the old Ree that the Sioux knew they were being followed.

For the Crows and Arikaras, what had once been the powerful medicine of this journey to whip their old enemies with the pony soldiers had slowly turned sour in their mouths. Instead of Custer leading them to a great victory and a trip to Washington City, the Long Hair was taking them with him into a valley shadowed by the wings of death.

Bloody Knife, Red Star, Stabbed, and others gazed at the half-dozen Crow scouts when Fred Gerard wasn't watching or Lieutenant Varnum was busy chattering with Custer. Neither group could speak the other's tongue. They didn't have to. There was a universal language any man could read, plain as paint on every scout's face—red eyes flinty and stoic so as not to betray the dark secret the white men simply refused to believe.

One young Ree named Horns-in-Front actually began to whimper quietly when he and Bloody Knife came across a huge stone at the site of one of the abandoned villages. The stone had been painted with primitive glyphics symbolizing two buffalo bulls. One had been drawn beside a bullet, and the other held a lance—both animals charging one another. Horns-in-Front trembled as he listened to Bloody Knife and the old man Stabbed discuss the symbolism in the Sioux drawing.

Then the young scout whimpered in fear.

Spotted-Horn-Cloud rushed the shambling, shaken youngster and slapped Horns-in-Front hard across the mouth, drawing blood.

That got Custer's attention.

Bloody Knife turned as well, watching the general drop from his big horse. Custer strode up quickly, examined the stone for himself, then asked his question in sign of his old friend, The Knife.

"What does this mean?" His freckled hand pointed to the drawings.

"Pony chief"—the aging Arikara's hands moved more slowly than usual—"it says there will be a hard and long fight for any enemy who chooses to follow the Sioux on this trail."

Instead of replying, Custer slipped off the big hat and ran a palm over the reddish blond stubble on his head. More trail weary than exasperated, he remounted his mare and loped out of the murmuring ring of scouts without another word.

A few hours later the scouts reached the largest camping site yet seen on the march up the Rosebud.

What now gave them all pause was the sight of the close-cropped grass extending for miles around in all directions across the rolling hills and timbered meadows beside the creek. Clearly the scouts could see that this site had been used for many days.

And then the general's brown-skinned trackers came to understand why the tribes had halted their leisurely march here at this beautiful spot in the shadow of the Wolf Mountains.

Close by the river on a grassy bottom that, come every spring, was buried beneath the swirl of winter's runoff stood the huge Sun Dance arbor of the Lakota nations.

Mitch Bouyer slipped up silently to stand near a speech-less Custer just inside the outer reaches of that massive framework of poles. It was not until the general rose from the ground, a handful of hard-packed earth cupped in his deerskin glove, that he finally noticed the half-breed scout at his shoulder.

"Tell me about this, Bouyer."

The Crow interpreter was a few moments before answering. Then his words filled the brittle, dry silence surrounding the Sun Dance Lodge with a stifling gloom. "Custer, I've never seen one this big. Not in all my years living with the Sioux."

"That mean something?" Custer snapped, not looking Bouyer in the eye, but staring instead at the buffalo skulls and the monstrous center pole those skulls surrounded. "For it to be so big?"

"I think it's safe to say it means something, General."

The Crow interpreter felt moved by the immense size of the arbor constructed of pine boughs and lodgepole, every trunk showing its recent age and just now beginning to weather beneath the prairie's summer sun. But what was most impressive of all to the scouts and Bouyer both was the size of that massive center pole, where hung some of the tattered rawhide tethers still.

The tethers danced on the late-afternoon breezes.

Bouyer understood more than any man there that afternoon what all those hundreds of rawhide tethers meant. He had grown up with the Sioux. He had watched men sacrifice themselves and their bodies in thanksgiving to the sun in this way.

What swept over Mitch, shaking him to his core, was the realization that the Lakota were preparing as never before some powerful medicine for a most special purpose.

If the Sioux of Sitting Bull truly did know soldiers were dogging their back trail, then the Lakota were making medicine as they never had for one powerful big fight.

Near the huge center pole's base the Sioux had driven a tall stake into the hard-packed earth.

Tom Custer passed his brother and the half-breed Sioux scout, the first to dare venture into the bowels of the Sun

Dance Lodge itself. Sergeant Jeremiah Finley of Custer's C Company joined Tom.

Crossing the pounded, baked ground to the center of the lodge now shadow-striped by the afternoon sun, Finley knelt to touch the hair tied to that single stake at the foot of the monstrous pole.

"Captain Custer! C'mon over here, sir!"

"What is it, Sergeant—" Tom began, watching Finley get to his feet, holding the dried scalp up at the end of his arm for all to see. "I'll be go to hell. Will you look at that sonuvabitch."

Wasn't a man gathered round Finley in grim silence who didn't realize that the sergeant had found a white man's scalp.

"Take it." Tom gritted his words out between clenched teeth. "Show it to Autie."

"Autie, sir?"

"The general, goddammit! My brother!" Tom snapped like a brittle twig, his eyes never straying from the brown hair.

After George Armstrong Custer had viewed the scalp in silence and showed it to his scouts, he asked Finley to pass it among the troops.

"Why you wanna do that, Autie?" Tom asked as Finley strode away.

"Don't you understand, dear brother—just what kind of effect that scrap of bloody hair will have on the men?"

Though he would never be famous for being as smart as his older brother, Tom Custer could never be accused of being on the slow side. A smile crossed his sun-raw face.

"Good," he whispered, approving. "Not a soul knows whose goddamned scalp that is . . . even when it was taken. But every one of the men will see that it was a white man's head of hair."

"You read sign savvy enough, Tom."

Near the huge Sun Dance Lodge, Bear-in-Timber, another young Arikara scout, found a sandbar at the bank of the creek where the surface had been purposely smoothed so pictures could be drawn in the flat, sandy surface.

Figures heading south, up the Rosebud, unshod ponies all. Behind them a smaller group rode on shod horses—soldiers, it was plain to see. It didn't take an experienced plainsman like Fred Gerard to understand that.

"They're telling all the Sioux who are still coming to join up, that there's a small bunch of soldiers dogging the main camp's tail," Gerard interpreted for Custer as Bloody Knife and Stabbed bent over the drawing, slowly tracing the lines with their scarred fingertips.

"You telling me the Sioux know we're on their trail?" His voice rose a pitch.

"No, General," he replied, shaking his head. "Funny thing of it, from what these Rees are saying, we aren't the soldiers the Sioux know are following 'em. Maybe so—there are some other soldiers this far south, some of Gibbon's boys, you suppose?"

"Crook!" he roared. "That's got to be it. I'll be horn-swoggled. Crook's got thirteen hundred troops marching up from Laramie to join with Gibbon and Terry." His look cut into Gerard's red-rimmed, hung-over eyes. "Ask Bloody Knife—if the Sioux know about Crook, do they know about us?"

Gerard could tell Custer's whole day depended on the answer to that solitary question.

"Stabbed says the Sioux haven't got an idea one we're on their back trail," Fred answered.

"By God's back teeth, that's good news!" Custer leapt to his feet, clapping. His smile disappeared. "Except—if Crook gets there ahead of me to snatch my victory right out of my hands!"

Custer wheeled, his boots plowing through the sandbar pictures. "*Saddle up, boys!* We're on the march!"

In the twinkling of an eye, Gerard had watched Custer go from whispering and worried to bellowing like a cas-trated calf.

"General!" Myles Keogh's peat-moss brogue brought Custer up short of climbing in the saddle.

"What is it, Captain!" he barked.

"The Crows over there," and Keogh threw a thumb back to indicate Bouyer and the Absarokas gathered round a framework of willow boughs. "They found something you should take a look at, sir."

"Another wickiup, Myles? I've seen quite enough of them in the last couple days." He leapt smoothly atop Vic. "Let's be moving out, gentlemen."

Keogh snagged Vic's bridle, halting Custer. "Sir, I think you should take a wee peek at what them Crows wanna show you . . . now, sir."

Gerard himself heard the anvil-hardened sound of the Irishman's words. Custer must have heard it too, for he studied the big captain's black eyes only briefly.

Whatever Myles Keogh might be accused of, he would never be accused of frivolity. As well as any man, Fred Gerard knew the Irishman's reputation for being a hard drinker and having a way with the ladies but Keogh always meant what he said.

Custer followed the Irishman, Gerard not two steps behind them both.

"Another wickiup, Bouyer?"

The Crow interpreter wagged his head as he looked up at the general. "No. A sweat lodge. Pit in the center. Warriors heat up the rocks in this hole over that fire pit there. They carry 'em in here . . . dribble some water on 'em to make steam."

"Don't lecture me now, Bouyer!" he barked. "I know what a sweat lodge is. Get on with it and tell me why this one is worth my time."

Mitch Bouyer squinted at Custer, a look narrowed as hard and as straight as his words had ever been spoken to a white man. Half his blood, after all, came from a white father. Trouble was, that Sioux half to his blood didn't take kindly to any man dressing him down, especially if that man was an army officer.

You're not here to work for this Custer, he kept reminding himself.

Still he couldn't quite escape the feeling that his own ass was about to be slung over the very same fire as Custer's.

"General, what I do is for your soldiers. Not for you."

Custer turned on Bouyer, a strange look in those sapphire eyes. Mitch figured he had struck some nerve someplace beneath that raw-boarded exterior.

"Just so you understand, I know you don't like me, Custer. But that don't bother me a damn. 'Cause I'm learning there's not much to like about you either. But what I'm gonna do is put away that bad taste in my mouth while I tell you what the Crow found here. I'll do what I promised No Hip Gibbon I'd do."

"So why don't you help me, Bouyer? I want this regiment moving again, and plenty fast. I've got Sioux to catch."

That interruption brought Bouyer up short, like someone had grabbed hold of his testicles and yanked on them with a jerk.

"Sioux to catch, General? Well, why don't you take a look over there? Step on up where them Crow boys are. Good. You take a look, and you'll notice a ridge of sand those Sioux've piled up there to snag your attention."

"Mine?"

"That's right. Now on the other side of that hump of sand, you see some horses drawn with iron shoes."

"Cavalry?" Custer asked, smiling.

"Ain't Brigham Young's Mormons chasing Sioux this far north, General," Bouyer replied, his voice dripping with scorn.

When a few soldiers behind him snickered at Mitch's joke, Custer whirled and glared flints. The troopers snapped silent, as startled as if the general had flung January ice water on them all.

"Now you see on the other side of that ridge there . . . the Sioux've scratched some pony tracks—Indians. This time you make no mistake of it."

"What are those figures in the middle?" Custer bent over the bank, peering down at the drawings scratched in the sun-cured sand.

"Soldiers, General. Your soldiers."

Custer straightened. "I see."

"No, Custer," Bouyer bit his words off. "You don't see. Least, you don't see with the eyes of these Sioux warriors you're hell-bent on cornering."

"What's that supposed to mean?"

"Look again there, and you'll see the soldiers are all pointing headfirst into that Indian camp."

The general reluctantly tore his eyes from Bouyer's copper face to peer down at the sand drawing while the silent Crows rose, creeping off to their ponies as if some unspoken cue had been given.

"I understand their simple drawings, Bouyer. The Sioux show my soldiers charging their camp."

"*No!*" Bouyer blared. "Dammit! These Sioux are showing your little ragtag outfit here falling right into their camp. To these Sioux falling headfirst means *dead*. You get it, General? Your men are falling into the Sioux camp like fish flopping on the bank of this river. Dead and drying in the sun."

For a long moment Bouyer's words stunned Custer and his officers into a granite silence. But as suddenly the general himself started to chuckle. It's bitter sound filled the hot void surrounding them all.

"Well, Mitch . . ." He laughed louder and strolled up to Bouyer. There he amiably slapped a hand on the short half-breed's shoulder, knocking some powdery alkali dust from the hair-on calfskin vest the interpreter wore. "The joke's on you this time!"

Bouyer's dark eyes flashed over the officers grouped behind Custer. Their faces showed the same sudden relief as their leader's. They too started to laugh with the general.

"General, I'm going to say this simple as I can." So quiet were Bouyer's words that his voice shut them all up as quickly as he began to talk.

"Over yonder by the river, that drawing on the sandbar might be some other army, a real big one. Maybe the one you say Red Beard Crook is leading north. But this one," and he pointed a gnarled finger down at the sweat-lodge scratchings, "the Sioux drew themselves as a huge force of warriors butchering a small bunch of soldiers. And that is just what *we* are, goddammit. Counting every last one of your men, we got less than half the strength of Crook."

He let that sink in a moment. "You think on that,

General. We haven't got Gibbon along—and you better believe the Sioux know that too. So you've got plans for us to prance right on in and flop headfirst into their camps, don't you?"

"Balderdash!" Custer spat.

Angrily Custer kicked at the sand ridge, sending grains of sand skidding across the sweat lodge and into the air, scattering those soldiers who stood close to him.

"We've got some Sioux to find, gentlemen!" he announced sharply, ripping Vic's reins from Burkman's hand. "Let's be about it. Sergeant Voss? You find trumpeter Martini. The two of you see that 'Officers' Call' is given by voice to each company. I want to talk to my officers. Right over there. And right now."

CHAPTER 12

As trumpeters Voss and Martini made their way through the command, Custer marched confidently toward a patch of willow and sage beside the gurgling Rosebud, where he drove the flagstaff for his personal standard into the dry, rocky soil.

Lieutenant Edward Godfrey had been close enough to hear the whole thing between Custer and Bouyer. Now Godfrey found himself one of the first waiting for Custer's hastily called conference to get under way.

"Gentlemen, the Crows tell me that they've found some fresh sign ahead."

It was as if he had dropped a sulfur-head Lucifer on a powder keg, waiting to see who would pounce first.

"I figure that's the news we've been waiting to hear, General," Lieutenant Algernon E. Smith rose to the bait.

He wheeled on Smith. "That's right. Trouble is, there's only three or four ponies. And one on foot."

"Dammit, Autie. Sounds like the scouts ran across some beggar's string-along outfit!" Tom said.

He stopped while many of the officers laughed at his comparison of forces. Godfrey knew that such laughter only goaded jokester Tom Custer on all the more.

"Autie, how can we get excited over some fresh sign after seeing where all these Indians camped—when that sign is just five poor Injuns?"

"If I may be so bold, General." James Calhoun stepped forward. "It appears the Crows are getting desperate to have some fresh sign to show you."

Custer held up his hand for quiet. "I for one find the news most cheering. Why, those of you who were with me will remember our winter down in Indian Territory chasing the Cheyenne."

"By God, that's right, General!" Godfrey piped up, watching Bouyer and Gerard join the officers' conference. "California Joe and his Osages ran across an old trail. Better than a month old, it was. And only one lodge to boot. But we followed it."

Custer beamed. "Did that trail pay off, Ed?"

"By damn, it did, General!" Godfrey answered on cue. "We caught old Medicine Arrow and all his Cheyennes napping!"

"By glory we did!" Tom echoed.

"Exactly," Custer replied quietly. "I want you to realize what happened on the Sweetwater is about to happen here, fellas. The fresh trail we've run across may only be four or five Indians, but that handful will lead us to the mother lode."

With a brutal, dry gust of wind at that exact moment, Custer's personal standard blew down, falling so that it pointed toward the rear of the column's march.

Back down the Rosebud.

For a moment not a single soldier, officer, or general alike realized the potent symbolism of that fallen flag. But Mitch Bouyer clamped his dark hand over his mouth, Indian fashion, to prevent his half-Sioux soul from flying out in awe and fear.

Godfrey stood where he could watch both Gerard and Bouyer. The Ree interpreter knit his brow, staring at the fallen standard gravely. But what Ed Godfrey read on

Bouyer's face frightened him. The lieutenant swallowed hard, then knelt to retrieve Custer's flag from the dirt.

He drove it in the dry ground once more.

No sooner than he let it go and turned back to the conference, another short gust of wind huffed out of nowhere, tearing through that officers' assembly, toppling Custer's standard a second time.

No longer was Ed Godfrey merely nervous. He was spooked as he plucked the flag from the ground and bored the shaft down into the summer-crusted, hard-packed surface the Indians had beaten with their moccasins. Only then did he lean the staff back against some sagebrush for additional support.

Godfrey raised his eyes and there met Lieutenant Wallace's sad expression, a look filled with the tale of something grave and foreboding.

Anxiously Godfrey glanced down at the standard. He suddenly remembered Wallace's warning on the evening of the twenty-second.

"I think General Custer is going to be killed."

Swirling, swarming, and burning with fiery torment, tiny red buffalo gnats descended once again on the troopers as they plodded, forever plodded, through the dust and sweltering mirages of the Montana high-plains summer. A bright one-eyed sun glared down on the columns with unmerciful intensity, chapping raw the faces that weren't already covered by a protective coating of talc-fine dust kicked up by the hooves of animals ahead in the long columns.

Damn gnats . . . mosquitoes! grumbled Mitch Bouyer.

Biting, stinging, sucking until it nearly drove a man mad for want of relief. The gnats swelled his eyes half-shut to where he could barely see, forced to suck at the swirling, buzzing air through a silk bandanna tied round his face. Burning with the sting of mosquitoes and the bites of monster horseflies everywhere, a chunk of the half-breed's flesh still lay exposed.

Never had he been able to bring himself to do what the old teamsters had done for years, up and down the Platte

River Road and the Bozeman Trail. They dabbed a potion of coal oil on the corners of their bandannas and hung those neckerchiefs from their sweat-weary hats just below their eyes to cover the rest of the face. That coal oil smelled bad enough to drive all but the hardiest pest away from the eyes. Bad enough that most men like Mitch Bouyer wondered just what was worse: the heat and dust and buffalo gnats . . . or the heat and dust and coal oil under your nose.

There were too many halts through that long afternoon, each one signaled by Custer so his troops would not overrun the Ree and Crow scouts. Not that any of the soldiers had noticed, but Bouyer took mark of it. Custer's Indian trackers were inching ahead a bit more slowly than they had the first two days of their march up the Rosebud. To top it off, they weren't ranging all that far afield on the flanks either. Seemed they stayed in sight of the dusty columns now.

No, Mitch decided, most soldiers too blind to recognize the face of fear anyway.

But Gerard saw it. Bouyer recognized it too. The Indians were tracking no longer. They simply followed that fresh trail working itself up toward the Wolf Mountains. On the other side of the divide spread that valley of the Greasy Grass, long a popular Cheyenne hunting ground for buffalo and antelope.

Throughout the beginning of their climb up the high, rugged land that erupted itself between the Rosebud and the Little Bighorn, the Indians kept a particular eye on that country off to their right—the drainage of Tullock's Creek. It was this piece of country scout George Herendeen knew so well. It would be here he could pay for his keep when they reached the Forks sometime tomorrow. But for now the scouts kept a wary eye on that drainage. Some of the jumpier, younger Rees even thought they saw smoke signals off to the right, up the Tullock's, far in the distance. But no older Arikara saw that smoke. They merely chuckled at the youngsters' vivid war-trail imaginations. It was funny, watching the young ones hour by hour grow spookier and spookier.

Without any rainfall in this part of the country for the past three days, the ground lay parched again, crumbling beneath the ponies' hoofs. Forced to follow a trail beaten by thousands upon thousands of horses and plowed up by uncountable travois only made the march worse for the dust-caked troopers. Custer ordered column-of-fours where he could, spreading the companies out as wide as practicable, attempting to keep the rising dust to a minimum.

Word was he didn't want to be spotted—not just yet anyway.

Without a breeze the thick cloud persisted over the regiment. More and more the saddle galls and sweat-crusted underwear of the soldiers rubbed and chafed and burned at their weary, blistered rumps. Some of the oiled McClellans were beginning to dry and crack.

Faces burned and lips bled, oozing and stinging when a trooper repeatedly licked his tongue across the salty source of his misery for some momentary relief.

Bouyer listened to the soldiers grumble, complaining how bad Custer was making it on them.

You ain't see the worst of it yet, Bouyer brooded in the privacy of his thoughts. *None of you seen just how bad Custer can make it for you yet.*

By sundown on the twenty-fourth, Custer had given the order to camp, placing his entire command under a long, irregular bluff to minimize the chance of being spotted by Sioux scouts roaming the slopes above.

The regiment had marched some twenty-eight miles that day, and still the general told his adjutant, W. W. Cooke, he wasn't satisfied with the pace. To Canadian Cooke, a tall, handsome, dead-shot woman's man, it seemed Custer hungered like a wolf on a hot trail—the scent growing stronger and headier in his nose each time they had come across campsite after abandoned campsite.

"Cookey." Custer turned suddenly as his adjutant dropped from his horse. "Don't dismount. Carry my compliments to the commands. Inform them all supper fires will be extinguished as soon as they're finished with their meals. Most important, they're to be prepared to move out again at eleven-thirty P.M."

Cooke jerked out his watch, the shimmering fob dangling from his palm. In the fading light of a summer's evening, he stared at the hands. His eyes climbed to find Custer staring back at him. "Sir—eleven-thirty? That's not but three hours from now, General."

"I well understand that, Billy," Custer rasped with a dust-scaled throat. His own lips burned and bled as much as the next man's. The cheeks above his own three-day-old stubble felt much like winter rawhide, stiff and unforgiving when he tried to smile.

But smile he did. "We'll find time to sleep, Billy. Make no mistake about that. We find that Sioux camp . . . we can lie in wait until time for our attack. The troops won't lose much sleep, really they won't. Now be off with you. Inform the men."

Cooke turned and rode off, thinking back to the long winter gone down on the Washita. The Osage trackers led Custer to that Cheyenne village of Black Kettle's the general had hoped to find, then lay his regiment in wait until the time was right for attack.

By damn, he'll do the same bloody thing here, Cooke ruminated as he rode back along the bluff. *Find the camp, then rest up the men before we ride in there and wipe them out . . . just the way we destroyed ol' Black Kettle's band of brigands!*

Although the columns had not covered as many miles as Custer had planned, it had been a long, difficult day nonetheless. In fact, three long and difficult days behind them now. And still the general prepared to march some more.

Three bleeming hours from now, Myles Keogh grumbled to himself, hearing word from Billy Cooke.

As quickly Myles figured there was no sense wasting what little time a man had by bellyaching about it. Use that precious time out of the saddle for all that couldn't be done on the march—like boiling coffee, what old files like Keogh called their skalljaw. Or forcing down their pasty hardtack and some dried salt pork as they squatted around their smoky little fires.

Or simply finding enough flat ground that would allow a man to stretch out his tired frame, pull his slouch hat down over his scalded face, and close his eyes to the world for a few delicious hours of sleep.

Myles invited Benteen and others to his quarters, in reality nothing more than a small chunk of canvas Keogh tied to a bush, lean-to fashion. But the lack of spacious accommodations didn't stop any of the guests from squatting in a circle to tell stories in that inky darkness slithering like a prairie wolf along the base of the bluff. Tom Custer even brought along a canteen full of whiskey he decided to crack open with his fellows. The whiskey scalded the parched throats and seared the cracked lips . . . but damn, if it wasn't tasty after the day's march.

While some shared their opinions of the Crow and Ree versions of the Sioux drawings, Lieutenant Calhoun worked at a huge blister at the back of a heel. His feet tended to sweat more than the normal man's, and with damp stockings his boots invariably irritated his feet. Up and down, up and down—constant movement rubbed his boot heel while the ball of his foot rested in the oxbow stirrup, working up a sizable blister that nearly wrapped itself around the back of his heel.

With one end of a woolen thread he had poked through the eye of a needle, Calhoun carefully evened the strand and began his surgery by lancing the blister. But instead of merely pricking the skin, Calhoun drove the needle on through and out the other side so that the woolen thread itself lay in the irritated fluid. In this way he could watch the thread absorb the moisture before pulling the wool strand from the blister.

Lieutenant Charles DeRudio finally piped up, wanting to tell a story about his days fighting under Garibaldi in the Italian army. His fellow officers passed Tom Custer's whiskey canteen the rounds once more.

This was a time in the west when most men carried some whiskey in a saddlebag or possibles pouch, after all—even those who might classify themselves as nondrinkers. John

Barleycorn was the proven specific taken for the "summer cholera" or "prairie dysentery," really nothing more than bowel cramps often caused by a change in diet or water.

There was a lot of whiskey in that starless camp this night. And somehow that trader's whiskey made the idea of the coming night march seem not so bad after all.

> I enlisted to sojur,
> And I'm willing to fight—
> Not to whack government mules
> And stay out half the night!

In his thick, peaty brogue, Keogh sang the words from the popular soldiering ditty currently making the rounds of the western posts. Practically every line brought a chorus of hoots and jeers and guffaws from the rest of his fellows.

> I've sojured for years,
> Fit during the War,
> But I never did see
> Sich fatiguing before.
> One day I'm on guard,
> The next cuttin' ice,
> Then on Kitchen Police,
> Which ain't over-nice!
> A fourth layin' brick
> (I ain't used to the thing),
> A fifth day on guard,
> With just three nights in!

On the second time through, the whole bunch joined in, raising a raucous noise down below that dark, fireless bluff.

> I enlisted to sojur,
> Not stay out half the night!

As the Crows and a handful of Ree scouts lumbered in from the surrounding hills, they could hear the singing in the camp. The nervous scouts had been moving more and more slowly as the Sioux trail widened and its dust lay deeper, scarred by thousands of travois poles plowing a wide road up the divide into the hulking darkness of the Wolf Mountains.

Cooke ran to fetch Mitch Bouyer when the Crows solemnly rode into Custer's bivouac and slid tight-lipped from their ponies.

Each man squatted on the ground, still clutching the reins to his pony. Not a word would be spoken until the interpreter arrived. Eerie hung the silence in that end of camp while the young Absaroka trackers sat chewing on their silent, morbid red thoughts, waiting for the half-breed.

"They say they have some things to show you, General," Bouyer started his translation for Custer. He nodded to Half-Yellow-Face.

From beneath their belts or pockets and out of their simple cotton shirts bought off trader Coleman at the Yellowstone, the Crows pulled hanks of hair still embedded in bloody flesh.

"Wait a minute here!" Custer muttered, squinting beneath the poor starlight. "Striker—bring me a lantern!"

Beneath the candle's glow Custer could see at last the scouts had brought him the scalps and beards of white men.

Bouyer cleared his throat. "They tell me they run onto a spot where the Sioux were celebrating a recent victory over white soldiers."

"White soldiers?" Custer's voice rose, his eyes narrowing on Bouyer in the flickering candlelight. "Where's the trail heading? Ask them that."

White-Man-Runs-Him pointed as he growled in Absaroka, his arm thrown up the divide.

"Over the Wolf Mountains."

"Would the Sioux camp on the Little Horn?"

"*Greasy Grass*, Custer," Bouyer corrected sullenly, in a whisper. Mitch had read far more in what the Crow had said than he was telling the soldier-chief.

Still, the tone of the half-breed's voice hadn't been lost on the Seventh's commander. "Out with it, Bouyer. There's something you're not telling me."

"Just this," said the beefy half-breed as he brought his dark eyes to square on Custer. "If the Sioux are celebrating a victory over some soldiers, it's only going to make 'em full of spit and vinegar to have a go at your small bunch. I figure they've whipped that bigger outfit the Sun Dance camp drawings told us about today."

"You're forgetting one important fact, Bouyer."

"What's that?"

"They may—I say *may*—have whipped a bigger detachment of soldiers. But—" Custer paused for that dramatic effect he had studied in public speaking. "Those Sioux warriors haven't fought a *better* regiment of soldiers than the Seventh."

Bouyer snorted. "If I didn't know better, I'd say you're intending to follow that trail over the mountains to the Greasy Grass."

"Bouyer . . ." Custer held up the lantern so the Crow interpreter better saw his face. "I intend to follow that trail straight into hell if I have to. Now, you just ask these boys here about that trail, will you? You ask them if all these other trails that they claimed to see, show the Sioux to be splitting up now that they've whipped some white soldiers—or are those trails coming together?"

After conferring with the Crows and getting his answer from young Curley, Mitch turned back to Custer. "The trails are coming together. The Sioux gather on the Greasy Grass."

Custer clapped his hands and leapt into a quick jig. "By Jehoshaphat! That's the news I want!"

Bouyer wagged his head. "I don't think there's enough time left for me to begin understanding you, Custer. Here you ought to be worrying about all those trails coming together—I mean worrying. Instead you—"

"The only thing that would worry me now, Bouyer," Custer interrupted the half-breed with a snarl, "is if those trails break apart. That'd mean the village I seek is splitting up. And if the village did that, we couldn't find the Sioux. At the very least we'd have to chase after them. No, Mr. Bouyer." He snapped his back rigid and slung the lantern toward striker Burkman. "I'm overjoyed to hear the Sioux are gathering. My prayer is that they not find out about our coming. I pray I find them sitting in their camp on the Greasy Grass when I come riding up at a gallop to do what a soldier does best."

"What's that, General Custer?" Bouyer squinted, measuring the soldier-chief in the pale, fluted candlelight, dim starshine splaying down from the dark summer canopy overhead.

"Why, Mr. Bouyer—a soldier's job is to find the Indians and capture them."

"Suppose they don't want to be captured. What then?"

"I suppose we'll have to do that other part of a soldier's job. And that's kill the ones who resist."

Without a single word of reply, the half-breed signaled for his scouts to rise and follow him. The seven were suddenly gone from the corona of firelight, drifting away on noiseless moccasins like the summer breezes that nudged their way along the high bluff.

CHAPTER 13

So it was, the mighty Lakota came together for the great buffalo hunt and a celebration of the old life as the great chief Bull had promised.

Lame Deer's Miniconjou were some of the first to join up. Later the Blackfeet Sioux and the Sans Arc. On and on they came, adding their camp circles and pony herds to that great procession streaming across the plains until they reached the cool waters of the Rosebud, where they would hunt the buffalo in the old way, as in the long-ago days of their fathers' grandfathers.

At long last summer hung like a whispered benediction over the vast sea of hills and creeks and red people. Moon When Chokecherries Grow Ripe for the Sioux. Moon of Fat Horses for the Cheyenne. June to the white man.

And one more time for the people to offer themselves up to the Great Mystery in thanksgiving.

Along the bubbling snow-melt waters of Rosebud Creek, the Sioux raised their circular arbor of some two hundred feet in circumference, its poles standing better than twenty feet high in supporting the roof beams in their crotches. In prayerful celebration the combined tribes dropped the monstrous center pole in the ground so that it stood more than fifty feet high, reaching in prayer for the sun. Around the pole's base lay a pile of painted buffalo skulls, their eye sockets open and staring, giving praise to the sun—as would those dancers who came in sacrifice to this place of honor.

Long, long ago . . . far back into any old man's memory, the Medicine Lodge of the Sioux was believed to have originated from the ancient Cheyenne people, when the Shahiyena first pushed out of the forests and onto the plains. A ceremony held only when all the bands came together for the celebration of life granted them through the Great Mystery.

A warrior noted for his superior courage in battle and his great generosity to those less fortunate than he would be given the single honor of selecting one of the four trees to stand in each of the four cardinal corners of the Medicine Lodge. After each of the four warriors had chosen his tree, he would strike it with his coup stick four times to signify the killing of an enemy for the mighty Wakan Tanka. Then other warriors chopped the trees down, trimming their branches, assisted all the time by a group of young virgin women.

After the four trees had been dragged back to the Rosebud camp, each was painted with its significant color: green for the east, where the sun arose each new day bringing life; yellow for the south, whence comes the land of summer each year; red for the west, where the sun hurries to bed each night; and blue for the northlands of the Winter Man and his brutal cold.

Beneath this huge arbor the tribes would give thanks, offer their flesh, sacrifice their blood as the sun was reborn again and again and again during the long summer days of dancing. Around and around that monstrous center pole with its ring of death-eyed buffalo skulls, each painted red with blue stripes or yellow circles, the young men would dance, praying for a vision and giving their thanks for another year of abundant life. A life lived in the old way on the lands of the ones gone before.

For each young man offering himself to the sun, the ordeal began by stripping to his breechclout and painting himself with his most powerful symbols. Only then could he present himself to the medicine men for the season's sacred ceremony.

As he lay in the Sun Dance arbor, the young warrior would have his chest gashed open above each nipple. After the medicine man dug his fingers beneath the pectoral muscles and the blood flowed freely, the shaman would shove a short stick of peeled willow through the wound and beneath that muscle. These small sticks would then be attached to the long rawhide tethers already lashed to the top of that tall pole erected in the center of the Sun Lodge.

Gradually the ropes would be drawn up and tightened until the dancer was forced to stand on his toes, eventually drawing the bleeding, torn muscles of his chest out five inches or more. Between his grim lips would then be placed an eagle wing-bone whistle he would blow upon to draw the attention of the spirits to his prayers.

One after another in that hushed and prayerful sanctuary of the sun, the dancers rose to their feet and began to pull at the rawhide tethers binding them to the center pole they slowly circled, driven by the rhythm of the incessant drums. One after another the warriors joined in that grim, bitter-sweet dance around that pole, accompanied by the throbbing chant of the spectators and the high, eerie shriek of those bone whistles. With the power of the eagle at his lips, each young warrior raised his private call to the heavens above.

Here they would dance for hour upon hour, staring into the sun as it made its slow, fiery track across the sky. Praise be to the life-giver to all things.

On the afternoon of that second day of dancing and offering, Sitting Bull surprised everyone gathered at the arbor by presenting himself for this mystic ritual of denial and sacrifice. Never before had he taken part in the Sun Dance. While Crazy Horse himself had never participated either, the decision to dance beneath the sun was considered a highly personal matter by the Sioux, and no man was ever criticized for not joining in the sacrifice of his flesh.

But today The Bull stripped naked and stretched himself upon the ground with his back to the center pole as the drums and the singing and high-pitched whistles droned on hypnotically.

His adopted brother tore at Bull's flesh, in every move as exact as were the great visionary's instructions. He was to use only a bone awl and a stone knife. No metal implement of the white man must touch his body. And with those tools of old, The Bull directed his brother to take fifty bits of flesh from each arm, beginning at the wrist and climbing to the curve of the shoulder; those hundred bits of flesh were to be placed solemnly round the base of the center pole on the painted buffalo skulls circled in offering to the sun and the greatest of all mysteries . . . life for the red man himself.

While most of the young dancers eventually struggled against their rawhide tethers so they might end their agonizing torture and self-mutilation—and escape the pain—The Bull instead danced on and on.

For the rest of that day and into the night. Then a second sun rose and fell, stealing its light from the face of the great Sioux mystic. After another night and spectacular sunrise, The Bull danced on with a strength that no man would know unless he himself had been touched by the greatest of all mysteries.

Blood trickling down his arms and off his barrel chest, Sitting Bull continued to send his prayers heavenward.

"May the People live as they once did, Great One! May the white man let us be!"

Yes, he danced for guidance in leading his people in the old ways. Yes, he danced to plead for wisdom in stopping the white man's further encroachment on the old lands.

So it was on that morning of the third day that at last he fainted from hunger and thirst and utter fatigue. Sitting Bull crumpled to the hard-packed earth at his feet, ripping the willow sticks from his torn flesh.

As he lay there beneath the arbor of the sun, The Bull finally received his sacred vision.

Hundreds upon hundreds of enemy soldiers falling into the Sioux camp, headfirst to signify their death before the Lakota people.

And with this mysterious event came the voice of the sun itself ringing in Bull's ears, telling him:

"These I give you . . . because they have no ears to hear they are wrong."

Hours later when Sitting Bull had revived, returning from the land of spirits to tell others of that dream's great portent, the story was pictured on the smooth sand of a sweat lodge. Crude pictographs showing soldiers careening head down into the Hunkpapa camp. Now the Sioux came to know Sitting Bull had long been right. There was to be one last great fight against the white man. Through the power of the Great Mystery, it was told they would defeat the soldiers who marched against them.

So great was the renewed celebration for this coming fight that inside another sweat lodge three round stones were painted red and set in a row to signify a great victory in war.

Likewise a large cairn of rocks gathered up from the banks of the Rosebud was constructed with the skull of a buffalo bull on one side and the skull of a buffalo cow on the other. The bull was painted red, the color of war, and there was an arrow left pointing at the cow to show all who passed this place that Sioux warriors would fall upon the soldiers like mighty bulls while the white men would run like frightened cows.

And the final offering was placed just outside the Sun Dance arbor itself: four upright and painted stakes upon which this summer's medicine men stretched a buffalo calfskin that had been tied with strips of bright trade cloth and hung with large beads . . . all to show that the Sioux understood the Great Powers were granting them a momentous victory over the white man. Even more so this primitive offering boasted that if the white man did not come to hunt the Sioux, the great Lakota nations would themselves hunt down the soldiers and destroy them.

The awesome power of one man's prophetic vision surged through the veins of all, pumping them full with the fire of fight and courage. Sitting Bull had electrified his people and made them one against that white tide seeking to sweep over their ancient lands.

Their time had come.

There would be no other.

After learning the Crows had discovered the hostiles' trail leading over the divide, Custer ordered an officers' meeting, dispatching Cooke to announce the assembly without the use of bugles.

"The general's compliments," Cooke said breathlessly as he loped up to a group of friends near Godfrey's Company K. "He wants to see all officers at headquarters immediately."

Some of those Cooke rousted had just eased back on their bedrolls to get a fix on some sleep without dreams of their tired, sore asses plastered to sweat-dampened saddles. Others had just dipped their nightly tobacco quid in snuff or trader's whiskey or even sweet fruit brandy. Still others wanted only to settle back to watch the fireflies or the stars swirling overhead like a slow, blazing pinwheel; they were content to listen to the gurgle of the Rosebud and that growing silence of the Montana prairie.

No moon yet. Still too early this time of the year. So without even that sliver of light overhead to guide their way, Custer's officers groped their way through the snoring troops and picketed horses, doggedly stumbling upstream toward the general's bivouac.

"You know, there's one characteristic I'll long remember as something that is truly Custer," Ed Godfrey explained to lieutenants Wallace and DeRudio as the trio crept along the meadow. "His restless energy is back. Pushing, pushing—forever driving without stop. In a way it's good to have the old man back again."

"Have him back again?" DeRudio replied with his Italian inflection. The subtleties of the English language continued to elude him.

"Yes, have the old Custer back with us. Seems ever since

we hit the Powder, even more since we crossed the Tongue and ran into those burial scaffolds, the old man got more and more distant. Quiet, withdrawn. Not his old self."

"Tell you the truth, Ed," Wallace said, "I don't know which Custer I like best—even if I had a choice!"

"As for me, it's a blessing to see that restless abandon surging through him once more. Why, after finding that Sun Dance Lodge today and all the rest, I got to thinking hard on it. The general's mind is right on course after all—straight and true. And that's just the way Custer's been able to get things done down through the years, fellas. He keeps his mind focused on one thing, and one thing only."

"So? You going to tell us what Custer's got his mind on?"

"He's not thinking of another damned thing but finding and crushing those Sioux."

"Still," Wallace sighed, "something about the way he's acting keeps nagging at me. . . ."

"You still haunted—still believe he's going to be killed?"

"Now more than ever, Ed. The man's got death written on his face, dripping from his every word."

Ed stopped, grabbing hold of Wallace's arm and hauling him up short. He whispered harshly, "Mind what I say, for your own good. Just don't let any one of his inner circle hear you say anything like that. You best keep that kind of talk quiet."

At that point they recognized the booming voice of Myles Keogh mixing with the high, contagious laughter of Tom Custer. Rounding the next clump of bullberry, Godfrey spotted a solitary candle lantern and the hulking shadows of officers gathering for Custer's meeting.

"From all that the scouts have told me," the general began, pacing before the assembly, "the Sioux are gathering in the valley on the other side of these mountains above us. We're almost there, by jiggers!"

Godfrey saw how worked up Custer was, perhaps more so than at any time since leaving the Yellowstone.

"Fellas, what I've come up with is that we're going to march as far as we can this evening, pushing up as close to the crest of that divide as possible. I want to find out where that Indian camp is . . . determine its size and strength.

Only then can I formulate a plan of attack. While I work that out, the regiment will conceal itself for the next day and night. Then attack at dawn on the twenty-sixth and catch the Sioux between us and Gibbon's forces when they run."

Custer slapped his hands together, rubbing them. "We've got to hope Terry and Gibbon got off as planned, boys. If not, that'll put our attack for the twenty-sixth in a totally different light. If the Sioux try to flee north, and Gibbon's not yet in position . . ."

As Custer's voice dropped off in contemplation, Captain Myles Moylan stepped forward into the soft candlelight.

"General, what did the Crows tell you about the strength of the village? How strong is it?"

He turned to his former adjutant. Moylan was not all that popular among his fellows, something that had to do with the man's Civil War record and a reenlistment under an assumed name. But Custer had taken Myles under his own wing at the beginning, when the Seventh Cavalry was formed, recognizing that Moylan had the makings of a good officer. The dark-haired Irishman never once let Custer down during that long winter campaign in Indian Territory.

"Myles, the Crow confirm we might meet fifteen hundred warriors at most. Seems they've found evidence of about four hundred lodges now. In their count they're including the young warriors bedding down in wickiups. All that's on the fresh trail heading over the divide."

"So, boys!" Tom Custer leaned forward. "Are we gonna whip 'em?"

"Not a question of whipping 'em, little brother," Custer chuckled in that bray of his. "Merely a question of keeping them from running on me before we can attack. Now remember what we'll do—go over the divide and reconnoiter tomorrow, laying the regiment in wait until dawn of the twenty-sixth. Then we can hammer these Sioux for brother Tom here!"

"Goddamn right!" Tom cried. "Hammer Sitting Bull and finally head back to that wonderful summer holiday-land called Fort Abraham Lincoln!"

Godfrey had to laugh. He always laughed at Tom

Custer's humor down through the years. There was much to admire about the general's younger brother. Always the joker. Charming and witty, forever having his way with the ladies. The life of any party, or any campaign into hostile territory.

"We won't go back until we've told the world about our victory," Custer added quickly. "Not until the world knows we've defeated the mighty Sioux of Sitting Bull!"

"Are we going to get close enough to the buggers that they won't be able to run on us?" Keogh growled darkly. "I'm ready for a good, dirty scrap of it, myself—so I don't want none of 'em scooting out on me!"

"Precisely what we're going to make sure of, Myles," Custer answered. "The Crows speak of a high spot on the mountains up ahead, some sort of rocky prominence that will allow a man to view the whole valley of the Little Horn. From there they tell me we can see the rising of smoke up and down the entire valley. And that smoke will confirm the location of the Sioux village."

The general strolled to Varnum's side. "I'm going to send some of the Crow and Ree boys to this rocky knob the Indians call the Crow's Nest. But most important, I need to have a white man along with the Indians to learn if the scouts do indeed see the Sioux down in that valley. I want verification, and I want someone who can send back some specifics to me."

With Custer standing directly before him, Lieutenant Charles Varnum slowly became aware that everyone else stared at him as well. He scratched nervously at the new beard just beginning to bristle over his sharp chin. To the Rees, Varnum was known as Pointed Face. But he was always ready to let others joke about his chin easily enough. The same way he was going to joke about Custer drafting him for this important mission.

"So, General, you want a white man along. I suppose that means me, eh?"

"Correct, Charlie, I want you in charge of the detail. Beside Bouyer and Gerard, take Reynolds along with you. I want as many trustworthy eyes as possible on that valley come first light."

"Understood, sir."

"Then I suggest you move out at once." Custer's tone was solemn once again. "What time is it, Billy?"

"Just after nine o'clock," Cooke answered.

"Good. The rest of us will set off after eleven as planned. I'll proceed to the base of the mountain below this Crow's Nest and await word sent down by you. As soon as you know anything, Charlie—anything at all—send me word by one of the Rees. I'll be waiting."

"Yes, General." With a salute Varnum parted the officers and disappeared into the darkness to fetch eight of his Rees, along with five Crow; Custer's favorite, Charlie Reynolds; and the half-breed, Mitch Bouyer.

Varnum never found Fred Gerard that night and didn't really waste any time searching for him. If he had, the lieutenant would have found the interpreter dead drunk beneath an outlying bullberry bush, sleeping off a bellyful of his patent whiskey.

The Crows, Rees, and Bouyer followed Varnum and white scout Reynolds out of camp on foot, leading their horses toward the hulking mass of the Wolf Mountains. A swinging pinpoint of light became a candle lantern looming out of the night.

"Lieutenant?"

It was Custer's voice. Mitch Bouyer would recognize that high-pitched, excited call anywhere.

"Over here, General," Varnum responded.

"Charlie, I just thought of something. Glad I caught you before you were gone. I wanted to ask something of the Crows. Where's Bouyer? Is he here?"

"I'm here," Mitch answered, stepping out of the pony shadows. He didn't even want to get near the general, still itching from their argument earlier in the day.

Custer gazed past the half-breed to the nearest Absaroka scout. "You, what's your name?"

"White-Man-Runs-Him," Mitch replied.

"Bouyer, ask this one where does his tribe stay. I mean . . . where's his home?"

Bouyer was confused at the reason for the question, studying Custer's face for some explanation and reading there a strange light aglow behind the blue candlelit eyes.

"We live along the Bighorn River. Up to the lodge-grass country—down to the valley of the Greasy Grass, what the white man called the Little Horn."

"Ahhh," Custer replied. "Exactly as I supposed. This regiment's approaching your ancestral homeland, aren't we, White-Man-Runs-Him?"

The Crow nodded with Bouyer's translation, his eyes flicking up to the Wolf Mountains. "On the other side lies the Greasy Grass. I am close to the land of those gone before. Yes."

"Then understand this." Custer spoke slowly, purposefully, so that Bouyer could translate as he went along. "I want you Crows to believe me. If I have to die to do it, you will get this land back from your longtime enemies, the Sioux. If you die in the coming battle, at least you will be buried on the land of your own people."

To Mitch's surprise Custer waited for no reply from the Indians or from Bouyer. He turned on his heel instead and was gone into the night. The scouts remained speechless a few moments until White-Man-Runs-Him muttered something. His exact words were chorused by the other five Absarokas. All six moved out toward the edge of camp.

Lonesome Charley Reynolds, who rarely talked to anyone at all, hung back to walk beside Bouyer, who had to keep tugging at his small Crow pony to keep it moving. After more than twelve hours of scouting up and down ridges already today, the animal wasn't in the least eager for a night ride up the rocky slopes of these mountains.

"What that Injun say back there?" Reynolds whispered to Bouyer.

Mitch stared at the white scout a moment, deciding he could talk to Charley. *He is a good man, after all*, Bouyer decided.

"White-Man-Runs-Him said something about Custer."

"Yeah? What'd he say about the general?"

"He said Custer's wearing some mighty bad medicine hung like a buffalo robe over his shoulders."

CHAPTER 14

Since the march would be resumed shortly after eleven P.M., so the command could inch as close to the Sioux as possible before daylight and thereby choose the best concealment for the day, many of the men didn't see any sense in trying to get back to sleep.

From Custer's meeting, some of the officers headed off in small groups, groping their way through the dark back to their companies. A larger group stayed the shank of the evening with reporter Mark Kellogg, who enthusiastically led a political discussion on the questionable future of the frontier army should a nonarmy president be elected come fall.

Nearby, a lonely soldier licked the nub of his pencil, then scratched in his journal beneath the pale light of a candle:

> The political discussions are still going on. Kellogg gets in a real sweat, as do some others. There's a lot hangs on

what's done at the conventions. St. Louis will tell whether the army is cut, rumors report.

Captain Myles Moylan, one of the few original officers with the Seventh, invited his friends to his bivouac to sing some songs before they would have to be off rousting their units for the night march. After "Little Footsteps Slow and Gentle," and the ever-popular "Annie Laurie" were given voice, the young officers ended with "The Good-bye at the Door" and the "Olde Hundredth." Then, to the surprise of most, a few began to belt out "For He's a Jolly Good Fellow," dedicated to Custer.

Back in the shadows a few of the old-timers solemnly discussed what scout Charley Reynolds had done to surprise them earlier in the evening before riding off with Varnum's scouts to ascend the Crow's Nest. While the lieutenant's Indians huddled in wait nearby, Lonesome Charley, as he was widely known, committed himself to a path of far-reaching consequence.

Reynolds distributed the contents of his personal haversack among his best friends.

"I damn well don't want your shirt, Charley! How many times I'm gonna tell you?" an old line-sergeant friend had ranted. He was angry simply because Charley's actions made him feel mighty uneasy. "You going and giving away everything you own in the goddamn world like this—I just don't know!"

"You and me been down some roads together, Rufus," Charley quietly pleaded with Sergeant Hutchinson of B Company. "Please, I want you to have the shirt."

It had been just like touching the cold hand of death itself to take that shirt from his quiet friend, but Hutchinson eventually tore it out of Reynolds's paw and raced off for his own unit, not knowing what else to say to an old friend who in his heart believed he was to die in the coming battle.

"You, Riley—you've always admired this, ain't you?" Charley asked, pulling a denim shirt from his war bag and holding it beneath a lantern.

Sergeant Riley had tried sneaking off when it became plain why Reynolds had invited some of his old friends to visit him this evening. The sergeant had to admit he had always liked the shirt—its preacher pleats running down the front to surround the buttons like neat rows of farmer's crops laid out in a plowed field. But he had never wanted the shirt that bad.

For an experienced plainsman like Reynolds to believe he was staring his last fight in the face was enough to shake even a veteran old file down to his sweaty boots.

Most of the troopers left their stock under saddle that night. Not much sense in removing the McClellans for the short time those saddles would stay empty. Only a few of the old hands thought enough of their animals to remove the saddles and sweated indigo blankets before they ripped up handfuls of twisted grass to scour the horses' sweaty backs. All round those sleepless, cold-gutted old-timers the rest of the camp snored and rumbled, grabbing what relief sleep could give them.

Over at Tom Custer's C Company, Private Peter Thompson had fallen asleep not long after the officers' meeting ended and the serenade concluded. Sometime later he awakened in total darkness from a dream about riding with a detachment of cavalry attacked by warriors.

Thompson bolted upright from his saddle blanket, dripping cold and with a dry mouth. He blinked, then blinked again—surprised to find his friends still asleep on the ground. He splashed some cool water on his face from a canteen while he calmed down. Then laid his head on an arm and closed his eyes. As Thompson drifted off to sleep, the horrifying dream picked up where it had left off.

The only difference now was that Thompson watched his fellow soldiers chased over the hill. Suddenly the private was left alone, surrounded by a horde of warriors. A blood-chilling scream shattered his ears. He whirled around to find a Sioux charging up, war-ax brandished as he raced toward the lone trooper. Just as the wildly painted Sioux drew close enough to strike—Thompson awoke, stunned and muttering his prayers for deliverance from death, sweating like a whiskey cooler on a humid summer's day.

When he could finally rise on his trembling legs, shaken

and unable to speak, Thompson knew he'd never fall asleep again in his life, afraid of what he'd see when he closed his eyes.

Determined to walk to the picket-line where his horse was tethered, Thompson wandered through the camp of sleeping men scattered on the ground, appearing to him as if they were dead. Among the mounts the frightened soldier noticed for the first time how gaunt and poor the animals all were becoming under the severity of the regiment's march up the Rosebud.

And under his breath, Private Peter Thompson cursed General George Armstrong Custer for punishing those animals and his men so damned hard right before he would ask them to fight the Sioux.

Then he prayed some more.

Down near the southern end of camp, striker Burkman had seen no sense in curling up beneath his coat for an hour or so before the command would push off up the divide. Instead, John stayed up with Custer while the general scribbled in his journal, from time to time sipping at the cool creek water he poured from Burkman's battered, blackened coffee pot.

Across his taut, sunburned cheeks, the orderly sensed the breeze darting past like a snowshoe hare scampering off from a winter-gaunt wolf. Here, there . . . then gone.

At times a quick burst of phosphorescent green lightning would illuminate the starless canopy overhead, eerie fire igniting itself out of the low, solid cloud banks that made Burkman feel closed in, surrounded. Smothered. Anxious and afraid, Burkman decided he would wait up with his boss, his commander, his master. And see the new day in as they drove over the divide to corner their quarry.

Custer had been confiding matters to his journals, words and thoughts he knew someday would see the public eye. From his hand, on those pages, were discussions he held with himself about this person or that, often wrenching up from his bowels his deepest and most sensitive feelings about where he had been and where he was certain Destiny herself called him.

And while Custer knew the coming battle was his road to Olympus, another part of him hinted that he might be marching to Valhalla, that sacred hall of Odin, the Norse god of war. There Odin—the supreme deity of Norse legend—received the souls of heroes slain in glorious battle. Odin would forever be there to welcome the heroes home.

Custer set his pencil back to work beneath the flickering candlelight as the breezes tousled the paper where he struggled to put down his thoughts upon this lonely, lonely night of homecoming:

> I have never prayed as others do. Yet on the eve of every battle in which I have been engaged, I have never omitted to pray inwardly, devoutly. Never have I failed to commend myself to God's keeping, asking him to forgive my past sins, and to watch over me while in danger. . . . After having done so, all anxiety for myself, here or hereafter, is dispelled. I feel that my destiny is in the hands of the Almighty. This belief, more than any other fact or reason, makes me brave and fearless as I am.

As General George Armstrong Custer closed his leather-covered journal and rose to his feet, stretching the kinks out of his trail-weary back, his dog Tuck raised her muzzle to the low, ominous sky overhead, howling.

The hair along Burkman's spine stood on end. Then the striker began to cry quietly. So the general would not hear.

John oft understood animals better than he understood the ways of man. Frightened, with a crushing sense of dread, Private John Burkman remembered dogs can sense death coming a long, long way off.

All along the bluffs their brassy voices ricocheted.

Horse guard roused company sergeants from their brief, troubled sleep. Sergeants nudged men from their slumber with a tap of a toe and an urgent word. And with that spreading commotion, the horses and mules grew excited until it seemed the whole valley reverberated with the noise of men and animals as an army began a new march.

Because of that thick dust adding to the black inkiness of the night, Myles Keogh's I Company and others had to grope blindly along the trail, listening to the plunk of a carbine, the rhythmic ping-ping-ping of a bouncing tin cup tied to someone's saddle or the comforting clatter of iron-shod horses scuffing over the rocks up ahead. Still, at times some of the lagging troops had to stop and whistle or holler out to the men ahead just to get a response so they could resume their ride into the darkest jaws of night.

At long last the march became more struggle than it was worth, and Custer's quiet command was whispered back along the strung-out columns.

"We're to rest here for the rest of the night, boys," Keogh growled. "Pass it along. Take care of your mount, then grab some winks."

Another blessed halt, the Irishman ruminated, pulling a flask from his three-strap saddlebag.

They had marched some ten miles in total darkness and would wait here for the coming of morning in this deep defile at the foot of the divide. Most of Keogh's men went about unsaddling their weary mounts as suggested, rubbing them down with twists of dried grass. Some of I Company realized only too well how their lives were irretrievably tied to their horses. All the good care a soldier gave his animal today just might save his life tomorrow or the day after.

Here and there other troopers built small fires in the lee of brush or rocks. Coffee was boiled, a black potion strong enough to disguise most of the bitter tang of alkali in the water of the creek they followed up the slopes of the Wolf Mountains.

A potion more fit for the likes of hell than those poor souls about to descend the valley of doom come first light.

Close to two-thirty A.M. Varnum and his scouts reached the Crow's Nest, some twenty-five miles from where they left the columns behind. Red Star, the young Ree, along with a Crow named Hairy Moccasin, was assigned to push into the highest reaches of the Nest, there to watch for the graying of the sky at dawn.

Meanwhile the rest would lay their heads upon a curled arm and sleep down in a pocket at the foot of the Nest, awaiting word from the two with eyes at the top of the divide looking into the valley of the Greasy Grass.

That first faint light to touch this northern prairie was slipping out of the east when Hairy Moccasin hooted soft as a night owl to his fellow Crows. Below him just some twenty feet, scattered upon the ground like sleeping children, the Crow scouts stirred from their cold beds, attentive to the mournful owl hoot from above. Quietly, one by one, the Crows began to chant their personal death songs, singing their prayers to the Grandfather Above.

To the eerie wail of those songs the Rees awakened. Several rushed to try squeezing into the narrow neck at the top of the Nest. The Crows, flushed with anger, bitterly shoved the Rees back, huskily jabbering in Absaroka.

The Crow asked for Varnum. No one else would they allow to the top but Custer's pony soldier.

Wiping gritty sleep from his eyes, the lieutenant elbowed his way through the anxious Rees and scrambled up to join Hairy Moccasin and Red Star. White-Man-Runs-Him breathed hot on Varnum's neck, standing right behind the white man to peer into the awakening valley below. In the graying light Charlie thought he was able to spot those two Indian lodges the scouts told him they had run across in their travels last evening before returning to the command with the portentous news for Custer.

Then the scouts directed Varnum to look far beyond and to the north, into that distant valley of the Little Bighorn.

"Look for *worms*," they signed with their hands, fingers a wriggling mass of movement.

Again the soldier strained his tired eyes, this time looking for worms they said would be wriggling across the valley floor. Still he could see nothing of the herd, blaming his trail-weary eyes, reddened and irritated by the gritty dust of the march. Besides, he rationalized, he had just ridden some seventy-five miles without much sleep to speak of. No wonder his eyes weren't working as they should.

In disgust Varnum slid back down to the pocket below

the Nest and drew out his tablet and pencil he used to scratch a hurried message to Custer.

"Here, Red Star," Charlie whispered, holding up the dispatch for the Arikara scout to see, using his poor sign language to explain the important mission. "I want you to go to the pony chief—"

The growing excitement and buzz among the Crows and Rees diverted Varnum's attention at that moment. On his feet he could himself see why the Indians were hopping mad. Down below on the east slope of the divide, the regiment's camp fires could be plainly seen only ten miles off, glowing like hundreds of pinpricks of orange red light scattered across the landscape. A purple twist of smoke curled lazily from each fire into the cool dawn air.

"I understand," the white man tried to explain with his hands. "If we can see those fires, then the Sioux can see them too."

The angry scouts bobbed their heads, grim faces a mixture of rage and fear. Varnum pulled his watch out of a pants pocket and noted the time. Four forty-five A.M.

"Red Star. Go. Give to Custer." He tapped the folded paper one more time, nudging the young scout off toward the ponies.

By now some of the Rees had climbed into the Crow's Nest themselves, studying the wide valley of the Greasy Grass beyond. Eventually the light grew more and more favorable for spotting the villages. Still, the scouts watched until absolutely certain. Then the Rees too filled the air with their own death chants.

"*Otoe Sioux! Otoe Sioux!*"

Varnum listened, frantically trying to sort out the babble, trying to remember the meaning of the Arikara words.

"*Otoe Sioux!*"

"Plenty!" the soldier whispered to himself, snapping his fingers as he recalled. "No," he muttered. "More than plenty. *Otoe* means *too many!*"

Charlie gulped unconsciously, staring up at those Rees crowded in the Crow's Nest, each one moaning with the sad refrains of his private death chant. Some scratched their

faces, drawing blood, while others tugged at their unbraided hair, pulling strands out.

"Sioux everywhere," Varnum murmured his own death
song that cool dawn. "Too many Sioux."

Because of some recent fears that Red Beard Crook would
follow them over from the Rosebud after Crazy Horse's
warriors had battled the white soldiers to a standstill only
eight suns ago, the Lakota chiefs kept a constant string of
young scouts riding out from the camps in the valley of the
Greasy Grass west of the divide.

Day and night, the scouts came and went.

Following little Ash Creek east up the divide from the
Greasy Grass, Standing Bear and a handful of Hunkpapa
warriors ran across a startling discovery: iron-shod horse
tracks! And they were very fresh. A trail coming up to the
crest of the divide, from below on the Rosebud.

Eighteen ponies, maybe more, Standing Bear concluded.

"Perhaps Red Beard is returning for another try at our
great gathering of tribes, little brothers!" Standing Bear
whispered to his scouts.

"One thing about the white man," laughed Round-Face-
Woman, a young warrior, "they can be very persistent."

"Pretty stupid at times," snorted another young scout.

"But—always persistent," Standing Bear echoed, ending
the discussion.

Just beyond the eastern slope of the crest, the scouts
spotted the smoke rising from the regiment's fires, the
distinct smell of bacon and coffee carried on the morning
breeze as the cool air was harried up and out of the valley
toward the high places.

Yet this fresh trail seemed to lead off to their right.

Strange, Standing Bear brooded, *those soldiers are camped
below and to our left . . . while this fresh trail wanders up the
divide to our right—*

"*Aiyeee!* There!" Round-Face-Woman shouted, pointing
up the slope, toward a pinnacle of rocks high on the divide
to their right.

It was true. Several Indians hid themselves up there,

looking over the edge into the valley of the Greasy Grass as the sun slipped its red ball of fire over the edge of the earth far to the east. Indians by their dress and hair . . . mostly their hair.

Sparrowhawks! Standing Bear figured. *Maybe some corn eaters along by the look of things. And yes! A white man with them.*

"Little brothers, these surely must be spies from Red Beard Crook's soldiers."

"We will ride back and give warning," Grass-That-Sings cried out, urging his pony aside.

"I do not think Red Beard will attack this day," Standing Bear whispered confidently. "He would not get close enough to our villages until the sun stands high in the heavens. And we all know soldiers prefer to attack at dawn. Have no fear, little brothers, that Red Beard will try our warriors in battle this day."

The younger scouts agreed and snatched up their reins.

Up, up through the trees they climbed until coming to those bare rocks they had to cross before they could descend into the cover of shady trees and concealing shadows on the far side of the divide.

And that's when Varnum spotted them: A handful of Sioux hurrying into the valley of the Little Bighorn with their urgent message of warning.

At daylight there were still a few soldiers and officers stretched out on the ground, some curled under a bush or with a saddle blanket pulled over them. Most of the troops hunkered red-eyed and wasted, clutching cups of strong, alkaline coffee and content not to have to think about much of anything at all.

Only a handful of these half-dead soldiers paid any attention to the lone Arikara scout who loped into camp, searching for the pony soldier-chief himself.

Tom Custer saw him coming first. He stood at the fire Burkman fed to heat some coffee the general wanted.

"Autie, you best quit wetting those bushes down now. Button up your britches and come on over here."

Custer came back to the fire as he buttoned up his

buckskinned pants. Tom pointed out the Ree scout headed their way on horseback, coming in at a slow walk now.

"You remember that one's name, Tom?"

"Can't say as I do."

"Find Fred Gerard, wherever he might be sleeping off last night's whiskey. Bring him here immediately. I figure we've got us some news coming down from Varnum."

As Tom loped off on foot to search for the interpreter, Custer held out his tin cup, not even looking back at Burkman.

"Striker! Coffee, please."

John watched the young Indian dismount, then poured a cup for Custer. The general signed his offer of coffee. Red Star nodded and held out his hands; from them the single rawhide rein looped back to the lower jaw of his horse. Burkman picked up his own tin cup and poured the thick, scalding brew into it for the scout.

As he squatted down at the fire with his cup cradled in one hand, Red Star reached inside the neck of his shirt and pulled out the dispatch scribbled by Varnum.

Custer ripped the tablet page open with more eagerness than most men would know in a lifetime.

Crows see *LARGE* pony herd in the valley.

North on Little Horn. I have not spotted it, but all the scouts see the herd north in valley. They see dust—smoke too. Come see.

"You damned bet I'll come see for myself, Lieutenant Varnum!" Custer danced a little jig around the morning fire for Red Star and Burkman right then and there.

"This is just the news I've been waiting for!" He stuffed the message inside his shirt.

Bellowing like a bull elk in the rut, Custer raced over to Vic and leapt upon the mare bareback. Seizing the reins, he tore off through the regiment's camp to spread the word all by himself. The fringe on his buckskins snapped and popped like corn parching as the blaze-faced sorrel's mane fluttered, creating a stirring sight for those grumbling soldiers rousted from their sleep by the general himself.

"Get up! Get up you lady-thumping rummies! We're marching at eight!" he hollered at the top of his lungs.

"General . . . over here!" It was Calhoun's recognizable baritone. Keogh dashed up beside him, winded from his run.

"By God, we've got them cornered now, Jimbo!" Custer gushed happily. "The scouts have spotted the village just on the other side of the divide. They're within reach!"

Custer hammered his heels against Vic's ribs and burst off to continue spreading the word.

"How far away, General?" Myles Moyian asked, sensing the familiar fever of impending battle already pumping in his veins.

"Twelve, maybe fifteen miles on the other side of the divide!"

"We'll whip 'em for sure, General!" Moylan cheered, throwing his huge fist into the air.

"Pray they don't run, Myles," Custer reminded him anxiously, his sunburned face suddenly serious. "Just pray they don't run on me now. I so desperately need to catch them right where they are."

Back at his fire a few officers had already gathered with Tom.

"Where's Gerard, Tom?" Custer demanded gruffly, eyes scanning the group for his interpreter.

"Couldn't find him," Tom shrugged, staring back into his coffee cup.

"You just didn't look under the right bush!" Custer flared.

He wanted Gerard, and he wanted him now. The general was certain Red Star had more to tell than Varnum's terse note could ever say. And Custer wanted that too. All of it.

He wheeled and tore off, never dismounting.

"Whaaaa!" Gerard growled moments later, blinking as he peered up into bright morning light and that tall man standing over him, thumping the heel of his boot with the toe of his own. "What in glory hell's wrong with you, Custer?"

"Get your flea-bitten, hung-over ass moving, Gerard!" he barked. "You're holding up my victory."

Gerard allowed his aching head to plop back to the saddle blanket he had pulled into the bushes with him. "Ohhh . . ." he moaned. "That's all, is it? Well, General, when you find the Sioux, you come tell me then."

"How'd you like to ride back to Lincoln in irons, Gerard? If you make it back alive at all."

Frederic F. Gerard opened one raw, bloody eye again and stared up into the new light of day shimmering round the tall man towering over his bed in the bullberry thicket. He had known Custer for most of three years now. Long enough to know the general was damned well dead serious.

"I'm coming, General." He struggled to sit up, feeling of a sudden he might lose last night's supper . . . then remembered he didn't have any supper last night. While others had eaten, Fred had only nursed his deep, abiding thirst.

Running a thick tongue over sandpaper teeth, it felt like a guard had tramped back and forth all night long inside his mouth . . . and with a pair of muddy boots on as well.

"I'll tell you what. I'll wait five minutes at my headquarter's fire," Custer advised sternly, climbing to the saddle. "Then, I'll send a guard detail to fetch you, Gerard."

Custer was gone as quickly as he had come, through the trees and milling troopers preparing horses and mules for the march that would be ordered at eight.

By the time Gerard staggered up, bleary-eyed and heavy-headed, Bloody Knife, Stabbed, One Feather, Soldier, Curly Hair, and others were gathered at Custer's fire. Each one talked low and solemn with young Red Star.

No longer wearing a light, easy expression on his face, Custer was intent on the business at hand. He handed his reins over to Burkman and dropped to one knee in the circle of solemn Arikara scouts. Their somber expressions and grave speech generally went unnoticed as Godfrey, Moylan, Keogh, Calhoun, and others eased up to listen in on Custer's discussion with the Rees.

"What's that he said?" Custer interrupted Gerard. He recognized something in Bloody Knife's tone from their years together. After all, the bold Ree scout had ridden this trail with Custer many times in the past. Custer could sense something serious in the color of the aging Ree's words.

Gerard turned back to Bloody Knife. When the scout had finished, the dry-mouthed interpreter blinked at Custer.

"Bloody Knife says there're too many Sioux over in that valley."

"Yes?" Custer replied, feeling a surge of anger. "We know there are many—"

"He says, General," Gerard interrupted uncharacteristically, "we'll find enough Sioux over there to keep us fighting for two, maybe three days."

"Oh, now . . ." Custer wagged his head as the peg-toothed smile widened, azure eyes twinkling distantly at the officers round him. "I guess we'll just have to get through them in one day."

Rising to his feet, Custer dusted his hands off on his buckskin britches. He simply didn't have more than one day to get the job done.

Even if the Sioux village was a little strong, the warriors would probably wage only a staying action, merely holding the troops off while their women and children and old people escaped into the hills. Like the Washita the men would fight only until the weak ones had escaped.

"Let's go to the valley!" Custer commanded. "Saddle up your men, fellas. We're moving out to catch us some Sioux!"

CHAPTER 15

CHARLEY Reynolds watched Custer coming that last mile up the rocky slope. For better than forty-five minutes the general had been in the saddle. He slid from Dandy's back and jogged stiffly up the last seventy-five yards of slope with that renowned restless energy of his.

Reynolds smiled beneath his sun-bleached mustache. While lesser men might feel the effects of a night march and the rigors of three long days on the trail, Custer was a special breed. His kind never tired. The closer he drew to his quarry, the more energy he always seemed to exude. Custer drew life from the hunt, the close, and the kill.

You just might need some of his energy yourself, Charley—before this day's out. Reynolds chewed on his thoughts as he watched Custer climb toward him. *Tomorrow if the general whips these Sioux, you could be riding to spread the news again.*

Two years back when Custer wanted to spread the news of gold found in the Black Hills of Dakota Territory, he had asked his Indian scouts to carry the news south to Fort Laramie. Trouble was, between the Black Hills and the fort lay Sioux country, swarming with hostiles. Bloody Knife and the rest refused to ride Custer's suicidal mission, even with the general's offer of gold.

But Charley Reynolds had stepped up and said quietly, in that way of his, "General, I'll carry your mail for you."

What had astounded those present was that Charley said it as if he were volunteering to do nothing more than take a ride into Bismarck.

Reynolds made his hair-raising ride through Lakota land and carved himself a niche forever in Custer's heart. Last day or so he had heard rumors that the general was about to single him out again to carry some crucial news back to the States.

While the Indian scouts made way for Custer at the top, Reynolds, Bouyer, and Varnum clung at the rocks. When the general was ready, Charley pointed where he should look through the field glasses loaned him by Lieutenant Charles DeRudio.

After several minutes adjusting the focus and straining his tired, wind-burned eyes, Custer was still unable to make out that dark carpet of worms they wanted him to see, nor could he claim that he recognized the smoke curling up from all the fires to be found along the banks of the Greasy Grass.

Eventually Custer pulled DeRudio's glasses from his eyes, disappointed. "I'm sorry, boys. Seems like a blind trail, because I can't see a thing that tells me there's Sioux camped in that valley yonder."

"You don't see the herd?" Bouyer inquired, astounded. "The biggest herd there's ever—"

"General," Reynolds interrupted, seeing that Bouyer grew testier by the minute, "you can plainly see the dust of the herd slowly moving north—most likely."

"Listen, fellas," Custer replied, jamming the field glasses back into their case, "I've been on the prairie for a good number of years already. I'll have you know my eyes are as clear and just as good as the next man's, but—I can't see what you claim to be a Sioux herd."

"But, General . . . it's right—"

"I told you, Reynolds! I can't see a thing. Don't you understand?"

Custer's snap caused the soulful Charley to purse his lips tight, swallowing down his anger.

But the bull-faced Bouyer wasn't about to give up without a fight. He had Sioux blood in his veins, which some would later say gave him a temperament hot enough to push for a scrap with Custer.

"Listen, you pompous ass!" Mitch spat, dark eyes flaring with bright anger. "If you don't find more goddamned Sioux down in that valley of the Greasy Grass—more than you've ever seen in all your goddamned years on the plains—why, you get a rope and string me from the highest tree you can find down below!"

His unbridled fury shocked not only Reynolds and the scouts listening a few feet away, but it shocked Varnum and Custer as well.

"All right, Bouyer . . ." the general soothed. "It isn't going to do anyone a bit of good for me to hang you. I'm after Sioux, and you're not Sioux enough for me to hang!"

Charley couldn't help it. He found himself chuckling along with Varnum at Custer's joke.

"Now, let's suppose there are Sioux down in that valley yonder," Custer said as he dropped to his rump to slide toward the pocket below them. "I'm certain they haven't seen us, Lieutenant Varnum."

"What about those Indians I told you spotted us near daybreak, General?" Charles Varnum protested. "Along that ridge right over there."

"I can't believe you saw any warriors, Charlie," Custer replied acidly. "Most likely, it was nothing more than the new light playing tricks on you."

"Wasn't only me who saw 'em, sir." Varnum realized he was beaten before he got started. "Crow boys saw 'em too."

Custer shrugged it off, not even looking at the young lieutenant only four summers out of West Point. "Light plays tricks on everyone, Lieutenant."

"They had to spot our tracks, General," Varnum fought on vainly. "From where we saw 'em, they had to cross our trail getting up to those rocks."

"You haven't told me a thing to convince—"

"Goddammit, Custer!" Bouyer roared, shoving himself up beside the soldier-chief, his shoulders trembling in rage. "You best listen to what Half-Yellow-Face has to tell you. He says you better attack now."

"Why the blazes should I attack now when my plans are to wait through the day and hit them come dawn?"

"Because these Crow realize the Sioux scouts they saw are carrying word back to their villages at this very moment. In fact, those villages down there already know about you, most likely. We—the Crow scouts and me—were given to you to do a job. You best let us do our job. And remember, I've got Sioux blood running through my veins. I grew up in Sioux and Cheyenne camps. I know the people. So for a herd that size kicking up that much dust down below—it can mean only one thing."

"What?"

"The great summer council," Bouyer replied stiffly. "A time when all the tribes come together, whether they're on the reservations or not. This year Sitting Bull called them to join him up here. That isn't just a single village down there—one you can strike and be done with while you wash your hands in the waters of the Greasy Grass. Custer, that down there is the greatest gathering of Indians any white man will ever lay eyes on and live to tell the tale!"

"Utter . . . rubbish! My reports state there couldn't be any such camp. Yet I'll agree with you on one thing, Bouyer—you were sent along with my regiment to help me. And nothing more. Best you get back to your scouting now and leave the military operations to me!"

"There isn't a man in your command who would know, Custer," the feisty Bouyer protested, "but I've spent over thirty years among the Indians, either living or trading with them. If that ain't the biggest camp there ever was any-where, you can cut my heart out and feed it to your dogs."

"We aren't getting anywhere with this—"

"Sitting Bull himself has offered a hundred fine ponies for my head! You'd better understand that, Custer. I know what I'm talking about! Them Sioux'll kill me if they ever get their hands on me alive. And it won't be a pretty thing to watch!"

"You're saying that very same fate awaits my command, Bouyer?"

Bouyer grinned at Custer wolfishly. "You understand, don't you? The Sioux know all about you soldier-chiefs. There's Red Beard Crook and No Hip Gibbon . . . and you, Custer. They call you Peoushi. Among the Sioux you are called the Long Hair."

"And years ago the Cheyenne called me Hiestzi—Yellow Hair." Taking off his hat, Custer began to chuckle. "Pretty funny, don't you think, Mr. Bouyer? The bloody joke's on them! They won't have an idea one who's charging their camp. I don't have long hair anymore!"

Reynolds found himself snickering with Custer's sour joke at his own expense. Varnum laughed loud and easy, like a colicky bullfrog.

Bouyer was patient. He waited until the white men were through with their fun. "If you're going to be so goddamned bull stupid—I've just got one last suggestion for you, Custer, then I'll keep my mouth shut."

"If that's a promise, Bouyer—to keep your mouth shut— I'll hear your last suggestion," the commander replied haughtily.

"Get your exhausted men and beat-down outfit out of here as fast as their wore-out horses can carry 'em. You go down there into that valley, Custer—you and too many others never coming out."

They watched the half-breed stomp off toward the horses.

Custer muttered to Reynolds and Varnum, "Let 'im go where he damned well pleases."

Then, to Reynolds's surprise, the general bolted after the whiskered half-breed.

Behind them all Ree scout Spotted-Horn-Cloud sitting solemn as an owl, having watched the white men argue before Bouyer raced off in anger. Slowly he scooped up handful after handful of dirt, pouring it over his head like water, mournfully singing out to the climbing sun. "Old friend of many, many seasons . . . I shall not see you go down behind the hills this night."

"Bouyer! Hold up there!" Custer shouted, reaching the picketed horses at the foot of the Nest.

Mitch whirled like he was shot. "You hold it, General!" He leapt aboard his Crow pony, taking up the slack in the reins.

"You needn't—"

"You know, Custer, a lot of folks tried to tell me about you—how goddamned right you always think you are. Said you get right on a trail like a winter wolf with the smell of fresh blood in your nose, and you just can't back off, can you?"

"I've never allowed myself to back off, Bouyer."

"They say some people learn quickly. Others . . . well, I've found they learn more slowly than most. Like preachers and schoolteachers—army officers learn most slow of all."

Custer and the others watched Bouyer tear downhill toward the waiting troops.

"If it were up to army scouts like you, Bouyer," Custer hollered after the half-breed, "the army wouldn't get a bloody thing done at all!"

After Custer left his troops behind to climb to the Crow's Nest, his command prepared to march to the base of the rocky bluffs as ordered and await the general's descent after he had personally studied the valley of the Little Bighorn.

While packing the mules for the march of F Company, Sergeant William A. Curtis discovered that not only had a small bundle of clothing worked itself loose from his bedroll during last night's blind climb up the dark and rugged trail from the Rosebud, but Corporal John Briody reported a box of hardtack missing from one of the company mules.

With a hand-picked detail ready and mounted behind him, Sergeant Curtis reported to Captain George Yates that he volunteered to retrieve both clothing and bread box.

"Very well, Sergeant," Yates replied without enthusiasm. In fact, it seemed he didn't relish sending his men along the back trail in the slightest. "Just be quick about it.

I don't want F Company strung out all over the divide if we run into some action."

"Understood, sir!" Curtis saluted and vaulted aboard his mount, leading the detail downhill toward the Rosebud.

Pensive and anxious, his stomach churning the way it did whenever he faced combat, Yates stared after the squad of men disappearing through the trees. A Civil War veteran who was not only a Custer hometown boy, but one who had served on Custer's staff during the war, Yates realized how important retrieving the clothing and bread box could be.

If any wandering hostiles discovered those items dropped along a fresh trail of iron-shod hoofs . . .

Curtis and Briody led their four green recruits down the back trail, sharing between them ribald jokes they had heard many a time before, occasionally whistling songs that pleased a soldier beneath the high, thin overcast foretelling of another sweltering day.

"Say, you boys know the words to—"

"*Goddamn!*" Curtis bellowed, reining back with one hand, throwing his right up to signal a halt.

"Jeeeesuuuus!" gulped one of the privates, yanking his mount's bit so harshly that the animal stumbled and fell to the side, neck twisted around, spilling its rider into the grass and spiny cactus.

He rolled in the cactus as the other three troopers bumped their horses into one another, all trying to retreat at once while Curtis and Briody attempted to maintain some semblance of order in their disheveled ranks.

Down the trail less than forty yards away, another small group of young men had also been surprised. They darted for their nearby ponies. Four warriors, wearing nothing but breechclouts and moccasins in the midmorning heat, had been intent on chopping at the wooden box of hardtack with a camp ax when Curtis's troops rounded the brow of the hill and discovered them.

The warriors didn't know whether to mount and ride or stand and fight. But it appeared the soldiers were dismounting and going to make a fight of it. Without waiting for much more than a brave yelp or two to spring from their throats, the half-dozen warriors leapt aboard their small ponies and kicked dust across the shallow creek, fleeing up the hill.

All but one of the warriors disappeared over the top of the knoll, pushing on west for the Little Bighorn. That solitary rider sat silhouetted against the pale corn-flower blue summer sky and raised his arm defiantly in the air, yelling out his challenge and ridicule. At the end of that arm hung one of the new Henry repeaters the Sioux had traded for at Spotted Tail Agency.

With the hairs on the back of his neck bristling at attention, Curtis ordered the de-horsed private to climb back on his mount or run the risk of getting left behind. This was one sergeant who wouldn't have his detail wiped out because a greenhorn shavetail had some cactus stuck in his ass.

"Cactus or lead, Private!" Curtis bellowed, swatting the soldier's horse with the butt of his carbine. "You'll have one or the other in your ass before this day's done. Now, *ride!*"

The greenhorn's animal bolted forward, its white-knuckled rider clinging for his life, every bounce on that wild, mule-eyed ride a series of excruciating jolts as the cactus spines drove deeper into his ample buttocks.

By the time Curtis's detail scampered back into the regiment's camp, every man spurring his lathered mount as if the devil himself were right behind them, they had covered more ground than they had in their entire march last night.

After listening to Curtis's story and ordering the suffering private to find himself a regimental surgeon, Captain Yates conferred with Major Marcus Reno and two other captains on a course of action. It was their considered opinion that they should recommence the march immediately, without waiting for the general's return.

They had been discovered by the hostiles, they figured. And with those fleeing warriors scampering now to warn the village, Custer's Sioux would slip from his noose. The general was going to be mad enough as it was. Best not to waste time getting over the divide and down into that valley.

As Custer himself descended the long slope from the

Crow's Nest, he could see the twisting, snaking columns climbing up from Davis Creek toward the spine of the divide. A hundred eighty degrees from what he had ordered.

"Major!" Custer called as he came racing into sight of the columns. "Reno! What's the meaning of this?"

"Begging pardon, General," Yates interrupted with an apologetic grin. Lord, how he hated admitting this to Custer. "We thought it best to ride on up to meet you. We got us some sticky news to tell you, sir."

As Yates explained the Indians' discovery of the box and clothing along their back trail, the color slowly drained from Custer's face. Then, as Yates watched, a sudden light began to flicker behind his azure eyes once more.

"Good," Custer replied when Yates finished explaining his orders for the regiment to mount up and march instead of waiting on their commanding officer. "You did right."

If that don't beat all, Yates considered. *We've just been handed the biggest problem spoiling our opportunity for surprise, and here Custer's smiling like the cat what ate the canary.*

Tom Custer dropped from his horse nearby. He strode up, wiping his glove around the sweatband of his gray slouch hat. "What you figure to do now, Autie? Lay out on this side till dark?"

"What I figure to do, Tom—is talk to my officers right now. This regiment needs to be ready for a fight!" He wheeled, hollering back along the columns. "Sergeant Voss! Find trumpeter Martini. Bring 'im here—he's scheduled for duty with me today."

"Sir?"

"The both of you—sound 'Officers' Call.' "

"Sir?" the veteran Henry Voss gulped. "The Indians, they'll hear the trumpets!"

"Dammit all, Voss! The red buggers already know where we are! So blow it!" Custer snapped, wrenching the bugle from Voss's saddlebags and practically stuffing it in the man's mouth.

Up and down the columns many of the men glanced at one another with those first few notes out of the tin horns. The first such trumpet call in over two days now. Trotting

forward along the excited columns, there wasn't a one of
Custer's officers who didn't fully understand the time for
secrecy and silence had come and gone. The blowing of
that one, solitary bugle call meant the time for battle had
arrived.

Custer gripped Dandy's reins tightly as he paced on foot
in one direction three steps, then retraced those steps in
another direction.

"Gentlemen, you recall the Crows reported seeing the
village from the Crow's Nest. They claim to see smoke and
dust, a big village. I, on the other hand, was unable to see
a bloody thing. I really doubted the Indians were down
there along the Little Horn, so I kept looking up north, in
the direction of Tullock's Forks.

"At least in those valleys we could bottle the tribe up,
and they couldn't escape me so easily. However, the scouts
tell me I'll find them in the valley of the Little Horn. And
down there the Indians can run and scatter two ways of
Sunday without us having a ghost of a chance to run them
down."

For a moment the only sounds filling the hot, dry air
came from the general's boots scuffing at the dry ground, or
his horse munching on the brittle grass, even the scratchy
cough of some man's trail-raw throat.

"All along I meant to surprise that hostile camp," Custer
went on. "We've got a command riddled with green recruits
of the rawest order. Our mounts are about as weary as any
could get, while the warriors we'll soon face are going to
ride fresh ponies. Yet do any of you see sense in my original
plan to wait out a day and attack at dawn tomorrow?"

"Yes, General. I do," James Calhoun finally gave a
cautious response.

"But we can't now, Lieutenant!" Custer snapped.

Like only a handful of the rest, Yates realized the general
had addressed his brother-in-law by rank. Custer was angry,
disappointed, and now veering close to fury.

"Gentlemen, despite the fact that we're not fully prepared for battle, and that we surely are not going to have the
advantage of surprise on those warriors, we nonetheless
have one advantage. We are the Seventh, a proven fighting

machine—and never before has our grand republic really seen what we can do when asked to perform above and beyond the call of duty."

"General Custer?"

"Who are you?" Custer asked, squinting at the tall, thin civilian looking out of place in dusty frontier clothes.

"George Herendeen. Assigned you from Colonel Gibbon and General Terry."

"Ahhh, yes . . . I remember now," he replied absently, an eye twitching as he appraised the man. "You came along to communicate with the other column, right?"

"Yes, but—"

"Too late for that now, Herendeen." Custer crossed his arms emphatically, eyes filling with the icy fire of a zealot, waiting for the scout's response.

"Too late, General?" the startled Herendeen protested with the rolling bass of his voice. "The head of Tullock's Creek is right over the hills yonder. We can have your men down that valley in no time and meet up with Gibbon's men. If you aren't going to send me with word as you promised General Terry, best you get all these men heading north that way right now—north where you'll have Gibbon's support."

"*Gibbon's support!*" Custer bristled. "What the devil do I need his help for? Tullock's Fork may very well be up north, but there are no Indians in that direction, Herendeen! They're in our front—and they've discovered us. It would serve no purpose dispatching you down the Tullock's now."

Custer wheeled to face his men once more. "The way I see it, fellas—the only thing to do is push ahead and attack the camp as soon as possible."

There it was, Yates figured. Custer had finally put into words what every officer had been fearing the general would decide on his own.

"General." Herendeen stepped closer, a lean, hard wisp of a man, his wrinkled face like well-soaped leather. "Haven't your scouts been telling you for days that you're bound to run onto more than you can handle?"

"I've listened to all their ghosty stories. What of it?"

"Those scouts told you how many Sioux there are. The Crow even showed you how big the village is down there in that valley where you're dragging these men. Right?"

"You're forgetting that I didn't see a blessed thing that could be taken for a huge Indian camp—and I had the field glasses!"

"Dammit, General!" Herendeen's sudden anger silenced them all like a slap across the mouth. "If you wanna play dumb to everything your scouts tell you, then there'll be a helluva lot of blood on your hands. If you're going to let your hot-blooded stupidity and eagerness to attack that summer gathering of the whole goddamned Sioux nation— with nothing more than a handful of worn-out men and trail-busted stock—then you might well be damned by that decision for all of eternity."

"Why, Mr. Herendeen," Custer drew back, strangely calm at the moment. "What would you know about military strategy?"

"Not a god . . . damned . . . thing . . . General Custer." Herendeen allowed Custer his smirk. "But I can count. As good as the next man. And I can see your ragtag outfit ain't ready for any kind of scrap, much less a fight against the best warriors these northern plains can throw at you."

"Are you quite done, Herendeen? Because if you are, you can ride with us to attack the village in that valley below. Or you can skedaddle up to the Tullock's Fork. You see, we're going to attack the Sioux before they scatter, and all those warriors you talk about can't be found."

"For these past three days, I was beginning to think all they'd said about you couldn't be true, that you weren't really such a goddamned arrogant asshole when it comes to following orders.

"Exactly what General Terry didn't want done, you're doing up in fine style. Instead of continuing south up the Rosebud, you've followed the Indian trail straight to their village. You've dogged this trail with your nose to the ground, and it's hard for me to believe you didn't intend to attack this village on your own from the start. So you see, General Custer—I, for one, don't buy your claim that you ever intended to obey Terry's orders, and you've never given a god-bloody-damn where Gibbon's forces are because you want the whole pie for yourself!"

Every man there stood in stunned silence. After a long, brutally painful moment, Custer allowed a smile to crease his face.

"Perhaps you aren't as dumb as I thought you were, Mr. Herendeen." Custer turned, slipping a boot into his stirrup. "One thing you are right about. I want the coming action for myself. For the Seventh—these men. Right, fellas?"

George Yates yelled and whistled as loudly as any other. Custer held up a gloved hand for silence atop Dandy.

"I'll return in a few minutes, boys. After I've discussed our plans with the Rees." His blue eyes darkened as he narrowed his attention on the civilian scout below him.

"And as for you, Mr. Herendeen—I suggest you either fall back with the rest of the scouts, or you can plan on bucking over to that Tullock's Fork you speak so highly of. You've got your choice to make now, and make it fast—because this outfit's going into battle!"

CHAPTER 16

C USTER yanked savagely on Dandy's reins, tearing back along the columns in search of Gerard's scouts.

By the time he found the Rees, they already understood that the command was preparing for battle.

A few of the older scouts squatted on the ground, tearing up the tall, dry grass at their knees, wailing as they tossed the brittle stalks into the hot breezes. Their death songs made for a melancholy background as Custer reined up before Bloody Knife, Stabbed, and Frederic Gerard himself.

"Gerard, tell them the time has come. Soon we fight the Sioux. You all came from Lincoln's Fort to help me find the Sioux. You've done your job. If you will not fight your enemies beside my soldiers, then at the very least I want you to race in and hit the Sioux pony herd. Drive them all off so your enemies cannot use them in battle. You can keep them as I promised you."

Custer stepped beside Bloody Knife. "But no matter what, my old friend—there will be a home for you, as I have promised Bloody Knife, if you fight alongside me. Bloody Knife will have a home I make for him. He is my good friend."

Instead of speaking for himself once the soldier-chief had finished, Bloody Knife grunted for Stabbed to speak for him. The old man nudged his tired pony out front of the other Arikaras to begin his high-pitched harangue.

"My brothers and nephews," Stabbed announced in his thin, reedy voice, "the fight we stare in the eyes will be a difficult one for most of you." The light breezes tousled his unbraided hair already marked with the iron of many winters. "I know many of you have never been tried in battle before this day. You have never had to kill an enemy before. Never heard the song of bullets whistling past your faces."

After lifting his chin to the sky for a moment as if in prayer, Stabbed went on, exhorting his men. "Your older brothers and uncles have done all we could to prepare you for this day. Nothing more can we do now but dress you in the sacred colors as we prepare to fight our old, old enemies. These sacred colors will guard you against the arrow, blade, or bullet that comes your way. Colors calling upon your spirit helpers to protect your bodies in this coming-time of madness."

With Bloody Knife's help, the old man mixed dried clay and earth pigment in his palm, smearing the pigment and bear grease and spit mixture onto every young warrior's face and chest. One after another, each scout stoically presented himself to the old warrior for this painting ceremony, while the others gathered round him, chanting.

One by one they ripped open their cloth shirts or tugged up the long tails of their buckskin war shirts so the old man could paint his mystical symbols on their flesh. At last Bloody Knife smeared red paint on those wounds scarred across Stabbed's chest and back: not only the scars suffered in his many Sun Dance sacrifices, but also knife and lance wounds of many scalp raids and war parties.

Finally Custer's most trusted Ree scout presented himself to the silent soldier-chief.

Bloody Knife held up his hands to Custer, showing him the smeared paint left in his palms.

"He wants you to paint him, General," Gerard whispered huskily as he pulled the flask bottle from his mouth, amber drops glistening on his lips. Ever since daybreak, when Custer himself awoke him with word that the Sioux were close enough to kill with spit, Fred Gerard had been drinking harder than ever.

Custer beamed at this singular honor. Kicking one leg over his saddle, he dropped to the ground and dabbed his fingers in what was left of the greasepaint in Bloody Knife's palms. When he was finished, Custer stepped back to admire his work.

"It is good," he signed for his old friend, The Knife.

"Yes, Long Hair," the Ree answered with his hands. "It is good for you to paint me before I go into battle at your side."

Bloody Knife laid a finger on that striking black silk scarf resplendent with blue stars tied at his neck. "One time, long ago, you gave this young tracker this fine present. I have worn it always with good thoughts of you in my mind. But—I can never escape the thought that by riding with you, death almost touched me once before. Does Long Hair remember?"

Custer shook his head. Bloody Knife went on solemnly speaking in sign.

"We traveled into the Sioux's Paha Sapa—their Black Hills—when one of the wagons I was leading got stuck in crossing a stream. You blamed me for the mud sucking that wagon into the creek bank. So crazy were you for that wagon that you aimed your rifle at me and fired a bullet. I ran away, not knowing what to do now that Long Hair's blood was mad at me and he wanted to kill me. There I was deep in the land of my enemies, and my good friend Custer was trying to kill me."

"I remember." The commander nodded gravely, his thin lips pursed beneath the corn-silk yellow mustache. "It is true what you say, Bloody Knife. I did get angry and shoot at you with a bad temper. But you must remember that I later asked you to come back and be my trusted wolf, my scout, once more. And—" He swallowed hard, for it appeared as hard now to spit out these words as it had been back in the Black Hills. "I apologized to you, Bloody Knife."

"I heard your apology and told you shooting at me was not a good thing for a man to do to his friend," the aging scout replied sadly. "Then I said that if I got crazy-mad like you, you would not see another sunset. Bloody Knife does not miss when he shoots, Long Hair. Do you remember all this?"

Gerard watched the rest of the Rees. Those young scouts had never heard of this dramatic incident. Now they muttered among themselves fearfully. Better than any other, Fred knew the Arikara. For these young trackers nothing else could pucker their bowels more here on the precipice of battle with their old enemies—than to learn that Long Hair shot at his old friend, The Knife.

Gradually their death songs grew louder, more insistent. Fred alone knew the Rees believed they were being led into a valley crawling with Sioux warriors by a man who had tried to kill their beloved and revered scout-chief.

Paying no attention to the rising cries of the other scouts, Custer gazed into Bloody Knife's eyes. "Trusted wolf, we both lived to see another sunset—and many more after that black day. I am certain the setting of this day's sun will be one of glory for us both. You will leave that valley below with me, Bloody Knife. We will be going home together, old friend."

Instead of smiling at Custer's bright optimism, the old Ree said, "Long Hair, my friend, I am going home today—yes. Not by the way we came, but in spirit. I am going home to my people. Before the sun sets this day, I will see all my relatives gone before to the spirit world. You and I will not ride together to Washington City. We are soon to journey to join the old ones gone before."

"Indian superstition," Custer muttered from the corner of his mouth, forcing a smile. "Simply superstition." He spat on the ground to emphasize it, then turned from Bloody Knife.

"Gerard, you tell your Rees if they don't want to fight

with my men, then they can chase after the enemy herd and fight the young boys who watch over those Sioux ponies."

As he translated, Fred watched how Custer's words slapped many of the older scouts. Still, the young ones remained too fearful to care about shame. Reluctantly, as if cutting a long-standing bond, The Knife pulled his horse from Custer to rejoin Stabbed and the rest.

"Gerard, tell them there are others coming, other soldiers," Custer said. "I want the Rees to understand these other soldiers are coming to attack the village, and I want to be the first because I want the honors of fighting the Sioux alone. I need to defeat them myself."

No expressions on those stony copper faces changed as Custer's words became Ree words. Dark, black-cherry eyes burned between Custer's shoulder blades as the soldier-chief finally yanked on the reins and led Dandy back to the head of the columns.

Gerard watched Custer prance away. He sucked again at the hot whiskey, not minding what dribbled onto his chin, into his beard. The whiskey no longer helped Fred Gerard.

Now he was as afraid as the next man.

The army surgeon's belly ached and his rectum burned. Raw, red, on fire.

You've got dysentery, Dr. Lord, he told himself. *Pure and simple dysentery.*

Dr. George Edward Lord, a strikingly handsome young physician who had accepted a short-term army surgeon's commission so he could revel in the glory of army blue on the frontier, diagnosed his own infirmity exactly. Every jolting step his mule took sent a wave of nausea through him. With insistent taps of his heels, Lord urged the reluctant animal toward the front of the columns, where he would find Custer.

"Cooke!" Custer hollered as Lord drew close. "I want every troop to call out six men and a noncom. They're to join B Company under Captain McDougall in guarding the pack-train mules carrying our ammunition at the rear of the march."

"Understood, General!"

"Get them cracking, Billy!"

"General Custer?" Lord's voice broke as he reined up.

Custer wheeled. "Doctor! Good day! How can I be of service to you?"

"I—I'm merely reporting—"

"Great God, man!" Custer interrupted, studying the doctor's peaked appearance. "You look about as green as high meat."

"Yes . . . quite. I—"

Custer laid his bare palm against the physician's forehead. "You're burning up, Doctor! I want you back with the supply mules. B Company. Immediately."

"Please, General," Lord protested lamely. "Had I any idea you'd send me back, I wouldn't have come to you. Today is what I accepted commission for, after all. To ride into battle with *this* regiment. All the excitement from here on out will surely take my mind off my infirmities."

"Hmmm," Custer thought on it, tapping a finger against his lips. "Perhaps it will at that. Very well, you'll stay with my command throughout this day, Doctor."

"I was hoping I could, sir!" Lord cheered slightly with a brave attempt at his own smile. "I believe it's only a touch of this prairie dysentery catching up with me. Bad water the past few days. Can't keep anything down, or in me."

Custer slapped the physician fraternally on the shoulder. "You stay close, Doctor. I'll divide DeWolf and Porter to the other commands when the time comes. But you—you'll go with me this day, and I'll show you enough bloody action to pucker up any bunghole!"

"Thank you, General." Lord offered a weak smile. "I'd be forever in your debt . . . if you could only pucker this problem hole I've been sitting on!"

During the short break that Custer called, the troops had laughed, joked, and kidded one another. Some even laid odds, betting future pay on who among them would come out of the fight with the most scalps hanging from his belt.

They were a rugged, Falstaffian group by now—some five weeks out of Lincoln, marching that trail west through spring snows, rain, and hail, not to mention the scorching heat of the past few days.

Round sunburned, cracked lips new beards sprouted on every face. Those floppy straw hats on their heads provided the only shade for the red dust-raw eyes that ofttimes now looked vacantly toward the wide valley yawning far below them.

Uniforms were worn and dusty if not ragged now, along with boots scuffed and cracked and far from black. Back at the mouth of the Rosebud, most soldiers had shed their blue tunics in favor of a civilian shirt. To watch them cross that fateful divide, an observer would think this regiment looked more like a band of vagabond gypsies than the legendary Seventh. Had it not been for the majority still wearing their yellow-striped cavalry britches and the company horses matched by color, not to mention those crimson-striped guidons snapping in the warm breeze, this might have been any group of ragtag riders.

Custer took a moment to reach inside his saddlebags, pulling out his pair of gold spurs. He straightened after strapping them over his dusty knee-high boots. He smoothed his jacket and admired the spurs privately before he met John Burkman's pinched expression.

Custer grinned. "What's the problem, dog-robber? Don't you agree these are a splendid and fitting addition to my battle outfit?"

"The spurs, General?" Burkman squeaked.

"Certainly," Custer replied cheerfully, still admiring how they added a martial note to his buckskin outfit. "They are my good luck charm, you see, Nutriment," he explained, calling his orderly by the nickname given Burkman for his love of eating. "You see, I wore them on the Washita. And you'll remember I wore them next with Stanley on the Yellowstone and down with Calamity Jane herself in the Black Hills. They're quite the item—don't you agree?"

"You said 'good luck,' General?" Burkman stammered with a serious case of the willies. "But you don't seriously wanna . . . you told me General Santa Anna lost them to a U.S. officer as spoils of war at the end of the fight down in Mexico . . . then that same officer sided with the Rebs, and you whipped him in the war."

"Correct in every respect, John."

"Then them spurs ain't really all that lucky, seems to me, General. Every respect intended. Looks like every man that's worn them spurs lost a battle they fought with 'em on."

"Silly superstition—just more willy-nilly claptrap!" he scoffed, peering down at his spurs beneath the high overcast of this late-June morning. "And to think of it, John— I'll proudly wear them as I parade down the streets of Philadelphia on my triumphant journey to the nation's centennial birthday party . . . even gallop once more down the streets of Washington City amid the cheers of millions of adoring citizens!"

Burkman glanced at the officers gathered near, as mute as he.

"Then, Striker—I suppose I've got no other choice but to break Medicine Arrow's silly Indian curse with Custer's Luck!"

Without another word Custer tore the reins from Burkman's hand and leapt aboard Dandy.

Poor, simple Burkman realized he was close to crying. He hid his face, welcoming the hot stinging release of tears.

As Custer loped off, Lieutenant James Calhoun turned to Ed Godfrey, a gnawing knot tightening in his gut. He whispered, "What the devil's Custer talking about? What have his gold spurs got to do with some Injun curse?"

Godfrey wagged his head. His own eyes clouded with the remembrance of that winter campaign down in Cheyenne country. "Goes back to the winter of sixty-nine, down in the Territories, Jim."

"What the hell is it, Ed?" Calhoun gazed anxiously at Godfrey. "Tell me, dammit!"

"A goddamned chief put a curse on the General—"

"Curse?" Calhoun shrieked in a hoarse whisper.

"Chief claimed Custer and all his men would get wiped out."

Calhoun gulped and tried a grin. "A curse. Shit! Silly pagan superstition, what it is. Right, Ed?"

Godfrey didn't return Calhoun's tin-plated smile. "Right, Jim. Nothing but silly superstition."

Jim was a big man, the kind any plainsman or hard case might think twice about taking on.

Calhoun watched Ed Godfrey turn and ride off. "Say, Ed . . . so how come you don't think it's just superstition, eh? So how come?"

Moments later Custer whirled back up to Burkman. "Remember, dog-robber, we'll be back by dinner for a good feed. These men'll be hungry, and I more than they! A good scrap does wonders for my appetite!"

Burkman watched the general wink as Autie Reed and Boston Custer loped up at that moment, followed into the intimate gathering by Custer's brother.

"Uncle Tom suggested I come ask you if I can ride at the front of the columns with you!" exclaimed ruddy-cheeked Harry Reed.

"Oh, he did—did he? Well, your uncle Tom is nothing more than a lady-humping rascal and a trouble-making rounder!" Custer smiled widely, teeth gleaming. "Of course, I can't grant you permission to ride at the front of the columns."

"Can't?" Autie stammered as if slapped.

"That's right," he answered, his face going as grave as a church warden's. "You'll ride right behind me with my personal staff!"

"Thank you, Uncle! Damn—did you hear that, Boston?"

"Don't you think it'd be a lot safer if you stay back in the pack train with me, Autie?" Burkman interrupted, stepping up to the young Reed boy, who looked quite the out-of-place innocent in his dirty and prairie-worn eastern clothing.

Pulling a foot out of a stirrup so he could swing his boot at the striker, Autie Reed chided, "You're just mad 'cause you can't go along with the general yourself!"

Burkman turned to Custer, finding sense in the youngster's words. "General, surely I oughtta be going along, you know."

For a long moment Custer did not answer. Instead, he straightened himself and gazed down at his striker. At last he leaned over, placing a gloved hand on Burkman's shoulder. When he spoke, the words came out quiet, as if what he had to say was something shared only between the two of them.

"Your place really is with Captain McDougall and his pack train, John. Safer there by a long shot. I need someone to stay behind to watch over Dandy and the dogs, after all. What you do best—looking after my animals for me. But"—he flashed that peg-toothed grin again—"if we should have to send back for some more ammunition during the fight, you can come in with the pack train for the home stretch. What say to that?"

"If that's what your orders are, sir." Burkman bowed his head, crushed.

The man John adored, the man he had centered the last six years of his life on, was abandoning him as he rode into battle. And Burkman knew, somewhere deep inside the tar black melancholy pit of him, that he would never see the general alive again.

"That's a good solider." Custer snapped a salute, waiting for Burkman's response. "A good soldier always follows orders."

"Yes, . . . sir," John croaked, then turned to trudge off, heading back to the pack train. The tears were coming again. God! how he wanted to turn around and beg the general not to ride into that valley.

But if the general's of one mind to ride down into that place of evil—then at least he should take me, Burkman brooded darkly. *Then at least I can die beside him. . . .*

"Private?"

Burkman turned to find Custer coming up on horseback.

"You'll take proper care to see that Vic is ready when it comes time to ride down upon the village, won't you?"

"Yes, sir." Burkman found his voice strained, dry as the dust beneath his feet. His eyes moistened in gazing upon Custer's haggard face. *Damn!* The tears stung his eyes as he stared up into the sunlight at the general.

"Those dogs of mine, you'll always see they're cared for, won't you, Private?"

Something in the way the general said it, something on Custer's face told Burkman that Custer knew.

He wants Missus Custer's favorite horse out of it come the fight. Come the finish, he wants Dandy safe.

And perhaps most of all, Custer wanted his staghounds protected. *General always had a special thing for those dogs, nothing ever closer than he had with them two, Bluech and Tuck. He said farewell to both of 'em back at Lincoln before marching out . . . and they surprised him by loping up to the column hours later, tongues lolling and tails wagging like schoolchildren playing hooky. Custer just didn't have the heart to refuse 'em their romp west at his side. They were so much like . . . like his own dear children.*

So now Burkman was assigned the task of holding the dogs' thick latigo collars while they whined and whimpered piteously, watching their glorious master gallop out of sight, down into the valley of the everlasting sun.

"Front into line, gentlemen! Center at a walk—*let's ride!*" Custer shouted, turning from Burkman to gallop back to the front of the columns.

He stood in the stirrups, waving an arm and signaling the start down off the divide, as if it were no more than a march across Lincoln's parade.

Most of the officers who waited nearby found themselves staring after their flamboyant commander with his fringe flying and gold spurs flashing. Time to move now.

Quickly they gulped at canteens of stale alkali water or pulled long at some trail-warm whiskey before swiping dirty fingers round the sticky sweatbands of their hats.

The Seventh Cavalry was moving into the valley.

CHAPTER 17

Aᴳᴬɪɴ and again across the short-grass time The Bull had taunted the agency Indians at Red Cloud or Spotted Tail, daring them to jump their reservations and join him in their old way of life.

"See, I am rich while you are poor . . . having to beg for the white man's coffee and sugar. I need none of that. I need none of the *wasichu*'s flour. I need only the buffalo and the old ways. Come join us!"

Like the mighty gathering of the shaggy buffalo itself into herds with numbers beyond count, all the more Sioux came to the Rosebud those first cool days of early June. The tribes gathered on the prairie uplands, marching but a few miles each day toward that ages-blessed crescent of the Mountains of the Wolves.

There this year the cool waters of the Rosebud had trickled beside the great Sun Dance ceremony and given The Bull his electrifying vision.

Here the people celebrated anew at each camp among the hills and bluffs, mesas and bottomlands strewn with

conifers and aspen, birch and alder, all lifting their heady
perfumes to the summer blue above. Here the people
joined in races and wrestling, the dancing and singing, the
drumming and always the courting by the young ones.

As was custom the head men hosted great councils of
war, welcoming in each new band as it arrived, opening
their arms to the visiting cousins: more Northern Cheyenne
and even some Arapaho who had wandered north to remain
free of the white invasion of their ancient tribal lands.

This last great council of war, declaring the People's
adherence to the old ways.

They would follow the buffalo.

At the age of twenty-eight summers, Oglalla warrior White-
Cow-Bull had yet to marry. But of late he had set his roving
eye on a very pretty Cheyenne woman living this summer
with her relatives among the Shahiyena, or Northern
Cheyenne, camp circle. Ever since Old Bear's people had
escaped Red Beard Crook's soldiers during the Black Night
March of the Sore-Eye Moon, White-Cow-Bull had hungered to make young Monaseetah his wife.

Cheyenne chiefs Ice Bear and Two Moons had many
times told the brave Oglalla warrior that the woman had
once belonged to the white man all Sioux called the Long
Hair. The story the chiefs told said this soldier-chief had
wanted to keep the young Cheyenne maiden as his second
wife, but that his first wife had grown angry, commanding
him to throw the Indian girl away.

Monaseetah had two boys, each by a different husband.
One Indian, a full-blood Cheyenne through and through,
and Yellow Bird, the son of Hiestzi, the Yellow Hair.

None of that really mattered to White-Cow-Bull. Un-
daunted, he persisted in courting the young mother now in
her twenty-fifth summer. Yet it was difficult for him to
spend time alone with Monaseetah. Never far from her side
was young Yellow Bird with his hypnotically pale eyes and
his light-colored curly hair. Only at night after her sons had
fallen asleep would Monaseetah speak at all with the
Oglalla warrior, talking through the lodge skins, for she
refused to come out, afraid to come to his blanket.

At long last in what his Sioux people called the Moon When Chokecherries Grow Ripe, she had at last worked up the strength to tell the young warrior that she had something important to say to him when the sun rested behind the mountains.

Giddily, flushed with the promise, White-Cow-Bull promised he would return that evening as the stars whirled in the foamy sky overhead.

Eagerly he dressed in his finest buckskins and brushed his hair until it gleamed like his well-oiled rifle. He was as certain as he had ever been about anything that tonight Monaseetah would finally profess her love for him. Across four moons the young warrior had courted her, ever since that camp of Old Bear's over on the headwaters of the Powder. Ever since that cold Black Night March.

But instead of giving her heart to White-Cow-Bull as he had hoped, Monaseetah declared that, though it hurt her to tell him, the Oglalla warrior must court another for his wife.

"In my heart," she explained, "it is not right for me to let you pursue me while I belong to another."

"Who is this other?" the warrior snapped, ready to challenge that man.

"I am waiting for Hiestzi to return for me as he promised." The memories were still fresh and raw, like a wound kept from healing.

The thick pain behind her words made the young Oglalla wonder if she truly believed the soldier-chief would actually come back for her.

"Only death will keep him from coming for me as he promised. Someday, he will come," she told him.

Monaseetah straightened and muffled her sobbing bravely. "You are very kind to offer your life to me, White-Cow-Bull. It is an honor for any woman to hear your words of love. But still—I must wait for Hiestzi to fulfill his promise to me. I can take no other. I must wait for my husband to return."

The great, shaggy horned uncle Pte had brought the tribes to this place. And it was the buffalo the great village now followed.

Tens of thousands carpeted the plains some ten miles south of the camps pitched along the Greasy Grass. The warriors could hunt at leisure each summer day following the massive herd north until it came time to hunt antelope up on the Yellowstone. Even a young child couldn't mistake where the great herd grazed in its journey—the dust hung like a thick winter blanket above the curly dark humps of these animals that spelled life itself for the nomads of the prairie.

So much like the dust of this great migration of the tribes. From their first camp along the Greasy Grass, the tribes moved a few miles north. That dust from their journey rose into the bone yellow sky above a trail a half mile wide and many more times that long.

In the van of the march rode those courageous young warriors, each wearing his finest feathers and scalps, brandishing their shields and new rifles aflutter with eagle feathers and hair. Behind that watchful vanguard of warriors came the women and children riding or walking among pack-laden and travois-dragging horses. Then behind the old ones tramped the huge pony herd, watched over by the boys too young to go to war, but old enough to show their bravery in caring for the thousands beyond count of Sioux ponies.

They had crossed the divide from the Rosebud, not in fear, but to find the buffalo. Not in fear that Red Beard Crook would find their great village. No, not in fear had they come to the valley of the Greasy Grass. For they had already whipped the soldiers across the time it took the sun to walk over the sky.

Like a bolt of summer lightning sent into the huge encampment that sixteenth day of June, 1876, as white men would reckon time—Crazy Horse's scouts had come tearing among the lodge circles on the Rosebud with their electrifying news.

"Soldiers! Soldiers! Sitting Bull told us of this—his vision! The soldiers come!"

So it was that Crazy Horse gathered his young warriors and sped out to greet the soldiers under Red Beard Crook, who had been marching north with thirteen hundred men to rendezvous with General Terry from Dakota and Colonel Gibbon of Montana. Some twenty-five miles south of their combined villages, the Sioux and Cheyenne scouts located the long blue columns along the Rosebud. They would wait till morning to throw themselves on these foolish white men.

Come daylight, Crazy Horse led the screaming, shrieking riders into battle.

It was battle as Red-Beard Crook had never seen it: naked brown horsemen whirling madly about his grim blue ranks, pressing the frustrated soldier-chief to a stalemate.

After nearly an entire day of fighting, during which Crazy Horse and his young field generals continually stymied Crook and his officers, both armies abandoned the field, taking their wounded and dead with them.

Crook had decided against either continuing the chase or plunging ahead to meet up with the other two columns. He preferred instead to pull back to the south where he could lick his wounds. At the same time Sitting Bull and his advisers had decided to push over the rugged divide between the Rosebud and that sparkling river just on the other side of those Mountains of the Wolves.

They would march, The Bull told them. They would march over the mountains to the Pa-zees-la-wak-pa.

The Greasy Grass.

"Let us celebrate our great victory over the soldiers!" thousands of Sitting Bull's people shouted. *"The victory you dreamed of and shared with us!"*

"No! Hear me!" The Bull cried above their praises. "We go because we have not yet struggled with the battle of my vision. We must march to the Greasy Grass. This fight on the Rosebud was not the battle in my vision, brothers!"

Still the warriors, young and old alike, persisted in their celebration. They had driven Red Beard's troops clear out of the country!

"We have won, Sitting Bull! Long it has been since there has been such singing in our camps—we have won a great, great victory!"

"Hear me! It was not the great victory still to be given us on the Greasy Grass," The Bull answered once they had fallen silent around him, intent on every word. "The dream showed me the soldiers would fall into our camp. Not on the field of battle. The soldiers would fall into our *camp.* Not only that—my dream showed our camp on the Pa-zees-la-wak-pa. Bull leads his people to . . . the Greasy ⸗Grass!"

So it came to pass that on the next day the people tore their lodges down and began their trek west. Over the Mountains of the Wolves they would come to the Greasy Grass, where they could hunt more buffalo, slowly working their way north to the land of the Yellowstone, where they could hunt antelope for meat and hides.

From that first warm day of spring, through the long weeks of wandering, that growing camp hummed with a constant activity, a drone of comings and goings. Not only were there the constant arrivals of cousins from the reservations and agencies, but there were the incessant departures of the young men on scouts and hunts. Not to mention those bands of warriors who led away pack animals burdened under dressed hides and thick robes, returning weeks later with their ponies swaybacked beneath loads of meat and blankets, provisions and guns, from the agency traders.

From the first day of late winter, when The Bull's warriors had been able to travel east across a trackless, frozen landscape, they had bartered for more guns and ammunition.

Too, with each trip to the reservations for provisions, the warriors returned with more men. More and more the young ones, tough like resilient sinew, came to pitch their wickiups beside the waters of the Rosebud and later the Greasy Grass. Came to enjoy that time of endless celebration: each lazy summer day filled with hunting and scouting—each long, warm night of courting and storytelling and coup counting, and planning for The Bull's glorious fight when the soldiers would fall headfirst into their camp on the Greasy Grass.

The valley of the Pa-zees-la-wak-pa lay blanketed with buffalo. A massive herd slowly inched south and west toward the hazy bulk of the Bighorn Mountains. By now little over a decade had passed since the white man began his wholesale slaughter of the black, shaggy beasts. But here this summer these herds were another blessing of the all-powerful Wakan Tanka.

Here in this valley the people would stay . . . far to the west from the white man. Here they could follow the buffalo as they had for time beyond remembering.

Eating the flesh of Pte to make themselves strong as a people once more.

"At last we are out of the white man's land," they all agreed, and smoked together each night on the Greasy Grass. "Let the *wasichu* stay over on his side of the land. We will stay here on our ancient hunting grounds. This is our last ground. From here we will not be moved."

With some three hundred lodges and better than three thousand people themselves, the Northern Cheyenne led the Sioux bands down the west slope of the Wolf Mountains to what the Cheyenne had always called Goat River. And in that valley of the Little Bighorn, they created a sight never before seen by Sioux and Shahiyena alike: eight huge, graceful camp circles rising along the Greasy Grass, the horns of each circle open to the east in prayerful greeting to the rising sun.

At the extreme north end of this greatest of all congregations, the direction the tribes were marching, stood those Cheyenne lodges. Next to them were raised the lodges of the Sans Arcs, the Miniconjou, then a small camp circle of the Brule Sioux. Beyond them spread the huge camp circle of Crazy Horse's Oglallas, the Blackfeet Sioux, another small circle of Santee Sioux, who without fail always pitched their camp next to the last tribe, Sitting Bull's Hunkpapas.

That name long ago given to The Bull's tribe had significance as "the edge" or "the border," for it identified the group that traditionally camped at the village entrance. In the parlance of the old days, the Hunkpapas were "The Ones Who Camp by Themselves."

Like Sitting Bull's huge black-and-red lodge, the Sioux tepees were tall and narrow with a big smoke-flap opening at the top, whereas the lodges of the Northern Cheyenne were larger in circumference, yet sat a bit squatter and were topped with smaller ventilating smoke flaps. Sioux lodge or Cheyenne—there were better than two thousand lodges scattered along that silver ribbon of river. And nestled back in the thick willow and alder and creepers were huddled those wickiups that served as small brush-and-blanket shelters for the young warriors fresh off the reservations without families of their own.

To the west beyond the eight lodge circles, the huge pony herds had been put out to pasture on the rich green belly-high grasses. More than thirty thousand animals in all. No man had an accurate means of counting just how many ponies roamed those fertile bench-land pastures.

A man would have to say they were as thick as the ticks on an old buffalo bull's back.

Off the divide at last a beautiful panorama opened up before the command.

The regiment had crossed a series of ridges some fifteen to eighteen miles wide, which separated the drainages of the Rosebud from the Little Bighorn. Far below their feet now spread a green, grassy plain extending a little more than fifty miles to the Bighorn Mountains, resting stoic and silent in a snowcapped majesty, pale and hazy beneath a summer sun that relentlessly worked at the high overcast to make for a hot day. By now the clouds above the column were burning off. The air about the men droned lazily with that buzz of summer's retribution upon the high plains.

Down the slopes of gray rock sprouting with stunted sage and sparse bunchgrass, they wound their way, weaving round the dark green of jack-brush and pine and cedar clustered in clumps like old squaws gossiping over the army columns coming their way.

Lieutenant W. W. Cooke felt the first drops of sweat rolling down his long, flowing Dundrearies that spilled off his jaws. All the rage back east at the time, the long sideburns had proven quite a hit with the young ladies come visiting Fort Abraham Lincoln. For a man handsome to begin with, the Dundrearies only accented his dark good looks. He swiped a hand across his handlebar mustache as

Custer called a halt on the open tableland where the column could enjoy the beckoning green of the lush grass calling seductively from the valley below.

"Not far now, General," Cooke commented, reining in beside his commander.

"Billy, I want to see the officers. Promptly."

"Right away," replied the Canadian-born adventurer, who had come south to America when the Civil War offered excitement. He quickly gathered Custer's officers at the head of the march.

"We're close now, fellas," Custer began. "I'm going to form the columns for the attack should we be presented any surprises. Therefore, the first troop commander to report back to me that his pack detail is complete and that each of his troopers does indeed carry a hundred rounds of carbine ammo and twenty-four rounds for his pistol will ride the advance of the column. It seems the honor of this position should go to the command who have done their best to obey my order against grumbling and is best prepared. I'll wait here for a company commander to report—"

"I take the lead, General!"

Custer jerked sideways in his saddle to stare at Benteen.

The stocky Missourian's H Company had been marching right behind Custer since the climb over the divide began.

Eventually Custer answered Benteen's salute. "By all means, Colonel Benteen," he stammered, flustered and referring to the captain's brevet rank awarded during an illustrious Civil War career. "You have the advance for our attack, sir."

"Thank you, General." For the first time in many, many years since he had joined the Seventh in its early days, there rang the genuine sound of appreciation in Benteen's voice.

That sound struck Cooke as odd, if not a bit off-key.

"Lead off, Colonel." Custer waved Benteen forward, sitting atop Dandy beside Cooke while H Company trooped past.

"The man hates you," Cooke whispered from the corner of his mouth as the dusty, ragged soldiers clambered by.

Custer never took his eyes off Benteen's men to reply.

"He doesn't have to like me, Cookey. He's a bloody good soldier. Perhaps the most experienced and levelheaded company commander I've got.

"Keep in mind we will all rely on each other today. Besides, it suits me that Benteen's up front. If we're confronted with the hostiles—Benteen hits them first. And if I have time to split my command for the attack as we did at Washita, then I can always count on the captain to come to my aid if I need him. No matter what you might call him—Captain Frederick Benteen is a soldier first."

The insides of George Herendeen's thighs were sweating. Tiny rivulets of cold water poured down the back of his knees and into his stockings already soaked and chafing. He was sure he'd never pull his feet from his boots come evening. Perhaps he could soak his feet in the cool waters of the Little Horn tonight.

But that meant this regiment under Custer would have to wade on into these Sioux and get finished with them before evening. George Herendeen didn't want to think anymore about his sweaty feet.

It didn't take long before the regiment descending the divide in column-of-fours started marching a little too fast for Custer's liking. Herendeen figured whoever was setting the pace up there was just as anxious as he was to reach the beckoning green pastures down in the valley along that bright, silvery ribbon of the river.

But Custer wasn't as patient as George Herendeen. He nudged Dandy into a gallop, racing to the head of command, where he could reassume the front of the march itself.

Through the pastel sego lilies and bright sunset orange of the paintbrush, down past the buttermilk-pale hanging globes of the yellow lady slipper and the twilight purple cockleshells of spiderwort, around the sage and through the tall grasses, Custer led his troops, on and on into the widening jaws of the Little Bighorn valley. Including the Arikaras and Crows, his civilian scouts and mule packers, along with those fire-hardened veterans and bowel-puckered greenhorns, Custer was leading approximately six hundred seventy-five men into the shimmering haze as forenoon settled over the sleepy summer valley.

Herendeen twisted in the saddle at the grunt-bellied sounds of the young mule clambering up behind him.

Mark Kellogg reined alongside the scout, bouncing like a buggy spring on a washboard road.

He pulled in so he could ride with the scouts whose place it was to form the front of the march. "George, could I ask you for the use of your spurs? I noticed you're not using them."

Herendeen glanced down at the reporter's boots, then at the wide-eyed young mule Kellogg battled for control. "Not having much good with that salt-pork mule, eh, Mr. Kellogg?"

Mark chortled in that nervous way of his, jabbing his wire-framed spectacles back on the bridge of his large nose. "I want to stay up with the lead. That's what I want."

"Here." George pulled the unused spurs from his saddlebag. "But I can only advise you not to put them on or use them, Mr. Kellogg."

"Why not?" Kellogg wiped sweat off his upper lip.

"It's best from here on out you pull back to the rear of the column and stay put there. Not the healthiest place up here in the front with the scouts."

Kellogg chirped, "Oh, George—you had me scared for a moment there! I'm expecting some interesting developments soon, and I want to keep up with you scouts so I can report on everything I'm able to see far ahead. You must understand—I've promised my readers back east that I'll report the full and explosive details of this encounter with Sioux warriors. In those dispatches and stories I've shipped east already, you understand. I can't let my readers down."

"Mr. Kellogg," Herendeen said, "take my spurs, if not my advice. Use one if not the other. If my guess is right, we'll soon be seeing more action than you'll be able to describe in a month of Sundays. Whoa, now! See there— the Crow boys are stopping ahead. They'll wait for Custer himself to come up. You should be able to hear what they say to him for yourself."

Mark Kellogg's eyes widened as General Custer loped

past, standing in the stirrups, his knees flexing easily. *The man's meant to be on horseback,* Kellogg thought to himself as he buckled the second spur over his round-toed boot. He decided to take Herendeen's suggestion. *Just stay close to Custer. That's where the action will be. That's where the best story of your life will be found.*

The Crow scouts had ground to a halt on the bank of the Ash Creek and even dismounted, waiting for Custer and the troops to come up. There in the dust of the wide, beaten trail they had been following, the scouts scratched the soldier-chief a map.

"They say this creek flows down to the Little Horn," Mitch Bouyer interpreted, watching the reporter move closer to the group. "The Greasy Grass of the Sioux, where Sitting Bull's waiting for you and your boys, General."

To Kellogg it sounded as if the half-breed still smarted from some old injury done him by Custer.

"They're waiting for me, you say—eh, Bouyer?"

Kellogg had become a practiced observer. Without really thinking about it, he studied faces, the way people held and carried themselves. More important than learning what a person had to tell about a story, Kellogg had found out some time ago, was learning what a person didn't want you to know.

From the look he read on Custer's face at this moment, as the general knelt staring at the Crow interpreter, Kellogg learned something about the cracks widening in Custer's command.

Mark Kellogg could tell that Custer didn't much like Mitch Bouyer, perhaps more so than he had ever disliked any man in his life. Even the nagging Benteen.

But then the reporter remembered that a man like Custer would revel in being hated by them both—Benteen and Bouyer: brave men and worthy adversaries.

Custer dusted his hands on his buckskin britches. "The Sioux, Mr. Bouyer—they can wait until ice water is served in hell itself for all I care. I'm going to slip 'em a Custer surprise!"

BOOK III

TIIE BATTLE

CHAPTER 18

Adjutant Cooke watched Custer rise from the dust where Bouyer and his Crows had drawn their map. The general snatched up his reins and leapt atop Dandy.

"Cookey, c'mon over here. I want a private word with you."

Off to the side out of earshot, Custer and Cooke discussed their plan for deployment of the command. After pulling some maps from his saddlebags and handing them over to Custer for his inspection, Cooke scrawled notes in the small notebook he carried.

"I'm glad you're in agreement," Custer sighed. "You remember the Washita, don't you, Billy?"

Cooke smiled with those straight, pearly teeth of his. Years ago at the Washita, his special crack unit of forty handpicked sharpshooters had bottled up Black Kettle's fleeing Cheyenne just as Custer had planned it. They had laid down a murderous fire across the river, so very few Cheyenne had made it downstream to the Kiowa and Arapaho camps on foot. Most who tried had ended up floating down the icy waters of the Washita, their bodies riddled by Spencer-rifle fire at the command of marksman W. W. Cooke.

"A glorious rout, General! And we're about to pull another one out of your hat, aren't we, sir?"

"That's why I like you, Billy. Always thinking like a soldier."

"I've learned from the best, General."

Custer nodded. "We'll use three wings to execute this attack again. And I'll divide off the first wing at this time. It is—?"

Cooke yanked his watch out. "Twelve-oh-seven."

"Very good. Let's get this show on the road. Bring Benteen up."

When Cooke had gathered the captain, along with Captain Thomas Weir and Lieutenant Edward Godfrey, he announced that Custer wanted to see them at the head of the march immediately. "The general's compliments, Captain Benteen. We're ready to deploy for the attack."

Surrounded by the three officers and his adjutant a few yards from the column, Custer issued his orders. "For the purpose of our attack, Captain Weir's D Company and Lieutenant Godfrey's K Company are placed under your command, Captain Benteen."

"Begging pardon, General." Benteen cleared his dry throat, straightening himself in the saddle. "Don't you think we'd better keep the regiment together? If it's truly as big a camp as the scouts claim it is, you're going to need the whole regiment standing together."

Cooke watched a cloud pass over Custer's face before he answered.

"Thank you for your consideration of my orders, Captain," he replied acidly, eyes filled with icy fire. "Right now I can't think of a reason why my battle plan would fail. Suppose you just remember that I give the commands, and you follow them."

"Very good, General," Benteen replied stiffly. "Where am I headed?"

Custer pointed to the southwest, toward the rolling hills,

deep valleys, and endless bare ridges that rose to meet the pale, sun-bleached prairie sky.

"Take your battalion in that direction. Watch for an Indian village, and pitch into anything you run across."

Benteen gulped, staring off into that nothingness of rugged draws and coulees. "Begging consideration, General—why there?"

Custer bit his lip. Cooke figured the general forced himself to keep from swearing at this white-headed pain in the ass.

"I want you to continuously feel to our left, if for no other reason than to assure myself that the hostiles—which we know have been warned already—won't flee upriver to the south. That's all I'm going to say, Captain Benteen. You, better than any man I command, ought to know I'm not in the habit of explaining myself."

The captain must have understood that plain enough, Cooke figured, for Benteen saluted, spoke, "Very well, sir. Understood. As you ordered."

Benteen nodded at Weir and Godfrey. They followed.

Ed Godfrey slipped his watch from his unbuttoned tunic pocket. Twelve-fifteen P.M.

How long will we have to ride through these bare, rocky hills before Benteen will figure out this is a fool's errand Custer's got him on? Is Custer paying Benteen back for his public criticism following the Elliott affair at the Washita? Or does Custer want to get Benteen's hundred twenty men massacred?

Godfrey felt the cold trickle of water dripping all the way down to the base of his spine and hoped it was only sweat—not his first taste of outright fear. Hell, he hadn't been afraid even when his small platoon had been practically surrounded at the Battle of the Washita. Not even then.

But this is something different, he had to admit. The only reason he could figure that Custer had sent them on this fool's errand chasing down the wind itself, was that Custer wanted Benteen out of the way.

Or killed . . .

As Benteen's three companies splashed across the summer trickle of Ash Creek, then plodded away beneath a cloud of choking dust, Custer turned back upstream with Cooke at his side to find a suitable place for Dandy to drink. Soon enough they were joined by more of the thirsty command and their dry-mouthed animals.

Custer struggled to pull a reluctant Dandy back from the creek.

"Don't let them get too much, men!" he called to soldiers nearby. "They'll get loggy on you, if you're not careful."

In turn, each of the remaining companies were given a few minutes at the scummy pools along the mossy banks of Ash Creek. As Dandy rested, Custer stared into the luminous, bone yellow sky at that relentless, one-eyed demon spewing fire across a breathless, choking landscape. Giving in, he removed his buckskin coat, tying it behind the cantle of his saddle.

Once more he carefully tucked his pants into the tall, dusty boots. His light gray army fatigue shirt already bore the dark blotches beneath each arm, between his shoulder blades, and in a necklace beneath his strawberry chin stubble. He wiped his blood red kerchief around the sweatband of the cream-colored hat, then rerolled the brim up on the right side in the event he would have to sight his Remington sporting rifle from horseback. When the kerchief was properly knotted round his neck once more, Custer ordered the columns to move out.

Behind him plodded those other hot, dusty, dry troops, their mouths caked and puckering with the alkali of Ash Creek. Most men had already lashed their blue tunics behind their saddles. A motley gypsy gang of good and ugly heading down, down, down into that valley of cool, sparkling waters and inviting green grass extending clear to the Bighorns. A valley beckoning Custer's army onward. Down to the green and cool.

This unsettling mixture of veterans and raw, untried recruits followed him into the maw. Rogues and rascals . . . even innocents and children who had no conception of what war with the Sioux was all about. Sobering for the hard-files to brood on the men around them—some thirty to sixty percent of each company unseasoned and scared enough right now to worry about wetting their britches.

Yet any man present would have said he trusted Custer. The general's reputation protected them all with a brassy aura of invincibility as they rode on and on, following that big cream-colored hat and that bright scarlet scarf fluttering on the hot breeze.

Custer had never lost a fight. So they followed.

Some sweated in those white shirts first used during the Civil War and still issued on the frontier posts eleven years later. Others dampened dark blue shirts simply because the white ones got all too dirty much too fast. These indigo shirts made it pleasantly convenient for a trooper: He got away with going longer between washings than did the simple-minded, who wore white and far too often had to pay a call on the post laundresses along Soapsuds Row.

Even a scattering of these soldiers sported the coarse gray pullover of the variety Custer himself wore this day. In addition, there appeared a lively mixture of the checkered hickory shirts some had purchased from trader Coleman at the Yellowstone. Such lightweight cloth made for a more comfortable ride in the summer heat of this hunt for the Sioux.

From time to time the troopers worked at some saddle rations, choking down hardtack or cooked pork with swallows of the warm, stinking creek water from their canteens. Their noses reddened and crusted with alkali dust, none could smell the earthy aromas of man and animal on the dust anyway. Those rank odors of lathered horses and played-out mules, along with the well-known and all-too-familiar pungent stench of men too long without a bath, mingled with the perfume of the tiny wildflowers trampled underfoot.

An army on the prowl.

Every man sweltered beneath a wide sky, accompanied down trail by the familiar thunk and clink of saddle leather and bridle chain. Not to mention the reassuring plap of their reliable weapons at their sides. While officers carried .45-caliber Colts, the troopers were issued .44-caliber Remington pistols, both of which could drop a man at seventy paces if a soldier could aim and fire without jerking the trigger. Those sidearms were usually worn butt forward on the right side of the body so the pistol could be withdrawn by the left hand, as the right normally wielded the near-obsolete saber.

Every soldier carried the 1873 trapdoor Springfield chambered for .45–.70 ammunition. Some men toted what they fondly called their knitting bag, a wool-lined cartridge box worn on the belt, used to carry more of that carbine ammunition: a .45-caliber bullet backed with seventy grains of powder that could kill at better than three hundred yards, making a tight six-inch group at a hundred. With a hundred rounds of Springfield ammunition assigned to each man, most soldiers filled the loops in their cartridge belts and allowed the rest of the shells to rattle loose in their leather saddlebags.

In the hands of a cool veteran, the Springfield trapdoors could fire seven shots in twelve to fifteen seconds. Enough to keep any band of charging warriors at bay.

With a rattle and thunk, a plodding clop of iron-shod hooves, and the snapping pop of the striped regimental pennants, the troops followed Custer down to the Greasy Grass. Beneath an oppressive summer sky, every man suffered a knotting belly and that nauseating ache from bad water, not to mention the agony of eyes scalded from alkali dust and a face burned raw by sun and wind.

The gallant Seventh marched down into the maw of that valley as surely as if it had been the cool, shady, beckoning halls of Valhalla itself. Less like an army of avenging Norse gods commanded by the all-powerful Odin himself—more like a roving band of renegade gypsies—Custer's Cavalry plodded down into the seductive valley of the Greasy Grass while Destiny herself opened her arms at last.

"The general's compliments, Major," Adjutant Cooke began with a smile, his long, flowing Dundrearies tousled by the hot breeze clinging to the Ash Creek drainage. "He wishes you to take command of Company A under Captain Moylan, G under Lieutenant McIntosh, and M under Captain French, sir. In addition, the general wishes to transfer to your command the services of Crow scouts White Swan and Half-Yellow-Face—also the Arikara interpreter, Gerard."

"Then he wants me to keep the Ree scouts with my command?" Reno inquired suspiciously, scratching his beard.

"It's my opinion that he does—yes, sir," Cooke replied. "He's keeping four of the Crows and Bouyer with him. The rest, I assume, are now to go with you."

"Anything more? Something in the way of orders?"

"No, Major." Billy Cooke glanced back at Custer, sitting loosely atop Dandy on the rise above them. *Strange, now that I think about it—*

"Custer just wants me in command of three companies . . . is that right?"

Cooke thought Reno sounded more than a bit anxious. But then the skin around the major's eyes sagged again. *The bastard's relieved that he's not ordered into battle immediately. If I had my way—*

"Correct, Major," Cooke answered. "He orders you to proceed down the left bank of the stream."

"Very good, Lieutenant." Reno turned toward his three companies.

By the time Cooke galloped back to the head of the columns to rejoin the general, Custer was sending the short, shy Charley Reynolds off to ride with Reno as well. The scout's soulful blue eyes twinkled with a melancholy light as he waved farewell to the general and the swarthy Bouyer, kicking his mount back along the dark snake of cavalry waiting patiently for Custer to complete this division of the troops for what most officers realized was to become a three-winged attack.

"Captain Yates?"

"Yes, sir!" he replied in his best Michigan Yankee accent.

"You and Captain Keogh will be in charge of the five remaining companies under my aegis."

"Sir?" Yates appeared startled.

"You'll take command of C Company under Captain

Custer, E under Lieutenant Smith, along with your own F Company, Captain Yates."

The eyes of the officers studied Custer as he in turn studied the valley beyond.

Billy Cooke understood why he wanted George Yates to command the lion's share of companies under Custer's personal aegis. Besides being a hometown Monroe, Michigan boy, Yates had served on Custer's staff during the war. He was a rock-steady hand, proven in battle. Yet, as Cooke thought on it now, there still remained the hint of stain. Guilt by association. George's brother, Fred, was the head trader for the Sioux at the Red Cloud Agency down in Nebraska, a fact that had not escaped the attention of many in high places during the graft-and-corruption scandals still rocking the War Department since the past winter.

If George does well in the coming fight, Cooke thought, looking at the two men, *then Custer's faith in him will be vindicated—and all taint removed from Yate's career. That's the kind of soldier the old man is.*

"Meanwhile," Custer continued, bringing his eyes back to the big Irishman, who sat sweltering in his own coarse gray-woolen pullover, "immediate command to fall under Captain Keogh will be his own and Lieutenant Calhoun's companies."

James Calhoun grinned as he reached over swinging a fist, slugging Keogh on the shoulder. They had long been the best of friends and drinking partners. Together they repeatedly boasted that their two companies alone could whip thrice their weight in Sioux.

"I want your command to be prepared for a rearguard action, gentlemen," Custer went on. "No telling what the sneaking hostiles might do in coming up our backsides. They know we're coming." His eyes scanned the far hills to the north, then moved back up the divide behind them. "I can't think of any better commanders to protect this regiment's backsides."

Keogh snorted that rollicking bray of his that characterized his lust for life. He never shied from anything thrown his way. "Jimmy and me—we're ready and able to watch over anyone's arses, we are, sir!"

"Splendid," Custer said with a smile. "Now that Reno's moving across the creek, you'll see that I've kept my family with me. Just as I've long envisioned it on such a day of glory. You'll all ride with me today. What say you, friends?"

"I'm one bastard fotching to spill some Sioux blood first, General!" Keogh rattled. "Washington City can wait till I get that outta my gawdamned system. Gimme more whiskey and bring on Crazy Horse!"

Custer said, "You'll have your wish shortly, Myles. Let's see if the Sioux are going to cooperate with us or not. I can't shake this worry that they're going to run on me."

"How can we assure that they don't, sir?" Calhoun piped in.

"Jimbo, I have a plan that might just work when we come in sight of the village," Custer whispered, lending a mysterious air to his answer. "But for the time being—ah, good. Here comes Vic now!"

Minutes ago he had dispatched Saddler Sergeant John Tritten from his personal headquarters command to ride back to the pack train with Dandy and fetch Vic, Custer's favorite chestnut sorrel, from Private Burkman. Back in the days of his Civil War battles Custer had learned the advantage in taking a fresh animal into a fight. Such a tactic had worked well for him in past campaigns, so he was not one about to break a string of good fortune now that he stood on the precipice of glory.

On Sergeant Tritten's tail loped angel-faced Boston Custer and young Autie Reed, the eighteen-year-old bullyboy who had come to watch his uncles butcher some Sioux. Beside them rode Mark Kellogg, still raking his worn-out army-issue mule with Herendeen's spurs. Taking their cue from the general's stern face, the three civilians fell silent, not anxious to interrupt the proceedings. They reined to a halt. Tritten switched Custer's saddle to Vic's back atop a dry blanket. At the same time, other officers and enlisted tightened cinches, patted their horses' sweaty necks, or adjusted their own damp clothing. Belts were wrenched up a notch, yellow-striped britches restuffed into scuffed boots.

Then Custer was up in the saddle once more, looking

bigger than life atop Vic, the blaze-faced sorrel standing better than sixteen hands high. After tugging his hat down over his hogged strawberry haircut, Custer waved his officers and their commands to follow him downstream.

"Billy, you'll see the troops are put to the march, then rejoin me?" Set deep within that sun-rawed, wind-scalded face were a pair of eyes burned red with alkali dust, hollowed and black-rimmed with characteristic lack of sleep.

"Will do, General," Cooke answered. "We'll follow your lead!"

And as Custer turned from his officers' conference, he pointed Vic's nose to the right—to every man's surprise. For now he no longer led his men down that wide, well-marked Indian road scoured by thousands upon thousands of hooves across the dusty, dry breast of the Ash Creek trail.

Custer ducked behind some low hills, hills that for a time put him out of Major Reno's sight.

With every bend and twist of the trail down into the valley, Marcus Reno grew a bit more apprehensive.

What if Custer's taken off, and I suddenly confront the Sioux on my own? Reno's mind raced, burdened by all the dreadful possibilities.

Several miles down the creek, both commands passed through a swampy morass. Here lay a steamy bog that over the centuries filled with stagnant seepage trapped as the spring rain and winter runoff trickled down from the Wolf Mountains. At this stage of the year, the morass by and large had already gone dry, its surface cracking beneath summer's retribution upon the land.

Over the damp belly of the bog hung a stifling stench. Unmistakable—some poor animal had blundered into the marsh, seeking relief from the heat, instead found no way out. Even the wary predators of these high plains had left the old buffalo bull to rot beneath the hot sun. The stench of its decaying flesh clung to the place as the soldiers hurried past, choking down their stomach's revolt at not only the smell, but the sight of maggots and blowflies busy at the blackened meat.

Shortly before two o'clock, Reno decided he would move his companies back to the north bank to ride in concert with Custer. Both the terrain itself and the major's own nervousness dictated his change of heart. Even the veterans tensed up on their reins, wary and alert when a few minutes later arose the frightened cries of the scouts.

They were pointing ahead. Shouting.

Reno's eyes shot up and down his columns. Every soldier had ears alert. Sour tongues raked dry lips. Sweaty hands yanked carbines into readiness.

Yet for all the tension and excitement, what the scouts had discovered was not a buffalo or antelope—much less a Sioux warrior.

All that stood astride the wide, well-plowed Indian trail pointing itself down the dry, cracked bottomland of Ash Creek was a solitary painted Indian lodge.

At first the Arikara scouts milled about nervously, bumping their mounts against one another, unsure of what to make of this startling discovery, more so afraid of what the existence of this lone tepee foretold. They shouted to scare off any evil spirits from the place. Then one of their number finally realized there were no Sioux here.

Only then did that solitary young warrior rattle heels against his pony's flanks.

With a whoop and a high-throated cry, Strikes Two charged down on the solitary lodge, swinging by it at a full gallop, slapping his quirt across the dry buffalo hides. He whirled about in a dust spray, bringing his snorting pony up sharply. He smiled, quite proud of himself as the first man of this campaign, white or red, brave enough to count coup on an enemy's lodge.

His strutting turn ended in time for him to watch his childhood friend, Young Hawk, leap from his pony at a full run and race on foot to the lodge, yanking his huge scalping knife from his belt. With one swift slash he had the lodge skins opened from the smoke flaps down to the stakes that were pounded into the dry, crumbly earth. Suddenly freed through that new wound in the old lodge, the stench of death and rotting flesh escaped, surrounding the tepee as Young Hawk stumbled back, his hand covering his nose.

More brown-skinned riders dashed up, striking the lodge
with quirts as Young Hawk and Red Bear tore aside the
lodge entrance. Inside on a low scaffold lay the body of a
dead warrior, his heat-bloated carcass wrapped in a beaded
ceremonial buffalo robe.

With both hips shattered by a soldier bullet, Old-She-
Bear, a renowned Sans Arc Sioux, had been dragged from
the Rosebud battlefield as Crook's troops struggled to hold
their ground against the maddening horsemen under Crazy
Horse barely eight suns ago. Because he had clung tena-
ciously to life at the time, Old-She-Bear had been loaded on
a travois and pulled from the scene of the fight to the
Rosebud camps. From there over the divide when the
bands moved toward the Greasy Grass. The dying warrior
slung behind a pony beneath the sun for each day's journey,
until his family and friends decided the old warrior was in
fact looking out at them from eyes filled with shadows.

Here along this boggy creek the Sans Arc warrior had
clung to life for several days, nursed by family who
patiently waited out the old man's slow death walk to the
Other Side.

After his final breath had escaped the old man's lungs,
the relatives painted Old-She-Bear's face with red clay and
dressed him in his finest ceremonial elk-skin war shirt and
leggings. Alongside the scaffold on which they laid his
body, the family placed his feather-draped shield, bow, and
quiver. Before leaving this death lodge for the last time, his
relatives had placed some cooked meat and blood soup for
Old-She-Bear's trip to see his grandfathers.

As a final tribute the warrior's favorite pipe, tobacco, and
tender bag were laid beside him. When at last his journey
to the Other Side was complete, the old man would enjoy
having a smoke and talking with friends gone before.

To further desecrate this enemy's lodge, Red Feather
chewed the dried meat and swilled down the cold, scummy
blood soup before he pulled his breechclout aside. He
urinated on the body of Old-She-Bear and those sacred
articles left behind by family and friends in celebration of a
brave warrior.

Custer reined up as Red Feather stooped from the torn

lodge, gripping his penis and spraying the side of the buffalo hides.

"Gerard!"

From all the way back with Reno and Reynolds, the Arikara interpreter heard his name screamed as if it were some black curse. By the time Fred rode up to the lone tepee, Custer trembled with an uncontrollable rage.

"You tell these poor excuses for men, these Rees, that I've ordered them to ride on! By God, they were told not to stop for anything! They've disobeyed me once too often! Long Hair has been shamed by a bunch of ragged Arikarees, and I won't have it!"

Custer was nearly shrieking, the color of his cheeks redder than a high-plains sunburn. Flecks of spittle dotted his rosy chapped lips. When Gerard started to speak, Custer plunged ahead, his fury still unspent.

"Gerard, you inform them they belong to you now." Custer spit so the Rees would make no mistake understanding that he symbolically rid himself of them. "I do not want them. Tell these red bastards to step aside and let my soldiers through. My troops will take the lead if the Rees won't. Tell your Arikaras I think they are women if they won't fight the Sioux. And if they are a bunch of cowardly squaws, I'll take their guns from them and send them back to their lodges, where their children can make fun of them for all the rest of their days. To laugh at them because they didn't fight beside Long Hair when he destroyed the mighty Sioux!"

Instead of answering the general's challenge, translated on Gerard lips, Bloody Knife and Stabbed both pulled their ponies out of the column and plodded off some distance from the soldiers. But Bear-in-Timber had long had a powder-keg temper. As the interpreter finished, the young warrior stood and shouted back at Custer, his own copper face flushed with anger.

"Long Hair, hear me! You take our weapons and send us home as cowards because we fear too many Sioux. You yourself told us we did not have to fight these Sioux, but that we owned their horses. Did you speak to us with two tongues, Long Hair? Do you now change your heart again and call us squaws? If you would tell your own young soldiers of the Sioux beyond count waiting for them in the valley below . . . they would surely act the same as we. You keep that from your men. If the soldier-chief spoke the truth to your own soldiers, you would be many days taking their rifles from them and beating them back to your fort."

Many of the Rees laughed behind their hands as Gerard translated that portion of the harangue.

Custer squinted his hollow, sleepless eyes, fuming. Gerard had seen the general angry before, but never this furious.

Gerard was afraid Custer might make an example of Bear-in-Timber for the others, to maintain discipline among his scouts. To let both Indian and trooper alike know that he wasn't about to take any of their guff.

"Just tell them this, Gerard," Custer growled like a hound with its guard hair up. He swallowed once, throttling some of his anger. "Tell them they can stay with us if they will fight. I don't want them otherwise."

At the moment Fred Gerard opened his mouth to speak, a young Ree scout called Good Face, along with an older warrior named Boychief, hollered out, signaling from a nearby knoll not far up the trail. Gerard leapt atop his horse and tore up the hill. He got to the top of the knoll, his own horse prancing barely under his control as he peered down the far slope for a moment, then kicked the horse back down the slope. The two Rees rode right on his heels.

"Indians, General!" Fred shouted.

"What? Where?"

"Maybe forty of them . . . could be more!" Gerard rasped breathlessly as he yanked on the reins, his mount sliding to a dusty halt.

Reno galloped up from his position. He had spotted the same hostile warriors. "They're sitting just out of our rifle range, General!" he shouted, genuine fear constricting his throat.

"Funny thing, Custer," Gerard added, wiping his hand across a parched mouth, thirsting for the liquid treasure in his saddlebags. "They just sat there, looking at us, like they expected us to be here."

Custer studied Gerard carefully as the interpreter stuck his hand into his three-strap saddlebag to pull out another tin flask. Custer couldn't help but smell the sweetish odor of the sour-mash whiskey as Gerard drew long and hard on the fiery elixir.

From the look on the general's face at that moment, Gerard was certain Custer—a notorious teetotaler—wanted a drink.

From behind them arose that sudden shrill cry Custer had known as a boy growing up in Ohio and Michigan, then again when he attacked Confederate cavalry and artillery positions during the war. This shrill and famous Custer shout leapt from Tom Custer's lips as he tore up on his charger.

Little brother had caught sight of the quarry himself.

Without invitation Tom held out his hand to Gerard, yanking the flask away from him. He drank every bit as long on the potent whiskey as had Gerard. When he handed the canteen back, Tom rattled the sagebrush hills once again with his wild war cry, a screech that would scour any white man's throat. Any but Custer's.

"Thirty days furlough for the first goddamned soldier who raises a scalp!" Tom shouted.

Down the waiting columns those who could hear young Custer's promise raised their own cries of battle lust. It was part of the fever they must each experience, working themselves into a lather for the coming battle.

Custer said, "Good, Tom! Work some fight up in 'em!"

Tom took the flask again and threw some more whiskey down his throat, peering up the knoll . . . then down the dry coulee that Ash Creek followed in the rainy season.

A *small bunch of Indians, eh?* he thought.

Tom gave the flask back to Gerard. They would share. Tom had never been selfish when it came to drinking. Whiskey was, after all, for sharing. For friends.

And he thought on those forty Sioux he had watched disappear over the knoll, riding out of reach.

Perhaps those Indians who had darted over the hill were nothing more than enticing decoys. After all, Tom knew as well as the next man how Crazy Horse had lured Fetterman and eighty men over Lodge Trail Ridge ten winters ago. It was the oldest Indian trick in the book.

Tom glanced up, feeling the whiskey warm his hot, knotted belly. The Rees mounted their horses.

"Gerard!" Custer shouted. "Why aren't your lazy Arikarees going after those Sioux? There are horses to be taken! Scalps and honors to be won!"

Tom climbed back into the saddle as Fred Gerard cursed his scouts prancing atop their skittish horses. Perhaps the horses themselves sensed the visceral fear of their riders. Gerard got no response from the younger members of his detail. On the ground nearby hunkered some of the older Rees, Bloody Knife and Stabbed among them. They tore up handfuls of the dry grass, tossing the blades into the hot breeze.

Otoe Sioux! Otoe Sioux!

"They claim there's too many Sioux again, General. More than there are blades of grass."

"You take them—take them all and ride with Reno!" Custer bellowed in disgust. "I don't want the Rees with me. Nowhere near me!"

"They don't want to fight so many," Gerard explained weakly, whispering so that only Custer and Tom could hear his plea. "Not with you or Reno. There's more Sioux than we can handle, General."

"Bullshit!" Tom shouted.

Gerard almost said something to young Custer but turned instead to the general. "None of the Rees want to go any—"

"Take their guns, boys!" Custer suddenly spat in the direction of the Arikara scouts. "Take their horses too! Give them their old ponies back. I have no more use for these whining squaws! We've found the Sioux, yet these miserable wretches don't want to fight. So be it, Tom. I'll send them home to their lodges, where they can die toothless old men."

Minutes later after a detail from Tom's C Troop loped up with the Rees' ponies, and the exchange of animals had taken place, the scouts still refused to ride the back trail. Instead, they clustered in a knot, afraid to leave the

protection of the soldiers. Many wailed their death songs
against a background of horse snorts and blue-tongued
curses from the stable sergeant retrieving the army mounts.

An eerie, wailing, profane chorus—fitting background
itself for Custer's descent into the valley.

Somewhere behind Custer's own standard and the regimental guidons, back down the columns in those faceless
rows of soldiers, a single voice rose strongly, clear in its
baritone plea. A trooper, singing the words to "Out of the
Wilderness":

> If you want to smell hell,
> Just join the cavalry,
> Just join the cavalry.
> If you want to smell hell,
> Then join the cavalry,
> 'Cause we're not going home.

CHAPTER 19

"CAPTAIN Keogh! Take Cookey with you to Reno's command," Custer ordered, now fully in sight of the Little Bighorn.

About time he started stirring things up, Keogh thought. *Time to get this bleeming attack under way.*

"And when I get there, General?"

"Inform the major I want him to take his men across the river below and attack the village as fast as he deems prudent, he's to charge the village. Tell him he will be supported by the whole unit."

Turning from the wide-eyed major minutes later after delivering Custer's message, Keogh and Cooke watched Reno lead his men down the dry bluffs of Ash Creek toward the Little Bighorn for about half a mile before the pair wheeled and kicked their mounts back to Custer's outfit waiting some three-quarters of a mile up the Ash Creek trail. They hadn't ridden far when the sound of clattering hooves made them turn and rein up.

Its nostrils flaring in the staggering heat, Gerard's mount

lagged wearily, already lathered from its valiant charge up the back trail. All the two officers could now see of Reno's men was a heavy dust cloud over the red-eyed bluffs hugging the river below. It appeared the major had made his crossing of the Little Bighorn.

"Cooke!" Gerard croaked, licking his lips as he reined up between the two soldiers.

"What t'is it, Gerard?" Keogh's brogue peeled off the rolling R's.

"Major Reno sent me with his compliments—"

"What's the news?" Cooke bit his words off impatiently.

"He's already met the Indians." Gerard offered his whiskey canteen to Cooke.

Cooke shook his head, but Keogh greedily scooped it from the interpreter's hand with his own big paw.

"I pass up no man's whiskey!" he bawled with a sour grin.

Cooke watched the Irishman swallow, then went back to studying Gerard. "Reno's spotted the Indians, you say?"

"We crossed the river. Spotted the bastards then. Lots of the red bastards. You can see their naked bodies as they ride to and fro down in the river bottom, down in the trees and marsh as we was crossing. We also seen the tips of their lodges downriver a throw or two."

"Damn," Cooke whispered, "but the queen's got her a one-eyed jack sneaking into her bedchambers, eh! Custer'll be tickled!" He slapped his thigh in amusement, startling his own skittish mount.

"You'll take the major's message on to Custer, won't you? Reno's desperate for the general's promised support—"

"Make no mistake," Cooke answered enthusiastically. He glanced at Keogh. "The general will want to hear all about this, he will."

"Here, my good man," Keogh belched, holding his arm out with the empty canteen at the end of it.

Gerard shook the canteen. "My God! You've emptied the damned thing."

"'Ave any more about you, Gerard?" Keogh interrupted him, feeling the warm whiskey jolting against the pasty hardtack and greasy salt pork in his belly like clashing lines of calvary. "I'd be willing to have me a go at another one of them, if you're willing to sell."

Gerard eyed him severely, then his face lightened. "When would I have my money?" he asked suspiciously.

"Soon as we hit Lincoln."

"I don't know—"

"I'm good for it, Gerard," the big Irishman said gruffly, sticking out his hand impatiently.

"Oh . . . all right, Captain. I suppose it won't hurt a thing, will it now?"

"Not when you've been drinking a goodly bit of it your own self," Cooke admonished.

"You'll get Reno's message to Custer now, won't you?" Gerard implored with his dark eyes, handing a full canteen over to Keogh. "Like the general promised—bringing his support to the major?"

Keogh dropped the canteen into his saddlebag, smacking his lips as he kicked his horse about. "C'mon, Cookey—we've got us a message to deliver to the old man hisself, we 'ave."

By the time his two officers had scaled the sunny hills back to Custer's position, the commander had already dispatched three young Crows under Bouyer to ride to the top of those bluffs rising above the river for the purpose of taking a look at the Sioux village below. But instead of heading uphill behind Bouyer, Half-Yellow-Face and White Swan kicked their ponies down into the Ash Creek drainage, following Reno and his men. In some mystical sense of order, they must have figured that going with the major was decidedly safer than riding with Custer.

The blue-eyed general watched the two Crows skedaddle downhill, his eyes glowering. He then turned back to see young Curley and Mitch Bouyer reach the top of the hill north along the bluffs.

Good. Maybe that half-breed Bouyer will work out after all.

The pair did not stay atop the hill but a moment before they came galloping back with their news.

Far beyond up the valley, they had spotted the village itself, seen through the thick trees clustered along the bends of the Greasy Grass. Many lodgepoles reaching into

the summer sky . . . more than many lodges . . . much
dust. Some mounted Indians dashed back and forth, riding
as if they were trying to warn others of the cavalry attack.

Young Curley politely waited for Bouyer to finish with
the pressing matters at hand, then asked the interpreter to
speak to the general on his behalf.

"Long Hair." The young Crow's face clouded, creased
with worry. "You and I are going home today by a trail we
do not know."

"He says he's going home today?" Custer asked as he
studied the Absaroka scout.

Bouyer nodded.

"Maybe he's right, Mitch. Maybe he will go home with
glory about his shoulders. Soon to be a chief of the mighty
Crow. By jiggers! We are going to win this land back for
these Indians. You will be a chief too, Mr. Bouyer!"

His sapphire eyes flicked to the right, straining to see
something, perhaps hoping to spot those hostile Indians
seen by the others far to the north, at least to see the dust
from all those hooves.

"Off to the north, eh?" Custer repeated rhetorically, a
plan already forming, congealing, solidifying in his quicksilver mind.

Custer visualized the river flowing north and the village
at the upper end of this green valley, the brown lodges
squatting in the sun—but a handful of miles away now. The
warriors Reno had run into must surely be some of the first
fighting men spurring out to defend their village because of
the advance warning from those forty Sioux they had
spotted back up Ash Creek.

Surely, the camp now knows soldiers are coming, he brooded,
an eye twitching. *With Reno attacking from the foot of the
village, I'll take my five companies and go after the head! Pound
them solidly while Reno holds their feet to the ground.*

"Clausewitz, you genius! You'd be mighty proud of your
best pupil this day!" Custer muttered excitedly.

"What's that, sir?" Cooke asked, still breathless after his
climb up from Reno's crossing of the river.

"Nothing, Lieutenant." He blinked nervously. The way
he always did once the excitement set in. "Let's ride!"

"General, rider approaching!" called Sergeant Major Sharrow, who clutched a beefy hand round Custer's personal flag.

Intently they watched the man's lathered mount labor up the slope, lunging, resting for a moment, kicked again into another furious series of weary lunges. Across the dusty slope the mount carried its rider with the last bit of bottom it had to give.

"Private Archibald McIlhargey, sir!" the soldier gasped as his horse stumbled, nearly collapsing beside Custer's mount. "Reporting from Major Reno."

"What's your message, boy?" Custer asked, swiping a finger around the sweatband of the cream-colored hat.

"The major wanted to report he's in the thick of it now, sir," McIlhargey gulped dryly. "Lots of warriors swarming on 'em down there."

"Swarming, you say?"

"Like a nest of mad hornets!"

"Good!" Custer slapped his knee. "Perfect, in fact. We'll let Reno have at them a bit here while we make a go of it at the head, up north a ways near the village."

"S-sir?" the young soldier stammered.

"We're going to ride north, young man, and attack the village."

"Major Reno asked for your support, General!" McIlhargey pleaded. He was scared as hell, talking to the regiment's commander. He had ridden away from Reno with the screams of the Sioux and the frightened cries of his fellow troopers ringing in his ears. Now he sensed his heart pounding in his throat as he glared at the general. "Your support, sir?"

"And that's just what I'll give him, Private."

Custer peered to the north and breathed deep, swelling his chest against the sweat-stained gray pullover. "I'm fixing to chop the head off this beast for the major."

"He—the major was thinking—aren't you coming down to help him, General?"

"Of course not, Private. I'm going to attack as I've always attacked. Reno's gone in and dealt them the first blow, and I'm going in to finish the job. Now, son—you report back to the major . . . or you can come with me. Frankly, I think you should ride with me. Appears your mount won't make it back to Reno's command."

"Thank you, sir," McIlhargey replied, sensing the winded mount sagging beneath him. "I'll report back to Captain Keogh and I Company."

Custer yanked on Vic's reins and galloped off past the private. The strong, well-fed thoroughbred lunged along the lines of troops waiting for some word on the Indians and news of Reno's attack on the village. He brought them the news they hungered for. Up and down the columns he loped, shouting of the discovery by the Crow scouts—the village far to the north—and that Reno was in the thick of it.

"We've got the village in our sights now, boys!" Custer cheered, standing tall in the stirrups, every bit as ragged as any of them, but more regal at this moment than ever before in his life.

Destiny waited for him downriver. Close at hand. Beckoning him on with her sweet perfume and seductive come hither.

He watched his effect on the men, loving it, knowing he could stir them as no one else could at this critical moment.

"Reno's got them tied down at the river . . . so, we'll go on to make a crossing where we can cut their head off! What say you, fellas? Reno's already in the thick of it! And we'll have some of that glory for ourselves in a few minutes! Just be patient . . . hold those mounts. What say—are you boys ready to ride the Seventh into gloryland?"

Many of those two-hundred-odd soldiers cheered and whistled their enthusiasm right back at the general. Some even tossed their hats into the air or tucked them away into their saddlebags with that loose ammunition for their carbines. Around their heads some troopers tied the brightly-colored bandannas bought off trader Coleman back at the Yellowstone.

Those five companies of old files and raw, frightened shavetails stripped for a fight worthy of the mighty Seventh U.S. Cavalry.

They prepared to ride into gloryland behind General George Armstrong Custer.

So now the Long Hair set off like a winter-gaunt wolf on a trail that smelled of snowshoe hare.

Into that scooped-out depression carved just behind the high ridges that rose up from the river, Custer led his five companies. Through the windless, suffocating coulees and red-eyed gullies, the dust stinging thickly in their nostrils by the time the last man loped up Custer's trail. From time to time they heard the bunching of low, resonant carbine shots creeping up the ridges from the river valley below. These soldiers riding behind the bluffs realized Reno's men were having themselves a hot time of it. All but the greenest of Custer's two hundred wished he himself were down with the major right about now having a go at the Sioux.

From the top of one of the coulees, Custer's men glanced down at the shining silvery river as they marched past. Reno's soldiers seen through the shimmering summer haze were mere specks on the green sward beyond, bugs scurrying back and forth, swallowed by dust and the gray blue of burnt powder smoke. The sight of that distant, impersonal battle was a bit more than some of the veterans and shavetails could take. Hearing now and then the booming reports of carbine and rifle fire was one thing—but seeing it firsthand . . . that was another altogether.

Some of those in Custer's command cheered spontaneously as they tromped along behind their leader's blue-and-crimson banner. Others cried out, allowing their weary, lathered mounts to have their heads for just a moment. One by one more soldiers joined in the raucous disorder, their horses charging out of formation around the head of the column. Up where Custer rode, leading them north.

"Hold your horses back, boys!" he shouted in a dust-ravaged voice. "Just hold 'em back for now! And don't worry—there's enough Indians down there for us all!"

By the saints, Lieutenant Cooke thought, riding beside his commander, *this has to be the finest fight you've ever taken part in, Billy Cooke! Reno's pounding hell out of 'em down there—and we'll slip behind 'em to hammer their asses to the ground.*

Custer reached over and slapped Cooke at that moment, clenching a fist in exuberance.

Damn, but my life bodes well now. Riding with Custer to glory. Beginning at the Washita, now along this river the Sioux call their Greasy Grass.

Custer turned in the saddle and waved, urging the troops out at a gallop this time, cutting more to his right, heading for the higher bluffs and ridges.

"These bluffs just might hide us from the villages below, Billy!" the general shouted above the clatter of hooves and the jangle of bit and saddle gear.

"Damn right, sir!" Cooke answered, every bit as lusty.

"I intend to surprise the warriors at the head of the village while Reno batters their feet," Custer explained, shouting above the hubbub, "But to do that, they must think Reno's attack is all there is."

Cooke turned for a last glimpse of the valley as Custer cut more sharply to the right again, far behind the bluffs. A last glimpse of the valley. What he saw was Mitch Bouyer and his Crow scout Curley, nodding gravely to one another.

Billy did not like the look on their copper faces at all.

What are they thinking? Cooke wondered. *Do they figure Custer's turning off from the attack . . . away from the river now?*

He watched the two exchange quick words, a few signs, before they both kicked their ponies into a faster lope to catch up to the columns.

Cooke felt the cold shaft of ice water spill down his spine as he turned away from those two copper faces clouded with doubt and confusion as they all followed Custer into the coarse, grassy bluffs ahead.

When the command was at last hidden behind the high ground, Tom Custer heard himself hailed ahead by his brother.

"Tom, get up here!"

He flushed, that scarlet spot on his cheek from Saylor's Creek blushing beneath his excitement. "Yeah, Autie?"

"Choose one of your trusted men. . . ." Custer looked

away from Tom, staring down their back trail. "I want you to have him send a message back to the pack train."

As soon as Custer had finished his instructions, Tom whirled and tore away, headed back to his C Company.

"Sergeant Knipe! Need you to ride back to the pack train."

Daniel Knipe grew mule-eyed. "Sir?"

"Hurry back to McDougall. Tell the captain to rush his pack train along, directly across country to our position. He must come now. And if some of the packs come loose, he has the general's orders to cut them loose and leave 'em behind. He must come on at all haste. Quick, Sergeant! There's a big Indian village directly ahead of us. Tell McDougall that! And if you spot Benteen down there, tell that sonuvabitch to hurry his ass up here too!"

"Yes, sir!" Knipe answered. He jammed his square-toed jackboots more snugly in the oxbow stirrups for the hard ride he would have of it over broken country. He short-reined his mount, twisting away, but young Custer suddenly seized his bridle.

"Sergeant!" Tom hollered into Knipe's face with the sour smell of stale whiskey. "Remember to tell him—it's a *big* village."

"Will do, sir!"

Knipe sawed his reins again. The animal leapt forward as if it had been shot, its rider raking the big heaving flanks with his spurs. Sergeant Knipe was on his way back to the pack train. Only once did he glance back over his shoulder for a last look at those five companies of soldiers and friends, their bright bandannas and glittering carbines flashing beneath a midday sun.

Not much farther along the jagged bluffs, Custer scanned the ground to his left.

"Hoping to find a place where I can see Reno's fight," the general explained to Tom and Cooke at his side.

"I see it, Autie," Tom said, pointing. "That flat table, jutting out into the valley looks like the spot."

Custer twisted in the saddle, ordering a halt and waving for Keogh to come up. The four galloped eagerly to the edge of the bluff.

From this high point Custer studied the valley below through field glasses. "Strange," he muttered absently, the glasses clamped against his red, burning eyes. "Very strange. I can't see a single warrior in that village. I wonder where they all could be. . . ."

"Let me have a look at it, General?" Cooke inquired, taking the glasses.

Little did Custer and the others realize that the only village they could see was the Northern Cheyennes', the others hidden by the tall cottonwoods along the Little Bighorn.

"What do you make of it, Myles?" Tom handed the glasses to Keogh after he had scanned the lodges, wickiups, and camp smoke of the distant village.

"Appears to be nothing more than a camp of women and children." Cooke scratched a long sideburn.

"Where'd all them goddamned bloody warriors come from?" Keogh growled. "The friggin' bastards what are giving Reno hell down there?"

"I suppose they're only the camp guard," Tom replied. "The warriors left behind while all the others gone out to hunt buffalo—"

"Buffalo?" Keogh spouted.

"That's right, you stupid, thick-headed Mick!" Tom barked with a slap to Keogh's shoulder. "Remember? That skinned carcass we ran across yesterday."

The dark Irishman nodded. "Ahhh, yes. The buggers're out hunting, aren't they, Tommy me boy? Leaving the home fires under the care of the camp guard."

"A most reasonable assumption, fellas," Custer added, putting the field glasses to his eyes once more.

The Cheyenne village popped into focus for him again. Only now the camp was in motion, women and children scurrying to and fro, hurrying west from the village, scampering into the meadowlands and rolling hills stretching toward the Bighorns. Other figures wrangled ponies into camp or were loading travois.

"Damn! They're tearing down and fixing to escape as we speak!" Custer jammed the Austrian binoculars into his saddlebags. "Best we get down there now and make a crossing so we can get a noose around that village before it slips off on us."

"Damn right," Tom agreed. "That weak-kneed bastard Reno has botched his attack. The frigging Sioux got him penned down while the village escapes."

"The second-oldest trick in the Indian book," Cooke said.

"And the first?" Tom asked.

Cooke swung a fist at young Custer's shoulder. "Sucking the army into an ambush with a decoy, you stupid, whiskey-fogged poltroon!"

Tom swung back playfully as Custer pulled Vic off the bluff.

"C'mon, boys," the general shouted. "I must get down there and now! My worst fear is that the Sioux have already slipped through my grasp!"

"Don't worry about a goddamned thing, Autie!" Tom cried. "We'll go capture the village, and when the warriors return, they'll have to surrender to us without a shot! We'll have their women and children as hostages!"

"Capital idea, Tommy!" Cooke cried.

"And this time, Autie," Tom said as he galloped up beside his older brother, "*I'll* take me a pretty Injun squaw to warm my robes!"

Keogh and Cooke laughed along with young Custer, but the general was too far into his battle plans to care that he had been made the butt of his brother's joke. Everything as clear as rinsed crystal now: north to capture the village . . . as all the pieces fell into place.

What Custer and his officers simply didn't realize at that moment was that most of the warriors in the camps below, who were only then receiving the news of Reno's attack, had been sleeping off a long night of dancing and celebrating over their recent victory against Red Beard Crook.

"By God's own back teeth, boys!" Custer shouted. "We've caught them napping!"

As he galloped back to his five companies waiting impatiently for action, the three officers close on Vic's heels, Custer stood in the stirrups, shouting, "Hurraw, boys! We'll get these Sioux in a blink of an eye! And soon as we've thumped 'em soundly, we'll go back to our station!"

"Lincoln! Lincoln! Lincoln!" yelled those ready for a victorious homecoming.

CHAPTER 20

As the cheering died, the dusty soldiers in Custer's five companies listened. The low booms of the trapdoor carbines were swallowed up by the higher crack of Henry and Winchester repeaters down in the valley.

A matter of heartbeats more, and that carbine fire started moving south—no longer driving north in the direction of Reno's attack.

"Cooke!" Custer wheeled Vic. "Dammit, man—follow me! The rest of you—prepare to move out at a charge on my return!" He raked his spurs into the sorrel's flanks viciously.

Something cold in Billy Cooke's guts told him he had better start worrying. Not just the sounds rising from the fight in the valley. But that cloud crossing Custer's face. *Custer knows*, Cooke thought. *He knows.*

The general skidded to a halt on the bluff once again, straining his eyes directly below, to his left. South. And for the very first time he saw the rest of the village.

"How'd we miss them before?" he muttered to Cooke, wagging his head. "In haste."

"Or hope, General," Billy replied.

"But there they are . . . hidden for the most part."

Even with his naked eyes, as red and tired and strained as Custer's, the adjutant could pick out some of the blanket-covered wickiups along the river.

More frightening still was the sight of the riders racing out of that thick timber after Reno's retreating cavalry—hundreds of warriors in a yellow cloud of dust, waving their blankets and robes. Naked for the most part. Brandishing rifles or lances, bows and pistols. From every throat rose a horrendous war cry as they spilled across the open ground toward the retreating draggle of Reno's demoralized soldiers.

Like hornets spilling out of an overturned nest, massing for the kill.

"My God!" Custer sputtered under his breath, hand at his silky mustache in frustration.

"What now, General?" Cooke swallowed, stoically straightening himself in the saddle.

Custer gazed at him with those cold blue eyes. "This village is bigger than anything . . . why, it's as big as our bloody scouts tried to tell me!"

Cooke watched him blink repeatedly, trying to clear his eyes of the stinging tears of anger clouding his vision.

"What now, you ask?" Custer repeated Cooke's question. He grit his teeth together, as if chewing some tough piece of jerky, something even harder to swallow.

Then Custer answered himself and Cooke both. "We proceed with our attack, Mr. Cooke. Just as planned."

The general yanked off his big hat, hoping someone below, some officer would see him high atop this ridge, would realize that though Custer's five companies were not charging in direct support of Reno's men, that Custer's troops were preparing to leap into the fray nonetheless—to pull the major's butt out of the fire.

Maybe some man below would see him waving . . . and know Custer wanted them to pull back to a single defensive position until he came up with support.

"Bring up the pack train. Yes." he said. "The pack train and Benteen. By god, bring Benteen up!"

Back and forth in the dry, hot air he waved that huge, cream-colored hat for them all to see. Not waving goodbye as many below would think. But, waving as if to say:

"Stop, you damned fools! Hold up and defend yourselves! By god—we'll come! Ride right through hell if we have to . . . but—we're coming! *We're coming!*"

As Custer yanked Vic back toward the columns, his guts felt about as heavy and cold as a stone. He needed that pack train to come up.

If McDougall will only race overland . . . he might make it here in time.

Custer realized as he raced back that his five companies would need that ammunition to make a stand of it so the pressure could be cut loose from Reno.

His eyes scoured the country ahead, measuring, considering, and deciding to take the five companies right behind him until he could find where to make a crossing and divert some of the warriors in his direction, taking pressure off the demoralized Reno forces.

And then he found it. A wide, shallow coulee, running to his left. *The river!*

Yes, in the direction of the river. *And at the mouth of a coulee, I can find a ford! By jiggers, this is a godsend . . . a bloody miracle!*

Sawing the big mare's head hard to the left, Custer led his column-of-twos down into the wide coulee to that rhythmic clatter of iron-shod hoofs on hard-baked ground, to that familiar jingle and clink of harness, to that hard squeak of dry McClellans.

Reassuring sounds to an old soldier.

Two by two by two . . .

The five companies turned quarter flank and left oblique, following their general down Medicine Tail Coulee until at last they could see the first glimmer of the river below. That's when the first shots whistled overhead; that's when the first arrows hissed past, smacking a horse here and there.

To their right, above the columns on the sage-covered

hillside, pranced half-a-hundred naked warriors, stripped for action in the tall grass. All round Custer the yelling broke out, confused and frightened men shouting, swamping the hard-boiled, calming orders of the veterans. He had to get a grip on the men before the raw ones broke.

"Captain Keogh!" Custer bellowed, racing back along the columns until he reached the Irishman. "Dismount your battalion! Fall behind the horses! Skirmish by fours!"

"Aye, General! 'Bout gawdamned time I give these bleeming bastards a what-for!" Keogh raged.

Custer turned away as Keogh's and Calhoun's companies dropped from their horses at the rear of the march, every fourth man holding four mounts while the other three soldiers jogged a distance up the northern slope of Medicine Trail Coulee. There under Keogh's command on the left and Calhoun's command farther up the slope on the right, the order to fire in volleys rose above the clamor of confusion and pain.

"First platoon! *Fire!*" Keogh shouted, arm waving as he moved amid his riflemen.

"Second platoon! *Fire! By God, Fire!*" Jimmy Calhoun hollered every bit as loudly.

"Cut the bastards apart!" Keogh screamed, flecks of spittle dotting his red lips he wiped now, wishing for a drink.

"We'll butcher the sonsabitches, Myles!" Calhoun shouted back to his partner.

"Teach 'em what-for, we will, Jimbo!"

Volley after volley fired into the Indian position as the warriors spread out a bit more, dropping back uphill, a bit more concealed. Then some more heads appeared over the rise. More arrived from beyond the top of the ridge. Halfway again to a hundred of them now.

Custer's mind worked quickly as he galloped back to the head of the columns where Tom, Yates, and Smith waited. *Better not get yourself pinned down here in this bloody coulee . . . you'll never get out. Just get Benteen back here. He's the one who can help.*

"*Tom!*" he yelled. Just seeing Tom's bright, smiling face, his eyes alive with the glory of the coming fight, did his heart good.

"By God, Autie—we're going to cut them up today!" Tom tore up, skidding a dusty cascade over his older brother.

His blue eyes darted round. "Cooke, get me Martini!"

"Trumpeter!" The Canadian wheeled about, shouting.

The Italian bugler nudged his horse forward from Yates's command, halted before the general, saluting. He had stayed close to Custer, as ordered, assigned to duty under the general's banner for the day.

"Trumpeter, you're charged with carrying a vital message!" Custer blurted it out, not remembering John Martini had enough trouble with English as it was, much less stuttered, angry English. The words continued like a Gatling gun of speech. "Get back to Benteen as fast as you can ride. Tell him to come on quick and bring the packs of ammunition from the train. We've got a big village, and we'll need his support."

Adjutant Cooke chewed his thirst-swollen tongue as he listened to Custer's sour prediction of their odds at coming out of the fight. As quickly Cooke realized bugler Martini would never remember the whole message, much less understand it to the point of spitting it back for Benteen or McDougall.

Meanwhile a numbed and very frightened Martini nodded dumbly at the general, saluted, and turned to dash off blindly on his mission.

Cooke caught the bugler up short. "Martini! Hold there! Just a minute, boy!" he barked, ripping open his shirt pocket and tearing out a small tablet on which he scribbled his message with the short nub of a pencil.

Pressing the notebook down on a knee, Cooke rammed the pencil across the page, finishing his desperate plea, then tore the page from his tablet.

> *Benteen:*
> *Come on. Big village.*
> *Be quick. Bring packs.*
> *W. W. Cooke*
> *P.S. Bring Pacs.*

"Now get this to Captain Benteen. You go quick. Benteen. Ride fast!"

With a sharp nudge Cooke pushed Martini on his way.

The bugler's horse leapt round in a tight circle. He was gone up the far side of the coulee, away from the firing and confusion and noise and fear, riding as fast as his played-out horse could carry him.

"What's that all about, General?" Cooke asked, his attention snagged up the side of the coulee where Tom Custer berated Private Peter Thompson.

"Appears the horse has marched its last," Custer replied calmly as he studied the hilltop warriors harassing Keogh and Calhoun.

After Tom had ordered Private Thompson to abandon his played-out horse and make his way on foot back to the pack train, he reminded the young soldier to be sure he took along his extra ammunition. Best not to leave it on the horse still struggling in vain to rise on its front legs. Plain for any horseman to see the animal was done in from the intense heat and long march over the divide.

Terrified, the young private lumbered off to the south on foot, following in the dust of trumpeter Martini and obsessed with the vivid details of the dream that had troubled his sleep last night: Sioux surrounding troopers on their worn-out horses; screeching warriors lifting scalping knives and tomahawks above the bloody bodies of his butchered friends; the feel of an Indian's hot breath close at his neck as the Sioux raised his club above him.

Thompson shuddered, deciding to stay to the coulees. He was alone now. Alone except for the sun and sage . . . and the sounds of Reno's men being butchered on the slopes below.

Hell, Thompson thought. *I'm really alone after all.*

Most of the young, raw soldiers who had watched Thompson's ordeal now turned their attention back to the fight raging in the upper end of the Medicine Tail. They studied the older veterans, men such as Keogh and Calhoun, Fresh Smith and Sergeant Major Sharrow. Then those young recruits too dropped to tighten saddle cinches for a hard ride ahead. Perhaps even a hard fight of it should any more warriors pop over that rise to the north.

Up and down the line the green, uninitiated soldiers

completed that same mechanical process in the midst of the rifle fire and cursing, sure that this horse-work had to be part of some mystical ritual in preparation for battle.

It won't hurt, some of them thought. *Won't hurt at all to do just what the veterans do.*

"Bugler!" Custer called to Sergeant Voss. "'Boots and Saddles'! To horse, men!"

"Seventh Cavalry! Prepare to mount!" Cooke shouted after Voss blew his command.

Up and down the columns came the rattle of carbine and bit chain.

"Cooke! Get back to Keogh and Jimmy—have them hold the hillside for a bit more; then have them to break it off and follow, guarding the rear of our march. We're going into the village!"

"The village, General?" Cooke gasped.

"There," Custer pointed down the coulee at the tiny sliver of river they could see between the sides of the mouth.

"To the river, General."

"And, Billy," he barely whispered. "Tell them both to keep an eye on our backsides. What with all the new boys—see that we aren't cut up from behind until I have our position in the village assured."

"Rear guard, sir. Right. Until Benteen and McDougall come up."

He slapped a hand on Cooke's broad shoulder, staring up into the Canadian's handsome face. "You got it, soldier. Let's ride!"

Cooke twisted round in the saddle to fling his voice back at the columns of dusty blue. "Mount!"

Stretching up the neck of the Upper Medicine Tail Coulee, sergeants bawled their commands. "MOUNT!"

"We're riding down on 'em, boys!"

"MOUNT!"

"By God—it's what we've waited for!"

"MOUNT!"

"—right into hell if we have to!"

Behind those hundred twenty odd voices rustled and squeaked saddle leather as the troops pushed into their

McClellans and steadied their snorting, wide-eyed horses. It wasn't only the smell of water nearby that made the animals skittish. They must have sensed the growing tension in the air, felt that unfamiliar rigidity of the riders atop their backs. In some way those big, muscular horses knew the moment was at hand.

What they had been trained to do would now be put to the test.

Custer smiled grimly as he heard that reassuring sound of men and animals merging into one four-legged, double-fisted fighting machine.

His dust-reddened eyes hidden beneath the shadow of his big hat, he peered down the coulee at that narrow sliver of river.

The crossing, Autie. Just make it to the crossing. . . .

Down below was the ford where he could cross into the village, thereby drawing pressure from Reno in hopes that his five companies could push the warriors back. He had practiced the maneuver enough during the war, just the way his instructors at the academy had drilled it into his head. Just as the great Clausewitz had written. Indeed, all those great European masters of tactical warfare had preached the same thing.

You pinch an army at its waist, or better yet—nail an enemy's feet to the ground while you battered its head.

Too late now to pinch the village at its waist, Custer realized.

All that was left for him to do to save this campaign—and his destiny—was to hope that Reno occupied the Sioux downstream while his own five companies flailed at the head of the enemy camps. He sensed that head was right down this coulee at the ford of the Little Bighorn.

To do what he hoped would require fast action from both McDougall and Benteen. If there was the slightest delay by either one, his five companies would be swallowed—

"Mr. Cooke: troops—front into line!" he bellowed back at Cooke and the rest, Vic prancing round and round in a tight circle, her master tall in the stirrups, hat waving. "Seventh Cavalry . . . ahead by column-of-twos . . . *center guide*—at a gallop! *Forward—ho!*"

Mitch Bouyer heard Custer bellow the command, but he sat a moment watching as the soldiers burst away at a hand gallop. It had to be one thing or another, the half-breed scout decided.

Seeing the general's brother riding past, the half-breed heeled his Crow pony into motion, galloping alongside Tom.

"Bouyer!" young Custer hollered out, a wolf-slash smile cutting his face above the pointed blond beard.

"I tell you what I think of your brother."

Tom's smile disappeared. "What!"

"Either Custer's insane, or he's bent on committing suicide."

"You bastard!"

"And he's just mad enough to take a couple hundred men with him straight into hell."

"I swear you'll get—"

"Tom!" Custer shouted from the head of the columns, waving to bring his brother up beside him as they ground out of the upper Medicine Tail and down onto a flat leading toward the lower coulee that would take them directly to the river ford.

"For Reno . . . it can only be a footrace now!" he yelled at his younger brother when Tom reached his side.

"There's no fight left in the man!"

"We're going to attack with everything we have. Remember. Should anything happen—I'm counting on you. Always have, Tom."

"I know—"

"Hush!" Custer commanded. "Get back to Keogh and Calhoun. Remind them I'm counting on them too—to support the rear of the command. Whatever they do—guard our rear!"

As they raced into the neck of the lower Medicine Tail, the ford came into view. Beyond the river, over on the west bank, stood hundreds upon hundreds of lodges.

"May God have mercy on our souls, Autie!" Tom whispered under his breath as he yanked his horse around in a haunch-sliding circle that took him up the sharp side of the coulee. He kicked savagely at the animal so he could spur back to give Keogh and Calhoun Autie's message. They must know they were in charge of protecting the rear flank of Autie's wild, hopeful charge into the village.

"May God have mercy on our souls!" he repeated to himself, remembering those were the same words he whispered to himself before every battle of the Civil War, before every wild charge into the face of enemy grapeshot and minié balls.

May God have mercy on our souls!

With the Gatling-gun pounding of iron-shod hoofs, the three companies hammered down the last few yards of the Medicine Tail, accompanied only by the whine of dry leather and the harsh jangle of bit and crupper. Carbines cried out like tired wagon springs as they were yanked from their scabbards.

And above the leader whipped that proud banner: the blood crimson and summer-sky blue crossed by a pair of silver white sabers. Custer wanted the Sioux to know Peoushi—the Long Hair—had arrived.

CHAPTER 21

Few of the *wasichu* scouts and soldiers riding into Miniconjou ford had any idea how frighteningly accurate were the scouts' predictions of the strength of the Sioux village across the river.

Custer himself knew of the venal Indian agents falsifying their counts on official reports sent to Washington City to assure an uninterrupted westward flow of goods and annuities. Yet in that summer of 1876, the army could only begin to guess how far the agents would go to cover their tracks.

Instead of nine thousand six hundred ten Indians residing that summer at the Spotted Tail Agency, there were in reality only two thousand three hundred fifteen.

The rest were gone visiting friends and relatives in that great summer encampment along the Greasy Grass.

Instead of twelve thousand eight hundred seventy-three at Red Cloud, there were only four thousand seven hundred sixty.

Down at Cheyenne River only two thousand two hundred eighty instead of seven thousand five hundred eighty-six. And over at Standing Rock, where there should have been seven thousand three hundred twenty-two Sioux that summer, all but two thousand three hundred five had left to join Sitting Bull.

The warriors were gathering, their souls burning for the fight of Bull's mighty vision. Still they came, more warriors and families had arrived each day to join up until this greatest of all villages stretched for more than three miles up and down the valley of the Pa-zees-la-wak-pa.

Already better than fifteen thousand joyous celebrants sharing the old life in the valley of the Greasy Grass this last week of the *Moon When Chokecherries Grow Ripe*. Using the ages-old means of counting three warriors of fighting age for every one of those two thousand lodges, a man could easily see how any soldier's bowels could pucker to consider that in that camp slept, ate, danced, and courted something between forty-five hundred and six thousand warriors ready to carry arms against any invading army.

And of those, better than half were seasoned, hardened veterans of plains warfare.

Not only the veterans—every fighting male snarled for a fight. Every one with a father, brother, uncle, or cousin who had been killed by the soldiers. In every male boiled blood hot for those soldiers destined by the Dream to ride down on their camp circles. For if any army was brazen and foolish enough to march down on this greatest of all gatherings in Lakota history, this epic encampment would be the last sight to greet their terrified, death-glazed white eyes.

In those few days it had taken them to cross the divide after fighting Red Beard Crook, the Sioux learned of another army in the country. Scouts had seen the Fireboat-That-Walks-on-Water up on the Yellowstone for days now. Some had even noticed the dust of a large compliment of soldiers marching on the Rosebud where Crazy Horse had scattered Red Beard's forces a few days earlier.

And now on this balmy evening a crippled and leathery old Sans Arc village crier hobbled through his camp. As white men reckoned with time, it was a Saturday, the twenty-fourth of June, in the year of 1876. The crier's high, reedy voice sang out that unthinkable news.

"Soldiers are coming, people! Heed my words! The Dream says it is so. Soldiers come with tomorrow's sun!"

Neither the Sans Arc nor any other camp circle paid the old man any heed. Surely Crook or any other soldier-chief wouldn't be crazy enough to attack so large a gathering. It would be unthinkable. Yet more than a few did remember the details of Bull's vision.

The soldiers would fall into camp almost as if committing suicide.

Others had heard that scouts reported seeing dust clouds on the divide. Some saw trails of iron-shod hoofprints.

That afternoon leaders of the various bands decided it best to post camp sentries on those ridges and bluffs east of the river to prevent any glory-seeking young warriors from dashing headlong out of camp to hunt down soldiers. If an army was indeed coming to fight the Sioux, then let those pony soldiers march all the way into the camps as Sitting Bull had foretold.

No warrior had the right to capture glory for himself by striking the first coup and ruining The Bull's vision. Instead, the old men wanted this to be a battle to cloak the entire nation in glory and honor.

By sundown that warm Saturday evening, camp guards rode along the bony ridges east of the Greasy Grass like the spine of a sway-backed old mare. Soldiers were coming. Everyone knew. The words sat on every lip. Nervous and impatient, the Sioux and Cheyenne would have to wait for the army to ride down on their camps.

Up at the northern end of that village in the Cheyenne camp, four young warriors announced they would sacrifice themselves during the coming battle with the pony soldiers. As twilight settled over their Goat River, a dance and celebration got under way for Little Whirlwind, Close Hand, Cut Belly, and Noisy Walking. This was to be their last night on earth. Their last night among friends, they boasted before everyone in camp. Tomorrow they would give their lives in battle.

As the sun sank like a red-earth ache behind the distant

Bighorn Mountains, a solitary figure slogged out of the river on foot, trudging up that slope at the far northern end of the long ridge. Up from the fragrant thickets of crabapple and plum and wild rose, he climbed into the tall grass and wild buffalo peas. Not a one of the posted camp guards challenged the lone Hunkpapa chief come here to sing his thunder songs and pray for guidance now that his great vision was about to see fulfillment.

With a purple sky deepening to black out of the east, this short, squat man left behind little bags of tobacco and red-willow bark, each bag tied to a short peeled willow shaft he had jammed into the ground near the crest of that hill at the northern end of the pony-back ridge. His powerful thunder medicine told him that here on this most hallowed ground, the last desperate fight would take place.

Here on the knoll, Sitting Bull prayed his final blessing for those *wasichu* soldier souls soon to be sacrificed, given to propitiate the Great Powers of the mighty Lakota nations.

Dawn of the next day stretched over the valley of the Greasy Grass, and with the first pale light to the east along the brown, hoary caps of the Wolf Mountains, a high, shrieking death wail erupted through the sleepy Hunkpapa camp.

Four Horns, the wife of Sitting Bull's uncle, had died as this new day was born.

Filled not only with grief but with a renewed awe at the mysterious workings of the Great Powers, The Bull knew this woman's death presaged the great victory of his dream.

Far back into the memory of any of the old ones, it had been told that with the death of the wife of an important man would come a momentous event.

Sitting Bull closed his eyes and prayed again for those blessings he had asked on the hill above the river. From that very knoll the soldiers would see the entire village spread before them.

From that dry, grassy crest the troopers would see why the powerful Wakan Tanka had turned them over to the fury of the Sioux.

★   ★   ★

Farther north in the Oglalla camp, a Canadian half-breed who spoke passable English sat at a smoky dawn fire, refusing to lay his head down for sleep. Unlike most of the warriors, who had gone to their robes just before dawn, this nameless one sat staring into those yellow licks of flame darting along the dry cottonwood limbs, sensing the portent of some great event. What stirred him most already this cool gray morning was the strange behavior of Crazy Horse.

Before most battles the great war chief was normally composed and reserved. Not today as the sun was born again in the eastern sky. The Horse stomped in and out of his lodge many times: scurrying back and forth around his pony, checking and rechecking his personal weapons, and repeatedly inspecting the war medicine he carried in a small pouch tied behind an ear.

With grease and a vermilion pigment, the war chief mixed his paints, plastering a brilliant handprint on each of the war pony's hips for speed this day. On one side of the animal's neck he drew a dripping scalp lock, on the other side his fingertip traced out a bloodied arrow.

Filled with nervous energy, he went for a ride to other nearby camp circles yet returned a short time later. In and out of his lodge he paced again.

Something refused to release its grip on his spirit. Something that told him this would be a day like none other before . . . or ever to be again.

Crazy Horse's most important fight was at hand.

A Miniconjou warrior called High Pipe drew himself from the icy water of the Greasy Grass and stood shivering beneath the first licks of sunlight breaking over the Mountains of the Wolf. When his morning prayer was spoken, and the air had warmed his body, the warrior strode back to his camp circle, finding his uncle, Hump, anxiously awaiting him.

"You must collect your horses, High Pipe," the old man solemnly advised, dark eyes darting suspiciously to that bony ridge east of the river.

"Why, Uncle?"

"Something is going to happen this day," Hump asserted. "Bring your horses into camp so your wives can pack them when trouble begins."

"Uncle, there are plans to move the camp circle today," High Pipe soothed, a hand on the old man's shoulder. "Farther north some, toward the country of the antelope. The Cheyenne lead the way. There is no need for alarm."

"Something bad will happen!" the old man protested, not understanding his nephew's sense of calm.

"What, Uncle? Tell me what you see."

"Many dead. Much blood. More than any one man has ever seen with two eyes! And I hear our people crying out in joy and sadness—both." Hump wagged his head and stared at the ridge.

"A day for celebrating, yet a day we will long remember with a stone of sadness upon our hearts."

Blackfoot Sioux chief Red Horse had awakened his lodge early and taken the women and children of relatives into the meadows and hills west of their own camp circle. There they would spend the long summer morning using antler-digging tools hunting for *tipsina*, a tasty wild turnip root filled with starch.

From those hills of their digging, they would eventually notice the dust cloud suspended above the soldiers marching north along the pony-back ridge east of the river.

And know that Bull's mighty vision had come to pass.

A wizened Cheyenne mystic named Box Elder had been troubled all night by a recurring dream in which he watched an advancing regiment of pony soldiers marching down off the ridges to the east of the river toward the Cheyenne camp. Again and again that same dream plagued him each time Box Elder closed his eyes to fall asleep.

At dawn he hobbled from lodge to lodge among his relatives and friends, warning them of what he had seen in his troubling dream. Some kept their mouths shut, while others chuckled behind his back as he tottered off to spread the tale.

But some Cheyenne "Crazy Dog" warriors openly howled

like rabid wolves at the old man—the supreme insult showing they believed the old man had finally gone mad, and it would be best if he was taken into the hills and left for wolf bait.

Since the great camp would be making another short march this day, some of the Cheyenne women had begun to dismantle their lodges and slowly pack household goods for the impending trek.

Monaseetah kept one eye on her older boy as he played with young friends near the lodge. Her younger, Yellow Bird, never wandered far. He clutched her skirt as the parade of four brave young warriors snaked its way through the Northern Cheyenne camp. Cut Belly and Noisy Walking, Close Hand and Little Whirlwind, marching proudly behind the camp crier, who sang out that these four boys would die in glory this day, die protecting their village.

"People! Look at these!" the old man cried that bright, cool morning. "You will not set eyes on them again. They go away to die this day! Never more will you look at them!"

Miles away up the Greasy Grass in the Hunkpapa camp, Rain-in-the-Face attended a late-morning feast at the lodge of a venerated old warrior. A few bites had been taken when they heard the first rattle of rifle fire and knew those many shots came not from Sioux guns. The rifles must belong to *wasichu* soldiers.

"They are coming into camp!" the great war chief Rain hollered as he leapt to his feet, swinging aloft the stone war club he carried at all times. "The Bull has told it. His dream has come to pass. The soldiers fall into our camp!"

Dashing back to his lodge, Rain snatched up his rifle, a bow and quiver filled with rosewood arrows, before leaping atop his favorite pony. Many of his friends clustered round him as they raced toward the valley action, catching but a brief glimpse of another group of soldiers loping north along the ridge beyond the river.

In a moment Rain's Hunkpapa warriors overtook a young woman named Tashenamini, or Moving Robe. This did not startle Rain in the least, for she had rescued her brother's body from the Red Beard battle a week before. Ever since

that time the Hunkpapas had called the Rosebud fight
"The Battle Where the Girl Saved Her Brother."

Rain smiled, singing out a blood-chilling greeting to the
young girl. She brandished her dead brother's coup stick
above her head, shouting again that she would avenge his
death this day.

"Many soldiers will fall!" she screamed into the noise
and the dust. "There will be much blood on my hands
before the sun has crossed this sky."

With a deep sense of pride, Rain bellowed a war cry for
all to hear. "Fear this pretty bird, *wasichu* soldiers! She may
be pretty as a sparrow, but she carries the talons of a war
eagle!"

"Behold!" shouted another. "A pretty bird rides among
us!"

Rain's grim smile broadened. The beautiful unmarried
girl would make his young men fight all the harder.

One final warning before Rain and his warriors reached
the soldiers falling headfirst into the Hunkpapa camp.

"Beware that no man hides behind her skirts!"

Just as Sitting Bull had dreamed that potent vision of his,
soldiers were falling into the Hunkpapa camp circle.

Unbelievable.

If the village had truly believed they would be attacked
by soldiers, perhaps more of them would have torn down,
packed up, and tramped off without delay during the
morning hours. Yet the only lodges coming down were
those belonging to families who wanted to get an early head
start on the day's journey down the valley. Another five or
eight miles more toward the Yellowstone.

So no more than a handful of women in each circle
busied themselves pulling their lodge skins from the poles
when pony soldiers charged toward the south end of camp.

As word spread through the villages, pandemonium and
confusion and fear raced on its heels like prairie fire along
the Greasy Grass. Women shrieked, children cried, and the
old ones wailed. And in the middle of it, war ponies
neighed and whinnied while warriors shouted their prayers
aloft into the singing air: Sioux praying to Wakan Tanka and

the young Cheyenne men to their Everywhere Spirit Above.

Dashing like water-striders across the flat surface of a pond, women scurried about to locate their children. Likewise the little ones darted in and around lodges, shrieking for their mothers. Amid the din, the old and the infirm struggled, hobbling along on their own if they could. Everyone beginning to head west, escaping from the camp circles. West, toward the hills and safety.

"Take what you can carry and flee before the pony soldiers ride into camp!"

With their frightened children in tow, the women yanked down their husband's most potent medicine bags and sacred objects to go with them into the western hills. No white soldiers must defile the power of their men.

Heralds scooted back and forth through the eight camp circles, shouting their news and mystical omens, raising their shrill and magical wishes for those young ones heading south into the fight. Hand-held drums throbbed their primitive beat as eagle wing-bone whistles sent an ear-piercing cry to the hot summer sky overhead.

In all the frightening noise and confusion, there nonetheless arose some sense of ages-old order: The women and children and frail ones must escape. Staying behind, the warriors would hold off the attack, giving those weaker ones a chance to flee.

"Will the pony soldiers stop at nothing?"

Each time the white man attacked, he threw his soldiers against a village of women and children . . . against the sick, tired, old ones.

"What kind of beast is this wasichu *anyway? What kind of savage makes war on women and children . . . and those ready to die?"*

Young Hunkpapa warrior One Bull drove his ponies east toward the river for morning watering, herding them in from their pasture, when he heard the first shots. Not too far to the south.

Leaping atop a pony bareback and gripping its mane with both hands in the shape of a narrow vee, he dashed into the camp circle to find the circle already in a wild disarray. Shouting and dust and screaming and a flurry of mad activity.

"One Bull!"

Turning, he saw Sitting Bull emerge from his tall red-and-black lodge, carrying a shield and stone war club.

"Give me your rifle, young one," the chief ordered quietly.

Obediently One Bull handed over his old muzzle loader. "Yes, Uncle."

"You will ride with these into battle, One Bull," the Hunkpapa mystic declared evenly. "My shield and my war club are my symbols of authority, my power in battle. Take these in my place and go meet the soldiers. Talk with them, if they will talk, so we can end this killing. Tell them I will talk peace to save the lives of our children. Go now! You carry the power of your chief. Lead your men wisely, Nephew!"

The young warrior leapt on The Bull's pony secured with a rawhide bridle and let fly a shrill war cry. He held high the coveted war shield of Sitting Bull, then vaulted away, leading close to a hundred warriors into the skirmish with Reno's charging troops.

After he watched the warriors gallop off to the fight, Sitting Bull buckled on his leather cartridge belt, stuffing an old cap-and-ball revolver in the holster. He then took up his Winchester carbine.

Yet before he would fight this day, The Bull knew he must find his old mother. He tore off into the choking dust kicked up by a thousand hooves galloping out of the Hunkpapa village. Before his eyes his own mystic vision swam with frightening reality.

At the center of all the screeching pandemonium, some camp guards were busy at their important task. One at a time the buffalo-hide sections of the huge Teton Sioux council lodge came down from their poles. It would not do to let the enemy cast their defiling eyes on this sacred lodge. As each section was bundled, it was hefted aboard the back of a pony and the animal led west into those coulees and hills, where the white soldiers would not find the lodge.

Past this calm, deliberate crew of Hunkpapa guards raced a middle-aged Cheyenne warrior, holding aloft a blue jacket he had stripped from one of the first soldiers killed as Reno began his frantic retreat into the timber at the river. Stone Calf wanted his Sioux cousins to see this battle trophy—and remember well.

"Look, my friends!" he bellowed with rage. "Heed this marking on the pony soldier's clothing!"

His gnarled finger pointed out the crossed sabers and that 7 nestled atop their apex.

"This is a good day for the Shahiyena, my cousins!" he roared. "A good day for the Cheyenne!"

A crowd of the curious gathered, slowing their dash to the battle or their flight into the hills for a moment to listen to the old Cheyenne's story.

"These soldiers are the same who attacked my village— when Black Kettle camped us along the Washita many years ago! *Aiyeee!* These are the very same pony soldiers who killed my mother! The ones who butchered my wife and children when they could not escape the soldier bullets that winter dawn before the sun rose above the blood and stink of our dead people! I have been alone since these soldiers murdered my family!"

Shouts of praise and wails of despair arose all round Stone Calf as he continued. "This day my heart is once again made whole. The *circle* is complete, my cousins! The *circle* begun on the Washita is now made whole once more!"

"Hear it! The *circle* is healed!" roared another warrior who took the bloody cavalry blouse from Stone Calf and brandished it aloft on his rifle.

A woman raised a fiery limb from her midday cookfire, torching the torn blue tunic. Once flames enveloped it, the blouse fell in shreds to the ground amid cheers and shouts of both Sioux and Cheyenne celebrating the thrashing given those white soldiers down in the timber at the river.

"Let us go show these soldiers what we do to evil men who attack a village of women and children!" one woman shrieked, in one hand brandishing a bloody knife and in the other an old cap-and-ball revolver. "Women! Do not run. We will fight and die alongside our men!"

Before she could lead the throng away, an Oglalla horseman galloped up and reined in his pony, cascading dust over them all.

"More horse soldiers!" he rasped hoarsely, pointing to the sun-bleached ridges to the east beyond the river. "More soldiers riding on the hills above! Come fight, or they will overrun the villages!"

"Where?" many asked, panic rising in their voices.

"We cannot see any horse soldiers!" an old man declared with some sarcasm.

"This is only wild talk," someone suggested. "Come, we must go kill those soldiers cowering in the timber to the south!"

"Wait! *Aiyeee!* It is true! Look!" a woman screamed, pointing at the grassy hills across the river.

Pouring out of the mouth of the upper Medicine Tail Coulee and into the lower gully that reached all the way to the Greasy Grass itself, rode a long column of pony soldiers.

"Soldiers come!" The Oglalla messenger beat frantic heels against his pony's flanks and tore off to carry his warning to the north.

"We must stop these soldiers," one of the Santee Sioux warriors shouted, rallying those around him. "To the ford! We will cut off their charge!"

As most of this crowd dashed off toward the river, a small, ugly mob rumpled into camp from south of the Hunkpapa circle. These Santees had just captured an old friend who long ago had married a Santee woman. Now that this prisoner rode with the pony soldiers, the Sioux realized they had every right to consider Isaiah Dorman a traitor.

A big black-skinned Arikara interpreter, Dorman begged for his captors to kill him quickly and be done with it, savvy enough to know what fate awaited him if they did not.

"Just kill me now and throw me away! Kill me!" he shouted in Sioux at his tormentors.

Instead, one of the Santee men spit into his shiny black face and rubbed his spittle on the soldier's eyes.

"You do not deserve to die like a man, *Teat!*" a warrior shouted Dorman's Santee name, given him because of the dark color to his skin, like a nursing mother's nipple.

"Instead, we will give you over to the women for their amusement. A traitor like you deserves no better than a camp dog's death." He turned to the women. "Tie him to a tree!"

After they lashed Dorman's arms and legs to a cotton-wood so he could not fall, they started using the soldier for target practice. The Santees filled his legs with so many bullets, he could no longer stand, collapsing suspended against his rope bindings. Only then did the archers begin their grisly work. Again and again they fired arrows into Dorman's body, but none of them enough to kill him right off.

"We don't want you to die quickly—not the death of an honorable man," an old man growled into the black face shiny with beads of sweat and pain. "You must die like a dog butchered for the pot. I want to hear you whine and whimper!"

When at last they cut him down from his tree, the Santees dragged the black soldier onto the prairie, where they stretched his body out among the hills of a prairie-dog town. Here the squaws continued their gruesome work, hacking little pieces of black-pink flesh from arms or legs or chest, bleeding him into tin cups that they repeatedly poured into an old blackened and battered coffee pot.

"*Wasichu sapa* must die slow!" one old hag spat into his face. "Black white man must die hard!"

In the midst of his painful torture, Isaiah Dorman harkened back to that last morning at Fort Lincoln, remembered his Santee wife tearfully telling him of her nightmare, begging him not to ride with Custer.

Now all the Negro soldier could do was die alone. His was a one-man job if ever there was one. Isaiah didn't have the strength to cry out anymore, not with all the pain he had to endure, not with all the blood seeped from his body, drop by tormented drop.

Dorman just didn't have the strength to do anything but die. And he did that just as bravely as he could.

Oglalla warrior White-Cow-Bull had stayed up into the early morning hours celebrating with the others their victory over Red Beard Crook.

His head ached from too little sleep and too much dancing as he lumbered up from the timber by the river, where he kept his wickiup with other young bachelors. The Cow wandered to a fire tended by an old woman, its greasy smoke rising to the hazy midmorning sun that boded a sultry summer day.

"Old woman," he declared as he stood over her hunched skeletal form, "give me some food."

For a long moment she stared up into the sunlight at the warrior, blinking her moist, rheumy eyes. Among the Sioux it was custom for young warriors without families of their own to be fed by those they supplied with camp meat. She-Runs-Him recognized White-Cow-Bull and speared some chunks of meat from her battered kettle for his breakfast.

"This day the attackers come to our village," she slurred, gumming the words from a toothless mouth as she presented him the steamy bowl.

"How is it you know this, Grandmother?" he addressed her in polite form.

"I know no more but what I see behind my eyes," she answered before disappearing into her lodge.

He knew she would not put her head out until he had finished his breakfast and was gone.

With nothing better to do this late morning, the young Oglalla determined to ride north to the Cheyenne camp in hopes of catching a glimpse of Monaseetah. When she had refused his offer of marriage, her words hurt like the cut of the Sun Dance knife—yet, if he tried again, perhaps he still might win her.

He must convince her that her soldier-husband would never return for her. It had been far too long already. Seven years should be long enough to wait for anyone. The soldier's son waited all this time at his mother's side.

Long enough to wait for any man—especially for a lying *wasichu* soldier.

"Let me help you with that," the Cow declared when he found Monaseetah dragging some deadfall up from the river with Yellow Bird at her side.

"I can manage." She smiled the brave, pretty smile of hers that lit up her face. "I have learned to manage on my own."

Rebuffed in a gentle way, White-Cow-Bull turned off to visit Roan Bear, a Cheyenne friend who this day as a member of the Fox clan was in charge of guarding his camp circle. The Bear sat protecting the lodge where his Northern Cheyenne people kept their Sacred Medicine Hat made of the hide of a buffalo head and its horns. While the Southern Cheyenne revered their holy Medicine Arrows, these northern cousins revered the Hat.

In the welcome shade of that sacred lodge, Roan Bear and White-Cow-Bull, proven warriors both, shared again their favorite war stories and tales of a first pony raid. Above their laughter the sharp crack of rifle shots came from the south on the dry breeze.

Both leapt to their feet about the time a young Oglalla rode into camp shouting.

"Pony soldiers! Pony soldiers! They attack the Hunk-papa circle! Come! Come help in Sitting Bull's vision!"

"We go!" The Cow shouted, grabbing his friend's shoulder.

"No," Roan Bear answered softly. "My duty is with the Medicine Hat. Because of the danger, I must take it far away to the prairie beyond the pony herd. There it will be safe from our enemy dirtying it. Only when another Fox warrior comes to relieve me, can I go fight the soldiers. Only when I know the Hat is safe, can I offer myself in battle as a Crazy Dog."

"Look here at the old one!" White-Cow-Bull pointed out the Cheyenne chief, Lame-White-Man, who rushed past with nothing but a small blanket wrapped at his waist.

"I was taking a sweat bath," the middle-aged chief announced with a self-conscious smile. "I do not have time to braid my hair, nor do I even take time to dress. With my rifle and this belt to hold my blanket up, I am ready to fight the pony soldiers."

"Go, old man!" Roan Bear exhorted. "Go and fight well this day!"

"Bear!" a young Fox warrior cried out, loping out. He carried an old smoothbore muzzle loader.

"Sleeps Late? Have you come to carry the Medicine Hat far from the evil ones?"

"Yes," he answered breathlessly, eyes blinking in the dust many others stirred up. "If you wish to fight, I will carry the Hat into the hills for our people. I would consider it a great honor, brother. A great honor to protect the Hat from our enemies."

"Go then, little brother." Bear handed the teenage warrior a fur-wrapped bundle enclosing the sacred object. "Protect it with your life."

Sleeps Late stopped and turned after a few steps. "Protect our village, Roan Bear. Protect our people with your life."

"*Aiyeee!*" Bear's voice rose above the tall cottonwoods with the power of a war eagle. "This is so, Sleeps Late! It is a good day to die!"

"*Nutskaveho!*" Cheyenne war chief Two Moons rushed by, leading his war pony he always kept tethered at his lodge. "White soldiers on the hills above! Run for your horses! Run for your horses!"

"What is this?" Roan Bear yelled at the chief.

"More soldiers are coming!" Two Moons shouted back over his shoulder. "Some fight the Hunkpapas, and now the others come to attack our own camp circle! *Nutskaveho!*"

The Cheyenne camp belched free its young warriors to join the valley fight near the Hunkpapa village as soldiers dismounted in the timber along the river. Roan Bear and White-Cow-Bull for the first time saw the two long columns of soldiers ride off the ridge into the upper Medicine Tail Coulee. Heartbeats later gunfire erupted, echoing from the coulee itself.

In the time it would take to kindle a pipe, the two young warriors watched the soldiers who led drop from their horses to return fire, then remount.

"*Nahetso!* They will ride straight into our camp if they cross the ford!" Roan Bear shouted at two of his young friends, throwing an arm up to show the pair those soldiers riding down from the hills, coming in their direction.

"If they cross, they will sweep our people away as the warm chinooks eat the winter snows!" Bob-Tail-Horse replied, knowing exactly what needed to be done. "We must guard the ford!"

"You cannot!" old man Mad Wolf hobbled up, crippled with age. "There are too many pony soldiers coming down to the river. We need help. You must go to the Sioux camps and tell them of the other soldiers coming to cross the river. You four cannot do this alone, Nephew! Those pony soldiers will kill you!"

"Perhaps," Bob-Tail-Horse replied calmly, a look of serenity crossing his face, giving it a strange light. "But only the heavens and the earth last forever, Uncle! A warrior is called upon to fight for his people and to give his life up for the Powers when he is called. Only the earth and sky will last. We who are warriors must die!"

"Hey! Hey! *Naonoatamo! Naonoatamo!* We honor you! We respect your bravery!" his three companions shouted as the four dashed toward the river crossing at Medicine Tail Coulee.

As soon as young Big Face tossed the old muzzle loader up to Bob-Tail-Horse, this oldest of the Cheyenne warriors galloped off toward the crossing. When they broke from the trees, the four were confronted with a flat, grassy bank that ran some twenty yards down to the river. Scattered across this grassy lip lay a jumble of cottonwood deadfall. As the warriors dropped from their ponies, three Crow on horseback appeared on the high bluff across the river, just above the ford itself.

"There are our enemies!" Bob-Tail-Horse exhorted his companions. "Shoot them, my brothers! Rip the wings from those Sparrowhawks!"

With the old muzzle loader he alone lobbed a shot up at the bluff. Before any of the others could fire their weapons, the fluttering tips of soldier flags were seen racing down the bottom of the coulee, while the air filled with that noisy rattle of shod hooves and soldier saddles.

"May you Sparrowhawks die a thousand endless deaths for bringing the soldiers down upon our women and children!" Roan Bear hurled his curse at the Crow scouts, who watched the soldiers approach the ford.

With the momentary appearance of the soldiers at the mouth of the coulee, the young Cheyenne warrior did a brave and provocative act: After handing his rifle away, Roan Bear turned his back to the three Crow horsemen and pulled his breechclout aside to expose his buttocks. It was a universal way to show what he thought of his enemies— daring the Crows to shoot him while he was disarmed and taunting them by presenting a round, and most inviting, target.

Then he challenged them further, shouting, telling the Crows what Cheyenne women would do to them once they got their hands on such despicable dogs unworthy of the title of warrior. At that moment Roan Bear had no more time to worry himself with the Crows.

The soldier column rattled to a noisy halt at the ford seconds before the lead horseman plunged his big, blaze-faced sorrel into the cool waters of the Greasy Grass.

This brave one riding in the front wore buckskin britches and had atop his head a big-brimmed hat that shielded his pink, sunburned face. Right behind the leader rode two others, both carrying small flags that snapped in the warm breeze.

With a jerky wave of his arm, the man on the big stocking-footed sorrel shouted something over his shoulder to his soldiers, urging them into the ford.

A mighty, chilling sound rose from the throats of those white men streaming down out of the coulee as they followed their leader into the river.

As quickly, another noisy challenge sailed across the river from the lips of those brave four who had chosen to sacrifice their lives at the crossing. Their shrill cries filled the air as they stared down the barrels of their weapons and knew only they could stem this cavalry charge. If the soldiers made it across the river and pushed through the undefended village, they would have the Indian forces cut in half. Defeat of the tribes would be assured.

One choice only—to turn the soldiers somehow, to force them back across the river until more warriors could come up. These four could not allow the pony soldiers to cross the Goat River and gain its western bank.

How pink and hairy these white soldiers are! The Cow marveled, gazing at the buckskinned cavalry leader splashing into the water, the white-stocking legs of his sorrel spraying a thousand tiny jewels over its rider's buckskin britches.

"This is a brave one!" Bob-Tail-Horse shouted to The Cow as he took aim on the leader. "I will wear his scalp proudly!"

Tom rode a few lengths behind Autie as the head of the column reached the mouth of the coulee. Custer surged ahead, into the river, splashing wildly and waving his arm for the others to follow.

"The villages are abandoned!" he shouted.

True enough. Or so it seemed to Tom. The lodges and camp ahead showed no activity. The village had fled.

Autie's two flag-bearers urged their horses down into the cool water, where they had to fight to keep the animals moving. So much water and so much thirst. The horses fought their bits.

Then the young bearer of the regimental standard spurred his animal. The horse struggled against the bit, then surged forward.

At the moment the trees ahead erupted with that single rifle shot, the standard-bearer's mount leapt alongside Custer's horse.

The big lead ball struck the young soldier in the side of the face. The exit wound left little of the back of his head. Blood and gray matter splattered the soldier-chief.

Tom watched his brother jerk his reins in. He wheeled crazily as Vic fought her bit, bringing the animal under control in the knee-deep water midstream. Custer gave Vic the business end of those gold spurs. The big animal lurched on across the middle of the cold, rushing stream.

Instinctively White-Cow-Bull pulled the trigger on his old Henry repeater. . . .

As his .44-caliber bullet smashed through George Armstrong Custer's chest, the shock wave sent the pink-faced soldier tumbling over the back of the big horse, into the turbulent water.

Almost by command his blaze-faced sorrel pranced once-round on the rocky bottom of the stream and loped back to where the soldiers skidded to a halt.

Their leader lay face down in the water. Some soldiers dropped from the saddle to fire their carbines at the Indians hidden behind their cottonwood fortress. At the same time, two other troopers stumbled along the rocky river bottom to retrieve the young soldier's body when it began to drift off on the bobbing current.

Three more soldiers dropped to the cold, tumbling waters beside their fallen leader. One of these wore buckskins too. His gray hat fell into the river.

"Autie!"

Tom's frantic cry bounced along the ragged river bluffs as he dashed forward, watching his brother pitch backward from his mount. As if it all happened in slow motion, Tom reached out—trying to check Custer's fall.

But he got there too late. Autie already floated in the water. Some soldiers at the head of the column dropped to the river, forming a protective barrier around the general, while the rest of the command milled and jostled—suddenly numbed and dumbstruck.

Lieutenant Smith was there in the river after the next beat of Tom's heart. George Yates right behind him.

The big blond captain from Monroe, Michigan, eased the general out of Tom's arms, turning Custer over, bringing his face out of the bloody water.

Tom stared, lips trembling and unable to talk, unable to move, staring at that huge red stain spreading like soft flower petals across the left side of Custer's gray shirt.

"Get his horse, goddammit!" Yates bellowed.

Tom didn't know what to do. Autie had always given the orders. Except in that wild unthinking charge at Saylor's Creek—when no one dared an assault on the Confederate artillery battery . . . no one, that is, until Tom cried out and led the charge himself.

"T-tom . . ."

He looked down into his brother's face clouded with pain, with confusion and fear. And watched a gush of blood pool at the corner of Autie's cracked lips, beneath that bushy, strawlike mustache.

"*Autie!*" The word slid like an elegy past Tom's lips. Never before had his older brother been seriously wounded in battle. So damned lucky, never suffering like the many, many others . . . "M-my God! You're shot!"

"Hill . . ." Custer bubbled his one-word command at the face swimming before his glazing eyes. "Get us back up the hill."

As his heavy head slowly drooped, the general fell silent.

"Is he dead?" Fresh Smith demanded coarsely, suddenly very afraid.

Those precious seconds at the ford became confusion. Then confusion gave itself to the beginnings of panic that spread through the ranks. Milling, shouting wildly, this headless army bottled itself at the mouth of Medicine Tail Coulee. While above them on the hillside, Calhoun and Keogh watched in concern.

Custer's own companies weren't moving across the river. Stalemated. And that spelled anything but hope in the hearts of Keogh's rear guard.

By now more warriors had slid behind the cottonwoods, returning the random soldier fire. Bullets pinged off the low bluffs directly behind the troopers or slashed into the river around them, sending up tiny eruptions.

Yates had been busy over the body, covering it while he felt at Custer's neck for a pulse. Then he pulled back momentarily, cursing himself. No wonder he couldn't sense a pulse beat . . . his gloves!

Instead, the captain bent to put an ear against Custer's chest. Almost as if they stood enclosed in some foggy dream, the shooting and shouting around the small knot of officers stopped suddenly, the horses quit neighing or fighting their bits, and the warriors across the river mysteriously fell silent.

There was powerful medicine made at this place.

"He's alive!" The Michigan soldier rose dripping from

the water, bawling to the bone-pale sky above. "By God in heaven—the general's alive!"

"Get his horse!" Tom cried out, instilled with hope, instilled with life himself now. And Vic was suddenly there. "Help me, dammit! Get Autie up! Up there on Vic. Get him on his horse!"

"It'll be all right," Lieutenant Smith droned over and over. "It'll be all right now."

Fresh Smith and George Yates helped sling the general over the saddle before Tom leapt atop Vic himself, squaring himself behind the cantle where he could cling onto his brother's body, steadying it for the coming ride. Lieutenant and captain caught up their own mounts, swinging into the saddle and splashing out of the stream.

From across the river, in their cottonwood deadfall fortress, the screams and shouts grew louder. And beyond them the shrieks grew more in number. Above a pounding of pony hoofbeats.

"We're in for a scrap of it now, Tommy!" Smith said it evenly, looking back over his shoulder.

"Sounds like the gates of hell have opened up, George!" Smith shouted to Yates.

"It's up to you, Tommy!" Yates said coolly, old hand that he was, his eyes set more serious and deadly than Tom had ever seen them. "Turn 'em around. Pick up Keogh and Calhoun after we're up the slope—"

"Slope?" Tom asked.

Yates swallowed, his eyes flicking up the slope past the point where companies L and I held off better than a hundred now. "Best you get us up that hill like the general wanted."

Tom made no mistake in reading the urgency in that veteran's no-nonsense declaration. He nodded automatically. Never had anything been so clear to him in his life. Autie had wanted him to get the men to the top of the hill. From where they stood right now down in the river, he wasn't all that sure how far away that hill really was, but he figured his older brother wanted to get there to make a stand until the reinforcements arrived.

The only chance they had was Benteen, returning with

his men, bringing McDougall's pack train. Tom figured they could hold out till then. Autie knew they could hold out.

That's what he tried to tell me, Tom thought. *Just get to the top of the hill. And whatever you do—hold on.*

CHAPTER 22

THE Hunkpapa and Santee camps thundered with victory cries now that the soldiers who had attacked them were cornered in the timber, retreating across the river and into the hills beyond.

More and more warriors rode back into the camps, returning from the battle in the valley, carrying scalps they brandished on their rifle muzzles or waved aloft from lances and coup sticks. A few even carried complete heads they had hacked from their victims. These were Santee warriors mostly, for they were the last tribe to practice this ancient ritual of decapitating an enemy.

Everywhere the women raised their high, shrill tremolos and ululating cries, sounding the ages-old approval for bravery and success in battle. A high-pitched trilling of the tongue was about all war chief Gall could hear—that and the pounding of blood hot at his ears.

Pizi, as Gall was known among the Sioux, had discovered his two wives and three young children dead near the southern edge of the Hunkpapa camp where they had gone to dig roots that morning.

Two women and three children dead. The first casualties of Major Marcus Reno's assault on that far fringe of the great gathering along the Greasy Grass. An ignoble beginning to a bloody little battle that would rage but two hours from the time Reno's soldiers fired their first shots, until there were no longer any alive on last-stand hill.

Trembling with primeval fury, Gall rose slowly from the bloody bodies of his family. He was alone. No wives now—no children to carry his line in their veins. His eyes afire with a blood-lust, the war chief finally heard that rifle fire coming from the northeast across the river.

He gazed up toward the hills, seeing the smoke from Indian and soldier guns alike near the top end of Lower Medicine Tail. Then to his wondering eyes came the most fantastic sight of all—frantic soldiers scattering in wild, disordered retreat up the hills leading away from the Miniconjou Ford, away from the Medicine Tail Coulee itself.

Soldiers in retreat, like a wolf spider trying to fight off the infuriating, overpowering charge of black ants. Their huge army mounts leapt and stumbled. Gall sensed what terror those *wasichus* must feel at this moment—easy enough for the soldiers to glance back over their shoulders and see what waited for the man who couldn't drag himself out of the mouth of that coulee.

Right behind the last frightened, white-knuckled trooper, the Cheyenne and Sioux were streaming across the shallow ford like maddened, vengeful wasps.

Surely many of Custer's soldiers must have blinked, and blinked again, after rubbing their eyes clear of dust and tears.

Could it be they really saw what galloped toward them?

Right in the middle of that horde of warriors splashing across the river rode a handful—no more than a dozen at most—screaming, riding their ponies backwards!

Completely naked, this dozen carried nothing more in their hands than long sticks aflutter with feathers and scalps. Hideously painted, they smacked the rumps of their ponies repeatedly to spur them after the retreating soldiers. Riding backwards, courting death, shrieking like a pack of banshees straight out of hell itself. The contraries' suicidal bravery pricked every other warrior into a wild charge across the ford and up the hillside.

Like a flock of wrens and sparrows suddenly wheeling about and chasing a troublesome, predatory hawk, the first warriors flung themselves after the screaming, crying, frightened soldiers, who kicked and whipped and beat their weary, lathered horses. No bottom left in those army mounts. It was too late—nowhere near enough time for grazing on their march up the Rosebud, and too little sleep crossing over the Wolf Mountains, not to mention no water to speak of in the last few hours. The horses were done in.

Gall rallied his warriors and led the hundreds of determined, blood-crazed Sioux, already hot from their battle in the timber, across the ford and up the slopes, dogging the cavalry's heels.

His blood aboil, the war chief knew his task was to push the pony soldiers back from the village, so no more women and children would have to die by soldier bullets. Then Gall would kill them . . . slowly, methodically . . . each and every one of them. Right down to the last soldier who had defiled their great camp and ridden down into this valley to attack a camp of the small and helpless ones.

Gall promised himself no *wasichu* soldier would remain alive to torture. He understood that for these frightened white men to see there was no chance for escape, for them to realize that the end was near and not know when that last bullet would come—all that was torture enough.

Pizi, the Sioux war chief, wanted to wallow in white blood the way a buffalo bull wallows in mud to rid himself of fleas and ticks. Already his nostrils filled with the stench of death . . . *wasichu* death.

"No one left standing!" he shouted now as his followers burst from the top of the lower Medicine Tail Coulee. "No soldier left alive!"

Many of the warriors glanced at their war chief for that fraction of a moment. Most knew he had lost his entire family to these soldiers he hungered to wipe from the earth.

It was right what Gall asked. The pony soldiers deserved to die.

"For our women and children!" Gall shrieked as the troopers above him stumbled, wheeled, and turned, dropping to the ground to set up a ragged skirmish line around some screaming officers.

"Wipe every last soldier from the breast of our Mother! KILL THEM ALL!"

Some two hundred twenty-five men had followed George Armstrong Custer in his march down the Medicine Tail Coulee.

Of that number only a handful of Crow scouts would live to tell of the horror on that ridge to disbelieving white ears in the decades to come.

In those first moments after Custer had been blown out of his saddle, the Sioux had shrieked down to the river crossing, bolstering the four brave Cheyenne warriors who had turned Custer's gallant charge into a harried retreat to certain death. With the smell of blood and victory fresh in their nostrils, the Sioux warriors had turned from the Reno fight in the valley and spurred their little ponies north toward the other soldiers who were reported ready to attack the villages.

So many hands were already bloody from the battle with the soldiers in the valley. Dark, wet scalps hung dripping from their belts. That paint they had quickly applied when the attack was sounded had now become smeared and furry with valley dust. Many were already drunk with victory. Most probably carried army carbines in their hands and wore those bloody blue-and-gray army shirts they had taken off the bodies of soldiers slaughtered down in the timber in the wake of Reno's mad retreat.

To wear a dead soldier's bloody tunic into battle with these others—such would work powerful medicine on these soldiers clustering in fear atop the hill.

While the young warriors charged up the slope, the women and old men scurried up to the high points of land east of the river to watch the battle take form.

This would truly be a fight. The soldiers in the valley

had turned and run away. These on the hill had nowhere to run. They had to turn and fight.

From the Medicine Tail Coulee the pony soldiers had struck out north by east, riding hell-bent for leather to the highest ground. Always take the high ground, they had been taught. Secure that high ground, General Custer's damp lips had reminded them before he slipped into blessed unconsciousness.

Once the soldiers reached that hilltop, the thousands upon thousands of spectators watched them spread out in a thin skirmish line along the ragged, grassy spine three-quarters of a mile long.

"Ride, you wolverines!" Tom Custer hollered to spur on the Michigan boys gathered tightly round him in their charge, like a blue fist sheltering the general slung over the saddle in front of Tom, his spirit oozing out of him with every drop that soaked his saddle red.

"Ride, goddammit!" Tom bellowed again, goading his men to the top of the ridge, where he could finally turn and look back into the valley.

There at the southern end of the spine, Tom gazed at the throbbing lines of black ants scurrying out of their anthills, streaming in a solid phalanx across the river, splashing up the slope toward the retreating cavalry.

"Troops, dismount!" he hollered, then his eyes darted over to Yates.

The big Michigander nodded and flashed him a huge, grim smile. It had been the proper order to give.

"Form skirmish lines—out—left flank! Out—right flank!" George Yates bellowed, already on the ground, pistol out and waving at the stragglers.

Not all the soldiers heard Tom Custer or George Yates. Not all could. There was simply too much sporadic shooting and yelling, besides all the horses neighing, bucking, and fighting their handlers. The animals had smelled the rippling water when they loped down into the Medicine Tail, then were refused a drink, lashed all the way to the top of this dry, dusty ridge without a chance to lap their muzzles in the cool river. Sadly the greenhorns didn't stand much of a chance controlling their wild mounts, rearing, fighting the bit—crazed with thirst.

Some soldiers clung to their saddles, while others stayed on the ground. A few riders spurred in and out of the skirmish formations, shouting orders, waving commands down the line—officers mostly, or veteran sergeants. Anyone who would take charge. Time and again a few cooler heads turned and glanced down the grassy slope into the river valley at those great camp circles spread like clusters of buffalo-hide jewels strewn across the green velvet of the meadows.

They knew in their guts that no man had ever seen such a gathering before and lived to tell of it.

"Form up that left flank! They'll sweep us off the top if you men don't hold!" Tom shouted at his end of the spine of high grass and cactus after the general had been placed in the care of his own C Troop.

Keogh, Yates, Smith, and Calhoun spread the word, working feverishly among their men, attempting to wrench some order out of the panic in their flight up the slope.

Frightened out of their wits, most of the raw recruits simply let the reins go. Horses reared away in the melee, dust, and noise, nostrils flaring and eyes wide as nose bags with fear—then galloped off downhill toward the river and water, big oxbow stirrups flapping. Ammunition jingled in every saddle pocket. The mounts of some were gone for good.

"Tommy boy!"

It was Keogh's voice young Custer recognized above the din of the first carbine shots as some of the veterans turned, dropped to their knees, and began to return the Sioux fire. He wheeled Vic on the mare's haunches, darting back to slide from the bloody saddle near the Irishman.

"Lookee there, man!" Myles pointed downhill. "We got them bastards stopped for a wee bitten moment or two!"

Sure enough the warriors were piling up behind the brow of the hill, most releasing their ponies, driving the animals back downhill to the river and the villages beyond. From a clump of grass or shadowy sage, the warriors tried to fire a potshot every now and then.

For the time being, the tall grass would hide a soldier lying prone, but only until that soldier fired his carbine. Then a burst of blue powder-smoke betrayed him. And the Indians returned his fire. Perhaps the noisy rattle of Henrys and Winchester.

For close to an hour the soldiers held Gall off while the warriors fired volley after volley from their repeaters or old muzzle loaders into the scattered lines of white troopers. Here and there a young soldier might hear for the first time that soapy smack of lead pounding into a human body. They were still breathing, and still alive—holding the Sioux at bay.

There wasn't any widespread nervousness or anxiety or fright . . . not just yet.

They had the Indians held down for the time being. Dr. Lord was working on Custer right up there in that ring of dead horses. The general would be on his feet again soon, and then they'd fight their way out of this red nightmare.

With Custer to lead them, they could fight their way right through the bleeding heart of hell. . . .

Beyond the throbbing movement just down the slope, Myles Keogh peered at warriors massing at the river, crossing the silvery ribbon of water before they streamed north, racing toward the far end of the swaybacked ridge.

If those red buggers sweep the end of this ridge . . .

He didn't want to think any longer on it.

"Myles!"

Keogh turned. Tom Custer was hollering, waving his pistol in the air. "George! Jimmy!"

When Tom called, the inner circle hunkered on the run to Tom's central position beside the general. Young Custer knelt in the grass and sage, his brother leaning against him. Dr. Lord sweated over a wet, blackened belly dressing that was drying about as fast as it was sopping up the flow that didn't seem to want to stop. A soldier's bloody tunic lay in Custer's lap.

"General!" Keogh growled in surprise as he knelt at Custer's side. Myles found himself marveling at the strength in the man.

He's never truly been wounded before . . . not a bullet hole in all this time . . . taking it now like it's something happens every day. Not many would take a close-range shot like that and still be breathing, much less rousing, eyes open, like he is—

"Myles . . ." Custer coughed up some blood, a pink froth bubbling over his lower lip.

"General," Dr. Lord whispered, pressing down on the compress all the harder, "don't try to talk now."

"End of the ridge . . ." Custer sputtered.

"You want us to go to the end of the ridge?" Tom asked anxiously, eyes darting nervously along the spine of grass and sage.

Custer nodded, weakly, eyes half-mast and watery.

"He's right," Keogh replied in a whisper. He pointed down the slope at the warriors streaming off to the north. "We don't get to the end of this ridge . . . north—the bastards can have full run at us when they ride up the north slope. Down there at least we keep them at bay."

Tom looked at each one in turn. "That means we'll have to protect both ends of the ridge."

Calhoun nodded.

Yates wiped a hand across his dry mouth. "Keogh's right. We don't keep 'em off both slopes . . . we're done."

"We're done as it is," Lord whined, his greenish face gone white with fear as his wet hands worked in the general's warm, sticky blood.

"We're not done, goddammit!" Tom snapped. He peered again at each of his old drinking partners, longtime friends who had lived so much life with him and the gallant Seventh.

"Up to you now, Tom," Calhoun said it for all of them.

"The gauntlet's passed, Tommy!" Keogh cheered as best he could.

Here we kneel, commanders of five of the best horse companies in the whole gawdamned world, Myles thought to himself. *We'll make it—by the saints—we'll make it!"*

"Don't you think we ought to be moving!" Lieutenant Algernon Smith suggested, shouldering in on the tight huddle around Custer. "Like the general ordered, Cap'n Custer?"

"Fresh is right, Tom," Yates replied.

"Yes." Tom gazed round at the others. His brother's most trusted officers.

Myles placed a big paw on Tom's chest, stopping him. "Who's to ride to the ridge?"

"Why . . . all—"

"No," Keogh growled low, like a wolf with a den to guard. "Cainnot be that way, Tommy. Who the hell's to support the retreat? Who'll stand behind to guard the rear?"

Tom remembered Autie's words. "Calhoun," he squeaked with a dust-dry throat ever tightening. "Autie asked you to stay and support our rear. Cover the retreat."

There wasn't a flinch of an eye nor a betraying muscle twitch along his jaw that said Jimmy Calhoun wasn't ready to do exactly as ordered. Stay behind and cover their backsides as the rest retreated along the dusty ridge.

"Yes, sir!" Calhoun shouted as he snapped a salute. Then he bit his lip a moment. "I told the general, Tom . . . told him personal I'd not be found wanting when it come time to prove how deeply I appreciated my commission he put me in for." He dragged a hand beneath one eye, smearing dust in a hot streak. "Suppose that time's come, ain't it?"

Before Tom could respond, Keogh rose to his feet beside Calhoun. Two big oaks hovered over them all like huge Doric columns.

"With your permission, Cap'n Custer," Keogh began, a smile on his thick lips above that black Vandyke beard, "I Company will assist Lieutenant Calhoun in the rearguard action, *sir!*"

Staring up into the cruel sunlight that sucked at his juices, sensing those two long shadows stretching out of the bone yellow sky, hulking shadows of his two friends, George Armstrong Custer fought back the tears. The warm syrup of his own blood choked him as he tried to spit some words out.

Still he knew he could show his men just what he thought, exactly how he felt, by doing something he had never done before in front of any of them. His tears told them all how deeply he had been touched by their time together. And how he felt about what they were ready to sacrifice for one another.

Tom looked up from his brother's silent, smeared face. "I think the general approves of your request, Myles." His quiet, choking voice sounded strange, distant, after Keogh's loud, lusty proclamation.

Tom saluted Keogh there in that bright light. "Permission granted to lay back in support of our march along with Lieutenant Calhoun."

"George . . ." the general whispered in a red bubble, vainly reaching for Yates's hand.

The captain bent so he could hear Custer's liquid whisper at his ear. When Yates leaned back and returned his hat to his head, Lieutenant Smith spoke that question every one of them shared.

"What'd he say?"

"Al, he told me to assume command . . . if Tom should fall."

Tom Custer nodded, saluting Yates. "Autie would want it that way: the Michigan boys around him. If I drop, you take care of the general, George. No matter what! You hear me? All of you? You damn well take care of the general. He must not fall into their hands—"

"He won't be left behind!" Smith shouted, fussing bravely with the bright crimson tie fluttering below Custer's neck.

Funny that I should notice it now, Keogh thought. *That tie's the same damned color as Custer's blood, bright and wet against the general's gray jersey pullover.*

"We'll see he goes with us," Yates replied softly. "Come the end, the general won't be taken alive."

Tom gulped. "I suppose we all know what's expected of us?" He straightened his Custer chin proudly. They all nodded without reply. "We make it to the end of the ridge, we can hole up till Benteen gets here with the pack train. Reinforcements. We'll last."

Suddenly Tom whirled, grabbing Keogh's shirt with one hand, clutching Calhoun with his left. "After Yates, Smith, and I have the end of the ridge secured, I want a protected retreat back to us from you two. Fall back—orderly."

Tommy's finding command a bit harder than he thought it'd be,

Keogh thought. *That whipped-dog look in his eye—save as many men as we can comes time we fall back*.

Keogh glanced at Calhoun, finding the blond lieutenant staring at him, smiling grimly. All three knew what the chances would be of the two ever rejoining the rest at the end of the ridge. Any man with but one good eye could peer down the slopes and see that where there once was a halting, a starting, and a stopping among the warriors, now a shrieking red wave rumbled up the hill.

It was time for Custer's command to move out—those who were lucky enough to be moving at all. Those who would have a little time bought dearly for them by Calhoun and Keogh and their two little companies of gallant soldiers.

Whittled down like dry grass before the winter wind.

Gall had led his warriors across the river. Flying pony hooves sent cascades of spraying, jewellike water and muddy sand high into the air over them. Sioux faces grim and hideously painted.

Death to them all!

Straight up the hillside they charged into the face of that terrible wall of soldier fire. Two warriors tumbled off their little mustangs in the first volley, the bodies rolling to a stop among the tall grass and cactus. Others rushed in to drag away the bodies of those fallen, out of range of the soldier's guns. Ahead of them along the spine, many of the soldiers were shouting, running for what horses were left them now.

Gall stood uneasily, watching. Some of the white men stayed behind—kneeling or stretched out on their bellies in the tall grass, firing their carbines as calmly as they could at any copper-skinned target that presented itself.

But those soldiers leaving to dash north along the spine—they were the frightened ones. Gall realized they were scared only because they had been given a chance to live now. Hope can be a terrible burden for a man with nothing else to cling to.

Those left behind—those men gathering about Calhoun and Keogh like cottonwood saplings round two tall, powerful oaks—they knew what their odds were. Perhaps best to take your bullet or arrow here and now rather than drag the damned thing out.

That's why such an eerie calm descended among those hardened veterans and green recruits that long afternoon on Calhoun Hill. Few men had ever experienced that singular feeling and lived to tell another soul of it. A peaceful, purposeful calm that passes over a man when he is finally reconciled to his own passing. Especially a soldier, young or old, when called upon by duty and friendship to cover the retreat of his brothers-in-arms. To give up his life so that others might have a better chance of holding onto theirs.

Something over an hour had crawled past since the Sioux and Cheyenne had driven the cavalry back from the river's edge and up that dusty slope. Gall was growing impatient. Along with Crow King, Iron Dog, and Big Road, he decided this popping their heads up to shoot at the soldiers was no smarter than suicide.

There is a better way, a safer way to fire into these soldiers clustered in tiny groups near the hill.

As word spread through the entrenched Sioux positions, the warriors brought out their bows in force at long last— and a storm of iron-tipped arrows began to rain death upon the troopers. While a warrior had to expose himself to fire his gun simply because a bullet travels in a straight path, an arrow could be sent into the sky in a graceful arc, whistling down to pierce horse or man alike.

Sergeant George Finckle lay his body over Custer's once more, protecting it from the shafts of darkness flittering down across the sun, falling from the sky in waves of iron-tipped hail. He watched others mount up behind Smith and Yates, fighting their horses, sprinting north if they had control.

"Get him loaded fast!" Tom Custer bellowed, dodging the red hail.

Arrows clattered into saddle gear and dead horses. Battering gear and piercing horses. *God, they make a racket!* Finckle thought as he knelt over the general. *Damn, he's out again.*

George looked around. Dr. Lord worked on a soldier

with a shaft all the way through the back of his neck. The man was drowning in his own blood, legs thrashing just the way Finckle remembered the chickens thrashing about the yard back home. Spraying bright hot blood just like this.

Jeezuz! A horse sounds just like a man screaming when it goes down, dying.

Men shouted as the arrows struck, or they cursed when the man next to them drew his last breath, yanking at that bloody shaft in his back or gut.

The soldiers who had leapt aboard their horses to escape the falling death from the sky didn't stand any better chance. They were hit as surely as those men left behind when the arrows rained. Saddles emptied, horses reared and broke free, bolting downhill in a noisy clatter.

For the first time bedlam began working its evil on that end of the ridge as soldiers scurried this way and that like sow bugs from an overturned buffalo chip. A few savvy old files even pulled the bodies of dead bunkies over themselves. The only protection from the iron-tipped messengers of red death.

"Buglers!" Tom's raspy rawhide voice carried over the melee.

He must want to be the last to ride outta here, Finckle considered. *He's staying till we get the general up on his horse. He'd not dare leave his brother's side.*

"Sound the charge, buglers!" Tom ordered, waving his pistol in the yellow dust that clung to everything in a sticky film.

From the saddlebags of the two company buglers came those shiny brass bugles they had not blown for three days now. In a stuttering, discordant melody, the buglers raised their tune along the grassy spine.

"If it's the last thing I'll do, Finckle . . ." young Custer snarled, "I'll organize this retreat, by God!"

"Cap'n?" Finckle gazed up through the dust and the powder smoke.

The general was conscious again when Tom slid up beside his brother in the tall grass.

"Blow for Benteen, Tom," he sputtered. "Benteen must hear us . . ."

Tom didn't answer. He leapt to his feet, dashing among Smith's gray-horse troop to find the buglers, whose brassy notes sailed over the slopes.

They weren't hard to find, not with those shiny instruments gleaming like mirrors strapped to a man's soul in the sun. Shiny and yellow beneath a bone-dry summer eye glaring down on their last hill.

Tom grabbed one cowering bugler hiding behind a horse carcass to blow his horn. Then Custer yanked the other trumpeter to his feet as well.

"Blow 'Assembly'!" Tom ordered flatly. "Then try 'Officers' Call.' Just keep blowing till I tell you to stop! Blow, goddammit—blow!"

CHAPTER 23

In a seeping gash along his cheek, the raw wound ached and pinched like puckered rawhide drying under this blazing sun.

Mitch Bouyer had been clipped by a bullet or fragment of one ricocheting off some rock down below him on the long slope to the river. Funny, but the cheek hurt one hell of a lot more than the bullet hole low in his belly.

It's just a little pain, he told himself. *Hurts only when I try to run.*

Bouyer laughed wildly, wickedly at that. *Only when I try to run! That's funny for a man to think of—now—isn't it?*

There couldn't be any running. Not for most of them anyway. But he looked over at Curley and young White-Man-Runs-Him. They were both related to Mitch's Crow wife. One was her younger brother, the other a cousin or something such.

Perhaps these two boys can make it out . . . spread the word of what happened in this place.

Calhoun had had it. That much was plain to see from

where Bouyer sat. The last few soldiers still up there at the end of this pony-back ridge where Calhoun's big fight had started were going down, one at a time like canvasback ducks on a high-plains pond diving for their lunch.

Except, Mitch realized, these ducks weren't coming back up for air . . . they weren't coming up at all.

Bouyer knew that wild-man Keogh would just have to hold the screeching Sioux off from the ridge when the warriors came swarming over Calhoun's position. That was the reality of it all. And that's when Bouyer knew he had to send the two boys off before they were vulture bait with the rest of Custer's soldiers.

In Absaroka, Bouyer shouted over his shoulder to get the youngest's attention—Curley.

Obediently the youth crawled up to sit beside Bouyer as the interpreter casually fired shot after shot with a dead soldier's carbine, and when it jammed, he crawled off in search of another. The soldiers he took the rifles from weren't going to be using their Springfields any longer— and besides, their stiffening, stinking bodies served as a shield for him while he fired back at the advancing warriors.

Smack, smack. The dull, wet thud of lead slamming into the lifeless white-soldier flesh—

"Curley," Mitch coughed, clearing his throat of the dust that threatened to choke him, "this fight does not go well for us." His Crow was spoken flat and hard, traveling with the speed of a carbine bullet itself. "The soldiers have lost this fight. We have lost this fight too, little brother."

Bouyer glared right into the young Crow's eyes. Curley did not flinch. He stared at the aging half-breed Sioux who was saying in his own way they all would be dead soon enough. Mitch, the old scout, his sister's husband. Curley dipped his fingers in the puddle of blood pooling beneath the half-breed's leg.

"My belly," Bouyer explained with a solid gulp of pain he swallowed down like it was some cod-liver oil to be taken, suffered, then gotten over. "That's why I can't come with you, my friend, my brother."

Mitch placed a powder-grimed hand on Curley's shoulder. "If you can get out of here, do it now. Do it quick. Get out of here before the Sioux have us fully surrounded. Go to the other soldiers up north. On the Bighorn. They are coming down the Bighorn to meet us in a few days. Go to No Hip Gibbon—tell him all of us are killed here."

"You can go with me," the young Crow begged with his eyes as well as his words. "I will carry you out of here. For my sister . . ."

"*No!*"

Bouyer clamped a dirty hand over the young man's mouth. "I will not go. This is where I am to die, don't you see? Old Man Above has brought me here—showing me this is where I am to die. I had many chances to leave Custer, but I came here with him. I can't go and leave the rest of these men by themselves now. Their souls will remain here. Mine too, Curley. My soul must find its place here, or it will forever wander. You know that."

"Yes, brother," Curley nodded, choking on the emotion. "When a man is shown his place to die by the spirits, he must stay there and wait for death."

Suddenly Mitch crimped with a spasm of pain at the gut wound, and more blood oozed from his mouth, dribbling into his barbed-wire whiskers. Curley lunged forward to help him as Bouyer toppled over to his side. The old scout pushed the youngster away. Always had been a tough little bantam rooster. Even ready to take General Custer on a time or two. And now the half-breed would go out on his own, with no help from any man.

Struggling to his knees, Mitch wrenched himself up and raised the carbine to his shoulder, teeth gritted against the hurt of it all. After he had fired two more shots at some Sioux down in a thicket of sage who were inching a mite too close for his comfort, Bouyer gazed into Curley's eyes one last time.

"That man over there . . ." He pointed at the top of the hill where Custer sat propped up against the body of a dead horse, officers kneeling all round him as a horse was brought up for brother Tom. Custer was lifted, slung over the horse in preparation for some movement along the ridge.

Probably running north, Bouyer brooded darkly, cursing Custer.

"That man Custer will stop at nothing. We warned him. But he has no ears to hear his scouts. We came to help him. No Hip saw to that. But this Peoushi does not want our help. Instead, he wanted only to attack the villages, the biggest damned camp any of us have ever seen on the face of the Great Mother. And now those villages spread at our feet will be the last thing any of us sees in this life."

His dark eyes studied the pained expression on Curley's face. "Except your eyes, little brother! Go now while you can escape," Bouyer ordered. "Go! Tell the world what happened at this place."

Without a word of reply, nothing more than a grave, watery look in his eye to betray his unspoken love for this Mitch Bouyer, Curley leaned over and hugged the aging half-breed. With that embrace he turned to leave his brother-in-law.

In all the maddening, swirling confusion, Curley's pony had been driven off by some Cheyenne scaring away the horses from Calhoun's position. As the young scout twisted and turned, wondering how to flee without his pony, a Cheyenne warrior began a ride up the hill toward the troops breaking loose from the end of Calhoun's hill. A sudden volley of carbine fire from the hilltop blew that young warrior into glory.

Curley was on his feet before the Cheyenne even smacked the ground.

Dashing through tall grass and around silver sage, the young Crow scout raced down the slope after that riderless Cheyenne pony. Bullets kicked up spouts of dirt near his heels. Arrows hissed past his bear-greased pompadour. With one desperate lunge Curley grabbed for the end of the rawhide lariat looped round the mustang's neck and held on for all he was worth, jerking the animal around, stopping it from running off.

Curley lay in the tall grass, catching his breath. Just moments ago he had discarded his dirty carbine because it had jammed. Tearing the army cartridge belt from his waist, Curley belly-crawled back uphill toward the dead

Cheyenne, poking his head up every now and then from the sage to check his bearings.

Making it to the crumpled warrior's body, Curley took the old Winchester '73 and the Cheyenne's half-empty belt of cartridges. Better this than nothing, and those cavalry carbines were as close to nothing as a man could get.

He pulled in the rawhide lariat tied to the pony until the animal grazed almost directly above him. Lucky that the Sioux could not pick him out through the dust and smoke . . . probably thinking the pony was merely grazing on the field of battle.

Curley glanced to the south and east. Unless he moved now, the end of the ridge would be surrounded. Hundreds upon hundreds swept up the Medicine Tail like maddened ants. He had to go now!

With one swift, smooth leap, the young Crow scout sailed onto the animal's back from the tall grass. He twisted the rawhide rein round one hand, urging the animal up and over the spine of the ridge while Cheyenne warriors howled in anger and utter dismay at the Sparrowhawk's escape aboard one of their own ponies.

"White-Man-Runs-Him!" Bouyer shouted in Crow as many soldiers turned to watch Curley gallop over the top of Calhoun's hill, through the soldiers and warriors and into the valley beyond.

"It is your turn, White-Man. Take one of the army horses that looks fresh enough to run. You have done all that you said you would do when No Hip hired you. I will tell your people in the land beyond how brave you are, but you must go back to the pack train now. Save yourself to tell this story. We are all dead men now."

White-Man nodded, a trace of confusion on his young face. He began to rise and dart away but was back in the next instant, grabbing Bouyer's collar, dragging him uphill toward the soldiers preparing to retreat north along the ridge.

"No!" Mitch barked, twisting painfully against the bullet hole gaping in his gut, a bubble of intestine protruding, puffy and purple. "I am done for. I go now to meet my people. Leave me to die here on this spot!"

Gently, almost as if Bouyer were a baby, White-Man lowered the half-breed Sioux down among the tall grass and touched Bouyer's hand where it lay drenched in blood oozing from the belly wound.

"Your people are my people now, Uncle," he told Bouyer. "I will see you again one day, in a valley not far from here. Remember this now, the journey you go on will not take long. The trail is easier than any trail you have ridden before. All your friends are there. Mother and father too. I will see you in that valley one day, brave one."

Then White-Man was darting uphill in a rooster crouch, heading for some horses held together by a grim bunch of recruits hunkered near Tom Custer's command. From what Bouyer could see over his shoulder through the swirling dust, the Crow scout fast-talked one of the recruits out of a horse and leapt aboard just as George Yates hollered out a warning.

Tom Custer whirled, yanking up his service revolver. Down the end of the muzzle he aimed at the scout's broad back but never pulled the trigger as the rider disappeared into the smoke and dust, galloping east as fast as the army horse could carry him.

Tom slowly stuffed the pistol in its holster before he dashed back to his brother's side.

Those high, clear notes sailing on the dry air, like cotton-wood down lifting over the ridge and the villages below, brought most of the warriors to a staggering halt for a few precious moments.

Soldier trumpets!

Their murderous fire slackened . . . shrieking cries died off.

Even some of the army horses near that hilltop acted as if they recalled something in their past, some tatter of memory stirred on this dusty slope by those brass horns.

From behind the trees and clumps of grass the old men, women, and young boys peeked to see just what was taking place with the pony soldiers up the hill.

Surely, this blowing of the shiny horns must be some powerful magic these soldiers are performing.

"This is no *medicine!*" Cheyenne warrior Old-Man-Coyote screamed bitterly. "We sing out our battle songs, the soldiers do the same with their death songs now! We have them beaten, brothers. They are singing in death. Join me now! Come spill their blood this fine day!"

First a handful, then a wave of Cheyenne and Sioux swept up Calhoun's hill behind Old-Man-Coyote.

Raggedly, grimly, the soldiers fired back. Not in volleys this time. Independent. More frantic now as the enemy tide swept upward.

The big horses reared. More broke free of men scrambling into the stirrups.

All of them headed for the river below.

Calhoun's troopers held—staying behind as the others scattered along the ridge, running north.

L Company laid down a destructive fire into the charging warriors, doing the best they could with the men they had left. Careful aim from a kneeling position—then plopping down behind the tall grass to reload and perhaps to struggle with the carbine's shell ejector. The shells they kept inside the leather pouches or on the cartridge belts were coated with a sticky verdigris that acted like a cement inside the superheated chamber of the Springfield carbines. Sometimes all the ejector did was to rip off the base of the shell from its tubing, leaving the soldier with a useless, army-issue club. Silently they fought a knife into the jammed breech beneath the trapdoor, in utter frustration breaking off the tips of knife blades.

Cursing as the Sioux worked their way closer up L Company's hill . . . ever closer.

The old ones hit a warrior near every time. Yet more came on—more still on painted, wide-eyed ponies looming out of the blue powder smoke and yellow dust like demons in a ghost charge. Some even rode the big army horses now instead of their Indian ponies. Better to lose a soldier horse to the soldiers' bullets than a prize war pony or buffalo runner. Most of these daring warriors wore the bloody blue tunics or gray shirts of Reno's dead.

A warrior wearing a tunic or blouse and riding an army horse found he could gallop that much closer to the hilltop positions before he was discovered and shot at. Slowly, inexorably—the warriors tightened the noose.

The bugle calls ended. More troopers darted like wild men along the ridge, following the general's body, following Tom Custer.

A retreat? No, the Sioux and Cheyenne watched these men running for their lives . . . running to steal a few more precious minutes of life.

A handful of those staying behind fired their carbines with one arm from the hip as they dragged wounded friends up the hillside until they reached the top, where Calhoun stood like a steadfast oak, bellowing orders all round, shouting encouragement.

He could afford to be courageous now, Jim Calhoun could.

Most of the men were throwing aside their useless Springfields and grabbing others, or pulling out their revolvers. The Indians inched close enough for pistol work now. Almost close enough for hand-to-hand—close enough that a man could hit them with chaw spit if his mouth hadn't gone dry.

Those wounded and dragged uphill cried out as they bounced over sage, yanked toward the spot where Calhoun's L Company remained behind to cover Custer's retreat down the ridge.

"Just hold 'em back, goddammit!" Calhoun hollered, his eyes straining to catch a glimpse of where his brother Fred had disappeared in the dust. "We've gotta hold the bastards off and buy our boys some time—*goddamn sonuvabitch!*"

Calhoun watched the corporal's brains splatter across the front of his checkered shirt but did not stop to wipe off the blood and gore. Jim sensed himself growing more numb with every click of the hammer on his pistol. Around him drew the last shreds of his gallant command. Crittenden was nowhere to be found.

Probably one of the many bodies I had to leave down the slope, he brooded, slamming cartridges into the cylinder. *Sergeants Mullen and Bender and Cashan—all gone now.*

Their bloodied bodies littered the thirsty soil just outside a ring of horses atop the knoll. Three veterans who had gone out to drag others to safety sacrificed their own lives in the process.

Try as he might, Calhoun couldn't locate Sergeant Findeisen through the smoke and dust that lent the hilltop an opaque, daguerreotype look. Nowhere in the blur could he see chevrons.

Doesn't matter much anyway. Calhoun already knew who he was going to choose for the ride. First Sergeant James . . .

"Butler!" Calhoun bellowed like a castrated calf, his left arm aching horribly where a bullet had raked a furrow along the elbow. Blood dripped off the hand. The arm hung useless now, swinging like a beef quarter, raw meat suspended lifeless from his big shoulder.

"Sir?" Butler crawled on his knees and hands, crabbing up. His leathery face was smudged with burnt powder and other men's blood.

"You're the last one left," Jim hissed breathlessly above the noise.

"Last, sir? Sergeants—oh . . . yes, sir. I'll rally the squads, sir."

"Shuddup and listen to me, Butler!" Calhoun said it more softly than he had expected. "A horse—not hit yet. Find one. Make the ride out of here. Save yourself if you can do it. I'll give you what cover fire I can. Ride south—off that way—yonder to find Benteen . . . the pack train. Just—get—somebody."

"Ride, Lieutenant?"

"Ride, Butler! Goddammit—like you never have before!"

"Yesssss*sir!*"

Butler appeared to come alive of a sudden, slapping a salute against his bloody, hatless brow and wheeling to find a mount. When he had one of the sorrels captured, he stuffed two extra pistols in his belt. Leaping atop the bloody McClellan saddle, the sergeant found the stirrups cinched much too short. A small man. Maybe one of the boys. But no matter.

He spurred back to Calhoun.

"Lieutenant—I'll bring 'em back, sir!" Butler shouted above the ear-splitting noise of battle and men dying.

Butler nearly brought the weary horse over on one haunch, yanking hard on the reins and kicking savagely at the animal's flanks. Probably figuring there was one last, mad dash left in the horse and nothing more. Tufts of yellow dust erupted from its flying hooves as Sergeant Butler sped away, butt in the air, head down along the animal's lathered neck. Like a jockey, reins clutched inches from the bit.

Off the spine of grassy ridge, right down into Two Eagle's Sans Arc warriors he rode, surprising hell out of the Sioux with his crazy courage.

Calhoun fought back the stinging tears of frustration and grief. Perhaps saddest that he would never again hold his dear Maggie.

Sweet, sweet Maggie Custer. Funny, he thought, swiping the hot sting from his eyes, *funny that I still think of her as a Custer and not a Calhoun. But—that woman will always be a Custer. She might've taken my name to wear for all the world to see, but beneath Maggie's freckles she remains a Custer through and through.*

He had lived for her, Jimmy Calhoun had. And now, he would die for her. For her brothers. For the general.

Jim just hoped Butler would be in time to save Keogh, Smith and the others up there . . . strung out along the ridge like dry beans scattered across his mother's floor back home.

Home. Maggie. God, I love you!

The tall, thick-shouldered lieutenant cursed his useless left arm and flung some more of the bright, sticky blood across the toes of his boots.

Damn, but I'm going to miss them all! Every goddamned one of you! We had a time, didn't we, boys!

"Ride, Butler!" he cried out with everything left in him at the disappearing back of the sergeant so far away, past the first warriors.

He might make it yet, Jim Calhoun prayed. *Too far away to hear me now.*

"Ride, Butler—goddammit, ride!"

If any man could make it through the Sioux, it would be

Sergeant James Butler. There wasn't a better horseman in the Seventh.

Sorry, Butler. It's just too late for L Company now. We've held 'em off long enough.

Calhoun turned and saw I Company in position north along the spine, Keogh's men hunkering along the east slope while the Indians worked their way up from the river side.

L Company just didn't have many men left now . . . men who could fire a weapon at the damned Sioux creeping closer and closer . . .

How many do I have left now?

He wondered that as the bullet smacked into the side of his gut with a wet thud. Slamming him with the power of a mule kick.

That was a funny sound. Something I've never heard before. Look, you're bleeding, goddammit, Jimmy. Don't hurt much though. Not like this goddamned arm!

Calhoun struggled to his feet.

"Uhhhnnnn!"

That one burns, dammit!

He fired at the warrior he figured had shot him in the lung. . . .

Right in the lights! Man don't live if he's shot in the lights. . . .

The warrior couldn't believe that the big soldier just stood there, rocking on the balls of his feet, refusing to go down.

But Calhoun's gun was empty long, hot minutes ago. He clicked the hammer over and over and . . .

"Ride, Butler, ride!"

Then two more rounds tore through his body, blowing huge, fist-sized holes out through the front of his chest. Jim Calhoun stared down at what was left of him. More numb than ever now.

Suddenly he felt the hot flourlike yellow dust beneath his wet cheek and wondered if he had been shot in the head. It was wet beneath his cheek.

Then Calhoun realized he was crying. *Good-bye, Maggie! Good-bye, Mother!*

Jimmy Calhoun heard the pounding of moccasined feet. Damned close now.

"We did our best, General!"

With the high, thin call of his eagle wing-bone whistle stuffed between his thick lips, Gall brought his warriors to their feet behind him.

As one they rose on command and surged toward the top of the hill where Calhoun had desperately held on as long as his men and his own strength could stem the tide. Some warriors knelt like sharpshooters with their rifles, covering the advance of the light cavalry that thundered past them toward the crest of the hill, whipping their ponies over Calhoun's handful of hold-outs.

The last few troopers alive were bowled over by the overwhelming onslaught, their screams of pain smothered beneath the hundreds of throats crying out with a vengeance for fifty years of broken promises and shattered treaties. Stone clubs swung against skull bone and shoulder blade. Old pistols fired point-blank into fear-taut, white faces. Hawk and stone alike smacked with a wet thud again and again and again as the wounded were toppled.

Soldiers scattered like so much chaff in the wind along the southern tip of their last ridge.

Hump killed the flag-bearer himself. At first he fired his Henry into the young man's chest. The private slumped to his knees near Calhoun. He was no more than a boy, really—barely eighteen and struggling to keep from falling any farther.

He gripped the shaky guidon pole as if it were life itself. Stars-and-stripes guidon—Company L. Calhoun's gallant men who stayed behind to cover the general's retreat.

Rally round the flag, boys!

Lieutenant Calhoun kept hollering at his standard-bearer there in the last moments, spitting up blood with every order.

Just keep that flag up, son—so the rest know we're still here. So Custer knows we're still fighting!

But Hump rode right over the boy, yanking the pole

from the youth's hands as the pony trampled the boy's body into the yellow dust already slick with other men's blood.

A wild Miniconjou war cry leapt from his throat as Hump heard the wet thrump of his pony's hoofs slash downward, crushing that young soldier's body.

All round the flag-bearer the last of the troopers went down as well. The smack of lead into flesh like a war song gone mad of its own.

At long last—they would teach the soldiers not to attack villages of women and children.

Near the north end of Calhoun's Hill there were still a few, just a handful who rose on cue and dashed off to the north, heading for Keogh and his I Company.

Kill Eagle, a Blackfoot Sioux, freed a primeval cry from his throat, pointing at the escaping few.

After them screamed the feathered hawks like predators swooping after fleeing field mice. Soldiers hoping to make it those few hundred yards . . . each one blinded by tears stinging his eyes from the hot wind, the dust—perhaps the pain of seeing your deepest, most fervent prayers go unanswered.

Then the warriors swooped down on these too from the back of their swift ponies—clubbing, slashing, gouging with their gore-soaked lances. When there were no more, the Sioux turned back to the hill where Calhoun's men had made their stand. Turned back to that bloody ground looking for more of the hated enemy to kill.

But here on Calhoun's Hill, there were no more. Only the hot breeze remained to whisper through the tall, wet grass. No one left to cry out now.

There were no more.

CHAPTER 24

DOWN in the Cheyenne village, Monaseetah came back from the prairie. She had fled to safety in the hills with the others when news of the attack raced like wildfire through the villages. Now she joined those who warily returned to their camps.

Twice before in her life soldiers had ridden down on her tribe's camp circle. Once she had escaped. The last time she'd been taken prisoner.

With the first shouts of warning that soldiers had attacked the Hunkpapa camp circle, Monaseetah remembered the terrifying image of the Little Dried River and how death had come charging into Black Kettle's winter village. She remembered how women and children had died beneath the slashing sabers and smoking guns, trampled beneath the bloody hooves that knew no difference between warrior and woman, young or old, in that dim light of a gray-winter dawn.

Thirteen summers old, she had been.

And four robe seasons later, Black Kettle's village on the

Washita again awoke to the same horror of blood-numbing cold and death. Women and children and the old ones were trampled beneath the big horses of the soldiers once more. Another winter dawn long ago.

Suspiciously now the Cheyenne women and old ones came back to their villages in guarded joy. The warriors said they had whipped the soldiers in the valley and sent them fleeing in disorderly retreat up the bluffs far to the south. Now the big fight was pressed against the pony soldiers who had dared to cross into the Shahiyena village itself . . . to slash through the lodges, killing women and children once more.

But they too had been turned back!

Anxiously she reentered her village, dashing across the camp circle to those cottonwoods that lined the riverbank. A boy under each arm, she watched the pony soldiers spread out along the top of the grassy ridge, some on horseback, others kneeling or lying down to fire their rifles at the warriors who kept up their never-ending pressure.

Minutes later the bugles called out with notes familiar from that long-ago winter far to the south.

Stirred to her soul by the brass horns, Monaseetah remembered those trumpet calls.

She sang, mimicking the quick, staccato notes along with the trumpets, much to the wide-eyed wonder of her sons. Their chins dropped to hear the high, clear, crystal-line notes lift from her throat. Sweeter compared to the brassy blare of the army bugles far up the noisy slope.

She remembered too the meaning of that war song. Officers coming together.

Another song—orders to mount. And another song calling the men to assemble so Yellow Hair could talk to all his pony soldiers. Mighty Yellow Hair.

She remembered.

Of a sudden her heart burned for him again . . . just to touch his pale face once more . . . to look into those eyes like a mountain pool of cold blue water. Water so cold it would set her teeth on edge to drink—

Then she saw the guidon.

It is his!

Yellow Hair's personal flag—the flag he had allowed her to touch and hold so many, many times during their long winter together. She above all others should know that banner.

I slept with that flag pillowing my head through many stormy nights.

She lunged forward a step, stumbling as the boys clung to her.

"Hiestzi!" The word flew from her lips more strongly, more hopefully than she had sung the bugle notes.

At her side both boys grew tense with apprehension. Was this Yellow Hair? Is that not what their mother had shouted? Who was this Yellow Hair? The one she spoke of so often?

Suddenly Monaseetah whirled, her eyes searching the throng of spectators. They came to rest on an old woman, Northern Cheyenne, whose father's relatives remained imprisoned on a reservation far to the south in the Territories.

"Talks-to-the-Moon!" Monaseetah shouted, dragging the two boys with her as she scuffed through the cotton-wood grove.

"Little mother!" the old woman gasped.

"Please—watch the children for me!" Her eyes pleaded. How could her old friend refuse?

"It is not safe yet," the old one said. "The killing has only started. See? There are too many soldiers fighting still. It will not be long now. Wait here."

"Watch the boys!" Monaseetah shouted, shaking her head sharply to shut the old woman off. "I must see these soldiers myself."

As Monaseetah turned to study the hill, more of the army horses stampeded, frightened away from the soldiers by youths fluttering blankets and robes. More thirsty animals bolted and clattered off toward the river, carrying their precious loads of ammunition far from the jamming carbines.

"I go look for a soldier! To see his face!" she admitted to the old woman. "He comes for me at last. Like a prayer, he comes for me!"

Talks-to-the-Moon found her mouth hanging open in

surprise as the young mother darted away, racing down the sharp bank into the river, where she splashed across the water, soaking her cloth dress above the waist. One plodding, slippery step after another, lumbering forward a foot at a time.

The ribbon of water separated her from him. This Goat River, slowing her desperate sprint toward the hill where Hiestzi waited for her.

She had seen his flag . . . that crimson, so like blood on winter's snow . . . and sky blue, so like the winter in his eyes.

It was *his* flag. It fluttered in the hot breeze up there on the spine of the swaybacked pony ridge, as if it meant to signal to her and her alone. Hiestzi had wanted her to see it. Monaseetah knew that—as surely as the dust stung her eyes and the powder stank in her nostrils.

Hiestzi has come back for me as he promised seven summers ago! My husband comes for me a last! His promise fulfilled . . .

Myles Keogh had watched Calhoun take the first fatal shot, marveling from afar at the stamina of his friend—not seeing the last, for the young lieutenant was lost in a swirl of dust and burnt powder smoke as the crimson wave swept up and over the burnt-sienna brow of the hill.

For a moment Myles wondered absently if that lone rider would make it.

Some yellow-livered coward, Myles cursed. *Running—rather than dying like a man . . .*

But Keogh had his own problems now.

The warriors who had overrun Calhoun were inching their way in ever-increasing numbers toward I Company. The big Irishman watched but a moment more, mesmerized, while some of the Sioux began to beat and pummel the wounded clustered on the brow of Calhoun's Hill. They shot the wounded and dying with their own weapons as the soldiers cried out for mercy. They fired arrow after arrow into the limp bodies, hacked at them with tomahawks and stone clubs. Close enough that Myles could see the enraged faces, painted and horrendous, every one distorted with blood-lust as they turned from the Calhoun dead to glare longingly up the spine toward Keogh's Wild I Company.

It was a sight that would make many a lesser man worry about losing his lunch or wetting his pants.

Hundreds upon hundreds, and still hundreds more, warriors streamed out of the villages now that they had driven Reno back up the bluffs, now that they had taken time to put on their paint and say their war-medicine prayers. Smeared with grease and charcoal, painting their faces black for victory. Skin painted yellow with blue hailstones . . . red with green horns surrounding their eyes . . . blue with red stripes down the chins.

Devil paint fuzzed with yellow dust and sweat . . . and smeared with white men's blood.

Some had charged up the hill totally naked, contraries mostly. They attacked the soldiers with little willow sticks hoping for a glorious death that would catapult their spirits into the other world of forever-happiness. Contraries ran naked through the tall grass, their cocks and scrotums bouncing as they leapt up the slope, offering their frail, naked copper bodies to Wakan Tanka after they had pledged their undying obedience in this personal vow of sacrifice.

Others rode up the hill with only a blanket or half robe lashed about their waists. Only a few wore feathers in their hair. Most simply did not have the time to ornament themselves at first for the valley fight. But by now many had stuffed hands into fire pits and dragged out charcoal to smear across their chests and shoulders. Perhaps mud at the riverbank. Anything to make themselves more hideous to those young, frightened soldiers laying eyes for the first time on battle-crazed warriors on this dusty Montana hillside.

There wasn't a green recruit kneeling behind his over-heated carbine on Keogh's slope who didn't imagine he had died already and been dragged kicking and screaming straight into the maw of hell.

While one warrior tied on his long headdress, its brim speckled with dragonflies and butterflies, another wore something much more primitive and provoking of fear in his enemy. Sun Bear strapped a single buffalo horn to the center of his forehead and dashed on foot up the hillside.

With the tall grasses waving beneath a gentle breeze across the entire slope, Keogh's men were able to watch those warriors still working over Calhoun's dead. Down below they saw the thousands of spectators—many young boys and old men riding back and forth just out of rifle range at the river. Women splashing across the Greasy Grass to join the swelling crowds of those who sang the young warriors on to greater feats of daring. Women who shook their skinning knives aloft, urging the warriors on so they could be about their own bloody work over the bodies of the slain soldiers.

Along the slope and the spine of the ridge, Keogh's soldiers heard the high, wailing cries of the women.

"Don't let them catch you alive!" one of Keogh's old files shouted to the frightened shavetails in his squads. "What I could tell you about Fetterman's poor boys . . . but—just don't let them bitches get their bloody hands on you!"

Slowly it sank in. A fate worse than a thousand deaths awaited the man who let the squaws get their hands on him.

Some of Gall's warriors broke off from the slaughter on Calhoun's hill and moved north along the ridge toward Keogh's position. The air filled with their blood-chilling cries, joining the screams and shrieks from the women below, mingled with the high-pitched prayer-sounds of the eagle-wingbone whistles constant and droning on the hot breeze that stirred the yellow dust and maddened the eyes.

Now and again that same breeze blew flecks of stinging foam off the handful of lathered horses left to Keogh's fear-riddled command. A man's ass tightened all by itself whenever an army mount galloped by, its saddle empty, wet with blood.

As the wild, crazed horses went down, thrashing in their death-throes, the mood along the ridge became more desperate still. A horse made a perfect target while the soldiers always did not. Men hid down in the grass. The horses could not.

Slowly, methodically, the warriors concentrated on the

big animals, whittling away at the horses, spilling their riders.

Funny how a soldier always stayed with his fallen horse, for protection from arrow and bullet alike, or simply because with his horse down and dying, there was no longer any means of escape. A few unhorsed troopers tried to run, out along that bumpy backbone of a ridge toward the last knoll far away—north, where the general had gone. The scared ones and the smart ones alike.

Most who had abandoned Company L hadn't made it. Those who fled I Company didn't make it either. They died like scattered kernels of corn on a threshing floor, shot and trampled and bludgeoned beneath the red onslaught before they had been up and running but a moment or more.

Riderless horses were allowed to break through the Indian lines, clattering down to the river where the young boys and old men captured them all. It was easy enough. Even though the big mounts did not like the smell of Indians, their intense thirst overpowered their instinctive sense of caution. Seized by young hands, these big, colorful horses were led across the river into the camps by proud new owners, their saddlebags jingling musically with ammunition to use in the army Springfields captured in the valley fight or on Calhoun's Hill.

More Springfields overheated, jamming along that ridge-top position Keogh had scratched out for his company. The verdigris coating the shells worked like cement, hardening under the heat of rapid firing until at last a shell refused to break free with the ejector. Several soldiers threw their rifles away in disgust and frustration after breaking knife blades on frozen shell casings.

Many of the warriors gathering below Keogh's ridge believed the soldiers were simply touched by the moon, gone crazy. There could be no other explanation for the troopers tossing aside their carbines.

All the while Keogh's men retreated into a smaller and smaller force near the crest on the east slope of the ridge. Their numbers slowly dwindled, exactly as Calhoun's position had before them. The handful of those left alive from Calhoun's Hill had run up the slope toward that big monolith of a man, Myles Keogh, like a lighthouse in the fog of that yellow-dust madness. Keogh kept calling out above the battle din, letting them all know he was standing there, rallying them round him like a group of schoolboys rallied beneath the spreading arms of a huge oak, strong, sturdy to the last.

"Goddamn their black hearts to perdition!" the Irishman hollered, his eyes watching some of his men abandoning their squads to pierce the smoke and dust shrouding Custer's companies farther north. On the last, very last, knoll.

"May the bastards spend their eternities quivering in hell's own furnace!"

Sergeant Bustard himself dragged up two wounded, one beneath each of the huge ham hocks he called hands. After slinging the soldiers behind the protection of a dead horse carcass already attracting its share of blowflies, James Bustard leapt into the smoke and dust once again to fetch more of his wounded and dying comrades.

"Give 'im a hand, will you, boys?" Keogh shouted as he waved two other veterans to follow Bustard downhill.

Sergeant Caddle leapt up and dashed off into the smoke on Bustard's tail. Mitch Caddle was the lucky one of the two.

As Sergeant George Gaffney jumped over the stiffening carcass of his horse, he was driven backwards into Keogh's little compound. His body writhed on the dusty grass a moment, his jaw blown off, the side of his head gone in a pulpy mass. As his bowels voided into the hot air, Gaffney quit trembling forever.

"Damn them all!" Keogh shouted. "Let them 'ave a go at me! C'mon now—you pagan bastirds . . . 'ave a shot at the likes of Myles Keogh!"

The captain darted side to side, waving his huge Catholic medal for all the nearby warriors to see beneath the shimmering sun in that buttermilk sky, as if to say he too wore some strange, powerful medicine to ward off their bullets and arrows.

"You can't kill *me!*" he called as a few more of his men

darted away into the smoke, intent on making it to Custer's lines.

The rear guard is falling. He fired his pistol at a warrior leaping after a soldier running north. Keogh nailed the warrior, really wanting to shoot the soldier in the back.

There's just too many, his mind raced clear and cool as any mountain stream surging out of the Bighorns. All round them howled ten times ten the number they had figured would be camped in this bloody valley.

Just too damned many for any of us to handle now. No way out—

With a snort the horse beside Keogh reared and in falling nearly knocked him over. Even the sure, gentle hands of the old files were failing to keep the horses from bolting now. They reared and fell back over the men, stumbling against each other in pure panic, breaking their hobbles, pinning and crushing soldiers beneath them, stomping on any unfortunate trooper who didn't roll out of their way fast enough.

Near Keogh's feet a young soldier knelt, sobbing, mumbling an incoherent prayer. As Myles watched, utterly mesmerized, unable to stop him, the young shavetail threw his rifle away and pulled out his service revolver. He handled the weapon as if it were some foreign, revered icon, juggling the heavy object into position alongside his head. The youngster pulled back the hammer, then calmly and without ceremony yanked on the trigger.

His brains splattered over three troopers nearby.

All three jerked round in fear and disgust, watching a comrade-in-arms fall into the yellow dust.

To Myles it was like watching one of Custer's short vignettes back at Fort Abraham Lincoln.

The captain stood spellbound, dumbstruck while the evil asserted its control on his company. More soldiers suddenly sagged, giving up to pull pistols themselves. Pointing muzzles at their temples or breasts, triggers squeezed with eyes fiercely clenched. They dispatched their mortal souls into limbo rather than suffer the possibility of torture at the hands of the Indians.

Save the last goddamned bullet for yourself.

Stunned, baffled by the suicides rippling the hillside around him, Keogh watched pairs of men point guns at each other's hearts in death pacts. Others died alone . . . no one to kill them . . . completing this last dirty little task for themselves. Slowly the staunch defense along Keogh's ridge began unraveling. Strange that even as his perimeter fell apart, most of the Indian fire slacked off.

Keogh could tell that the gunfire from Calhoun's Hill had faded.

Indeed, those warriors back along the ridge sat silently behind their tall clumps of sage and furry tufts of bunch-grass watching in frosty fascination as the pony soldiers fought among themselves, shooting each other until only a grim handful remained at the top of that dusty spine, a hardened knot gathered in a tight ring of corpses and horse carcasses.

Bitterly Keogh ordered a retreat with what was left of his Wild I Company. The first retreat he had ordered in his life.

Through the dust and smoke of this Sioux-made hell they crawled up on their knees and for a moment peered across the slopes toward the last hill less than a half mile away.

A few bolted away along the backbone, running hunched over like squat prairie cocks skittering through the sage ahead of a hungry coyote. First one, then another, darted off. Dust from hundreds of bullets kicked up funnels among their heels as they zigzagged their way through the sage. One was down, then another, now a third. And with those fallen soldiers sank the hope of Keogh's last command.

One trooper sighed with a death rattle and calmly replaced his six empty shells in his revolver with live ammunition. He then crawled over to a tight knot of four quivering, whimpering recruits. Two of them gazed up at the veteran's face, appealing to him with their tears and tortured expressions—imploring him with empty, quivering hands.

"This can't be happening!" one shouted.

"Whadda we do? Whadda we do now?" cried another.

Methodically, one at a time, the old file placed his pistol

against the back of each head. The fourth young trooper went down without protest or struggle.

Then, without warning, Sergeant Frank E. Varden suddenly turned the weapon on himself before Keogh leapt to stay him. The pistol tumbled from Varden's grip as his body twitched, then collapsed atop the bodies of the last four recruits left in his entire squad. Sergeant Varden had protected his men to the last.

Keogh knelt trembling in rage. Disbelief like a cold, hard stone clogged his throat. Revulsion soured his tongue, seeing his men blow their own brains out. Myles Keogh had seen enough wounds and battlefield action to numb him to blood and gore. This was something else entirely that twisted his stomach now and made him heave up what was left of the dry breakfast they had wolfed down before Custer had moved them up and over the divide. It all came out with a good dose of sour whiskey in gut-relieving lumps that lay in the dust and the grass, beside these men, joining their blood in the ocher soil on this lonely hillside in Montana.

And when his belly finished punishing him, Keogh took up Varden's bloodied pistol. Finding the sergeant had left one last live round in the cylinder. Keogh put the revolver to his forehead and rammed the hammer back, feeling how cool the muzzle felt against his sweating brow.

"Good man, Varden," he croaked, speaking to the dead man beside him. "You saved the last bullet for your ol' cap'n Keogh."

He couldn't bring himself to pull that trigger. Life had always been too damned precious for him.

Keogh allowed the weapon to fall out of his hand, knowing his only course now lay along the ragged spine . . . a half mile, perhaps a bit more.

Hell, it don't matter how far, Myles.

He'd join the others. He could rally them.

Tommy boy'll be there. Might even have a sip or two of whiskey about him. Tommy's always been that way. When it comes to whiskey and women—Tommy isn't stiff like his big brother.

Myles yanked cartridges from Varden's belt, loading one, then two, and finally four pistols with fresh rounds.

Then, with a war cry of his own, Captain Myles Keogh rose to his feet like a mighty oak. He stuffed two pistols in his belt, manhandling another pair. He emptied one as he bolted off, then flung it angrily at a charging warrior. With the first shot out of the second, Keogh brought another Sioux skidding to a stop to stare at the red hole in his chest before he crumpled to the sand like a wet sack of corn mash.

Lumbering with all the concealed grace of a draft horse, Myles was off on his big Irish feet, dashing as he had never run before, remembering the footraces he always lost to Billy Cooke.

This's one day ye'd not win again' me, Cookey!

Keogh fired left then right as warriors popped up, lunging for him with clubs and rifles. Each wanted to be the man to lay first coup on this mighty warrior who wore the metal bars on his shoulders and that shiny medicine disc round his bull neck.

Myles fired and ran, ran and fired, until the two pistols clicked and clicked again. He hurled them angrily at red targets, yanking the last one free and into action. He pulled the trigger again and again, his feet covering ground as if there were only wind beneath his boots.

All the dark Irishman knew for sure was that he was thirsty and Tom Custer just might have a drink or two about him.

On and on he ran, the bullets kicking up spurts of dirt around his big plodding boots. Bullets split the air about his black head like mad mosquitoes whistling on the Rosebud. The only thing Myles Keogh knew for certain was that he was thirsty . . . so thirsty he would do damned near any bidding for a drink right about now.

Captain Myles Keogh had always been like that, though. He would do anything for a drink.

In fact, he would race right into hell itself.

CHAPTER 25

CALHOUN'S Hill had fallen.

Keogh's ridge was no more.

One by one Custer's officers had gathered round the mortally wounded commander on the west slope at the north end of this bony ridge a few yards below the bare, windswept crest.

Even Keogh himself had lumbered in at the end, nicked and slightly the worse for wear, dragging behind him some screaming Sioux and Cheyenne warriors out of the nightmare of yellow haze.

Now this favored inner circle drew round their leader like old herd bulls protectively guarding their patriarch against snarling wolves. Tom, Cooke, Keogh, Smith, and Yates. Around these officers clustered the survivors from each company, their shrinking command post ringed by a wall of horse carcasses.

What goes through a man's mind when he feels the sweat pouring along his backbone, gazing down a dusty slope at the silvery river, and the village without end just beyond the cottonwoods?

Ringing in every soldier's ears above the shriek of warriors and the high-pitched whine of wing-bone whistles were those orders barked over the command by one officer or another. The refuse of battle littered their hillside. Wounded men cried out for water, for help, for a friend to come pull them to the top.

Water!

That's all the dying men needed as they gazed into a shapeless, shimmering sun suspended directly overhead, beating down unmercifully on their hilltop from a bone yellow sky. The sun stared back with one accusing eye at the soldiers who had come to raid camps of women and children and the old ones too weak to run.

There were other moans that afternoon on the hill. Cries of despair and utter hopelessness among the recruits of Smith's company, Custer's and Yates's commands too. Young men who saw utter futility in fighting on. At first they had clung to the hope in what their officers promised them once they reached the end of this ridge. At first they had believed in Custer—hoping they could hold out until Gibbon and Terry marched upriver with their reinforcements.

Wasn't a man on that bare hillside who didn't realize what price Calhoun's men had paid in buying some precious time for the remaining four companies under Custer's command.

And on the heels of that murderous slaughter, they had watched stunned and increasingly numb as Keogh's men put up the beginnings of a desperate fight. Gall pressing from the south. Lame-White-Man and Two Moons leading their Cheyennes from the west. And Crazy Horse's Oglalla cavalry hitting, slashing, tearing at I Company from the east.

On hot breezes came the death chants and songs of victory, drifting up the hill. The warriors had only to wait for the sun and time itself to do its evil on these last hold-outs near the top of the ridge. Songs the warriors sang to make themselves brave.

But those last few gathering round Custer near the crest didn't seem to remember any songs of their own to make them courageous that afternoon. They just couldn't remember the words anymore. Hard enough to keep breathing, or keep from soiling your army britches, much less try to remember some damned words to a song.

Tom Custer shot a soldier in the back of the head, stunning all those but the officers huddling nearby.

Try as he might, Fresh Smith trembled, watching the soldier's brains and blood soak into the parched earth.

"I told him!" young Custer roared, wagging the pistol at the dead man twitching at his feet in the last throes of death.

The young soldier lurched convulsively, his bowels voiding, then lay still in the stench and heat of that yellow hill.

Lieutenant Algernon E. Smith gulped. For years now he had it drummed into his head that an officer could kill a coward who refused to fight. He had never before seen any officer do it.

"Gave him a direct order!" Custer shrieked. "There'll be no cowardice on *this* hill, men! We're—not—going—to—fall!"

"By glory, we'll hang on!" George Yates shouted to show his support.

"Damned right!" Tom explained to the dumbfounded soldiers staring at him with different eyes now. "Just like the general says . . . we'll make it. I'll shoot the next one that talks of surrender to these savages!"

"Gimme a carbine and a belt, Tommy boy!"

Tom Custer scooped up a dead trooper's carbine and ammunition belt, flinging them both at Keogh.

Keogh spoke softly. "Ain't much better here, it 'pears. We're weakest back 'long the ridge. But, gimme a dozen men or so, I'll go shore up that south flank. They're pressing us that way and in a hard ditch of it too."

"Keogh?"

It was George Custer's croak, emerging from the dry, wounded pit of him.

Myles knelt beside his commander in the dust. "Right here, General. Too evil a bastard to die just yet, I am."

His Irish smile buoyed many a man struck silent on the side of that yellow hill as his big head shaded the general's dirty red-bristled face. Custer opened his eyes and, swallowed against the pain in his chest. Beneath that cat's-whisker brush of a mustache of his, Custer tried a grin, showing a little of his teeth before blood trickled across his cracked lips.

"Thank you, Myles," he sputtered softly. "See what you can do for us, will you?"

"Aye, General!" Keogh smiled, rising, casting his full shadow across Custer. "Told you before what it meant to have your trust and your friendship, Armstrong." He sighed as he called the general by name, something he had never done before.

Custer tried to salute but gave up. He couldn't get his right arm up that far.

"Sorry, Myles," he rasped. "Going a bit numb."

"That's all right, sir, you can salute me later. When we're all done here. But for now—I've got to send some of these bleeming h'athen savages straight back to the pits of hell for you!"

The recruits and officers alike watched the big brawler leap over a dead horse as if it were but a clump of sage. Keogh hunkered down the skirmish line, tapping a man here, another there, handpicking his defense force. When he had his dozen, Keogh led his squad south along the knotted spine, spacing them out in pockets here and there.

The southern flank would not fall if Myles Keogh and his hard-files had anything to say about it. Grim-eyed, sunburned, saddle-galled veterans every one, they fired slow and sure and steady at the advancing Sioux just the way they had worked over Confederates at Bull Run, Shiloh, Gettysburg.

One target at a time. One shot at a time. These men with Myles Keogh knew how to fight.

Myles Keogh would show the lot of them how to die.

"The canteens are dry, Autie," Tom whispered in a crackle near his brother's ear. "Too many wounded, can't keep 'em quiet. Hollering for water. It's beginning to drive the men mad." He knew Autie must be desperate for water himself.

"The river . . . just—get to the river," Custer sputtered, coughing. "Open a route down to the river . . . now. . . ."

Custer struggled again to rise, pulling on Tom until he sat upright, gritting those pearly teeth against the excruciating pain of that seeping hole in his chest.

He pointed. "Down there," indicating the deep scar of the ravine. "Send a detail down there to secure . . . the coulee . . . we get water . . . there—"

Custer collapsed. It was more than he could bear, holding himself up that long. Issuing orders to the end.

"I'll do it, Autie," Tom replied, the iron back in his voice.

"No, you won't, Captain," Lieutenant Smith slid in beside the general, his own words full of granite. "My men'll do it. We'll go down to secure that ravine for water carriers. If we intend to hold out as the general wants us to—we'll need water. Begging pardon, Tom, but you needs stay here. In command. With the general."

Tom sensed his heart swell with the courage of the young lieutenant's offer. "Very well, Fresh. I'm proud of you."

"Thank you, sir." He turned to go.

"Smith?" Sounding like a rusty iron wagon tire dragged down a gravel road, Tom's words caught the lieutenant up short.

Smith glanced over his shoulder, studying that red spot on Tom's cheek, remembering the bullet wound and a young cavalry officer single-handedly charging a Confederate artillery position at Saylor's Creek eleven long summers before.

"Good luck, Smith."

"Thank you, Cap'n. We really don't need luck though. Just the kind of sand you showed at Saylor's Creek, Tom. That, and some time."

"You'll buy the time for us, Fresh."

"Promise you—we'll give our best!"

Smith slapped a smart salute and headed downhill toward his chewed-up E. Company.

With sergeants John Ogden and James Riley, Smith selected thirty-six more men, three squads with a corporal to lead each. Without much ado the squads stood ready at horse. Sending a hearty wave back up the hillside to the commander, Smith's men mounted what was left of the big horses.

"Front into line . . . guide front . . . *center!* Forward at my command—*charge!*"

Into the maddening yellow dust that fuzzed the slope like dirty cotton gauze, the men dashed toward the river below.

Smith knew well enough that his brave action could serve to inspire those left behind on the hill, men whose spirits were flagging. If his detail could only show some aggressiveness against the circling red noose, the command might be able to hold the warriors off for another—who was to say?

Tom stood, saluting that mad dash. *God only knows if we can hold out long enough for Gibbon and Terry to come up,* he thought to himself, reloading both pistols now. *But first we have to cut and hold a route to the river. And that's just what Smith's about to do for me, and for Autie.*

Monaseetah watched the group of four-times-ten mount their big horses and gallop downhill from the hilltop, believing that Custer himself must surely be in that brave group on horseback.

Always leading his men.

"He comes for me!" she sang out with the certainty of it, clambering to her feet that he might see her.

"Hiestzi! I am here! Husband—I wait for you!"

A young Cheyenne warrior leapt to his feet nearby, dragging her down among the tall grasses as random carbine shots from the knoll lobbed her way, kicking up spouts of yellow dirt.

"He is my husband!" she protested at the warrior, who pinned her down in the grass.

He was sweaty and smelled of rancid bear grease in his

braids, in the paint smeared across his cheeks and under his mouth. All of it furred now with the dust everywhere. He stank.

"Hiestzi returns for me at last," she pleaded with the young warrior to understand, smelling his foul breath in her face, suffocating her. "He promised to come back for me. I must go to him!"

"Hiestzi is not here. The Red-Beard sent his soldiers against us again. Yellow Hair is far, far away." He tried to calm her, clamping a dirty, sweaty hand over her screaming mouth. But try as he might, Monaseetah remained hysterical, biting and kicking now. Shrieking at the top of her lungs when he yanked his hand back in pain.

"Hiestzi! I wait for you!"

She suddenly lay still, panting beneath the warrior's weight. "Don't you see? He has returned for me exactly as promised! He has come for me now in the Moon of Fat Horses!"

Right after propping himself up to watch Smith's charge down the hill, Custer thought he heard something out of place among the chants and curses, something not belonging with the wing-bone whistles and drums, or the cries and grunts of dying men. Something high-pitched, like an arrow in flight, yet sweet to his long-ago memory. A voice he recalled from the past . . . a long winter gone.

It can't be true, Custer decided, wrestling down the pain threatening to overwhelm him and drive him into blessed unconsciousness.

You're suffering too much, Autie . . . this wound . . . the blood spilled—that's all it is, he told himself. *It's just pain. You can fight it now the same way you've fought everything else all your life . . . scratched your way up from nothing to Boy General. Just fight the pain—*

"Yellow Hair!" There it came again.

That voice! Where? Ohhh, God . . . a man can only do so much! I tried to reach you. No! It's not true . . . not here . . . most certainly not now!

"*Yellow Hair!*"

The voice climbed again above the din of battle and the

cries of the dying—scratching at his ears without stop. He strained his dust-reddened eyes and licked at the blood-crusted, alkali-cracked lips, hungering suddenly for the taste of her mouth as if it had been yesterday's hot summer sun rising when last he saw her . . . waving from that wagon as he waved back—promising he would return for her.

Knowing now that he had never really stopped wanting her.

It cannot be, Custer's fevered mind burned. *But Lord! This hunger for her is like something solid I can't escape . . . aching across all these years.*

He struggled to prop himself up higher, ears pricking to locate the voice.

Downhill! Monaseetah's coming to take this all from me . . . ohhh, God!

The pain caused him to double up as he pushed himself to rise. He spit out a little stomach bile. All that was left in his stomach now.

Yes, Autie—you want her perhaps even more than life itself right now.

He wanted her to touch him one last time—now that everything was slowly fading out behind his eyelids, looking more and more like a gray pool of sleet on the northern plains that struggled to capture winter's light.

He could not have the presidency now . . . he could not reach out and touch Libbie. For so long Libbie had kept herself from him.

This Montana hillside held him prisoner as surely as his restless soul would wander no more. This is where he would die.

Yet . . . before he closed his eyes, Custer wanted her to hold him one last time.

Hold him just long enough to last into forever.

After charging downhill only five hundred yards, the first of Smith's men yanked on their reins, drawing to a halt after effectively scattering the Sioux and Cheyenne before them.

They had driven the warriors out of the ravine itself, flushing them down the slope before their wild charge—but the soldiers suddenly did something most unexpected by white or red alike. They stopped dead in their tracks for no apparent reason. At least no reason any man on that hill could figure out.

No reason at all—for they hadn't counted on Lame-White-Man and his Cheyenne Crazy Dog soldiers.

A Southern Cheyenne war chief, visiting relatives up north for that summer gathering of the great camp circles, Lame-White-Man had led a strong contingent of warriors from the upper camps across the river at the mouth of the deep ravine, throwing his force against the pony soldiers entrenched on the hill under Tom Custer. He was himself a many-scarred veteran and not likely to frighten easily, buckling as did the youngsters under the charge of Smith's forty.

"Brothers!" the Lame One shouted, rising to his feet. "We must stand our ground. Do not quail before these pony soldiers. They are but dust in the wind. We are many. We are mighty. Hold your ground! This is your day!"

Many of the warriors retreating in panic before the troopers halted, looking back over their shoulders. Now they saw for themselves. Exactly as Lame-White-Man declared—the soldiers were not many. And they were not following.

Perhaps by magic, some thought, *the Lame One has turned back the soldiers!*

With renewed courage the Cheyennes wheeled about, starting back up the slope to where the lone war chief stood his ground, exhorting his young men to join him in this battle against the forty.

The Lame One hobbled a bit, but despite his limp he marched steadily upward, closing on the place where the soldiers reined back, drawing their snorting horses together in a confused mob.

By the time the soldiers had dismounted near the side of the long ravine, Lame's warriors had edged closer under continued fire. The smell of Indians on the wind drove the big horses mad with fear. They reared and bucked and pulled at their holders.

Suddenly a few older Cheyenne boys leapt from the

sage, waving blankets and shouting at the frightened horses, scaring the encircled soldiers into full-scale panic.

First the horses bolted away, careening downhill toward the river, their stirrups and saddlebags of ammunition clattering through the tall grass and past screeching warriors. Thirsty far too long. It was easy work for the young boys and old men at the river to round these last horses up, head them downstream. The white man's animals wanted nothing more than to be near the water.

With dry throats of their own, Smith's soldiers gazed longingly downhill. Their mounts gone   any means of escape gone as well. Hope disappeared like a puff of yellow dust in the dry breeze.

Everywhere the air filled with sound, crushing at their ears. Burnt powder stung nostrils, clinging to the hillside like dirty coal-cotton gauze. Dust burnt eyes into dark, reddened sockets. And still more warriors splashed across the shining ribbon of the river, swarming over the hillside like red ants from a nest Custer had stirred with a big stick.

"Here!" Sergeant John Ogden's voice rose above the shrieks of the enemy and cries of panic among the young soldiers. "Follow me to the ravine!"

No one needed to suggest the ravine more than once to those men. Up here on the slope, they were helpless and exposed, naked to the painted enemy. Nearly all of them dashed off on Ogden's heels, scrambling downhill and sliding into the ravine they had intended to secure and hold until Gibbon's boys arrived.

As soon as the soldiers scrambled over the edge, Lame-White-Man exhorted his warriors into the mouth of the coulee itself, charging up toward the milling, frightened, trapped soldiers.

Panic began to spread its evil curse like wildfire among the thirty-eight at the bottom. With the charge of the Cheyennes up the ravine, the young soldiers began a furious scramble to escape their self-made trap. The sides of that gully were irregular, dotted with stunted cactus, bunchgrass, and gray-leafed sage. Not much for a man to hold onto in clawing his way out.

They found themselves caught like fish in a drying

puddle, ready for the killing. Better to try to clamber back uphill.

Time and again they pocked at the south wall with attempts to dig their way up the sides of the ravine. Kicking holes out for their boot-toes and digging furrows for their fingertips, some fought the side of that ravine as hard as they would fight their panic. Until they slid exhausted to the floor of the coulee, able to fight their fear no more. Confused and terrified, some fired aimlessly into the air. Then panic won the day.

As Smith himself crawled through sagebrush, he listened to the loud reports of carbine and pistol fire erupting from the ravine. He glanced back on that slash of a coulee as he pulled himself uphill at an agonizing pace, watching blue powder smoke belch from the ravine, thinking his troops were giving a hard time of it to the Cheyenne.

If only they'll hold out, Smith prayed, *I'll bring some more men down, and we can secure the route for the general.*

Just as he had promised he would.

Yet as the young lieutenant crawled away, an entirely different scene from the one he imagined occurred in the bottom of that ravine. Instead of shooting at the warriors crawling up the ravine, the desperate soldiers turned their weapons on themselves.

With a powerful and contagious despair, a single trooper put his pistol muzzle to his head and pulled the trigger. Mesmerized, his comrades watched, helpless to stop him. That lonely soldier's private panic now spread like cholera.

Another man jammed his pistol against his heart. Two soldiers up near the far mouth of the ravine shot each other in the head as the Cheyenne raced over their still-trembling bodies.

To the approaching warriors the troopers were touched by the Everywhere Spirit to kill themselves. In utter awe the young warriors watched, disbelieving—some rubbing their eyes, others holding hands over their mouths in awe so their souls would not fly away. Suicide was something far from the Indian experience.

Of a sudden Cheyenne chief Two Moons was among the

warriors on his pale horse, rallying the fighters to charge up the coulee behind Lame-White-Man. To throw themselves right into the milling, confused, suicidal soldiers. "This will be the last day you see your war chief, Two Moons! Come watch me! I die with honor!"

"Nastano!" Lame-White-Man hollered. "Come—Two Moons will lead us to kill these soldiers!"

"Hey! Hey!" Two Moons replied, his voice high and shrill and buoying above the commotion in the ravine. "These are only children. They are ready for us to kill them! Do not be afraid of children!"

With his words of encouragement ringing in their ears, the warriors rushed up the coulee, carrying hawks and lances and knives. Each one ready for hand-to-hand of it. Coup counting in close combat.

But not a single soldier remained standing to resist that Cheyenne charge. Every one lay dead.

The white men had killed themselves and each other.

CHAPTER 26

Farther up that bloody, carcass-littered hillside, the hold-outs watched it happen.

Angrily, bitterly now, they poured their fire down into the Cheyennes busy over the dead troopers, warriors pounding in the head of any white man still breathing. Stone clubs mashing heads with a soppy, wet thud. The carbine fire of those at the crest ultimately took its toll, forcing the Cheyenne back to the mouth of the ravine to seek cover.

There the warriors found the three casualties of their brief skirmish. Two young Cheyennes picked off by soldier marskmen up the hill. And Lame-White-Man himself.

A dark sense of despair descended upon the hill. Their plan to open up a route to the water supply had failed. What was worse, Custer's officers had to watch as friends committed suicide, giving in to panic and defeat exactly as they had done at Keogh's position.

Now all that was left for the hold-outs was to make a stand here on this last hill for as long as possible.

"Autie." Tom knelt beside his brother, whispering loud enough to be heard over the gunfire banging away on all sides. "There ain't many of us left now."

Custer struggled bravely against the pain in his chest and the waves of nausea that threatened to engulf him. By holding his brother's arm, Custer sat up a bit straighter, swallowing hard against the dry knot of blood coagulating at the back of his throat.

"Boston?" Custer asked.

Tom shooked his head, scratching his cheek stubble. He gazed downhill a few yards, silent.

"Autie?" Custer asked. "Young Autie?"

Tom only wagged his head of greasy hair, having lost his hat at the ford before their mad rush. He dared not try to speak just yet, afraid of what might spill out. Somewhere on that ride up from the river he had seen Autie's body, among the trampled grass and sagebrush and stunted cactus. Trampled in retreat.

"I never should've brought them," Autie whispered angrily. It was the longest sentence he had spoken in over an hour. Ever since he ordered them to follow him down the Medicine Tail and into the village.

"Never made the village," he coughed, then smiled weakly at Tom. "Never gonna make it to Washington. Not now, Tom—I'm sorry."

"Hush," Tom said gruffly. "Just be quiet now."

"How many . . ." He coughed the words free, clutching his bubbling chest. "How many left?"

"I'd say forty, maybe." Tom answered, slewing his eyes over the hillside. "Maybe as many as fifty. We're fairly chewed up, but—"

"Dr. Lord? God, can't he help me? Give me some laudanum, something so I can get on my feet? Must take command before it's too late for the rest! Find Lord for me!"

Tom pushed a struggling, emaciated brother back down, against the horse carcass. "It's too late for that now, Autie."

"Lord . . . too?"

"Yes. He did what he could for you. Told us that. Said it's a little too late for the rest of us too."

"Damn you, Tom! Goddamn you! We don't give up!" Custer sputtered, glazed eyes narrowing darkly.

Tom shook his head sadly. "No, Autie. We Custers don't ever give up, do we? It's just—the only thing left is to do as much damage as we can while men and ammunition hold out."

"I ordered every man to bring a hundred—"

"Not anymore," Tom interrupted, patting Custer's shoulder. "Most of the horses are gone too. Some carbines jamming badly. Men having to hunt through the bodies for a usable weapon . . . cartridges in the pockets, on belts."

"I see." Custer gritted his teeth as another wave of nausea hit him; he doubled over, supported by Tom as he puked up more yellow bile and pink froth.

When the grip of it had released him, Custer sagged against the stinking, bloated horse carcass, staring down the slope to the south and west. "My God! Where'd they all come from?"

"The village you were hunting, Autie."

At their feet lay the thousands upon thousands of lodges, erected in orderly camp circles along the twists and bends of the Little Bighorn. All the villages spread out before Custer like the mighty nations of the Sioux and Northern Cheyenne paying homage, bowing in reverence at his feet.

"Dammit, Tom! Where's Benteen with the . . ." And he sputtered up some more chunks of pink lung along with frothy blood, spitting them into the yellow dust at his side. "Benteen and the ammunition I ordered hours ago—"

"Less than two hours, Autie."

He gazed up at Tom, wonder mixed with fear in his eyes.

"We've been whipped in less than two hours?"

Tom nodded. "Yes. And Benteen hasn't come yet. Maybe we can hold out till that white-headed bastard does get his ass up here with ammo and more men. If . . ."

"If what, Tom?"

"If Benteen can break through the goddamned Sioux to get to us." His eyes held Autie's for a long, long moment.

"I understand," Custer replied gravely, lips spreading in

a thin red line of determination. "Help me sit up a bit more, will you, brother?"

Everywhere around their dusty command post, men were methodically butchered by arrow and bullet alike. Custer's own private desperation and long-hidden fear of failure finally overwhelmed him as he watched his men, beloved troopers of his Seventh dying all round him like dry leaves tumbling from a mighty oak at autumn's first slashing wind.

"Get the field glasses."

Through them Custer peered hopefully to the south and west, where he had left Reno and Benteen to their fates.

"By God, I need his ammunition," he finally exclaimed with a wet, gushing sound. "Benteen's gotta make it through to us."

"Gotta be soon, Autie."

"General?"

"George?" Custer was genuinely happy to see Yates, buoyed by a hometown face here beside him in the final minutes, when a lot of the pain subsided. He swallowed hard, releasing silent, salty tears as he peered into the grim, blackened face swimming before his.

"General, there's thirty-four of us left on the hill," Yates reported. "No telling how many Reno's got left now after he got cut up in the valley."

"I was planning to batter the head," Custer rambled, staring into the bone yellow sky. "If Reno had only held their feet down while I—"

"General? General Custer?" Yates grabbed Custer's chin, pulling his sunburned face so he could look Custer in the eye. "It's not Reno, it's not Benteen I'm worried about."

"Benteen?" Custer snapped alive with a spark ignited from some place deep within him. "Benteen's coming, you say?"

"No, sir," Yates answered. "I can't believe he's coming, not now."

With no small agony Custer pulled himself upright against the carcass, lifting DeRudio's Austrian field glasses to his eyes. For long, anxious moments he trained the glasses on the hills to the south and east. Suddenly the commander noticed shapes and color shimmering through the thick dust and haze rising off the landscape. Through the waves of heat he saw a mass of shimmery blue . . . then the mirage separated into column-of-twos.

"By the love of God!" he gasped, blood oozing from his lips. "It's Benteen! He's coming, boys! By all that's—Benteen's coming!"

Tom yanked the binoculars from his brother, disbelieving, knowing Autie was close to a rambling fool by now.

But he wanted to believe so badly himself. With everything he had in him, Tom wanted to believe. He strained his eyes on those hills far away and squinted through the haze. Sure enough, he found blue columns loping north, a motley mixture of companies on different colored mounts. The rescue columns galloped past a high point some few miles south of Custer's hill, marching north.

"Damn, if you aren't right, Autie!" he shouted.

Then Yates took up the cheer, scurrying here, then hunkering in a crab walk to carry the word elsewhere. With the captain's good news, each knot of hold-outs immediately raised tired voices and carbines in the air at the prospect of rescue. Even Keogh and his crew of old-files hollered along the spine with gritty joy.

"How long, sir?" Lieutenant Cooke asked, his dark, handsome eyes boring into Tom's.

Young Custer studied Cooke's face, remembering the times they had courted the Wadsworth sisters together—summer picnics and winter sleigh rides. Wondering now if Cookey had been as lucky as he to get his hand inside so many perfumed blouses, feel the soft coolness of so many naked alabaster thighs in the shadows of a shaded bower—

Tom brought the field glasses to his eyes, staring into the shimmering southlands. He could not believe what he was forced to watch now, refusing to accept what he saw happening on that faraway high-point. For the longest time he stared, numbed, his mouth hung half open, like a voyeur caught peeking at something obscene.

When he finally brought the glasses from his face, Tom swallowed down his own despair, gathering strength for what needed saying. Laying the glasses on Autie's chest, he told them. "Looks like Benteen won't be coming after all."

"Not coming?" Cooke growled.

"He's been overwhelmed," Tom explained, gazing now at his brother's gaping chest wound, wet and bright beneath the high light. "Turned around . . . a goddamned rout."

"Tom?"

He looked into Autie's questioning eyes, glazing and sunken ever more now. "Yes, brother. They're retreating. Trapped and surrounded. Just like us."

Within that stinking compound made of some seventy dead horses littering the hillside, just below its crest, the air went deathly silent while it all sank in.

The only sound for the longest time was the random Indian bullet smacking into those huge, bloating carcasses. With every hit noxious gas escaped with a moist hiss, adding to the despair creeping over that yellow slope.

Lieutenant W. W. Cooke—Canadian adventurer who came south to fight in the Civil War and afterwards joined Custer's newly formed Seventh U.S. Cavalry at Fort Riley to fight Indians rather than return home—rose awkwardly to one knee.

"Well, gentlemen," he began in that soft, winning way of his that had won the friendship of many a man and the heart of many a pretty lady. "General, sir. I've a job to do. And I'm still of one body and soul so, I'll be about it."

Cooke stood, a fairly large man for the time and exceedingly fleet of foot. He more than any other man had won regimental footraces held at forts Riley, Hays, and Abraham Lincoln. "Just this last month we celebrated my thirtieth birthday, boys."

"I remember it well, my friend," Tom said, placing a hand on Cooke's shoulder. "What a celebration that was. We truly drank the day away!"

"Aye." Cooke licked his burning lips. "Wish I had some of that whiskey right about now." He sounded sorry there wasn't any left after caring for the wounded with what whiskey had been carried to the hillside in some saddlebags. "But there's been many a time in the past that I knew for sure the way my life was going, I'd never make thirty.

And look at me!" He chuckled with dark humor. "I'm thirty now and stuck on some goddamned hillside in—who knows where? Going to buy myself a small piece of this goddamned barren ground! Made it to thirty—only to die a month later!" He started to cackle wildly.

Tom Custer lunged at Cooke, gripping his shoulders in a close, fierce embrace. When Tom pulled back, he said "Billy, why don't you go right over there?" He pointed out a position on the perimeter that needed some bolstering. "Looks like we could use a top shot covering that slope."

Behind his tears, Cooke swallowed hard. "I am a good shot, you know."

"The best, Billy." Custer himself struggled to raise a hand to his adjutant. "I ought to know . . . choosing you to lead our sharpshooters at the Washita." He winced with a swell of pain. The gray veil passed over his eyes. "You remember the Washita, don't you fellas? The high point for the Seventh Cavalry. You remember, don't you?"

Cooke knelt again beside Custer, wrapping one of the bloody freckled hands in both of his.

"Aye, General." Cooke nearly choked on the sob, some slow, fat tears rolling down his cheeks and into those thick black Dundrearies. "It's been a hell of a pleasure knowing you, sir! One hell of an honor too. May I shake your hand, General?"

"Of course, Billy Cooke." Custer did not fight to hide his tears any longer. "You've been one of my closest allies all along. I'm going to miss you too." His eyes gone gray searched each of them out now. "Miss all of you." Then he gazed back at Cooke. "Remember one thing for me, Lieutenant Cooke . . ." He waited, clenching his eyes against the pain like a hot poker dragged slowly through his rib cage. "Remember, we're taking no prisoners this time."

At first, none of them knew how to take that. Then the general opened his eyes. They seemed to sparkle with some renewed light. It wasn't only a glistening of tears. Some small flicker of fire still burned bright behind those sapphire eyes.

He was having a rough time breathing. So much pressure

on his chest that he wanted to cry out. Instead, he would issue his last orders.

"Spread out. Keep your heads down. And remember, we take no prisoners this trip out."

Cooke clutched the general's freckled hand quickly a last time, then was gone up the north slope in a crouch, crabbing in the direction where he would keep an eye on a band of warriors massing down the side of the hill.

God, it looks like better'n a thousand of the heathen bastards down there now, Cooke thought to himself as he skidded through the yellow dust and around stinking bodies.

And out front of them all sat a warrior with light-colored unbraided hair, perched regally atop a prancing horse painted with bloody handprints on its hips, an arrow and a scalp drawn along the neck of the animal. Close enough for Cooke to marvel at the princely bearing of this one.

If I didn't know better, Billy Cooke thought, *he looks grill enough to be a Fifth Royal Lancer, that one!*

That solitary warrior sat watching, studying the hold-outs upon the rise. As if deciding whether or not to crush such a pitiful last reserve of *wasichu* soldiers.

"Tom?"

"I'm right here, Autie. Not going to leave you now. Won't ever leave you, brother."

Custer reached out for him, his eyes glazed so badly he could barely see. And Tom, his hand was there, holding onto his own with a fierce grip. He fought down the bile that rose with the pressure filling his chest, heavy on his belly.

"G-get me . . . get me to the top," Custer gasped. "I've got to . . . just get me to the top."

"Sure, Autie," Tom answered, his voice wavering. He glanced up to the top. It was still some fifty feet away. "Should I drag you?"

"Yes . . ." He winced in more pain, sensing he didn't have long now. What with the effort it took to speak, to stay conscious. "Just get me to the top."

Tom Custer stuffed the pistol in his holster, then thought better. He picked up two more Colts from soldiers who wouldn't be needing them any longer and stuffed them both in his belt. Only then did he lean over and snag both hands around Custer's collar, beginning to pull him over the summer-cured grass and sage.

Up . . . up . . . up the hill.

He wants to be close to the top, Tom kept reminding himself as he dragged the deadweight behind him. *Get him to the top. Damn, but you're heavy,* he wanted to complain out loud.

But the exertion was enough. Tom didn't want to waste his energy in this heat by talking.

Just get Autie to the top of his god . . . damned . . . hill.

Late June in Montana Territory.

The hillside ablaze with the splash of tiny flowers and budding blossoms. Across the tall-grass slopes lay scattered patches of locoweed like carpets spread over hardwood floors. So many flowers strewn in wild profusion across the rumpled-bedspread hillsides: pink and rose, lavender and blue, each one sleepily nodding its head at him in the soft June breeze.

Custer knew exactly how they felt. He wanted to go to sleep too . . . wanted so badly to go to sleep for a long, long time.

But he could smell them. And with their seductive scent, those wildflowers reminded him the time for picking drew near.

Young Indian girls would come up this hillside and gather the sweet peas and buffalo beans, carrying their treasure back down to their camp circles, where they would boil and mash the fruit to be eaten greedily with a tender hump roast.

He could remember those meals, Custer could. Why, even now he could see her as one of those young girls skipping giddily up this slope, with each gay step working her way between the bodies of men or bloated, gassy horse carcasses, completely oblivious—as if death hadn't opened its fetid bowels and littered itself across this colorful hillside. As if the foul refuse of war really wasn't here at all to defile this slope where young girls went to play and whisper together about their young lovers down in the villages at the river below.

Flowers all purple and magenta, white and fire orange

and a delicate pink. The color of his own skin under this merciless sun. Pink.

He had to make it to the top of the hill. If only Tom could get him there.

Custer turned his head slightly, blinking several times, trying to clear his eyes.

There it was! Right under the edge of bright sky!

Just make it to the top of the ridge, Tom. I'll be safe there. See everything from up . . . higher. Keep climbing, Tom. Good, brother! We're getting close. Get me up there on the ridge where the earth touches the sky. I can see it! Lord, I can see it clearly now—earth as brown as her slim body . . . rising to meet the sky the way her musky earth-scent breasts rose to meet my lips as I covered her.

That's it, Tom! Up there where no man has ever gone before . . . your destiny, Custer. It's your destiny alone, always has been yours alone to go where no man has trod.

Up just a little higher . . . higher still . . . up where I can seize the sky.

Less than twenty of them still breathed on the hill under that hot, merciless sun. Twenty, if you counted the wounded who could still hold a gun.

When Tom Custer, George Yates, and Fresh Smith led the rest of them out of the Medicine Tail and up the slope to that hogback spine of grass-strewn ridge to join with Keogh and Calhoun, there had been something close to two hundred twenty-five soldiers and civilians riding hell-bent for election to cover their asses and get someplace where there weren't so damned many screaming Indians.

By the time Tom and the rest left James Calhoun and Myles Keogh behind along the ridge, Custer had with him about a hundred and twelve stragglers limping onto that last hill north along the hogback.

After Smith's men had slaughtered themselves in the ravine and the lieutenant himself struggled to crawl back to the general's position, there were about sixty soldiers left, grim-lipped and squint-eyed, to stare back down the slope at the warriors closing the noose. Time and again their fierce, resolute little ring tightened round the general's command. Each of those still alive by some cruel twist of fate's own sleight of hand, understood by now that none of them were walking out of this valley.

No man found breath to joke about riding out either. A couple of men had tried that earlier. Corporal Foley and another.

Harrington, Tom thought. *Maybe it was him. Haven't seen the man in a long time.*

Both riders had succeeded in getting off a ways, each followed by warriors on ponies fresh and spirited for the chase. Then each soldier shot himself in the head before the warriors could catch them alive.

So no man on that hillside joked now about riding out of here. There was no one laughing anymore.

Tom had about had it from the drag uphill. He stopped to rest and catch his breath, yanking at the big blue bandanna knotted round his neck. Already sopping wet. Still he used it to wipe his brow while he dropped to the dust and grass beside his brother. He had watched that horrifying whirlwind of frightened horses, panicked men, and finally the suicides sweeping west along the ridge. He had seen it nibble away at the will to live . . . the will to try.

How long ago?

How long had it been since Smith had led them down? How long since the lieutenant had been cut off on his retreat uphill?

Poor, sad, Fresh Smith, Tom thought dryly, running his gummy tongue around the inside of his mouth, sour with the taste of old whiskey.

With the scars of a horrendous wound suffered in the Civil War, Smith couldn't raise his left arm above his shoulder, couldn't even put on his tunic without a struggle. So when his right arm was mangled by a Cheyenne bullet as he crawled away from the suicides in the ravine, Smith found himself fair game for any glory-seeking young warrior.

A Cheyenne Crazy Dog had stood over him seconds later, reveling in his triumph. Poor Smith, hampered now by two useless arms, spread-eagled on the hillside while the warrior carved his scalp off. Still alive.

The *scream* . . .

Tom would always remember that paralyzing sound. A friend, this Lieutenant Algernon E. Smith. Yes, Fresh was one to always do his best. But he just couldn't make it back up the hill as his men slaughtered themselves in that ravine below. His scream . . .

So as the warrior did his gruesome work on Smith's scalp, Tom Custer ground his teeth, swiped the hot tears from his eyes, and sat down calmly, bracing Autie's hunting rifle over the bloated ribs of a dead horse. He drew and held his breath. Let half of it go.

When he had the side of Smith's head in his sights, he closed his eyes to the stinging tears and squeezed on the Remington's trigger.

Reluctantly he had opened his eyes to the bright, white-hot sunlight once more. The Cheyenne warrior was standing every bit as tall, flinging his anger up the side of the hill at the man above who had killed the helpless soldier, robbing him of pleasure in slowly butchering the *wasichu* trooper wearing metal bars on his shoulders.

"Goodbye, Lieutenant Smith," Tom had whispered, choking on gall, pulling the Remington back. Then he slumped behind the horse carcass until Autie moaned.

How long ago now?

Now nearing the top of the hill, dragging his brother, the sun seemed brighter.

All of the civilians gone now. . . . Had no damned business coming along, Tom brooded.

Kellogg was somewhere down by the river. He had never made it very far out of the Medicine Tail at all. Riding that poor slow mule he loved and coaxed all the way from Lincoln. The mule had cost the reporter his life as those five companies made their last mad dash up the slope out of the slopes and away from the river.

Boston and young Autie.

Harry. Just should've called you Harry. Not named you after your famous uncle. Maybe you'd still be back in Monroe right now if they'd let you be just plain Harry. You'd be flirting with girls down at the mercantile . . . or sneaking in for a swim up to Hansford's place . . . swinging on that rope and dropping into the cool, rippling water. Instead, you're lying dead, baking on the hot sand of a nameless Montana hillside.

Tom eventually gazed down at Autie. Custer was still breathing, but his eyes were half closed, as if he were asleep. Only the whites of his eyes showing. Sleeping through these last few minutes. Quickly Tom pulled all three pistols from his belt and checked them for live rounds. Replacing some spent cartridges, young Tom put one back in the holster, one in his belt, and the third he clutched in his sweaty hand.

Lord, the soft, pliant breasts I've held with this hand, he thought, staring down at it dirty, bloody now. *What pleasure you gave the girls, Tommy lad. No more of that now.*

Certain as the sun baked the back of his neck, Tom would see that the last two bullets weren't used on the Indians. He'd learned enough from Indian warfare to know that. Two bullets. One for Autie, one for himself.

Lord, am I crying? Shit! I've never cried. Not even at Saylor's Creek when half my face was blown off in that charge for the flag. I had to do it, goddammit! That artillery position was chewing Autie's cavalry to pieces. Crying?

He sighed and fought for control. He didn't want to cry in front of the men. Not now. *Jesus, is it noisy here!* Just listening to the sound of these few men on the hill. To the south Keogh was down to—

Hell, Myles has four men left.

Cooke was firing off into a pocket of some snipers to the west and still doing some damage. *Christ, Billy had only two others still with him now.*

Down the west slope in front of Tom sat perhaps a dozen more of his men nestled behind the bodies of comrades or horse carcasses. Up here he felt so alone . . . so goddamned alone. Then he looked down at Autie's unruly straw mustache and sunburned freckled cheeks. And suddenly he didn't feel so alone anymore.

Up here right near the top of Autie's goddamned hill.

He tried to spit. Nothing but cotton balls in his mouth now.

Shit! Can I make it to the top? Can I?

Custer wanted Tom to drag him to the top. He had

always done what Autie wanted him to do. From their earliest days as kids in Ohio right up to courting the proper girl—that Agnes Bates from Monroe last summer at Lincoln. He had always done just what Autie wanted, and he always would.

Autie . . . oh, Autie! You were always the fair-haired boy in town, the hero—even as kids. The one we were told to be like. And I was always the younger brother—trying to live at the edge of your bright light. It wasn't fair, Autie!

I was every bit as good as you. But the only way anyone would ever pay attention to me was for me to chew tobacco in school, get in trouble in town—stealing, drinking whiskey with the older boys, raising hell. But you—no, you never raised hell. I had to, just to get someone to pay attention to me.

That's why I did those reckless, stupid things for you in the war, Autie. You understand now, don't you? Two goddamned Medals of Honor for heroism. That's why I charged alone while the other men around me were cut down or turned back. Simply because I wanted everyone else to know I was every bit as good as you. But look at us! We're both waiting to die on some dirty little hillside on some dirty little nameless goddamned river in Montana Territory.

And no one is going to know I saved you as long as I could . . . down to the last war cry on this hill . . . and then put an army bullet in your brain.

CHAPTER 27

No one would ever know.

How could they? He had never talked about it with any Sioux or Cheyenne friends. And the only white men who had laid eyes on him were dead now.

He was Crazy Horse. No one would ever know what he kept buried inside.

What it was had left a searing impression that had burned inside the pit of him up to this very day as he sat atop his war pony, staring up the north side of this grass hill where the last ragtag squad of pony soldiers had themselves dug in, soldiers who fired a shot now and then from behind other dead *wasichu* soldiers and horse carcasses.

Only he would ever know what happened twenty-one summers ago.

Following an early-morning attack on a Brule Sioux village camped north of the Shell River, what the white man called his Platte, instead of taking scalps, General Harney's troopers had brutally slashed the pubic hair from the dead squaws littered among the smoking ruins of the village. Around those defiled bodies terrified children wailed as the soldiers completed their bloody task.

A fourteen-year-old Oglalla boy named Curly had been visiting cousins in the village Harney attacked. That frosty morning Curly was forced to witness this methodical butchery by Harney's crack infantry as they slashed and tore and laughed about the mutilated genitals.

Years later after the death of his only daughter to the white man's cholera, this young warrior changed his name. In a dream quest he was told he would ride a wild horse, leading his people to avenge the many wrongs of the pale-skinned earthmen.

Curly was no more. Crazy Horse was born.

Down below the soldier hill now, all along that grassy slope, crawled Miniconjou and Sans Arc warriors, along with a mixture of Left Hand's Arapahos and whoever else wanted to lob a few shots at the hold-outs.

In a rough crescent looping round that southern flank over the back of the ridge were stationed the angry, swarming-hornet Hunkpapa soldiers led by Gall and Iron Dog. They were bolstered by the strength of Cheyenne Crazy Dog warriors led by Bob-Tail Horse and war chief Two Moons, who had by this time had a horse shot out from under him.

On this far slope of soldier hill sat the impatient Oglalla warriors, itching for permission to charge on over the troopers. They would act as cavalry themselves, riding light and fast up that long north slope. Led by their spiritual master. Led by Crazy Horse.

With the latest Henry and Winchester rifles, both lever-action repeating weapons, in addition to those army carbines captured in the valley fight and on Calhoun's hill, the warriors encircling the last-stand hill had the soldiers out-gunned in those final minutes. For speed of firing the repeaters worked admirably. For long-range sniping the Springfield carbines were the best.

Earlier in the afternoon Crazy Horse had lost a handful of warriors in his first charge at the soldiers. As the troopers had been chased out of the coulee to the top of the spine, The Horse had led his Oglallas across the river and along the minty bottomlands. Like blackbirds swarming after a hawk, they followed him around the brow of the hill and up its north slope—just in time to meet Smith's E Company. Right then and there the surprised soldiers clattered to a halt and hunkered down for a stand. Crazy Horse had them bottled up but good. No longer any place to go, no place to run.

The Oglallas had swept on up through the soldier ranks, touching here, striking out there with lance and hawk and rifle . . . until the great yellow cloud of dust blinded everyone, and the screams and shouts and wild grunts grew deafening to the ears. Then, as suddenly as Crazy Horse had come, he was gone. His Oglallas with him, battering Keogh's I Company against Gall's Hunkpapa infantry.

Crazy Horse had stopped the frantic retreat of Custer's soldiers. With nowhere to run, no place to hide, the troopers milled about, confused and bewildered.

And frightened. For as the yellow-and-red dust lifted from the brow of the hill, the young soldiers with Tom Custer looked down to see the mighty Oglalla army waiting for them at the bottom of the north slope, taunting them, playing with the *wasichu* troopers the way a badger will play with a little brown field mouse before he gobbles it up alive.

For too long the Sioux and Cheyenne had waited to have such a victory as this. They wanted to savor it, knowing what that wait did to those few left atop the hill.

They swarmed round those hundred twenty troopers at first, noisy like enraged bees stirred from a hive someone has knocked with a stick. They swarmed on the north and west and south, hot for combat, their blood boiling for a chance at some close-in fighting. As the minutes dragged by, Crazy Horse and his Oglallas calmly watched pandemonium and insanity spread through the soldiers like winter's first frost slicking icy scum across a pond.

Officers darted here and there, trying to wrench some semblance of order from their frightened men. Army horses with empty saddles reared and bucked and tumbled, tearing away from their handlers, spooked by the waving blankets and the shrill cries and the bullets and arrows slapping their flanks like stinging wasps. And everywhere the white men began to fall—some screaming in pain at their wounds, others falling without any sound at all.

For some of those iron-gutted veterans, it became desperately clear that Custer had made a crucial mistake in judgment. When he had forged down that trail beside Ash Creek against the advice of his scouts, the general plainly intended to have his victory over the Sioux here and now—or he would die seeking his destiny along these flowered hillsides bordering the Greasy Grass.

No man could ever claim Custer had a fear of being wounded or a fear of death. Neither had ever been a part of George Armstrong Custer's life, and no such fear would attend his death.

The last twenty or so who remained huddled near Custer could watch how the general slowly, bravely slipped away without a yelp or cry of pain through that long afternoon. As they had admired him in life, so they would admire the way he died.

Those twenty rolled up their sleeves and burrowed down behind barricades of dead horses, some animals gut-shot and still trumpeting in pain, sounding so human as they thrashed their way into death, the stench from their ruptured bowels pungent on the hot, steamy air. Those last twenty worked quietly, fiercely at their weapons, prying the shells out if they could, and if that took too long, throwing aside a carbine and reaching for another. With but twenty men left on that hill, there were a lot of weapons to choose from.

By now some of them had both hands filled with the heavy Colt revolvers, like Billy Cooke, standing and plugging away methodically at the hundreds of warriors who snaked up through the tall grass to fire silent arrows into the air, watching their arc whistle down into the dead horses, the dead troopers, and hearing every now and then a muffled scream when a live soldier felt the iron sting.

And still that double handful kept the warriors at bay. It had been close to an hour and a half since the general had been slung over his McClellan, in his brother's grip while they rode like hell up the ridge. For these last twenty that hour and a half seemed like hell gone on forever. Eternity is something hard for a man to swallow when he's choking on his own bile.

Overhead the sun seemed to fall, not into the west, but easing right down on the hill itself. Hotter, drier—and the air got meaner with it. Filled with the buzz that is summer on the high plains. Blowflies and mosquitoes, beetles and ants, scurrying through the little desperate ring of soldiers. All matter of creature called to the sugar-sour blood spilled across the thirsty soil.

And everywhere the mean, scorching air roared with sound if a man stopped for a moment to listen.

All about them rang those thousand and one distinct sounds that added to the nightmare. The shrieking of the women, urging their warriors on. Those shrill cries of the warriors themselves. That high-pitched, constant keening of the eagle wing-bone whistles. The drum, drum, drumming of thousands of hooves racing back and forth along the slope. That mournful creak of dry saddle leather as a horse thrashed, working against its bloody cinch. The whimper of a soldier dying, forgotten by his bunkies and fellow troopers because they had their own problems at the moment . . . maybe because those bunkies were all dead anyway and beyond worry now.

Above it all rose that wild cry of the wind rushing down from the Wolf Mountains: stalking, hunting like a feral predator. Knowing there would soon be bones bleaching and burning beneath a hot sun—before the day was out. Bones for that feral wind to whistle and sing over for all time to come.

Most of the warriors could wait these last long moments. There was medicine made up on soldier hill. Already they had watched some of the troopers throw themselves away. Silently the warriors glanced at one another and nodded, spitting on their fingers, then blowing on their palms. The troopers had killed themselves and each other, so many lying in the grass and flopping around like white-bellied trout tossed on the stream bank to die beneath a hot sun.

"The Great Powers made these soldiers kill themselves," the Sioux explained to one another.

"Yes," replied the Cheyenne. "The Everywhere Spirit made these soldiers go mad because they attacked a village of women and children."

And even a few of those Cheyenne massing on that hillside remembered the legend of long ago begun far to the south in the Territories when old chief Medicine Arrow had told the soldier-chief Yellow Hair that he would be cursed with death should he ever break his word to the Cheyenne by bringing his soldiers to attack a Cheyenne camp of women and children. Perhaps only a handful could remember that curse and the dumping of ashes on Yellow Hair's boots to seal his fate.

"If only *that* soldier-chief Yellow Hair were here now," some whispered mystically, "he would finally see how it is for all these last brave soldiers to die around him, exactly as the old chief's curse predicted in that winter long ago."

Having watched Tom Custer dragging the general up the slope, stopping to pant in the smothering heat, Mitch Bouyer decided he had had enough.

He wasn't about to wait for death to come slinking of its own pace. He wanted to die now.

Down inside he knew this hillside had his name on it anyway, so why wait?

Attack death as you would attack any enemy itself, Mitch Bouyer, he thought to himself. *Grapple with it and go down singing your death song. The Sioux taught you that much in all your years growing up in their camps. Your Hunkpapa mother had done enough to pass that much on to you anyway.*

"General," Mitch whispered as he knelt over Custer, their blood mingling in the yellow dust at Custer's side.

Tom glared flatly at the dark half-breed.

"I'm leaving now, General." Bouyer sighed, ignoring Tom's shadow over him.

"He can't hear you now." Tom's voice came out tasteless and bland, even though his eyes flashed their contempt.

"S'pose it doesn't matter much now, anyway, does it?" Mitch replied without looking up.

Tom was not sure if the question deserved answer.

"I tried to tell you, Custer." Bouyer bit his lip against

pain. "But you were ready to throw away all these good men for the sake of taking your soul on a long, long journey. Some said to Washington City to hold power over all the whites. I say you were prepared to go all the way to hell if you had to. But now—you'll never make it out of this valley."

Tom grabbed the calfskin vest Bouyer wore.

Mitch turned and snarled. "Leave me be. I'm dead a'ready. And I ain't gonna take nothing from the time your brother's got left anyway."

Young Custer let the half-breed go. "Hurry. He wants me to drag him to the top."

Bouyer looked back to the sallow face, eyelids half-closed as death hovered near.

"I'm moving on now, Custer. Down toward the river. Sioux look thickest down there. I'll take two, maybe three of 'em with me as I go down. Got no idea how long this belly of mine will let me stay up on my wobbly pins. But I figure if I get started downhill with a bum gut spilling into my hands like it is, ain't much but a lot of lead gonna finally bring me down."

Mitch struggled to his feet and bent to shade Custer's face. He wobbled, then sighed as he struggled to keep his balance. "Guess it's time. I'll be seeing you in hell, General Custer."

Tom watched the half-breed career about, pulling two pistols from his sash.

As Mitch darted past stunned troopers and around the dark barricades of bloated horses, his calfskin vest flapping wild in the breeze, he began yelling at the top of his lungs. Yet it was more than a yell—more like a chant, a high, wild song.

Telling the devil he was coming in, like it or not. And the old boy damned well better open those bloody gates of hell for him.

Amazing both troopers and Sioux alike—Bouyer made it better than four hundred dusty yards down the hill, firing those pistols at every Indian who popped up from the sage and grass to halt his wild charge. He was angry, damned angry—and wasn't about to go down easy. Old Jim Bridger, mountain man and later guide for the army in the early days of the far west, had taught Bouyer well.

Mitch died with some grit.

He went down the way he had lived, both hands packed for bear, singing his own medicine song to the Devil himself.

Ordering the gates of hell itself opened to welcome him home.

Custer came to as moccasined feet padded off.

He had his lucid moments, when his mind ran as clear as a mountain stream.

This time he was lulled by the constant drone of noise filling the air with a golden hum.

As his eyes sought to focus, he initially saw nearby a young bugler, not a day over eighteen really, his ear blown away, the pulpy wound already crusted under the hot, juice-drying sun. Flies were at work on the flesh, crawling and buzzing in and out of the boy's open eyes as they stared off across that Montana landscape. A few flies worked in and out of the bugler's gaping mouth.

Nearby, somewhere to his left, out along the ridge, a trooper cried out and died noisy. Yelling about the arrows falling from the yellow sky. Yelling something wild and crazy and demented about death falling out of the sun.

All round Custer closed a narrowing fog. Not in much pain any longer. His chest had grown lighter for the first time in—ah, hell. He didn't know how long he'd been here anymore. Strange, but his mind seemed suddenly clear again, like a piece of crystal he had seen once at a museum back east in New York City—a piece of crystal displayed on a swatch of sapphire blue velvet. His mind just that clear—as he allowed his soul to slip on down, sensing those emotions these last few soldiers huddled tightly about him must surely be feeling.

A good man—that Bouyer, Custer thought.

Some men, he brooded darkly, *wallow through the muck of suffering if their wounds are painful like this chest of mine. Doesn't make the whole thing of dying any easier . . . having to hurt through it all. And when the pain gets to be a little more than you can bear . . . a man begins to wonder just when it will all end and the pain will go away. Can't death just come and take me now? Can't I just have it done?*

Down at the last when you're holding on by the last thread comes the peace . . . the welcoming. Death will come welcome and none too soon for most men left on this hillside.

Off somewhere in the corner of his mind, Custer heard Yates and Tom and Keogh nearby. Heard them bellowing "GarryOwen" together. Off-key as always. It was their medicine song, their fraternal death song.

Thought he could hear one of them guzzling noisily, drinking as if he'd never again get a drink in his life.

Hell, he probably won't now. . . .

Maybe if he could turn his head a little, look behind him, they would see he wanted to share a drink with them.

Just one last drink.

Damned shame . . . never had a drink with these good men . . . even my own brother. Never had the chance to toast to health . . . to toss one off to a friend's happiness. Not at any wedding . . . not even my own. Never made a chance to drink with these . . .

Through the narrowing gray mist, he finally recognized Tom staring down at him.

Dear brother Tom. That rambunctious, bighearted oaf of a hellious brother who loved the women and his whiskey both about as much as the other. Too much of a contest all Tom's life to see just who or what he would dedicate himself to—the whiskey or some woman.

"Whisk . . ."

"What'd he say?" Keogh suddenly knelt over the general opposite Tom.

"I think he's asking for whiskey," Tom answered, snatching the canteen from Keogh. Gingerly he placed it to his brother's cracked, bloody lips, trickling a little of the cheap amber fluid into the slack mouth.

Custer sputtered. His mind reeled, instantly recalling the strong taste that had made him act like an ass there in front of the Bacon place so many, many years ago—right in front of the judge and young Elizabeth Bacon herself. But he fought down the sickening bile of remembered pain, making his stomach not care any longer.

"More," he ordered. And swallowed it with lessening difficulty.

"Easy, brother," Tom replied, Custer's head draped across his left arm like a wet bag of oats.

"Toasting you boys," Custer stammered slowly. "You . . . good friends."

"Yes, General." Yates began to cry, openly at last.

"For you, George, and the Seventh." He watched those big, leaden Yankee tears pour down George's dirty face. Knowing sweet Annie back at Lincoln was going to have a tough time of it without this man. Knowing all those women back at . . .

"I'll drink to you, General." Keogh's thick brogue fell soft about his ringing ears. "Then I've got to return to me post, sir. I'm still kicking some red ass, ain't I, General? Them savages ain't got Myles yet."

"Ah . . . Myles. Bless you, you Catholic sonuvabitch." Custer seemed to smile somewhere behind those glassy blue eyes.

"Why, General—I've never had you swear at me before!" Keogh brought up a chuckle, thick and hearty and genuine. "It feels mighty good to have you cussing me out. I'm sure I've been deserving a good tongue-lashing before now, but you've not brought yourself to do it. Now"—and he suddenly grabbed the general's face within his own meaty paws and bent down to plant a kiss on both of Custer's cheeks—"I've still got some bullets, and I've still got hot Irish blood pumping through me body, so I won't let you down."

Keogh belched, reeling to the side, caught himself before he fell. "I've loved you, General—every one of you as well. Like the brawthers I never had. All and a one of you. This regiment's been the home I niver had." He choked, seeing that he had made the others self-conscious with the admissions of this big, mighty man. "Well, I couldn't be more proud to die with you, boys."

Unashamed, his big lips and bristling mustache raked the cheek of Tom Custer and George Yates and the general one last time before he was gone to a little plot of land some soldier had scooped out with the butt of a useless, jammed carbine. A little piece of ground where Myles Keogh could die.

"Myles?"

"He's gone, General—"

"*Shit!*" Tom shouted in a growl as Yates's voice broke off.

Custer felt something hot and wet slap his face, spraying across the side of his neck. Then slowly he felt the weight of a body slumping against him. He gazed up through the fog and saw that the side of Tom's face and shirt were splattered with blood and gray matter.

"George?" Custer croaked weakly, like he didn't want to know.

"Yes," Tom whispered close to his ear now. "Head shot. He never knew what hit him."

"Cookey?"

"He isn't here, Autie," Tom whispered again. "Not anymore."

"Are we at the top of the hill? I can't see. Are we on the top, close to the sky?"

"About as close as I can get you, Autie." Tom rose to one knee. "I don't dare get any closer . . . it's so damned bare and naked up there at the top and looks—goddammit— those horsemen below, massing on the north flank. They're finally coming, Autie!"

"That'll do it, won't it?" Custer asked.

"Yes . . . I expect it will." Tom smiled bravely behind those first tears. He had fought them so long—just as bravely as he'd fought these Sioux and Cheyenne. "There's a handful of us left at most. Some down each side, still working. It'll be over in a minute. Here comes the charge, Autie. Bastards're coming now!"

"Like Saylor's Creek—one last charge for Thomas Ward Custer?"

Tom choked at the heady memory dredged up from the depths of that madness that was their own family war against the Confederacy. "Yes. Saylor's Creek, Autie. I should've died there. Should've finished it there."

CHAPTER 28

"**I** made a mistake," Custer said it out loud.

Tom jerked around. He didn't believe it. But of a sudden Autie's voice had become strong and clear. Young Custer stared down into the dust-reddened eyes.

"Made a mistake, Tom. Leaving her behind," he sighed. "And about dividing the regiment. Never sent Benteen off . . . Reno, the worst mistake of all. If I'd had Benteen down in the valley, been a whole different story. And if I'd never left her behind, I'd be—"

"Made a lot of damned mistakes myself, Autie," Tom glanced down the slope at the horsemen coming, feeling an urgency now as never before. "If I'd kept Jim and Myles with me instead of leaving them off to cover the rear, the Seventh might've made a better show of it this afternoon."

"Not your fault. I spread 'em too thin—"

"No time to criticize yourself." Tom struggled up on both knees out of the dust. "Far as I'm concerned, sir . . . it's been a pleasure and an honor serving you, General."

Custer blinked as he stared up at that narrowing tunnel of bone white glare overhead, hearing the thunder drumming up the slope. "Tom? You called me *General* only once before."

"I've loved you, Autie, as I've loved no one else." Tom's voice tripped on the anguish. "Want you to remember that. Loved you more than anything on the face of this earth."

"I'll remember. For all time, Tom."

Custer realized now it would come by Tom's hand. The way he was talking. He was even more sure of it as Tom scrambled to his feet, two pistols in his hand. Custer's mind was clear here at the last, clear as polished isinglass. There was even a little reflection of some light bouncing off into a dark corner, reflected right into his soul like light splintering off a mirror.

Custer really didn't mind anymore, mind making this blood atonement for all the others. It had been coming for too long as it was. For all those years of broken promises and busted two-tongue treaties of the bureaucrats. Some payment was long overdue. Bound to happen sooner or later . . . bound to happen on this Montana hillside.

Damn, but the gods in Valhalla will finally mark their ledger closed at last . . . paid in full. Written in Custer's blood, by God! Written in Custer's blood—

"Hiestzi!"

Custer listened to her high, thin voice carried seductively over the chants and wing-bone whistles, over the growing thunder of hooves pounding up the long north slope.

It could be no one else. Custer was sure.

He turned this way, then struggling to twist in another. None of the others seemed to hear it—that solitary voice calling out to him.

Battling against his own arms that didn't want to work anymore, he finally fought his way onto an elbow and peered downhill over to the right, on that little outcrop, there in the tall grass—

"Hiestzi!"

It had to be . . . no one else would be calling to him. *The red bandanna . . . like a flag—*

Glory! Monaseetah's come at last! She knew, Lord, she knew how I wanted to keep my promise to return to her.

"Husband!"

He wanted to yell out so badly. Nothing came up but blood and chunks of lung and a little taste of that sour whiskey.

Come, Monaseetah! I want you. Oh, do I need you. God . . . how I loved you.

"Autie."

Tom's voice. Real close. Then he felt Tom's arm resting on his chest, right over the soggy wound. Gripping him tight. Hugging him.

No! Not hugging me . . . holding me down!

Custer tried to focus through the narrowing tunnel of gray, gazing up into the bright light at the end. Tom's face filled his vision. He wasn't feeling much pain in the gaping hole, no heaviness now. More and more light drawing closer round him all the time. He tried to struggle, sensing the muzzle against his temple.

Turn away from it!

But Tom held him tight, forcing the back of his head down into the grass and dirt and blood and—

No! he wanted to shout. *Not yet . . . not yet, Tom! Monaseetah's coming, can't you see? Everything will be all right now. She can help me . . . help us like before . . . together at last! She's coming for me—*

Tom pulled the trigger, refusing to look down at what he did—this last act of love for his brother. Hoping Autie would forgive him. Despairing now that he had forgotten to ask Autie for forgiveness before he pulled the trigger. But there wasn't time. The horsemen were practically on them.

He rose, staring down at the peaceful, resting body a moment.

"I love you, General. Love you like a brother."

With a resolute buoyancy, he leapt the last few yards to the top of the crest, firing off to the north as he ran. Already the Oglalla cavalry under Crazy Horse had overrun the spot where Cooke's body lay—slashing, cutting, pounding heads in with their stone clubs.

"Stand, goddammit!" Tom shouted to the handful limping to the top with him.

Some struggled on hands and knees to draw close to that final ring. Some weaving, clutching bloody hands over oozing holes, braving the last few yards to the top. Five, maybe six of them was all.

The Sioux came on, up that north slope in a red wave that had no end.

"Stand, you damned wolverines! Stare it in the face!"

Tom actually heard the soapy, thick smack of it hit him. Not like the one that had smashed through his jaw at Saylor's Creek. He hadn't heard that one.

This was different. He heard it. The bullet that had his name on it. *Thomas Ward Custer.*

For all these years he had been waiting for that one, solitary bullet. And when it came, he actually heard it tearing, slashing through his body, driving bone through his lungs as it opened up a hole as big as a man's fist in his back, taking a good chunk of his lung with it. He watched the others struggle to stand with him, forcing themselves up on their feet.

"Goddammit! Stand with me, wolverines! Stare 'em in the eye! Let the bastards know we're the Seventh—by God—Cavalry!"

Another huge chunk of army lead smacked into his body, then a third as he was finally driven down on his side.

Still, he came up on his knees, listening to that wolf-pack howl as the Oglalla achieved the top of the hill and poured over his handful of hold-outs. A great howling that deafened Tom's shouts of defiance beneath hooves and stone clubs. A charge that spun him around as he fired wildly into the air with both pistols singing.

It seemed that wave of ponies would never end as they thundered over the brow of the hill, trampling the survivors, the ones brave enough, the ones strong enough to have made it to the top of Custer's hill.

With a sudden ringing in his ears, Tom realized the Sioux had passed. And with its deafening chant eventually came a quiet that told him that last bullet had come from close range . . . it echoed inside his head. A fading, dying echo.

That last one so close it made his ears ring.

After waiting a few moments more while the ringing clatter of that last bullet gradually died away, Tom opened his eyes and gazed up into the clear, cloudless Montana sky.

He was surprised to find a cool breeze washing itself along his right cheek, over the rosy mark from that long-ago bullet at Saylor's Creek.

Eventually, after a long time, he heard them calling. Familiar voices—he knew the sound of each one as he knew his own moods.

Tom propped himself up on one elbow and grinned as big as he had ever grinned before. Never a sight like this in all his life . . .

There they stood. A few yards off and heading down to that silver ribbon of the Little Bighorn, where it would be cool and shady and they could get a drink of water at last. Myles with his big Irish hand held high and urging him to come on. Jimmy Calhoun, Maggie's grinning Adonis, right beside Myles, where he always wanted to be found. Billy Cooke and George Yates. Fresh Smith turning now, waving him on. Friends for all time.

All of them hallooing him on down the hill with them.

And Autie.

He stood right in the middle. Autie yanked off that big cream hat and waved it back and forth at his younger brother. It was as if . . . as if he had forgiven Tom already for that last bullet.

"C'mon, Tom!"

Autie's voice rose strong and clear above the green grass and gray sage and tiny flesh pink buffalo-bean flowers nodding their heads in the cool breeze awash across the grassy slope.

"C'mon, now—not going anywhere without my little brother!"

*T*wo women mourned that hot summer afternoon as a blood red sun settled with an ache over the Bighorns. Two strong, delicate, and beautiful women mourned.

One sobbing as her quaking voice raised itself in the words of the old Christian hymns that gave her strength and solace in her darkest hours. Now that she was truly alone at last. And forever more.

The other, wailing and shrieking her grief to the heavens in an ancient, primitive dirge, a song of prayer and longing that went back beyond summers to the womb of time. A song that went back to a long winter gone.

Both women prayed to the same God; both mourned the same man. Suffering the same loss. That loss of love and a man who always smiled when times were darkest.

His passing, their greatest loss.

Now Yellow Hair belonged to the ages.

AFTERWORD

IT was a time of romance with a capital *R*. A time in our country when adventure and the mysterious lure of the West had captured the Republic's attention.

At no other time could the Battle of the Little Bighorn have happened—a tragedy that struck during the very celebration of our nation's centennial. No novelist could hope to dream up any better drama. Nor any deeper tragedy.

As my friend Will Henry said of the last stand, "Its story has been told in more wrong ways than any other adventure of the Western past." Considering his deep appreciation of the native culture that found itself in conflict with an onrushing white migration, along with his lifelong dedication to historically portraying the tragic drama of that conflict played out during the Indian Wars, I think Will would approve of this telling of the story.

This novel is the first to deal with the Indian side of the Custer fight itself.

While there have been numerous historical novels deal-

ing with the Reno fight and hilltop seige, with details lifted
from the testimony of white survivors, and though there
have been some novels devoted to imagining what took
place on Battle Ridge—this is the first novel to reconcile
the latest in archeological data with the most cogent of
"Custer movement" theories, coupling that empirical information with the testimony taken from the only survivors of
the day.

The Sioux and the Cheyenne themselves.

For too long white historians and writers have ignored
the overwhelming Indian testimony of what happened on
Battle Ridge. Simply because they found that testimony at
times contradictory! Yet those same battle enthusiasts
neglect to apply the same standards to the testimony given
by white survivors from Reno's and Benteen's battalions.
Their accounts evidenced glaring conflicts—both immediately following the fight and years later during the Reno
Inquiry.

I don't find myself alone, therefore, in agreeing with
Stanley Vestal (whom I quote at the beginning of this
novel), when he called the plains warrior an astute and
practiced observer of war. War was, after all, the very focus
of his way of life. To listen to a warrior's rendition of a battle
is to see that fight through the eyes of a keen and objective
observer, one who views his role in the conflict only
through the lens of a very particular microscope: his entry
into the fracas, his coups, his wounds.

By piecing together the many of these stories collected
over the decades from veterans of that fight against the
soldiers along the Greasy Grass River, I have constructed
what I believe to be the most plausible rendition of that
battle which left no white survivors. In addition to the
testimony of Sioux and Cheyenne warriors used in this
novel, I relied heavily on the latest archeological and
historical research completed as recent as 1990—even while
this novel is being prepared for the publisher. So by
combining the best that historical research has offered with
the results of that methodical combing of the battlefield
during the recent research summers, and by painstakingly
sifting through the Indian testimony—plotting it all on a

tabletop topographical map—I am confident that what I present here is a most plausible scenario to take much of what has been a mystery out of that hot afternoon on Battle Ridge.

Mystery and tragedy both marked George Armstrong Custer's short life. Mystery and tragedy had been his life long companions even before the moment he led his five regiments away from Major Marcus Reno, marching into history and myth. Many questions and their unspoken answers have gone to the grave with Custer's two hundred. Even more answers to the puzzling contradictions of his life have gone to the grave with his officers who survived the disaster at the Little Bighorn, but who remained silent out of some nineteenth century code of honor that would not allow them to utter the truth while Elizabeth Custer still lived.

Ironic that Libbie Custer outlived all but one of them!

Gentlemen they were, carrying to their graves their gloomy story of the outcome of Custer's tragic affair in Indian Territory and how it led him to the banks of the Greasy Grass some seven years later. We amateur historians could not blame these men for their chivalrous silence. It was, after all, a time when soldiers gone off to war were permitted their dalliance with foreign women. A gentleman always kept quiet, for that Gilded Age was, after all, an era when the keeping of a mistress was widely accepted and generally practiced.

Custer had been sexually active as a young man in Monroe, Michigan, before marrying his Libbie.

Following the Civil War he was assigned leadership to clean out the nests of Confederates and hangers-on in Texas, 1865. It is generally believed Custer had a dalliance there with a daughter of the Old South.

Before coming to Fort Riley, Kansas, with Libbie the following year, Custer journeyed through St. Louis, where he shared another indiscretion with the wife of a fellow officer, one of Sheridan's staff.

And following his court martial and one-year suspension from active duty, Custer returned to the plains in the fall of 1868—only to continue his practice of infidelity, this time with a young Cheyenne woman taken prisoner at the defeat of Black Kettle's village.*

Finally, during those years Custer was stationed in the northern plains at Fort Abraham Lincoln, he not only appears to have continued his extramarital dalliances, but in fact flaunted them before his wife. Time and again he tells her of his indiscretions and improprieties during his visits to New York without Libbie.

To better understand our culture's continuing fascination with the man we must remember that Custer was a young hero who had captured the nation's attention and fancy during a most dramatic time in our collective history: the Civil War. After remarkable yet tumultous years of service on the plains, he became the nation's darling, a hero cut down at a particular and tragic moment in what had been a brilliant, meteoric career. Cut down in the company of two brothers and a nephew, a brother-in-law and his closest of friends: the Custer inner circle.

The entire family gone in one hot breath of red fury on that yellow hillside.

Perhaps the primary reason this battle remains so vividly etched for all time in the American psyche is that no white survivor lived to tell the story. Yet as dramatic as that may be, history has recorded other military tragedies of far greater magnitude and consequence: the British charge of their light cavalry during the Crimean War, when over six hundred rode hell-bent to their destruction into the fiery maw of enemy cannon; and, the three-hundred Spartans who sacrificed themselves at Thermopylae. Down through our history, there were other, many lesser-known battles in which no man survived.

Most of us in this closing decade of our 20th Century look back on 1876 as a time when *"the cavalry to the rescue!"* was the stirring watchword of not only the frontier . . . but a call exciting the pulse of Easterners as well. Still, to put that era in perspective, we must not fail to realize what exciting exhibits thrilled visitors to the Centennial Exposition in Philadelphia that same summer. Not only a device

---

*a story told in Son of the Plains, Volume 1: *Long Winter Gone*

that prepared a "ready-roll," or tailor-made, cigarette, but Alexander Graham Bell unveiled for the world his improved telephone. On and on, one could list the electronic and scientific marvels that astounded the world that summer. Yet with all that magic accompanying our nation's headlong rush into its second century, the citizens of the Republic nonetheless turned their eyes to their past, if not focusing their attention on the startling contradictions of their present.

All the more ironic, wasn't it, that the most popular, well-attended exhibit at the Centennial Exposition proved to be one sponsored by the Central Pacific Railroad—an authentic reconstruction of an 1876 buffalo-hunters' camp in the Colorado Rockies. The average citizen, east coast or west, trained his eye on the frontier West for glory and romance back then . . . every bit as much as we do to this day.

While the white man celebrated the Republic's one-hundredth birthday back East during that fateful summer, the Indian celebrated his most stunning victory for but two days—then disbanded, never to gather again in such strength or numbers. Never to share between them such accord and harmony, such *medicine*, as they had experienced that hot afternoon in Montana Territory when they ably defended their way of life. What had been the brief high-water mark recorded on every band's winter count, was for the white man an ugly, gaping, bloody interruption to the self-absorbed celebration back East—a terrible, annoying reminder to the white man of what he had to do before he would truly call this land his.

He had to recommit himself to subduing, if not crushing once and for all, the native cultures of the plains.

The Army of the West reaffirmed its dedication to doing just that only weeks after discovering the bloated, stinking carcasses of some two hundred twenty-five white soldiers on that yellow hillside. With a renewed fervor and blood-vengeance so strong that it echoed shrilly behind the chants of "Remember Custer! Remember the Seventh!"—the Army of the West hammered away relentlessly at the now-divided and conquerable bands dispersing across the plains on the four winds.

Why such fury on the part of the Army? The destruction of Custer's men at the Little Bighorn decided nothing. More men had been killed in other engagements. So, it was not simply that soldiers had been killed, even that there were no survivors. There were other instances of no white survivors on the Western frontier.

No, instead, what fascinated then and fascinates us still is that *he* was killed there on that hot afternoon. *He* alone conjures up specific, myth-loaded images in us all. Say *his* name aloud and our imaginations dance on cue—bobbing and weaving to the eerie scream of eagle wing-bone whistles and hand-held rawhide drums. Perhaps instead our imaginations march in formation to the rollicking but plaintive battle-cry of *his* favorite fighting song "Garry Owen."

Because of those images, so many who hear the word *Custer* or the name of the place where he was killed will never be able to sort myth from reality. Over the years, this much-discussed battle has taken on truly Olympic proportions. The historic Custer who was a genuine hero coming out of the Civil War gave way to the frontier Custer who struggled hard in that Washita winter of 1868–1869 to redeem himself and his standing before both his superiors and the American public.

But on that hot Montana hillside reeking with death, Custer's fate was sealed. Not that he would die by the hands of Cheyenne and Sioux—or even by the hand of his own brother—but that the frontier Custer was fated to become for all time the mythic Custer.

The man and the myth were to be caught up forever in a swirl of debate between those for whom Custer was a much-maligned, unsung demigod, and those for whom he was a strutting, arrogant, egotistical martinet.

In this novel I wanted only to have, in some way, the real Custer emerge—the man who was a little of all those things they say he is. More than anything, I wanted to make him seem a little more human than either plaster saint or devil incarnate—to show him as a man with the same hopes and fears, dreams and regrets, that we all know. Custer was, ultimately, a man who walked on stage at the most opportune moment, remaining for every curtain call.

Custer had feet of clay.

Like you, and like me.

In closing I want most to express my indebtedness to the primary sources used in writing my story of the Custer fight. After years of research done for this trilogy, from the reading of hundreds of books, articles and monographs written about the man and this battle, I have naturally come to some of my own conclusions. Do not curse the following for what they have contributed to this scenario of that bloody summer Sunday afternoon.

Both Dr. Thomas B. Marquis (in his *Keep the Last Bullet for Yourself*) and David Humphreys Miller (who wrote *Custer's Fall: The Indian Side of the Story*) invested lifetimes interviewing the Indian participants of the battle. While some continue to ignore those accounts, I am indebted not only to Marquis and Miller, but to those warriors who chose to tell their stories in the truthful, objective manner described by no less a scholar of the plains Indian than Stanley Vestal (Walter S. Campbell) himself.

If a reader were to ask me to suggest one book that would discuss both the climate of the times and the battle itself—making sense of the startling complexities, I would have to suggest three: telling them to devour *Custer's Luck* by Edgar I. Stewart; John S. Gray's *Centennial Campaign - The Sioux War of 1876*; and, *Cavalier in Buckskin—George Armstrong Custer and the Western Military Frontier* by Robert M. Utley.

Yet Stewart published his work in 1955, and much of the search for the truth of that bloody afternoon has since continued. John Gray picked up the torch with his most thoughtful and dispassionate search, resulting in a book that was first published in the battle's centennial year, 1976. The banner has since been hoisted by my esteemed friend and Western scholar, Robert M. Utley, who (besides writing very readable history) has, like Stewart and Gray, devoted his life to the quest of historic truth of that battle, using the finest of research methods, based on empirical data, to arrive at his own cogent thesis on the movement of Custer's troops and a scenario of the Custer fight.

To all five of these scholars, I offer my undying gratitude.

You must remember that the events herein portrayed are by and large drawn from the actual documents of the time and from eye-witness testimony, dealing with a short timespan from the moment the Seventh U.S. Cavalry marched out of Fort Abraham Lincoln in Dakota Territory until the setting of the sun on that bloody hillside in Montana Territory, 25 June, 1876. Certain conversations and descriptions have been supplied by the author where the silent tongues of the dead—red man and white alike—could not speak for themselves here one hundred fourteen years later.

Why is it that no other battle so captured the public imagination of its time? Why has no other single military event remained in our national memory as the Custer fight? It has, like no other event of its kind, come to symbolize, for good or bad perhaps, the essential character of the American Frontier West: the determination and grit of its characters, and the tragedy that always stood ready to challenge any man gutsy enough to pit himself against both the land and the redman who vowed to defend his last, best hunting ground.

This is essentially, in my estimation, a story of those ordinary men, both white and red, who dared pit themselves against a fate that drove so many to hurl their bodies against enemy iron, steel and lead that hot summer day. And thereby became heroic.

I believe that the essential facts herein presented are faithful not only to the gallant memories of the courageous officers and enlisted men of the Seventh Cavalry, but faithful as well to the memories of those valiant red horsemen who rode against Custer's pony soldiers in the name of freedom and their ancient way of life on this dusty, sage-covered ridge where I sit at this moment, on another afternoon of 25 June, these one hundred fourteen years later.

Back along the hilltop at the monument it is noisy today—what with the celebration of an anniversary, with the comings and goings of those who pull off the interstate highway to drive by in slow parade, for but a few minutes to stop and peer across this forlorn piece of ground, perhaps to read a stone here and there. But few will ever allow themselves the time and the quiet to listen to the ghosts.

Where I sit late this afternoon, it is quiet. Here on Calhoun's Hill. Where so many historians across this last century of controversy agree that the only real resistance was put up against the Sioux after Custer's two hundred fought their ragged way up this slope from the river below.

From here I can look to the north and make out the bustle and swarm of visitors around that huge stone monolith marking Last Stand Hill. From where I sit among the sage, I can gaze across the east slope of the ridge, see the white of the markers glaring beneath the high-plains sun, each stone tablet plotting the fall of one who stood and fought beside that irascible Irishman Keogh. In the end, as I always do, I turn and look southwest, across several folds of this rumpled blanket of a landscape, and I imagine I can see across that distance the mouth of Medicine Tail Coulee, where it opens at the Minniconjou Ford on the Greasy Grass itself.

Where Custer began singing his death song that hot afternoon.

Up here, where I sit alone, it is so quiet at this moment that I can hear the breeze nudge the grass into whispers, a breeze that taunts this hallowed ground, pushing gently through the gray-bellied sage with a mournful keening of memories too-long unspoken. Here, on this quiet, lonely hill, I stay while the sun sets, listening to the ghosts that will forever haunt this place.

Ultimately, it is the ghosts who have told their story here across the pages of my book.

This story is their whispers heard among the grass and sage that blankets this hallowed, bloody ground where they fought and fell.

Their whispers.

TERRY C. JOHNSTON

Custer Battlefield
Montana Territory, U.S.A.
25 June, 1990

Terry C. Johnston captures the spirit and
drama of a unique era in American history
in his magnificent novel,
DANCE ON THE WIND, which marks
the return of a great fictional character
by a storyteller at the height of his power.

DANCE ON THE WIND

Now, the award-winning author of *Dream Catcher* and
Carry the Wind presents a novel that marks the return
of one of the most beloved characters in frontier fiction—mountain man Titus Bass, made famous in the
bestselling, critically acclaimed trilogy *Carry the
Wind, BorderLords,* and *One-Eyed Dream.* In the first
book of an exciting new saga, Johnston takes us back
to the early years of this extraordinary individual as a
young Titus Bass blazes a trail of danger and adventure across the American Frontier. From the banks of
the upper Ohio to the vast, unexplored expanse of the
lower Mississippi, Bass comes of age on a journey
across a volatile, violent country of riverboatmen and
river bandits, knife fights and Indian raids, strong
liquor and stronger women. Like America itself, Titus
looks west and sees the future . . . and he's willing to
risk everything to seize it.

Turn the page for an exciting preview of Terry C.
Johnston's **DANCE ON THE WIND,** available now
in paperback wherever Bantam Books are sold.

ONE

Slick as quicksilver the boy stepped aside when the mule flung her rump in his direction.

Only problem was, he had forgotten about the root that arched out of the ground in a great bow nearly half as tall as he stood without his Sunday-meeting and schoolroom boots on. The end of it cruelly snagged his ankle, sure as one of his possum snares.

Spitting out the rich, black loam as fine as flour in this bottomland, Titus Bass pulled his face out of the fresh, warm earth he had been chewing up with a spade, blinking his gritty eyes. And glared over his shoulder at the mule.

Damn, if it didn't look as if she was smiling at him again. That muzzle of hers pulled back over those big front teeth the way she did at times just like this. Almost as if she was laughing at him when here he had just been thinking he was the one so damned smart.

"Why, you . . . ," the boy began as he dragged himself up to his knees, then to his bare feet in that moist earth chewed by the mule's hooves and his work with iron pike and spade.

On impulse he lunged for the fallen spade, swung it behind his shoulder in both hands.

"Put it down, Titus."

Trembling, the boy froze. Always had at the sound of that man's voice.

"Said: put it down."

The youth turned his head slightly, finding his father emerging from the trees at the far edge of the new meadow they were clearing. Titus weighed things, then bitterly flung the spade at that patch of ground between him and his father. The man stopped, stared down at it a moment, then bent to pick it up.

"You'd go and hit that mule with this," Thaddeus Bass

said as he strode up, stopped, and jammed the spade's bit down into the turned soil, "I'd have call to larrup you good, son." He leaned back with both strong, muscular hands wrapped around the space handle like knots on oiled ropes. "Thought I'd teached you better'n that."

"Better'n what?" the boy replied testily, but was sorry it came out with that much vinegar to it.

Thaddeus sighed. "Better'n to go be mean to your animals."

Titus stood there, caught without a thing to say, watching his father purse his lips and walk right on past to the old mule. Thaddeus Bass patted the big, powerful rump, stroked a hand down the spine, raising a small stir of lather near the harness, then scratched along the mare's neck as he cooed to the animal. She stood patiently in harness, hooked by leather and wood of singletree, the quiet murmur of her jangling chains—the whole of it lashed round a tree stump young Titus Bass had been wrenching out of a piece of ground that seemed too reluctant to leave go its purchase on the stubborn stump.

Titus flushed with indignation. "She was about to kick me, Pap."

Without looking back at his son, Bass said, "How you know that?"

"She was hitchin' her rump around to kick me," Titus retorted. "Know she was."

"How hard you working her?"

Dusting himself off, he replied in exasperation, "How hard I'm working her? You was the one sent me out here with her to finish the last of these goddamned stumps."

Thaddeus whirled on his son, yellow fire in his tired eyes. "Thought I told you I didn't wanna hear no such language come outta your mouth."

He watched his father turn back to the mule's harness, emboldened by the man's back, braver now that he did not have to look into those eyes so deeply ringed with the liver-colored flesh of fatigue. "Why? I ain't never figured that out, Pap. I hear it come from your mouth.

Out'n Uncle Cy's mouth too. I ain't no kid no more. Lookit me. I be nearly tall as you—near filled out as you too. Why you tell me I can't spit out a few bad words like you?"

"You ain't a man, Titus."

He felt the burn of embarrassment at his neck. "But I ain't no boy neither!"

"No, you rightly ain't. But for the life of me, I don't know what you are, Titus." Bass laid his arms over the back of the tall mule and glared at his son. "You ain't a man yet, that's for sure. A man takes good care of the animals what take care of him. But you, Titus? I don't know what you are."

"I ain't a man yet?" Titus felt himself seething, fought to control his temper. "If'n I ain't a man yet—how come you send me out to do a man's job then!"

"Onliest way I know to make you into a man, son."

He watched his father turn and survey the stump partly pulled free from the ground, some of its dark roots already splayed into the late-afternoon air like long, dark arthritic fingers caked with mud and clods of rich, black earth.

Thaddeus straightened. "You wanna be a farmer, Titus—the one lesson you gotta learn is take care of the animals gonna take care of you."

The words spilled out before he wanted them to. "Like I told you before, Pap: it's your idea I'm gonna be a farmer."

The old man's eyes narrowed, the lids all but hiding the pupils as he glowered at the youth. "You not gonna be a farmer like your pap, like your grandpap and all the Basses gone before you . . . just what in blue hell you figure on doing with your life?"

"I . . . I—"

"You ain't got it figured out, do you?" Thaddeus interrupted. "And you won't for some time to come, Titus. What else you think you can do?"

Titus watched his father step back in among the

leather, metal, and wood of the harness, tugging at it, straightening, adjusting the wrap of log chain his son had placed around the resistant stump.

"I like hunting, Pap."

Without raising his head from his work, Bass said, "Man can't make a living for his family by hunting."

"How you so damn sure?"

The eyes came up from the singletree and penetrated Titus like a pair of hot pokers that shamed him right where he stood.

"Sounds like you're getting a real bad mouth these days, son. Time was, I'd taken a strop of that harness leather to your backsides teach you to watch your tongue better."

Titus felt his cheeks burn. No, he wouldn't let his father raise a strap to him ever again. In as low and deep a voice as he could muster, the boy replied, "You'll never lay leather on me again."

For the longest moment they stared at one another, studying, measuring the heft of the other. Then his father nodded, his shoulders sagging a bit wearily. "You're right, Titus. If you ain't learned right from wrong by now, it ain't gonna be me what's teaching it to you. Too late now for me to try to straighten out what needs to be straightened."

Titus swallowed, blinking back the tears of anger that had begun to sting his eyes as he stood his ground before his father. Suddenly confused that his father had agreed with him. It was the first time in . . . He couldn't remember if his father had ever agreed with a single damned thing he had ever said or done.

Thaddeus Bass patted the mule on the rump and stepped closer to his son. "But you heed me and heed me well: if I ever hear of you using such words around your mam, if I ever catch you saying such things under my roof—then we'll see who's man enough to provide for his own self. You understand me, son?"

With that dressing Titus fumed under his damp collar.

"I ain't never cursed under your roof, and I sure as hell ain't never gonna curse in my mam's hearing."

"Just make sure you don't, son," his father replied, stepping back of the mule and taking up the harness reins. "It'd break your mother's heart to hear you use such talk—what with the way that woman's tried to raise you."

Turning, Thaddeus Bass laid the leather straps in his son's hands. "Now, get back to work. Sun's going down."

Titus pointed over at the nearby tree where he had stood the old longrifle. "I been at this all day, and I ain't had a chance to go fetch me no squirrel yet."

"It's fine you go playing longhunter when you get your work done, Titus. That stump comes out'n that ground and gets dragged off yonder to the trees afore you come in to sup at sundown."

His stomach flopped. "If'n I can't get the stump up afore the sun goes down?"

His father looked at the falling orb, wagged his head, and said, "Then you best be making yourself a bed right here, Titus."

Anger was like a clump of sticky porcupine quills clogging his throat with bile. Time and again he tried to swallow as he watched his father's retreat across the field. Thaddeus Bass never turned as he headed purposefully for the far trees. Above the verdant green canopy beyond the diminishing figure rose a thin, fluffy column of smoke from the stone chimney of their cabin. He wondered what his two brothers and sister were doing right then.

Grinding the leather straps in his hands, Titus seethed at the injustice. He knew the rest of them would eat that night and sleep on their grass ticks beneath their coverlets. While he'd be right here in the timber, sleeping with the old mule and the other critters. Mayhaps that wasn't all so bad—but his belly was sure hollering for fodder.

Maybeso he could slip off with his old rifle and shoot some supper for himself, bring it back to roast over an open fire—then at least his stomach would be full for the night.

Titus took a step behind the mule, then stopped, staring down at the reins in his hands.

If he set off on his hunt to fill his grumbling belly, just what in blazes would he do with the mule?

"Hell, she ain't going nowhere," he reasoned, looking over the harness that bound her to the stump. "Can't get that stump out, she sure as the devil ain't running off from here."

Quickly he tied off the reins to the harness and leaped around the tangle of upturned roots. The rifle came into his hands like an old friend. More like an accomplice who had helped him in hunts without number in these very woods—ever since he was big enough to hoist his grandpap's longrifle to his narrow, bony shoulder and stride right out the cabin door to disappear within the forest's leafy green shadows.

Dusk was settling on the woods in just the way the mist gathered in the low places by the time he stopped at the edge of the narrow stream and listened. Titus jerked at the sudden, shrill call from a shrike as it dived overhead and disappeared in the coming gloom of twilight. The forest fell silent once more.

He figured he was too late to catch any of the whitetail coming here to water before slipping off to their beds for the night. Their tracks pocked the damp earth at the bank near the natural salt lick the deer sought out. No matter anyhow. Titus hadn't really figured when he'd started out from that stump that he would scare up any critter at these riffles in the stream. More than anything, he had come here just to get away from the mule, and the stump, and the work, and his pap.

On the far bank a warbler set up a song as the spring light disappeared from the sky. Another joined in, then they both fell quiet. Far off he heard the cry of a riverman's tin horn on the Ohio. A boat plying the waters—coming down from Cincinnati, which lay a twisting forty-some miles from where he knelt in the damp coolness of that dark forest glen. Perhaps a big flatboat speeding downriver to Louisville, on down, down to the faraway Mississippi with its rolling ride south all the way to New Orleans. Maybe even one of those keelboats that would eventually point its prow north on the old river to St. Lou. Seemed everyone in nearby Rabbit Hash, here on the Kentucky side of the Ohio, was talking about St. Lou these days.

"The place holds promise," claimed one of the drummers who came to town regular from Belleview, just five miles upriver.

Thaddeus Bass had snorted and wagged his head as if that was the most ridiculous assertion ever made. "Maybeso for shop-folk like yourself. Not for this family. We be farmers. Work the soil. Worked it since my grandpap come into Kain-tuck and staked himself out a piece of ground he and others had to defend from the Injuns. Naw, let others rush on to St. Lou. They been rushing on west, right on by my ground for three generations already."

"Opportunity enough for any man, I'd imagine." The drummer smiled benignly, pulling at his leather galusses.

"To hell with opportunity," Bass retorted. "Opportunity's the retreat of a weak-spined sort. Hard work is what makes a man's life worthwhile. Ain't no better blessing for a man than to feed his family with the fruit of his sweat and toil."

Breathing lightly, Titus listened to the nightsounds, cradling the old flintlock, and wondered if he could ever forgive his father for keeping him chained to a mule, mired waist-deep in the muddy fields that surrounded their cabin and barn and outbuildings. Could he ever forgive his father for throwing cold water on his dreams?

"You'll get over it, son. Every boy does when he grows to be a man," Thaddeus had explained. "That's the difference between a whelp like you and a man like your pap here. Feller grows up to do what he has to do for them what counts on him, and he's a man for it. A boy just got him dreams he goes traipsing off after and he don't ever come to nothing 'cause dreams is something what cain't take him nowhere."

In the rising fog over the surface of the Ohio, the cry of the tin horn faded off. Titus closed his eyes, trying to imagine what sort of boat it was. Oh, he'd seen plenty of those flatboats and broadhorns, keels, and even those ungainly rafts of logs lashed together for the trip down-river, every small craft's wake lapping the surface of the Ohio against Titus's bare feet year after year. Summers without count had he wanted to hail a boat over and beg its crew to take him on.

But instead he sat there, listening until that horn was no more in the thickening fog that clogged the valley of the Ohio.

In the quiet that settled around him he heard the faintest rustle of brush. Held his breath. And a moment later his ears itched as something moved off into the night. Whatever critter it was had scented him.

Wind wasn't right, he decided, easing himself to his feet. Time to be moving off to home.

Times like these when he wasn't back to the cabin for supper, his father warned he'd get none. Still his mother always wrapped up a slice of cold ham and some corn dodgers, maybe even a sliver of dried apple pie, folding it all within a big square of cheesecloth before placing her treasure just back of the woodbox that sat to the left of the door on the front porch. Again tonight he knew he would be sitting in the dark, listening to the muffled voices of his family inside the firelit cabin as he chewed on his supper and washed it down with the cool, sweet water from the well his grandpap had dug generations before.

As much as he was certain he'd likely die early if he stayed on to become a farmer, Titus knew he'd feel like a rotted stump inside if he disappointed his father. So through the past few years he had walked this narrow line between what his pap expected of him and what he had to do just to keep from dying inside, a day at a time.

Warm, humid starshine streamed down through the leafy branches of the trees as he felt his way barefoot along the game trail that would take him back to the field and the stump and that old mule he realized had likely grown just as hungry as he himself had become. He stopped and listened a minute, leaning his empty hand against the bark of a smooth sumac tree. A frightened chirp overhead startled him. Black squirrel. Something amiss in that warning.

He did not stop again until he reached the edge of the meadow Thaddeus was having cleared for cultivation. Beneath the half-moon and the bright starlight he could make out the stump he had been uprooting across the open ground. But he could see no mule. Titus burst into a trot now. His throat seized with his thundering heart. Skidding to a halt on the turned and troubled ground around the stump, he found the singletree and chain harness still lashed around the wide trunk. But no mule.

Collapsing to his knees, he quickly inspected the leather for some sign that the old girl had snapped her way out of harness. Yet nothing there suggested she had freed herself. Around on his knees he crawled, inspecting the ground for hoofprints, bootprints, anything that might tell him how she got loose. Mayhaps some of grandpap's thieving Injuns. Or, worse yet, a white man come to steal the mule. But there was nothing untoward about that churned-up soil surrounding the stump.

"Take care of the animals gonna take care of you."

The voice seemed so real it near made him jump out of his skin. Titus turned this way, then that, just to be certain. Assuring himself he was alone, he settled on his rump, back against the stump, and cradled the rifle into his shoulder. As his head sagged, he struggled with what to do about the mule, about his running off into the woods and leaving her to get stole.

Finally he decided. If she was anywhere, she was chewing on some grass at that very moment. It made his stomach grumble in protest to think the mule was eating, and here he was worrying about her with an empty belly of his own.

In the starlit darkness it took something less than a half hour to reach the glen where the cabin stood, its chimney lifting a gray streamer to the night breeze. The wind was off from the wrong direction, but now and then he could pick up the faintest fragrance of supper. It made his belly growl in anticipation. Behind shutters and sashes drawn against the night outside, narrow ribbons of yellow lamplight squeezed free, a wee patch of light oozing out at the bottom of the door. Across the yard stood the separate kitchen, used from spring into the fall so the cabin wouldn't grow overly warm in those seasons of baking and cooking. Beside the kitchen stood the small smokehouse. Across the yard, the springhouse and corncrib. Beyond all of them still, the barn—taller even than the cabin with its sleeping loft.

Heading at an angle for the structure that blotted out a piece of that starry night sky, Titus kept to the shadows. Years before, so his father and grandpap had told him many times, the men of the family were required to keep an eye open at night for Injuns. Any shadow seen stealing across the yard was likely an enemy, and subject to be shot.

It had been years since the tribes had last made trouble. Back to the war with the Frenchies, later the revolt against the Englishers. It made his grandpap choke in anger to think that his father's own countrymen had made life so hard on their fellow English citizens that the colonists had gone and fought to throw King George right back into the sea. But as distasteful as it was to admit, grandpap's countrymen had turned out to be conniving, vicious lobsterbacks who had set the Injuns on the rebellious settlers. An army and all those Injun tribes come to make war against a few hundred farmers scattered over hundreds of miles of wilderness.

Titus slipped into the barn through the narrow door and held his breath.

His imagination soared as his eyes grew accustomed to the fragrant darkness. Recalling his grandpap's stories of how a few brave young men had carried word of an uprising or the English army's advance from settlement to settlement. How the farmers had reluctantly abandoned their fields and gathered families around them, hurrying to the nearby fort erected by a group of settlers for their mutual protection—each individual farmer's outlots in the fields surrounding that communal stockade. There had been one such stockade near Belleview where the Bass clan had gone in times of emergency. Where nearly everyone in Boone county fled when the British set their Shawnee and Mingoes loose on their own white-skinned countrymen.

Now Titus's eyes were big enough that he could make out the low walls of each stall, to discern the backs of some of the animals, the spines of a rake or a loop of harness draped over a nail. Enough light crept through tiny openings in the wall chinks that Titus could make his way down to the last stall, past the milk cows. One curious one came up and stuck her wet nose over the gate. He stroked it as he went past, feeling her long, coarse tongue lap over the back of his hand.

As he reached that last stall, he held his breath and hoped. It wouldn't be right to say he prayed, simply because he never had really prayed for anything. But at this moment he hoped harder than he had ever hoped for something before. And if such hoping was another man's prayer, so be it.

Daring to turn his head slowly, Titus looked into the stall.

Against the back wall stood the old mule. And on the nearby wall hung the harness.

Turning on his heel, his knees gone to mush, the youngster sank with his back against the stall door, where he leaned the rifle, catching his breath.

Leastwise the old mule was here. She wasn't took. He swallowed hard, knowing who had come to fetch her. Likely come to fetch him for supper. More likely, come to see how he was doing on that dad-blamed stump.

Titus wondered if his pap would count "dad-blamed" as cursing.

"I don't give a good goddamn if he does or not," Titus whispered to the lowing animals. "His damn ol' mule anyway—so he can take proper care of it hisself."

He listened as the mule moved closer, right up to the stall door. Looking up, he saw she had laid her bottom jaw atop the door and seemed to be peering down at him with one of those dark, iridescent eyes.

"I'm sorry, Lilly," he suddenly apologized. "Nothing against you. Shouldn't've left you be there all by yourself. Something might've happened to you. Sorry, girl."

Her head seemed to bob once before the mule retreated back into the stall once more.

Sometimes, he brooded, these animals were downright spooky. Like they understood what you spoke at 'em. Mayhaps—he feared—even able to outright read a person's mind.

Slowly clambering to his feet, he saw that she'd been fed. The bucket hung from a peg inside her stall where the mule could reach it, feeding herself from the grain provided her every night. His pap had done that too. Likely brushed her down good. Like Titus was supposed to each night after he worked over the stumps on the far edge of the ground they were clearing for next season's planting. Not time enough this year—what with the good ground already turned and the seed already covered, more than a dozen good, soaking rains already.

He put his hand in the canvas bucket and brought out a handful of the grain. Holding it beneath his nose, he drank in their faint sweetness of oats, the fragrance of molasses. Then he extended his hand to her. She came to the stall door, curled her lips back, and lapped at the offering as he patted the solid bone between her eyes.

When she finished, Titus swiped his damp palm across his worn britches and took up the rifle. It was time he had something to eat himself. Careful not to let the small door slam against the side of the barn as he eased it back into place, the youngster crept amongst the shadows toward the cabin. As he had done so many times before, he would eat his supper, then wait until all the lights were out before he would climb the roof and steal in through the window to find his bed in the dark.

After setting the longrifle against the side of the porch, Titus heaved himself up without using the steps. They were creaky with age and use, and more often than not apt to make more noise than one of the rooting pigs down in the pen behind the barn. Kneeling at the side of the woodbox, he reached around to the spot where his mother always left the cheesecloth bundle for him. He felt a little farther. Still nothing. Leaning all the way over the hinged flap atop the woodbox, he put both hands to work, stuffing both arms clear under the box. Nothing. No cheesecloth bundle. No supper.

At that moment his stomach growled so loud, he was sure they heard it inside the cabin.

Quickly hunching over and wrapping both arms over his belly, Titus limped away from the woodbox to the edge of the porch, where he sat dangling his bare feet while he stared up at the half-moon. It had climbed to near midsky, and the breeze was coming up. Damp, rich, rife with the smell of rain by morning despite the cloudless sky overhead.

In the starshine the edge of the hog pen stood out on the far side of the barn. Closer still, the small corral where his pap kept their wagon team. Titus had straddled the wide backs of those old, gentle horses ever since he could remember. As much excitement as it had been when he was a pup, these days he yearned to climb atop a real horse. Not one of those working draft animals. A lean, slim-haunched horse that would carry him across the fields and down the wooded trails with the speed of quicksilver. A real horse like those he saw from time to time in Belleview. And the once-a-year trip upriver to Cincinnati, only some twenty miles if a person took the overland route that dispensed with most of the meandering course of the Ohio.

Yes, sir. A real horse like fine folks rode. He deserved that, Titus decided. Here in his seventeenth summer, on the verge of manhood, a hunter like himself deserved a fine horse. After all, times were good. The Englishers were gone, thrown out for good, and when the men got together, they cheered one another with talk of times being good now for their young country as America slowly spread her arms to the west. Four summers back Lewis and Clark had returned from the far ocean, with unbelievable tales of tall mountains and icy streams teeming with fur-bearing animals. Stories and rumors and legends of fiercely painted Indians who attempted to block their journey every step of the way.

The only Indians Titus had seen were a few of the old ones he saw from time to time, come to Belleview or Rabbit Hash, civilized and docile Indians who no longer hunted scalps but tilled the land like white men. They came to the towns for supplies but for the most part kept to themselves when they did. Wouldn't even look the white folks in the eye.

"They're a beaten people," Grandpap had told young Titus. "We whupped 'em good when we whupped the lobsterbacks."

At first Titus had been scared whenever he saw one of those farmer Indians. Then, he grew afraid he never would see a real, honest-to-God Injun for himself, ever.

About as much chance of that as him ever forking his legs over a strong, graceful horse.

He sat in the darkness until the last lamp went out. Everything was quiet down below, quiet up in the loft where his two brothers and sister slept. Waiting while the moon moved a few more degrees off to the west to be sure all were asleep, just as he always did, the youngster crept back to the door, took hold of the iron latch, and carefully raised it, easing forward on it to crack open the door just wide enough to—

Damn!

He tried again, thinking perhaps he hadn't raised the iron latch high enough to clear the hasp. Titus pushed gently against the door again—

Goddamn!

It couldn't be stuck. He tried harder, noisier, as iron scraped against iron.

The door was barred from the inside. He was locked out.

This had never happened before. Always the door was left unlocked for him when he went hunting of a night, or off to gig frogs, or maybe only to wander down the road to Amy's place, hoping she would sit and talk with him about mostly nothing at all. But that door was never locked.

And his mam always had supper waiting under the woodbox in that piece of cheesecloth.

He leaned his forehead against the door, suddenly wanting to cry. So hungry he couldn't think what to do next. So tired from fighting the mule and the stump and his pap that day that he wanted only to lie down upon his tick, pull the covers over his head, and go to sleep despite his noisy, snoring brother.

With a sigh Titus turned from the locked door. Mayhaps he could pull himself up onto the porch roof and make his way across the cabin roof and lower himself onto the sill where a lone window opened into the sleeping loft. Maybe his old man wasn't as smart as he made out to be.

After hiding the rifle behind the woodbox, Titus shinnied up the pole and clawed his way onto the roof. As quietly as he could move across the creaking timbers and shakes, the youngster crept to the cabin roof itself and hoisted himself up. Keeping to the sides where the support beams had more strength and were therefore less likely to groan and protest his weight, Titus leaned over the edge and found the window. Lying on his belly, he scooted out as far as he dared and reached for the mullioned windowpanes. Nudging. Then pushing. Straining. Neither side would budge.

Frustrated, he tried again, and again. It acted as if it were nailed shut. It was always easy to open that window, he thought. Both sides flung open for summer breezes. Never before had it been so hard. He tried once more. Unable to budge it.

A nail or two could do that, he thought. Wouldn't take much to keep him from sneaking in that way.

As he dropped barefoot to the ground at the side of the porch, he boiled with indignation. Wrenching up the rifle from its hiding place behind the woodbox, Titus seethed to have it out with his pap. But as tired as he was, it could wait until morning.

Back across the damp shadows of the yard, he could already smell rain coming. Into the barn he crept once more and waited for his eyes to adjust to the darkness. To his right stood the faint hump of a hayrick. After leaning the rifle against a nearby post, Titus kicked at the soft hay with his bare feet until he had a pile long enough, and some four feet deep. On it he lay down and began pulling hay over him for warmth.

Curling an arm under his head, the youngster closed his eyes, his breathing slowing as the anger and disappointment and hunger drained from him. All he wanted now was some sleep. In the morning he would have words with his father about locking his son out of the cabin.

Even if he had gone off without tending to the stump and the old mule, nothing was so serious that he should be locked out of his own home.

Titus felt the warmth of the hay envelop him the way the cool of the swimming hole would wrap him on those hot summer days yet to come.

No matter how important any *thing* was to his pap, nothing should be more important than family.

Bringing the old girl home, feeding her, putting her up for the night in her stall. No two ways about it—that mule was getting better treatment from his pap than Thaddeus was giving his own son right now.

With the hay's heady fragrance filling his nostrils, the quiet lowing of the animals droning about him, and his dreams of riding one of those fast horses the woodsmen owned, Titus drifted off to sleep.

He shivered once and pulled more hay over him. Growing warm once again. Not to stir for what was left him of that short night.

"Get up, boy. You've got some righting of a wrong to be at."

He blinked into the gray light, then rubbed at his gritty eyes, staring up sidelong at his father, who stood over his bed of hay. Thaddeus had the collar to his wool coat turned up against the morning dew, a shallow-crowned, wide-brimmed hat of wool or castor felt pulled down on his hair.

It was cold in here, he thought. Damp too. Must have gone and rained.

"I said get up!" Thaddeus Bass repeated more urgently. And this time he added his own boot toe for emphasis.

Titus pulled back his bare foot. "I know I done wrong—"

"Get up! Afore I pull you up by your ears!"

The youngster stood, shedding hay as he clambered to his feet, shivering slightly, hunch-shouldered in dawn's dampness. His breath huffed before his face in wispy vapors. Outside a mockingbird called. "Jest lemme explain, Pap."

"Nothing to explain, Titus. You left off work to go traipsing the woods. Left off the mule too. No telling what'd become of her I didn't come back to see to your work at that stump."

The look in his father's eyes frightened him. He could

remember seeing that fire in those eyes before, yet no more in all of Titus's sixteen years than the fingers on one of his hands. "It was getting on late in the day anyhows—"

With a sudden shove his father pushed him down the path between the two rows of stalls in that log barn. "Grab that harness."

"Yes, sir," he said with a pasty mouth, too scared not to be dutiful and obedient.

A rain crow cawed on the beam above him. He shuddered as his bare feet moved along the cold, pounded clay of the barn floor. But he wasn't all that sure he trembled from the morning chill. Not knowing what would come next from his father's hand was all it took to make the youth quake. Alone Titus had faced most everything nature could throw at this gangly youth—out there in the woods and wilderness. But he had never been as frightened of anything wild as he was of his father when Thaddeus Bass grew truly angry.

As Titus took the old mule's harness down, his father said, "G'won, hitch her up."

The boy pushed through the stall door and moved into the corona of warmth that surrounded the big animal. She raised her head from a small stack of hay to eye him, frost venting from her great nostrils, then went back to her meal as he came alongside her neck and slipped the bridle and harness over her.

"Bring her out to me."

"Here, Pap," he said, almost like whimpering. "I . . . I'm sorry. Never run off on the work again, I swear—"

"I don't figure you ever will run off again, Titus," his father snapped. "Not after I've learned you your lesson about work and responsibility." He pointed to a nearby post. "Get you that harness."

"What for? I got the mule set—"

"Jest you get it and follow me."

He trudged after his father, out the barn door and into the muddy yard, where a faint drift of woodsmoke and frying pork greeted him as warmly as the dawn air did in cold fashion. How it did make his stomach grumble.

"Can I quick go and fetch me something to eat while we're off to the field, Pap?"

In the gray light shed by that overcast sky the man whirled on his son. "No. You ain't earned your breakfast yet."

"But—I didn't have no supper last night."

"Didn't earn that neither. Off lollygagging the way you was."

He swallowed and walked on behind his father, bearing south toward the new field they were clearing. Suddenly appearing out of the low, gray sky, the bright crimson blood-flash of a cardinal flapped overhead and cried out. In the distance Titus heard the faint call of a flatboat's horn rise out of the Ohio's gorge. Was it one of those new keels with a dozen polemen? Or was it one of those broadhorns nailed together of white oak planks the boatmen would soon be selling by the board-foot on the levee at far-off New Orleans?

"Here, girl," Thaddeus said as he put the mule ahead of the harnesstree and himself at her head, beginning to coax her back a step at a time. "Titus, hitch her up."

Titus hoisted the oiled hardwood and locked both harness traces in place. Then he straightened, watching his father pat the mule between the eyes.

Gesturing toward the tangle of leather and chain his son had dropped onto the ground, Thaddeus said, "Now you hook up that harness to the tree."

Maybe he didn't want to know any more than he already could guess. Maybe he refused to believe his father would really make him do it. No matter—Titus didn't ask, didn't say a thing as he bent over his work. His cold hands trembling, he found it was a tight fit lining up all the metal clasps into the harnesstree's lone eye, but he got it done and stood again. Shivering in the cold air as a breeze rustled the green leaves of the nearby elms.

"We gonna pull the stump out and then we go to breakfast?"

His father slapped the mule one time on the rump as he moved back to take up the reins. "We gonna pull out the stump, that's right. We'll see for ourselves what comes next, Titus. Now, step in that harness and cinch yourself up."

"M-me?"

"You heard me, son."

"Y-yes, Pap."

For a moment longer he stood there, gazing at his father. Thaddeus had taken the long, wide leather reins into his weathered hands, shifted it all to his left, then took one long double length into his right and began to wave it over the mule's wide back.

"You seen what your pap has to do if'n an animule ain't obeying, ain't you, Titus?"

Quickly, he turned and stepped into the harness. "Yes, Pap."

"Buckle yourself in and take up the slack," the man ordered, then ever so gently laid the long strap of leather onto the mule's back. Obediently she leaned into her harness and raised the harnesstree off the damp ground, then stopped, awaiting the next command.

"Aside her, I'm just gonna be in the way—"

"Lean into it, boy!"

"You ain't really gonna make me pull this stump out—"

"I'm gonna make a farmer outta you, Titus—or I'll kill you trying. Now, lean into it, goddammit!"

"Pap!"

"There's work you left afore it was finished, son." Thaddeus's eyes glowed like all-night coals.

"Lemme pull the stump out by my own self with the mule. I'll get it done—"

"Damn right, you'll pull it out with the mule," his father growled, savagely bringing the leather strap down on the animal's back.

FROM THE AUTHOR

I was born on the first day of 1947 in a small town on the plains of Kansas. That great rolling homeland of the nomadic buffalo has remained in my marrow across the years of my wandering.

From Nebraska, to Kansas and on to Oklahoma, I've spent a full third of my life on those Great Plains. Another third growing up in the desert southwest an arrow's-shot from the wild Apache domain of Cochise and Victorio. The most recent third of my life has passed among the majestic splendor of the Rocky Mountains—from Colorado to Montana and on to Washington state. In less than a year, I am back in Montana, here in the valley of the great Yellowstone River, in the veritable heart of the historic West. The plains and prairies at my feet, the great Rockies as my backrest.

The Great Plains runs in my blood and always will. More than merely growing up there, my roots go deep in the land that over the last hundred-odd years soaked up about as much blood and sweat as it did rain.

My maternal grandfather came from working-class stock in St. Joseph, Missouri, where he first became a carriage-riding sawbones doctor who as a young man moved to Oklahoma Territory, finding it necessary to pack two small .36-caliber pistols for his own protection while practicing his medical arts from his horse-drawn buggy. In later years he would be proud to say he never stepped foot in a motorized vehicle.

It wasn't long before Dr. David Yates met and fell in love with the school-marm teaching there in Osage country, Pearl Hinkle. My grandmother had bounced into The Strip, formerly called "Indian Territory" or "The Nations", in her parents' wagon in June of 1889 during the great land-rush that settled what is now the state of Oklahoma. With immense pride I tell you I go back five generations homesteading on the plains of Kansas—Hinkles, simple folk with rigid backbone and a belief in the Almighty, folk who witnessed the coming of the Kansas Pacific Railroad along with the terrifying raids of Cheyenne and Kiowa as the Plains tribes found themselves shoved south and west by the slow-moving tide of white migration.

My father's father wandered over to The Territory from the vicinity of Batesville, Arkansas when he first learned of the riches to be found in what would one day become south-central Oklahoma. It was an era of the "boomers"—when oil money ran local governments and bought law-enforcement officers both. Yet in that violent and lawless epoch, Oklahoma history notes a few brave men who stood the test of that time. I'm very proud to have coursing in my veins the blood of a grandfather who had the itchy feet of a home-steader turned Justice of the Peace in that oft-times rowdy, violent and unsettled frontier.

Still, it was more than what Scotch-Irish heritage ran in their veins that both my parents passed on to me—more so the character of those sturdy, austere folk who settled the Great Plains. From my father I believe I inherited the virtue of hard work and perseverance. And from my mother, besides her abiding love and reverence for the land, I have inherited a stamina to endure all the travesty that life can throw at simple folk. Those traits she has given me, along with a belief in the Almighty—the self-same belief that helped those hardy settlers endure through hailstorms and locust plagues, drought and barrel-bottom crop prices.

Brought up in the fifties during the era of Saturday matinees and some twenty hours of prime-time west-erns on those small boxes we fondly called TV, early on I found myself bitten by the seductive lure of the West. Yet, it was not until 1965 during my freshman year in college in Oklahoma where I was studying to become a history teacher that I was finally able to separate the History of the West from the *Myth of the West*. Over the intervening twenty-five years I have happily found the historic West every bit as fascinat-ing as the mythic frontier.

You would be hard pressed to find a man happier

than I—still teaching as I am thousands of readers outside the confines of the classroom about a magical epoch of expansion that roared rowdy and rambunctious across the plains and mountains of our Western frontier. A man is a success when he can put food on his family's table doing what he loves most to do.

Over the years I've been cursed with the itchiest of feet, moving on frequently as did the rounders and roamers of this mountain West more than a hundred-odd years before me. My wife Rhonda wants to stay put for awhile, here in Billings along the Yellowstone, under the sun hung in that Big Sky, while we raise our two children, son Noah and daughter Erinn.

There'll be time enough to move on, time enough for me to see what's over the next hill. Time enough still to follow the seductive lure of tomorrow and the next valley across the years to come . . .

ABOUT THE AUTHOR

<small>TERRY C. JOHNSTON</small> was born on the plains of Kansas and has immersed himself in the history of the early West. His first novel, *Carry the Wind,* won the Medicine Pipe Bearer's Award from the Western Writers of America, and his subsequent books, among them *Cry of the Hawk, Dream Catcher, Buffalo Palace, Crack in the Sky,* and the Son of the Plains trilogy, have appeared on bestseller lists throughout the country. Terry C. Johnston lives and writes in Big Sky country near Billings, Montana.